YOU CAN'T DIE BUT ONCE

PENNY MICKELBURY

Bywater
BOOKS

2020

Bywater Books

Copyright © 2020 Penny Mickelbury

Print ISBN: 978-1-61294-187-5

Bywater Books First Edition: December 2020

Printed in the United States of America on acid-free paper.

Cover designer: Ann McMan, TreeHouse Studio

Bywater Books
PO Box 3671
Ann Arbor MI 48106-3671
www.bywaterbooks.com

This book is dedicated to Marian Wright Edelman,
who founded the Children's Defense Fund 45 years ago,

To Patrisse Cullors, Alicia Garza, and Opal Tometi,
who founded Black Lives Matter seven years ago.

To all the children stolen from their families
along the U.S. border,
and to their families who continue to search for them
and work to secure their freedom.

To all the souls, everywhere in the world,
who work to keep children safe and loved.

WE WHO BELIEVE IN JUSTICE AND FREEDOM
WILL NOT REST UNTIL IT IS SAFE TO DO SO!

This book is also dedicated to those of you
who love Mimi and Gianna—they love you right back!

And lastly, to Peggy, who has my back.
Always has. Always will.

CHAPTER ONE

Mimi answered the phone even though she didn't recognize the number and choked on the mouthful of orange juice she'd just taken at what she heard:

I'm gonna whip your ass you stupid bitch!
No you ain't. Not no more you mean bastard.

Mimi put the phone on speaker so Gianna could hear just as a gun fired. The man's scream was as loud as the gun retort, causing Gianna to choke on the coffee she'd just sipped and to instinctively reach for the gun she didn't have: She didn't wear a holster at the breakfast table.

You shot me you stupid bitch! I can't believe you shot me! I'm gonna kill you!
No you ain't, and you ain't gonna hit me no more either. You or that stupid preacher. You ain't gonna do nothin' else to me, neither one of you!
How you gonna stop me, you stupid bitch!

The gun fired again, and the man screamed louder and began crying. Gianna gave Mimi a wide-eyed, questioning look across the table, and Mimi gave back a helpless shrug. She didn't know who was on the other end of the phone call. She hadn't recognized

1

the number, and she didn't recognize either of the voices. The man stopped crying and moaning. Despite his pain, he had no remorse.

You shot my hand off you crazy bitch!

You call me bitch again and I'm gonna shoot your mouth off.

Where you get a gun from anyway? And where you learn to shoot it? Who taught you to shoot a gun?

That ain't your business. Or that stupid preacher's.

I'm gonna kill that Connor bitch, too! You'uns been plottin' against me.

You think I don't know 'bout her?

Mimi dropped the phone at those words: Beverly Connor was a target of this man's rage! And suddenly she knew who the woman was: Jennifer somebody. She had met her in the waiting room of Bev's office a couple of months ago while both were waiting for their therapy appointments. As was often the case, the therapists were double-booked because clients often didn't show up. Today, however, both of Bev's appointments were present, on time: Mimi and Jennifer. Gianna grabbed the phone up, activated the display screen, and wrote down the number displayed there.

You ain't gonna kill nobody if you can't walk.

They were ready for the gunshot. The louder and more belli-cose the man was, the softer and quieter the woman's voice became. And then she fired the gun. This time the man didn't scream and curse the woman; he merely wept and mumbled. She said nothing, and Mimi and Gianna knew instinctively what was coming, and they both felt helpless because there was nothing they could do to prevent it. A final gun blast and a moment of eerie silence before the man began screaming and cursing again.

You stupid bitch! Call fuckin' 911! You better not be dead! Call 911!

2

As if she were a shape-shifter, Mimi's Gianna became the DC Police Department's Captain Maglione. While still holding Mimi's phone she snatched up her own, punched a button, and began calmly and precisely delivering the orders that would have the phone number traced and officers sent to that address. She hung up and looked at her watch, then at Mimi, who performed her own transformation, becoming the focused, fast-thinking newspaper reporter who had earned respect and awards in the days when truth mattered. She answered Gianna's question before it was asked.

"The woman's name is Jennifer, and I met her at Bev's maybe two months ago." Mimi now recalled the meeting with crystal clarity because it had happened during one of the worst times of her life, when she quit her job before she could be fired for refusing to apologize to a racist, sexist buffoon masquerading as a reporter. Gianna had been shot protecting Mimi from a drug-dealing lowlife wanting to stop the stories she was going to write about him. Gianna almost died and still walked with a slight limp, though both her surgeon and physical therapist assured her she'd regain full function in the leg ... but it would take time. In the meantime, she used a cane and went to physical therapy twice a week. Mimi, who couldn't forgive herself for being the reason Gianna almost died though nobody else—the chief of police and Mimi's editor included—blamed her for Gianna's injury, went to therapy once a week, but for help healing the emotional injuries, not the physical ones.

"That lowlife drug-dealing dirty cop is who's to blame for what happened to Gianna," Beverly Connors had told her more than once, followed by, "You've got enough work to do without using up our time feeling sorry for yourself, Mimi."

"That's not how a therapist should talk to her patient," Mimi would whine, to totally unsympathetic ears. Dr. Beverly Connors was more than her therapist. She was her former lover and closest friend.

"I need to call Bev and tell her about this," Mimi said, standing up.

"What can you tell me about this Jennifer?" Gianna asked.

"Young, white—"

"Bev has white clients in the middle of a totally Black and Latino community?"

"Surprised me, too," Mimi said, looking thoughtful as more of her conversation with Jennifer came back to her, and she told Gianna all she remembered. Jennifer lived in one of the large, new low-income City Housing Department developments on the East Side built for large low-income families, and she had told Mimi that one of her neighbors told her that talking to Bev would help her.

"Help her with what, Mimi?"

Mimi sighed. "She's nineteen, Gianna, and she has four children. Her husband won't let her have a cell phone or cable or go to the library. Or to the doctor. She's to be a traditional wife, but he hangs out with his pals every night after work—"

"She's not from DC, is she?" Gianna asked.

Mimi shook her head. "Somewhere in Pennsylvania—"

"You'uns!" Gianna exclaimed.

"What?"

"That's what he said—the husband. That 'you'uns' were plotting against him. I haven't heard that in years. It used to be common around Pittsburgh. What the hell are they doing in DC?" Gianna muttered as she limped out of the breakfast room because she was trying to walk too fast.

"Where's your cane?" Mimi called after her.

"Leave me alone, Mimi!"

Mimi grinned, then quickly sobered. She pulled her other phone from her pocket and sat back down. She'd call Bev as soon as she had called Tyler, the editor and friend she hadn't spoken to in more than three months. She inhaled deeply and punched a button. Tyler answered so quickly he could have been waiting for the call.

"Mimi?"

"Hi ya, Tyler. Do you have time for me to share something with you?"

4

"As much time as you need, Mimi," and he listened without interruption as she told him about the phone call, then as much as she knew about Jennifer. "Where, Mimi?"

"One of the East Side housing projects for large families," she answered, and heard him yell at somebody to monitor the police scanner. Then he asked her how she was doing and feeling.

"Can I come back to work, Tyler?"

"Is today too soon?" he asked, almost before the words were out of her mouth.

"Only if you buy me lunch. And at the French place, not the Chinese one."

"You don't like the French place."

"True but think how good it'll make you and your expense account look."

She could picture his confused face as he said, "I don't follow."

"You took me to an expensive lunch and *voila!* I came back to work."

"Nobody who knows you will believe that, Patterson."

She was back! He only called her Patterson when she was the reporter and he was the editor. So . . . since she was back . . . "The children, Tyler."

"What children?"

"Jennifer has four—"

"Had four. Just got the info: both parents are dead, and so far there's no sign of children, but the cops haven't completely cleared the scene yet."

"We gotta find those children, Tyler."

"See you at noon-thirty, Patterson. *Bonjour.*"

Tyler disconnected immediately so Mimi punched the button that would connect Bev and she, too, answered as if expecting the call. "Anything wrong, Mimi?"

"Yeah, but not with me," and she relayed the call from Jennifer, adding the latest info from Tyler. "But there were no children in the home. We gotta find those children, Bev."

Bev gave a deep sigh and because Mimi knew her even better than she knew Tyler, she could hear the sadness in her voice and

5

picture it in her face. "Jennifer's mother came and got the two youngest ones last weekend, and the older two probably are at school." She sighed again and almost whispered the words: "Jennifer, Jennifer. I am so very sorry."

"Sorry for what, Bev?"

"Sorry because sometimes, Mimi, there's nothing we can do to help."

"So ... women like Jennifer have to what, help themselves? Or do without help?"

Bev didn't say anything for a long moment, primarily because there was nothing to say. Then, "Am I gonna hear from the cops?"

"Not unless there's something in Jennifer's home with your name on it."

"Her husband even checks—checked—the garbage cans, so no, she wouldn't have left anything for him to find and question."

"Bev! He knew about you—"

Beverly snorted. "The difference between me and his wife is that I don't live in trembling fear of him."

"How awful to have to live that way," Mimi said.

"What's truly awful is how many women have to live that way," Bev said, adding, "I'm really grateful to you and Gianna for keeping me out of it. I can't afford to spend half my day listening to cops ask me questions I can't answer."

The two old friends declared their love for each other and ended the call, and Mimi got up and began loading the dishwasher. Starting today she'd no longer have the luxury of taking all day to clean the kitchen and breakfast nook just in time for dinner. Gianna entered in full uniform and while Mimi was admiring the sight, the eagle-eyed, leave-no-clue-unseen captain was clocking the clean kitchen. She didn't comment verbally but raised a questioning eyebrow.

"I'm having lunch with Tyler—"

Gianna wrapped her in a tight embrace before she could complete the sentence. "Good for you, sweetheart. I'm really glad."

"You're this happy I'm having lunch with Tyler?"

"I'm this happy you're going back to work."

Mimi pulled back just far enough to make eye contact without breaking the delightful full-body contact. "I didn't say I was going back to work."

"You didn't need to. Since you successfully transformed the junk heap that was the combined contents of our two homes into such a beautiful and fabulous living space while managing to conquer your entire to-read list, you have nothing to keep you occupied all day. You'd die of boredom before noon."

Mimi had to acknowledge the truth of that statement: There had been eight weeks of almost nonstop unpacking and organizing and often reorganizing once Gianna had returned home and offered a suggestion or two—or three—. Mimi had enjoyed the entire process. Because of her leg, Gianna was unable to manage any of the lifting and moving of boxes and furniture, but she did an award-winning job of finding new restaurants to order from and new wines to try, and they surprised each other with how well and how easily they managed to agree on how to arrange and organize their new living space. Each woman had had her own home when they met and though they often talked about moving in together, work always got in the way. Now they wondered why it had taken so long. Their closest friends—Beverly and Sylvia, and Freddie and Cedric—agreed that the new space looked as if they'd lived there for years instead of just two months.

"You know me too well, Captain," Mimi said, and kissed her appreciation before stepping out of the warm and wonderful embrace. "And unless you want that beautiful uniform wrinkled, not to mention being late for work—"

Gianna stepped away as quickly as her bad leg permitted and over to the rack at the kitchen door where her keys hung and where an elevator would take her down to the garage. She blew Mimi a kiss and opened the door. As much as she'd love to end up back in bed with Mimi, wrinkled uniform and tardy for work be damned, today was not the day for it.

"Don't forget your cane."

7

Gianna muttered something unintelligible, grabbed the cane, and left. Mimi smiled to herself and went to get ready for work for the first time in two months.

Gianna's boss, the DC Chief of Police, paced back and forth in front of the room full of the department's top brass: assistant chiefs, deputy chiefs, and commanders. Gianna and her seconds in command, Lt. Eric Ashby and Det. Jim Dudley, were the lowest ranks in the room. Every eye was on the chief. He was looking at the video screen that covered most of the front wall. As he paced, he jiggled the coins in his pockets, and anybody who'd known him for longer than fifteen minutes knew to pay close and careful attention. He proved the point when he spoke: "I know you all are tired of hearing this, and I'm more tired of saying it than you are of hearing it, but I'm gonna say it anyway." He stopped his pacing and coin-jiggling and made eye contact with the room. "I do not want a repeat of that Charlottesville horror at this demonstration on Saturday. The law says we have to let the little hatemongers have their demonstration, but you will see to it that things don't get out of hand, and you for damn sure will keep anybody from being killed. Their lawyers have been all over social media talking about their rights. Well, here's a right I got for 'em: They've got the right to obey the law as long as they're in my town! Otherwise they'll get their hate-spewing asses arrested. Period."

The chief resumed pacing and jiggling, the sound absurdly loud in the deadly quiet room. Then Deputy Chief for Operations Gerhardt Schmidt cleared his throat and stood up, but before he could speak the chief waved him back down. "We'll hear from you in a minute, Schmidt. I want to hear from Maglione first."

"But I'm Chief of Operations," Schmidt said, barely stopping short of whining.

"Since I gave you the job, I think I know that. Now have a seat," the chief said, looking at Gianna.

Without looking at Eric, she gave an imperceptible nod of her head and the newly minted lieutenant walked to the front of the room. He saluted his chief and started talking: "We will deploy our people on both sides of the demonstration. I'll lead one team and Det. Dudley will lead the other. Our people will wear mics and cameras, and they will be mobile—able to move about the crowd as necessary, especially in the event of a disturbance— relaying an audio and visual record of everything. They will be in constant contact with our Command Center, which will be in constant contact with Command Central—"

"I haven't issued that order," Schmidt said loudly.

"I'm issuing it," the chief snapped. "I want everybody in constant communication with everybody else. Is that clear? This is not the damn federal government! No unit of this police department operates in secret. Keep talking, Ashby."

"Yes, sir. If Chief Schmidt—or anyone—needs one or several of our people to change position, the order goes from Central to our Command—"

"And who's in charge there?" Schmidt demanded to know.

"I am," Gianna said quietly and without turning around so she didn't take her eyes off the chief. "All orders from Central go through me to my people."

Gianna had been a cop long enough that everyone in the room knew her. All of them respected her and most of them liked her. A couple, however, like Gerhardt Schmidt, were envious of her close relationship with the chief, but even they knew she'd earned his trust, even if they didn't know all the pertinent details. But that didn't prevent more than a few of them from wanting to see her up and moving, wanting to see some hint of vulnerability, to see her limping or, even better, using the cane, which was tucked under her arm when she entered the room. Wasn't gonna happen.

"All right, Schmidt. You can talk now, then ATTF. I see Andy Page but where's your boss, son?"

Page closed his eyes and inhaled. Then he squeezed his eyes tightly shut. "He's on his way back from a Homeland Security briefing—"

Everybody already knew what their chief thought about the federal law enforcement agencies of Washington, and most had worked with him long enough to have heard, if not felt, his displeasure. Still it was a revelation, and some insisted that he regularly invented new cuss words and especially creative new ways to express his feelings about the feds. Lt. Andy Page's eyes still were squeezed shut, but a tiny grin lifted his lips. He was glad not to be his boss.

"What are you grinning at, Patterson?"

"You, Tyler."

"Why?"

"'Cause you're funny, getting all worked up because I won't give into your whining and do the story on Jennifer when I told you before we ordered this pretentious . . . whatever it is . . . that I wouldn't do the story. You do have other reporters, you know."

Indignant replaced whining. "Do you know what this lunch is costing me?"

Grinning even wider. "Nothing," Mimi replied, "and I don't care what it cost the paper. Now, can we talk about Saturday's demonstration? That interests me."

Tyler's attitude did a graceful pirouette on the proverbial dime, and now he was the grinning Cheshire. Mimi groaned inwardly. She'd just been had. "Carolyn will be delighted to hear that, Mimi," he said, grin widening as he saw that she knew she'd been played. Yes, he was her boss, but he also was her friend. They'd worked together for years and knew each other well. Knew where all the buttons were and when to push them. She'd only been gone a few months. Had her gears rusted so quickly?

"I see your promotion has improved your skills, Tyler." Formerly the city editor, Tyler Carson now was the managing editor, and Mimi's abrupt and angry resignation three months earlier had a lot to do with that. "I'm gonna have to up my game."

He shook his head. "Your game is fine. Just don't leave me to my own devices again, please."

"Does that mean you missed me?"

He began a snarky riposte—their usual form of communication—but bit it back. "More than you'll ever know, Patterson," he said quietly.

"Hmmm. Maybe I should've gotten mad and quit sooner. I don't know how to handle all this love from you, Tyler. But then maybe you have so much more to give since you finally wised up and dumped the straight boyfriend. I don't know how or why you put up with his sorry ass for so long."

Tyler mumbled something that sounded a lot like "fuck you, Patterson." Mimi sighed. She was back and, truth be told, she was both happy and relieved. While quitting had been the right thing to do under the circumstances, and her unemployed status meant she was on hand to help Gianna heal and orchestrate their move into their wonderful new condo, at this point she was bored and antsy. She loved her job and she was good at it. She needed to be busy. She didn't know what exactly Tyler had in mind for her, but working the White Power demonstration story with Carolyn Warshawski as her editor was a good start.

It took but a moment for silence to descend on the normally noisy newsroom when they walked in. All eyes were on Mimi. The silent disbelief turned into beehive buzzing and then into a raucous cheer. "Fuck you Patterson!" Someone yelled the good-natured welcome from the back of the room, and Mimi yelled back a good-natured obscenity that involved the heckler's mother. She was home. And like the professionals they were, everybody returned to their work, and the cacophony of ringing phones and clacking keyboards and voices at all levels of conversation that made up the normal noise of the newsroom was as welcoming as a royal trumpet salute. Not to mention louder and less melodic.

"About time you brought your sorry ass back to work," Mimi heard from behind her, and she didn't need to turn around to know that Joe Zemekis would be there, trying to convert the joy in his face into a scowl. His anger at her resignation had almost caused her to walk back the words "I quit". Almost but not quite. She turned around to face him, and the scowl lost.

11

"Hi ya, Joe. Tyler's been keeping you busy, I see." Naturally she still read the paper every day, the print edition as well as the many digital ones. "You've been doing really good work."

"I'm really glad to see you, Mimi. Still pissed at you for quitting but glad to see you."

"I'm glad to see you, too, Joe. And if I hadn't quit, you'd have been fired, so I did you a favor. You should thank me instead of bustin' my chops."

"How do you figure you did me a favor?"

Mimi remembered the day more clearly than she wished to, and she saw that Joe did, too:

Well if it isn't JJZ! Where's the Queen B? Somewhere making beautiful music with the lieutenant who can do no wrong, leaving you to do all the work?" Ian had spoken loudly enough that everyone within a ten-food radius heard him, which was his intention. To call the man clueless was to grossly understate. "I just wish Patterson heard what he said, the little fuck. She'd have cleaned his clock and left the pieces on the floor." Joe had said. Carolyn made a sound and Henry looked up as Mimi headed toward them. "Patterson! A little afternoon delight with the lovely lieutenant? Give me an hour with her and I'll make her forget all about that wanna-be plastic dick you dykes use. Or is it rubber? I'll slide nine inches of the real thing into her—" Mimi's fist met his jaw with such speed and power that witnesses weren't sure he'd been hit until he was spiraling backward, yelling at the top of his voice.

"If I hadn't hit him you would have, and then you'd have been fired instead of me."

"You weren't fired, Patterson; you quit."

"And now I've un-quit and if you don't mind, I could do with no further talk of the Weasel and his disastrous effect on the operation of this newsroom." Mimi looked around. Everything was the same and yet everything was different. How one person could so totally and negatively affect an entire operation—the thought sickened her. For about the one-millionth time.

"Our ship has been righted," Joe said, and as proof that he was right their editor, Carolyn Warshawski, approached.

"I'm so glad you're back, Mimi," she said, offering a brief hug.

"Me, too, Carolyn. And I'm so glad that you're finally in the chair that should have been yours a long time ago."

"I couldn't be in this chair as long as Tyler was in it," Carolyn said with a smile. "But as soon as he moved his butt, I moved mine!" When the Weasel finally got shit-canned, Tyler was promoted to that job and he quickly promoted Carolyn to his. Back for just a few minutes and Mimi already could see that the newsroom was functioning better than it had in years. As if to prove the point Tyler joined their group—something the Weasel never would have done.

"Patterson will brief you and Joe on this morning's events. Then you and I can put our heads together and decide how we want to cover the clusterfuck they're calling a demonstration.

"You really think it'll devolve into a clusterfuck?" Joe asked.

"I live to be pleasantly surprised," Tyler said, his tone dry as desert dust, as he turned and headed toward his lair. Carolyn made for her own cubicle, beckoning for Mimi and Joe to join her.

"Please talk us through it, Mimi. How did she come to have your number? Did you know her? Was she a source?"

The waiting room of East Side Families First was packed, as always. No matter that Dr. Beverly Connors and the original partners of the Midtown Psychiatric Associates had moved across town, bought a small abandoned warehouse, and added half a dozen new therapists and social workers; the demand for services in one of the poorest parts of Washington, DC, would guarantee a permanently full waiting room. Appointment times were rarely kept because, as everyone knew, emergencies took precedence, and in a community where the women and children were as traumatized as those living in war zones, emergencies were the norm. Which is why Mimi always brought along a book.

"You're not poor," Mimi heard almost directly in her ear. She lifted her eyes from the book and turned to her right. She controlled her surprise.

"No, I'm not."

"So how come you're here? This place is supposed to be for poor people."

"I'm here because Dr. Connors is the best therapist in the city. Why are you here?"

13

Mimi's words had the desired effect: The young white woman, struck speechless for a moment, finally replied. "I'm damn near crazy and I'm for damn sure poor."

"And you're probably the only white person in this entire neighborhood."

The young woman gave a snaggle-toothed grin showing all the places where teeth were missing. "Which is why my mean bastard of a husband won't look for me here! I don't hate Colored people like he does!"

"But he'll live in a neighborhood with people he hates?"

The young woman shrugged. "If he can get free stuff."

"But he doesn't know you come here?"

"Gawd no! He'd kill me! I cain't go anywhere or see anything or read anything or hear anything that his dumbass church don't okay first. We ain't got no TV and no cell phone. He won't even let me take the children to the library 'cause there's computers there and computers got the internet."

"How many children do you have?" Mimi asked.

"Four and he wants me to have some more, but I ain't. I'm puttin' a stop to that shit. He'd kill me if knew. That dumbass preacher got him believin' we have to be old fashin. But if he wants more babies he can damn well have 'em hisself."

"Where is this church?"

The girl shook her head. "It ain't got a place. We meet in different places but mostly in the community room of the place where we live."

Mimi took a card from her pocket and offered it to the girl who reluctantly took it. She squinted at it, reminding Mimi of her friend Baby Doll—Marlene Jefferson—who couldn't read when Mimi met her. "I'd like to talk to you some more if that's okay—"

"What do this say?"

"That I'm a newspaper reporter—"

"Like that fake news?"

"Only if you believe that telling the truth about that shit for brains in the White House is fake news," Mimi snapped, standing up when the receptionist called her name.

"Do you see Dr. Connors for free?"

Mimi shook her head. "I pay full price."

14

"Do you remember when this was?" Joe asked.

Mimi shook her head. "But two things: On the call we over-heard the husband say 'you'ens' and Gianna recognized that as being an Eastern Pennsylvania speech pattern—"

"Kinda like 'y'all' or 'youse'," Joe said, nodding.

"And she called the church 'maga.' I thought she was saying 'mega,' like it was one of those huge places with thousands of members, but she was saying—"

"Oh shit!" Joe exclaimed. "MAGA church!"

"Do not say those words in my presence, Zemekis," Mimi growled at him.

"There could be more of them. Lots more of them!"

"Lots more of what, Joe?" Carolyn asked.

"People like this Jennifer—lots more of them living here in DC."

"Happy hunting, Z," Mimi said.

"Will Dr. Connors talk to me?"

"Nope," Mimi said.

"Will you ask her?"

"Nope. You're on your own."

"How old was this woman? How old are her children?" Joe Zemekis was thrumming like a tuning fork.

"The cops have had access to that place for a few hours now, Z. They'll have all the answers you have questions for."

"Thanks, Patterson. Later, Carolyn," and he was off and running—literally.

"He's a good reporter," Mimi said.

"One of the best," Carolyn agreed. "As are you, Mimi, and this could be a very good story. Why don't you—" The ringing phone saved Mimi from having to formulate a polite answer. "Tyler wants to see you. Then there's a meeting in the Exec's office to discuss how to cover the demo on Saturday."

Mimi looked around the newsroom and smiled. "Feels good in here. Again."

Carolyn Warshawski smiled and nodded her agreement. "Glad you're back."

Mimi exchanged welcome back greetings with several colleagues en route to Tyler, and she had to admit that she enjoyed the feel-good feeling. Under the Weasel's tenure the toxic level in the place had been dangerously high. The Weasel had fired some good people to make room for his hires—at best lazy reporters, at worst raging incompetents. He'd tried to fire Joe Zemekis who was stationed at the Central American Bureau, but Joe played his seniority card and forced his return to the States. Then Tyler blew away all of the Weasel's hires, all white men, and replaced them with a variety of women and men of a variety of colors and sexual preferences.

Mimi shook the ugly thoughts out of her brain and approached the cubicle Tyler maintained on the main newsroom floor, the place he was happiest and the most comfortable. He saw her coming, stood up, and entered his office, where he stood in the door waiting for her, then closed the door. "I just got back, Tyler, for crying out loud. I haven't had time to do anything that warrants a closed-door meeting."

"I don't want people to hear you scream when I tell you that part of your new assignment is to be one of the digital content editors—"

"I don't want to be a fuckin' editor, Tyler."

"Two days a week, Patterson. Two days a week for Zemekis. I do the other three. And it's just until we hire two permanent editors. And you know we have to do it. The world is a digital place."

She knew. She'd become a frequent reader of the paper's digital edition and had to admit that it was a quality operation. "Who's been doing it?"

"Carolyn, Zemekis, Henry and me. Now Henry and Carolyn can concentrate on their regular jobs. I'll give you a tutorial after the Exec's meeting."

Mimi hadn't screamed, but she was feeling as if she'd been slipped a mind-altering substance. A ninety-minute lunch with Tyler and back in the building less than an hour, and her reality was so different from the one she awoke to that perhaps screaming wasn't a bad idea. She startled the Exec when she knocked on his door, and he frowned when he checked his watch. "It's not time for the meeting, sir. I just wanted to check in with you."

He stood up. "Welcome back, Ms. Patterson."

"Thank you for having me back, sir."

"I'm not the one who wanted you gone," he snapped, "and nothing like that will ever happen again at this newspaper, I promise you that!"

"Yes, sir. Thank you, sir."

"Now go to the personnel department and see how they're handling your absence."

Personnel had been human resources for at least ten years . . . but who was counting? And she had quit. How many ways could that be handled? She posed that question to him as delicately as she knew how but he waved her away, muttering something that sounded like "nothing in writing." Then he called her back. "You gave that young woman your card. The one who killed her husband and herself. That means you were working for us at the time. Had been all along, for my money."

"So, you were on sick leave for a few weeks, and the rest of the time . . . what?" Gianna was as mystified by the outcome of Mimi's visit to human resources as was Mimi herself.

"Not sure I know, my love. At least about anything but the four weeks," Mimi said with an elaborate shrug and a crooked grin.

"But you understand the four weeks of sick leave?"

Mimi nodded. "According to the head of the personnel department, a.k.a. human resources, I have oodles—her word, not mine—of sick leave, but I seem to be one who believes in using her vacation time as soon as it accrues. Unlike someone I know," she said, shooting Gianna a dark look, one studiously ignored by the captain. "So, since she had to take time from me, she took it in the form of sick leave. And the rest of the time . . ." Mimi shrugged. "Tyler'll figure it out."

"No doubt."

"Can we eat now?"

"After you tell me about the digital editing job."

Mimi told her, and they both agreed that it certainly could prove to be interesting, if not enjoyable. While Gianna opened wine and fixed their plates Mimi read the latest update of the digital edition of the paper and felt a sliver of excitement creeping in. However, it was mitigated by a sliver of unease. She looked up from the laptop screen and caught Gianna's eye.

"And sweetheart? Don't turn your back on that Schmidt character. His long knives are out and sharpened."

CHAPTER TWO

"White power!"

"America for Americans!"

"White lives matter!"

"White is right! White is might!"

Heavy clouds, accompanied by heavy humidity, hung over the demonstration, but the threat of rain remained just that: a threat, no matter how many hopes, wishes and prayers for a downpour were sent to wherever the supplicants sent their pleas for a rain-out of the meager gathering.

"Fuckin' weather forecasters wrong again," was heard as often as the pleas for rain. The only correct prediction was the number of far-right demonstrators who answered their leaders' call to show up in DC: About five hundred of them, far below the ten thousand they themselves predicted. And as was almost always the case, the far right was greatly outnumbered by the other side. About five thousand counterdemonstrators out-shouted the hatemongers. Their voices were louder and they lasted longer, and they showed an impressive willingness to remain behind the police barricades that they could overrun at will should the mood strike them. Thankfully, that hadn't happened. Yet.

"Go back to the mist, gorillas!"

"Your mama is a gorilla!"

The right surged as one. The police line held as more than one person mused how often it happened that bullies and hatemongers were so thin-skinned. One of their favorite tactics was demeaning other people but when the name-calling was directed at them, they were hilarious in their hurt feelings and bruised egos. They shouted insults and obscenities that only the cops heard because now the counterdemonstrators were singing Freddie Mercury songs.

"What the fuck are you doing?" Gianna heard whispered in her ear and it startled her because the voice was that of Kenny Chang, and in all the years she'd worked with him she had never heard him curse.

"Eric, call me please," she whispered, and four seconds later he did.

"Boss?"

"Something has spooked Kenny. Leave Tim in charge of your post and reposition so that you can respond to whatever has upset Kenny if necessary." She heard his whispered acknowledgement, then went to stand near Kenny. She wanted him to know that she was there but that she was not interfering. She stood watching the ever shifting and changing images of the demonstration on the three huge monitors mounted on the wall. The images came from almost a dozen different camera feeds, including three drones. She'd been watching them since long before the official start of the demonstration, as much to be certain that her people and procedures were in place as to get the pulse of the crowd. But though she watched all the screens with their shifting images, her intense focus was on the one image that did not change—the one on the computer screen in front of Kenny. Three of her own people were in the group of white supremacists, so undercover that she almost didn't recognize them, and one, Randall Connelly, kept moving within the crowd, ducking and dodging, stooping low as if to conceal himself beneath them. *What the fuck are you doing indeed!* She sat down beside Vik Patel and whispered to him, "Pull up Connelly's coms."

He nodded, typed on his keyboard, frowned, typed some more, then shook his head in confusion. "Must've malfunctioned, Boss—"

"Bullshit," Gianna barked. "That's new equipment and it had better not malfunction. Can he shut it down if he wants to?"

"He's a tech-savvy guy, Boss, so I suppose so. But why would he?"

Why indeed. "Can you override whatever he did—without him knowing it—and get him back up?"

Patel was typing furiously, and nodding his head just as furiously, as if some fabulous beat that only he could hear reverberated in his head. Gianna resisted the urge to look down to see if his feet kept the rhythm. "I should be able to find him, Boss, but I can't! You think he's destroyed the com?"

"I'll destroy his ass if he has," Gianna responded, surprised to hear her words out loud. She'd intended only to think them. She returned her eyes to the big screens on the wall so as not to concentrate on what Kenny and Vik were doing. It seemed that the crowd of anti-demonstrators had grown in number and volume. The various camera feeds constantly shifted the crowd angle and she spotted Alice Long in the crowd, watching without seeming to watch. Alice was one of the best undercover cops Gianna had ever seen. Then the image shifted again and she saw Mimi, working the outskirts of the crowd. Mimi back at work—diligent, focused, and enjoying every moment of it, and for a brief instant Gianna forgot about Randall Connelly and his silent communication device.

"Boss!" Kenny Chang's shout brought her to his side as fast as she could manage, and she silently cursed the still-healing leg and the murderous young man whose bullet had almost cost her the leg—and her life.

"Show me, Kenny," she said calmly.

He pointed to his screen. "Watch these four guys . . . here they go . . . as a group they move exactly three steps to their left. Then they just seem to wait. No shouting or chanting. Like they're not really part of the demonstration."

Gianna watched the men. They all had shaved heads and visible Nazi symbols tattooed on their necks and arms. They were in the group of demonstrators, but did not seem to be part of the group.

"Have they been this way the whole time? More like spectators than participants?"

Kenny shook his head. "They were really into it in the beginning. They were closer to the front of the group and yelling and shouting with the rest of them."

"Then what changed, Kenny?"

"I don't know, Boss. They just started this shifting action about ten minutes ago." And as if on cue the four men now backed up. At the same time Kenny whispered, "Connelly! They started when Connelly started acting squirrelly."

"Where is Connelly now?"

"Don't see him, Boss," Kenny said.

"Vik. Do you have eyes on Connelly? Ears?"

Patel shook his head but like Kenny, his eyes never left his screen. Gianna had seen enough. She turned away from the screens and grabbed her phone. Eric answered in the middle of the first ring. She told him what she saw and what she thought: "They're moving to the back edge of the police barricade, and I think their intention is to get out of the enclosure. Move there, Eric, and I'll get you some backup." She then picked up a land-line, punched a button and connected to Command Central.

"Captain Maglione." The voice on the other end answered as quickly as Eric had.

"Will you connect me to Chief Schmidt, please? It's important."

"It had better be important, Maglione," Schmidt snarled almost a minute later.

"It is, Chief," she said, and told him what she'd seen and what she thought. "I've moved Lt. Ashby—"

"You put Ashby back where he was, and you don't move anybody without my order. My people are watching the screens and nobody has reported what you have—"

"Leave Ashby where you sent him, Maglione." Gianna and Schmidt heard the chief's snapped order. "I'll send Andy Page and his team as backup."

"But Chief!" Schmidt all but yelled.

"Don't argue with me, Gerry. If Maglione thinks there's some-

22

thing to worry about, then I'm gonna worry about it, and if you're smart, you will, too. Keep your eyes on this thing, Maglione, and call me directly if anything changes."

"Yes, sir," she said, but he'd already hung up, so she did, too, so as not to hear anything Gerhard Schmidt had to say. She called Eric and told him to watch for Andy Page. Then she returned to her spot behind Kenny Chang.

"Lt. Ashby is watching our guys," he said, watching the screen.

"Lt. Page from ATTF will join him in a minute," Gianna said, knowing she didn't have to tell him to keep his eyes glued to the screen.

Mimi watched Eric Ashby change positions after summoning Tim McCreedy to take up his original spot. She didn't think too much of it: A demonstration was a fluid, almost organic thing, constantly shifting and changing; and after the violence in Charlottesville a couple of years ago, she knew the chief of this department well enough to know that he would not allow this demonstration to get out of hand. Of course Gianna would move her top people around . . . but twice in a matter of minutes?

Ashby took off running toward the rear of the demonstration. Just as Mimi was deciding whether to follow, she saw the flak-jacketed members of the Anti-Terrorism Task Force break ranks and follow Ashby. That made up Mimi's mind and she followed, but slowly. She saw that some of the crowd noticed the cops. Curiosity was one thing, panic quite another, and if she ran in pursuit of the cops, panic could ensue, especially since she'd already identified herself as a reporter. First cops run; then the reporter runs after them? As the talking heads of the day liked to say, not good optics. So she walked—a bit faster than a stroll but short of a sprint. Her brain, however, was in overdrive. *What the hell was happening?*

* * *

Eric Ashby willed his brain to stop thinking and his eyes to watch and see. The four men shifted again, this time by backing up three steps, and four people behind them—all women—shifted to the side of the men. The four men backed up again and their backs were at the barricade. Escape was theirs and Eric could do nothing to stop it. Not alone. He couldn't pull his gun on them, not in a crowd. Nor could he yell at them to stop whatever it was they were planning. So he stood with his back against the wall that provided a natural barrier and watched, frustrated, angry and helpless.

The design of the demonstration had seemed like a good idea at the time: Confine it to a newly gentrified but still industrial area of lofts, galleries, tattoo parlors and brewhouses, close enough to the federal enclave that the Washington Monument was visible. Since few of the organizers had any real knowledge of the city's geography, they believed themselves to be close to their idol, so they didn't really understand that they were contained: A brick wall was one boundary, and a wall of armored, shielded police patrolled by mounted officers was another. The two crowds of demonstrators faced each other behind barricades about ten feet apart. But the rear barricade where the four men now stood was vulnerable, though it didn't look like it. It was thick, dense black plastic mesh bolted to half a dozen metal poles—a ten-foot-high structure backed by concrete planters to prevent a crazed driver from repeating the Charlottesville catastrophe.

"Oh shit! Boss!"

"What is it, Eric?" Gianna tried to sound calm, but since Eric sounded panicked, that was all but impossible.

"Where the hell is Andy Page? I need him here now!"

Where indeed, Gianna thought. It wouldn't help to tell Eric that Andy should be there, especially since she was looking at the same thing he was. The four men somehow cut through the wire mesh fence, like they knew to bring wire cutters . . . and there was Andy in the ATTF van, just in time. Andy and his crew piled out of the van just as the four men completed their escape—walking right into the waiting arms of eight DC police officers. They were so surprised they didn't even try to resist. In the few seconds before anyone else could escape, Eric summoned half a dozen mounted officers to secure the back boundary. And lo and behold, Randall Connelly was right in the middle of the crowd, shouting slogans and gesturing with his fists like any good demonstrator—including an undercover cop—should.

Gianna turned her attention back to the ATTF takedown of the escapees. All were handcuffed and face down on the ground and Eric and Andy were watching the ATTF team search them. Eric was standing close enough that she could hear some of what was going on, when she heard one of them yell, "LT look! Wire cutters!"

Andy Page rushed over, said something, and two of his team pulled one of the cuffed men to his feet. Eric hurried over in time for Gianna to hear the man say that he would say nothing, though he did demand a lawyer. Andy smacked him upside the head, ordered him to remove his shoes, and threw him into the van. His team grabbed the others and followed suit, including the shoe removal, which caused one of the men to kick out violently and attempt to escape. He was quickly subdued but the scuffle called attention to what was happening, especially for Randall Connelly, who was trying to get to the back of the crowd. Gianna saw him.

"Officer Connelly, if you break your cover, I will fire your ass."

He stopped in his tracks. She knew that he had reactivated his communication device, and while he remained in place he continued to try to see what was happening to his friends. But there was nothing to see. They were safely inside the ATTF van on their way to Central Lockup where the chief was waiting for them.

Gianna's phone rang. "Are you all right, Eric?"

"Yes, Captain, I'm fine, and it all looks calm here."

"Did they say anything?"

"Not a single word," and she knew the disgust in his face equaled that in his voice. "Maybe Connelly will give us something."

"Not bloody likely," she said, not masking her own disgust. "Get started on your report as soon as possible and reasonable, Eric. And good work today, as usual."

25

✳ ✳ ✳

It was the quiet that alerted Gianna. It was never quiet when both teams were present, even if a class was in session or, as was currently the case, they were watching a training video. Det. Alice Long, one of their trainers, likened them to a class of two-year-olds. Eric's favorite description was a basket of puppies or kittens. Bottom line, they were never still and quiet at the same time. Gianna looked up from her corner of the room and quickly stood. Striding toward her was Deputy Chief Gerhard Schmidt. She stepped from behind her desk and went to meet him.

"Chief."

"Captain," he said, and extended his hand. But there was no palm to shake. Instead he proffered what she recognized as personnel folders. She took them but did not take her eyes from his, forcing him to speak first. "This is the paperwork transferring Lt. Eric Ashby and Det. James Dudley to my command, effective immediately."

She held his gaze, which was becoming a snarl, for another three seconds before turning away to stand behind her desk. She picked up the phone and pressed a button. "Sgt. Bell, do you know if Lt. Ashby has left already?"

She heard Tommi Bell's deep inhalation, then, "He's here with me, Captain, with Lt. Page. Where you left them, working on their statement."

"Then with my apologies, Sergeant, please ask him to return immediately. And I need you to come look over some personnel files, please."

"Do you want Lt. Page to remain here?"

"Thanks, Sergeant," Gianna said, and hung up. She was angrier than she'd been in a long time, especially since Schmidt now was leaning across her desk glaring at her.

"Nobody needs to look over those personnel files, Captain," he snarled. "Surely you recognize an order when you hear one, and if you read those files, you'd see one. Unless it's not your habit to follow orders."

26

"It is my habit to follow protocol, Deputy Chief, and protocol dictates that I sign off on the personnel files when officers leave my command and that my administrative sergeant sign off as well. Which we will do. After we've read them."

"And you are not to inform Lt. Ashby and Det. Dudley. I will do that."

It was Gianna's habit to grow calm to the point of still, and quiet to the point of silent when she was angriest, so when she dropped the personnel files on her desk and headed across the room, away from Schmidt, she did so at a leisurely stroll, without a word. The stroll effect was to mask the limp that she was damned if she'd let Schmidt witness, and the silence was to prevent her from saying out loud what she was thinking. So when he yelled out, asking if she'd heard what he said—"of course, sir," she replied over her shoulder, not turning to face him. The farther she got from Schmidt the faster she walked until she was standing directly behind Jim Dudley. "Don't turn around, Jim. Go to my office—Sgt. Bell's office—immediately."

He followed orders, and she shifted position to block as much of him as possible as he exited in case Schmidt had decided to follow her. Then she followed Jim to the slow-as-molasses elevator, which they took up one floor because it was faster than waiting for her to walk, though maybe not for much longer. *STEPS* was next on her Physical Terrorist's to-do list. Gianna closed her eyes at the thought, and Det. Jim Dudley took advantage of the moment to take a good look at his boss. He'd known her for a long time and thought her one of the best and toughest cops he knew. He'd seen her beaten and shot by perps, and injured more than once in the line of duty. He'd seen her so angry that she punched a would-be rapist hard enough to break bones in her hand. He'd seen her tackle an IRA gunrunner on an icy street. He'd never seen her look like she did now: ready to cry.

The elevator door opened, and he followed her out. Eric Ashby and Andy Page were standing in the hall waiting. "Captain—"

She waved him quiet, asked Andy to excuse them, and both men followed her in. She closed the door and faced them.

"Deputy Chief Schmidt has requested your immediate transfers to his command. He is downstairs with the paperwork authorizing the transfer. I have no choice but to sign it. I don't know why this is happening—"

"I know exactly why it's happening," the usually mild-mannered Ashby snarled. "He's pissed because you've showed him up twice—"

"What the hell are you talking about, Eric?"

"In the command demo planning session when I gave the briefing instead of you, and then at the demonstration when you tried to alert him that something was wrong, and he didn't want to hear it and the chief overrode him and took your side. That's what this is about." Mimi's warning rang like a claxon in her head. *Watch your back. He's got the long knives out.*

"Let's go," Gianna said, opening the door and walking out. They could not but follow. They shared a glance, misery etched on their faces.

"Where the hell did you disappear to, Maglione?" Deputy Chief Schmidt's fury was huge. "I didn't expect—"

"Lt. Eric Ashby and Det. First Class James Dudley, at your service, Deputy Chief."

"I told you I wanted to make the transfer notification!"

"These men came to work for me at my request. I owe them the courtesy of informing them that—"

"And you owe me the courtesy of obeying a direct order, Captain."

Gianna worked to think of something to say that wouldn't get her fired. Then shouts of, "Boss! Boss!" with a few "oh shits" thrown in saved her, and she hurried over as fast as her leg would permit to watch the screens that had galvanized her team, moving faster than was wise. "Fuck a duck!" she exclaimed as her hurry-up gait morphed into a limp, bringing the pain that went with it. "What is it?"

"Alice is kicking some guy's ass!" Team Leader Bobby Gilliam exclaimed, sounding like a proud father instead of a role model for the young cops he commanded.

Sure enough, Detective Alice Long was kneeling in the middle of a perp's back while she cuffed him. He was fighting to topple her, all the while calling her black nigger bitch and black nigger cunt bitch over and over. Alice couldn't get the cuffs on, so she slapped him upside the head. Hard. He screamed in pain but stopped wriggling around long enough for Alice to lock the cuffs. She stood up, and when she turned around Gianna saw blood running from her nose and mouth.

"Is that one of your officers who just hit a cuffed man, Captain?" Deputy Chief Schmidt demanded.

Gianna ignored him. "Get a patrol car to that location," she ordered.

"It's already on the way, Boss," Bobby said, and a patrol car screeched to a halt. Two uniforms jumped out and hurried over to the cuffed perp on the ground who once again was yelling profanities and wriggling and writhing with all his might, even landing a blow on the uniforms. But Gianna was focused on Alice and the three young cops she was giving an undercover lesson. Something obviously had gone terribly wrong.

Schmidt was in her face now, snarling and growling at her. "I asked you a question, Captain, and I expect an answer."

"Since you saw exactly what I saw, when I saw it, you must know that I cannot answer your question, but I wouldn't anyway without written reports from the officers involved. And since I no longer have my lieutenant, who normally would be en route to that scene, I'll be going instead. With me, Bobby." And she turned away from Schmidt to find Sgt. Tommi Bell holding up her shoulder holster, which she slipped into and fastened, followed by her jacket. She accepted her phone from Tommi, thanked her, and headed for the door. "Kenny! Vik!" she called over her shoulder as she reached the door.

"Video will be cued up and ready for you when you get back, Boss," Kenny said, knowing what she wanted.

"I want to see that video right now!" Schmidt exclaimed. "And I want the reports from the demonstration as soon as they're ready."

Straw that broke the camel's back for Gianna. She whipped around. "The chief has the reports from the demonstration—"

29

Schmidt cut her off. "Why does the chief have them? And the written reports? They're already finished?"

Gianna looked at him like he was as nuts as he sounded. "Because he's the chief of police and he asked for them, and of course the reports are finished. That demo was three days ago."

He gave her a strange look. "You always have written reports back that fast?"

"Of course," she said, willing her face not to telegraph her thoughts. "Unless an involved officer is injured and unable to complete a report. And when the chief tells me to show you that video is when I'll do that," she said, and asked Tommi to get the chief on the phone. Schmidt almost knocked her over trying to beat her out of the door. Eric and Jim followed slowly, with backward looks at Gianna and their now former teammates—helpless, hopeless and angry looks. Gianna sighed deeply. "Order some food, Tommi, please. A lot of it. We're going to be here late tonight."

Mimi Patterson and Joe Zemekis were deeply into their reporter personas as they walked about the East Side neighborhood where Jennifer and Craig Goodloe lived when they were alive. Mimi had sworn off the story. Wanted no part of it. Until Zemekis told her that the real story might not be the influx of whites into the Black and Latino neighborhood on the east side of town, but the hostile—about to turn ugly and violent—reaction of longtime residents to the unchecked gentrification of the community. And the gentrifiers weren't a few poor white people from Pennsylvania who came to DC to collect welfare and live in subsidized housing. This story did interest Mimi. Beverly had been talking about it for the better part of a year, ever since she and her partners moved their practice from Midtown to the East Side. And they had moved because of gentrification. The once poor and dilapidated area in the middle of the city transformed so quickly and completely that the people who lived and worked there barely had time to pack up and move, and they'd *had* to pack and move because they couldn't afford to stay. Beverly and her partners owned adjoining brownstones in what had been such a drug- and crime-infested block that patrol cars were stationed outside to escort the doctors, nurses and social workers to and from their cars. Gates and bars covered every window and door to augment the huge "NO DRUGS KEPT HERE" signs that hung on the buildings, until they were defaced and ultimately destroyed. When developers had offered what Beverly called an obscene amount of money to purchase the two buildings, the partners had accepted and moved to the East Side. But the move wasn't about the money: The patients they treated had been bought or sold out, too, and most of them, if they'd been able to remain in the city, ended up on the East Side. The patient load, according to Bev, was heavier and more desperately in need than ever. And now gentrification was following. The big difference was that here, the residents were fighting back. The signs were everywhere:

NO!!! I'M NOT SELLING MY HOUSE SO DON'T ASK!!!
GET OFF MY PROPERTY!!!
NO TRESPASSING ALLOWED!!!
PRESERVE SAFE AND AFFORDABLE HOUSING!
LIFE, LIBERTY AND A DECENT PLACE TO LIVE!
WE PLEDGE TO UNIFY, NOT GENTRIFY!

Mimi and Joe took dozens of photographs and copious notes, always aware that they were closely observed from porches and yards outside, and from behind curtains, blinds, and shades inside.

"We don't look like developers, do we?" Joe asked when two men stopped blowing and bagging leaves and followed them for half a block, until they turned the corner.

"I don't," Mimi said with a smirk.

"All developers are not white men," Joe said hotly.

"I'm willing to bet that a good number are," Mimi responded.

"I'm keeping my money in my pocket," Joe muttered.

They turned off the residential block, crossed the street, and saw two things almost simultaneously. Above them the Metro train from downtown, headed east, pulled slowly out of the station, gaining speed as it cleared the platform and the discharged passengers headed for the exits. Ahead of them, across the street, the burned-out shell of a building claimed an entire corner. "I'm guessing that's what's left of the fire-bombed coffee shop you told me about," Mimi said.

Joe nodded but before he could speak, they both looked up as a downtown-bound train screeched into the station. Not many people exited, and those who boarded were left standing because the train was full of East Side and east suburban residents headed into the city. "As long as that train runs in and out of that station every few minutes, gentrification is coming along for the ride," Joe said in a matter-of-fact tone. "It can't be firebombed away. Slowed down maybe, but not stopped. Did you see how packed those cars were?"

They both were startled to hear, from very close, "Don't know what kind of business you all are considering but I'd advise against a coffee shop. This is not a lucky location for caffeine."

Mimi and Joe turned slowly, not wanting to show how spooked they were by the voice so close to them, and by the fact that someone had appeared behind them so totally unnoticed. There was no humor in the "not a lucky location for caffeine" comment and there was no humor in the face that confronted them, though they both were surprised by its youth. She was no more than mid-twenties and looked as if she'd time-traveled from the 1970s with her huge Afro, dashiki and wire-rimmed spectacles, not to mention the bell bottom jeans. She was a dead-ringer for the fiery Angela Davis of two generations ago. "Not looking to buy property—" Joe began.

"Then what are you looking for?" the young woman asked.

"A story—" Joe began again.

This time Mimi interrupted. "I'm Montgomery Patterson and this is Joe Zemekis—"

"The newspaper reporters," the young woman said. Then to Joe, "You wrote the story about the murder-suicide over in the housing development."

32

"That's right," Joe said.

The young woman gave a speculative head nod. "You got it right. For the most part."

"What part did I get wrong?" Joe asked.

"You didn't dig deep enough. You didn't ask why they're here—"

"I certainly did, and I included that in my story."

"You only asked the ones who'd talk to you," the young woman said, "You need to talk to the others, the ones who don't talk to outsiders. Especially from the fake news." Now she was laughing at them.

Joe smiled at her, a real smile. "Maybe you'd be kind enough to make the right introductions. And explain that I'm the real news. And the real difference between them."

Still smiling, the young woman said, "I just might."

"And maybe you'll help me find out who burned down the coffee shop."

Smile fading, the young woman said, "I wouldn't even if I wanted to know, and I don't. Nobody does because nobody cares. We're just glad the place is gone. They got what was coming to 'em."

Mimi frowned and shook her head. "Who deserves to have their business destroyed?"

"Anybody who refuses service to people because of their color twenty years into the twenty-first century."

"Say what?!" Mimi exclaimed.

"You heard me, and I'll be happy to introduce you to the people who were refused service, starting with myself and including my grandmother."

"Your grandmother?" Joe asked.

She nodded and explained that her grandmother was a DC native who had vivid memories of DC's Jim Crow days, when the nation's capital was as segregated as any American city. Mimi and Joe knew the history but, probably like most people, believed past practices like Jim Crow were in the past. To learn differently was shocking. Also shocking was the fact that their informant—

Melinda Franklin, working on a doctorate in International Studies at George Washington University—was not shocked. "Given what's been happening in the country in recent years it is to be expected. But dammit, not in my neighborhood! Let them practice their hatred where they live. In fact, let them stay where they live and they won't have a problem."

Mimi looked askance at Melinda Franklin. "And so . . . what? You plan to burn out all the newcomers?"

"There's more than one way to skin a cat."

"I hate that expression!"

"Actually, so do I," Melinda said sheepishly. "Especially since I'm owned by two of the hairy beasts. I apologize—to you and to them. What I mean to say is—"

Mimi whipped out her recorder. "What, exactly? I'm really interested to know since we just walked up and down blocks where it appears at least a third of the residents are newcomers—"

"Are white," Melinda insisted.

"A good number of them are," Mimi said, "but suppose some of them want to open a business? They live here. Are you saying they shouldn't be able to?"

"Not if they want to dictate who can patronize their business."

"But business owners can do that—" Joe began, and Melinda interrupted him.

"Yeah: No Shirt, No Shoes. No Service. I get that. It's that MAGA shit—"

"Whoa. What exactly are you talking about?" Joe asked.

Melinda Franklin took a backward step and gave Mimi and Joe a long, appraising look. They gave her one right back. Finally she said, "Just like Mr. Zemekis only scratched the surface in his story about the murder-suicide couple, you're about to make the same mistake about the gentrification of this community, Ms. Patterson. Look deeper." She reached into the slouch bag that hung on her slender shoulder, retrieved a notepad and pen, and began writing. A millennial with a fountain pen and pad. Maybe young Melinda was going to be all right. "I'm giving you my number and the names and numbers of people you should talk with. And the names of streets you should visit. Look closely and carefully. I'm sure you both are familiar with that old saying, 'The devil is in the details'?" She tore the page from the notebook and gave it to Mimi. "Nice to have met you both." And she started to turn away, but Joe called her back.

"Why International Studies?" And when Melinda looked confused, Joe said, "A woman with your knowledge and skills is surely more useful at home—"

"Bullshit!" Melinda exclaimed. "I come from at least four generations of people who remained in place and dedicated themselves to making things better. Then, less than a month ago, my seventy-year-old grandmother is refused service in a coffee shop under the pretext that all the tables were reserved. I won't be the fifth generation to waste my time." And she walked away.

"Well shit," Joe said.

"You think she burned down this place?" Mimi asked, studying the burned-out shell of the former coffee shop, realizing with the shift of the wind that the acrid smoke smell still lingered even after a month.

Joe shrugged. "I suppose it's possible. She's certainly angry enough."

"If someone did that to my grandmother, I'd be angry enough, too," Mimi said, studying the information on the notepaper Melinda gave her.

"Why did you get the info sheet?" Joe whined in a near pout.

Mimi grinned. "Solidarity," she said, raising an Angela Davis-like fist.

Sgt. Alice Long didn't want to keep the ice pack on her face and she didn't want to talk about the altercation that had resulted in her bruised face. The entire incident was recorded on her body camera for any and all to see. What she wanted to talk about was how it happened that Eric Ashby and Jim Dudley no longer were part of their unit. It's what every one of them wanted to talk about, even more than they wanted to eat all the food Sgt.

Tommi ordered, which was a first. So Gianna told them about it. She told them exactly what happened. "So now you know what I know."

"He can just do that?"

"That's so not fair!"

"Did you tell him he couldn't take Lt. Ashby and Det. Dudley?"

"Suppose they didn't want to go?"

"They definitely didn't want to go!"

Gianna held up her hand and quiet descended immediately. They were, for the most part, young cops, and they all had forged a tight bond in their unit. Maybe too tight. "Listen to me, all of you. The chief of police and the deputy chief for operations do not need my permission or approval to do *anything*, and they didn't ask for it. I will miss Eric and Jim as much as all of you, but a police department is like the military. We serve at the pleasure and we follow orders, whether we like them or not. Period, end of discussion about things we can do nothing about. We don't have to like it, but we do have to deal with it."

They were seated at the long tables that faced the two huge wall monitors and the two dry erase grease boards, and they looked a dangerous mixture of angry, sad, and sullen. Damn Deputy Chief Schmidt. She went to stand in front of the room. Every pair of eyes followed her.

"I worked with Eric Ashby for most of my career, and I've known Jim Dudley for almost that long. They are good friends as well as trusted colleagues. And they're gone. We, on the other hand, are still here and we have work to do. So . . ."

She walked over to Alice and put a hand on her shoulder. "I'd planned to have Eric ease you into the duties of the operations sergeant but, Sgt. Long, that ship has sailed, leaving you kinda on your own." Then she turned to face Sgt. Bell. "I'll help as much as I can with the administrative responsibilities," she said.

Tommi Bell stood up and saluted. "Yes, Boss. Whatever you and Sgt. Long need. Just as long as she doesn't expect me to join her in training for that iron woman triathlon thing." Tommi

36

mimicked a person with a body full of broken bones trying to run. And just like that the tension in the room broke. Good-natured hoots and catcalls rang out. Alice, the pain of her battered face forgotten, got up and ran over to Tommi, grabbed her up and mimicked jogging and weight lifting, and Tommi feigned fainting. Then they hugged each other, and Gianna knew that her two sergeants would be okay, but more importantly, she knew that each woman would be fully in command of her responsibilities to the unit as a whole, and to the individual teams whose members relied on one or the other of their sergeants for just about everything in the pursuit of their daily responsibilities.

"Tim, I'd like for you to assume leadership of what now will be Team T." The shock and surprise on Tim McCreedy's face was slowly, gradually replaced by pleasure and excitement, which was all his new team—his former teammates—needed to see. They pounced on him like he was a squeaky toy. They mobbed him. They hugged him. They climbed on his back. Then they pounced on the food, and Gianna had to make herself heard over the din claiming one of the turkey and Swiss cheese sandwiches, and warning Bobby Gilliam, a notorious potato chip thief, to leave her bag of chips alone. He gave her a sheepish grin; then, with one hand holding two sandwiches across Alice Long's shoulders and the other hand holding three bags of potato chips across Tim McCreedy's shoulders, he headed toward the corner of the room nearest her cubicle. Tim couldn't be in better hands. He'd be all right.

"Sounds like you averted a disaster," Mimi said later that night as they discussed the events of the day—a relatively new experience for them on two fronts. First, they'd both given up working the ridiculously long hours that always got them home at nine or ten o'clock at night, too exhausted to do anything but fall into bed—and to sleep. But perhaps more importantly, they now spent time talking with each other openly and honestly about—almost everything. They'd spent the early part of their relationship being

37

overly careful and cautious about each other's professional boundaries. Then they had a period when their jobs constantly clashed. The reporter insisted that the public had a right to know certain information and the cop insisted that releasing that information not only could jeopardize the public, but could compromise the investigation. They had more than a few tense times until they learned that they could trust each other completely and understood that neither would ever do anything to jeopardize the work of the other.

"I averted a mutiny," Gianna said, "but I fear the disaster still looms."

That got Mimi's attention. She stopped pouring wine and looked steadily at Gianna. She believed she'd heard a hint of fear in her voice—not only unexpected but unprecedented—and if Gianna was frightened by something, then Mimi was terrified. "Loom and disaster in the same sentence?" Mimi tried to sound light. "Talk to me, love. What exactly is going on? Whose butt do I have to kick?"

No matter how dire the circumstance, Mimi could almost always make her feel better and now was no exception. Gianna laughed, accepted more wine, and said the words she knew would be a conversation stopper: "Your friend the chief of police."

Mimi almost choked. She had never heard Gianna speak a negative word about the chief, or His Excellency as Mimi dubbed him. Gianna always defended him in every circumstance. Not only was he her mentor, her protector, but he was her friend. And she now was saying the chief was responsible for the potential disaster that was looming over her, for the near mutiny in her unit.

"How, exactly?" Mimi asked calmly, feeling anything but.

"I'm more concerned about the why," Gianna said. "Why would he allow Schmidt to take two of my top people without a word of warning? And an explanation would have been preferable, though I know he doesn't have to explain his actions to me. But if I've done something to warrant that treatment, I'd like to know what it was!"

38

Now Mimi realized it wasn't fear she'd heard in Gianna's voice; it was pain, and while she would readily kick the ass of anyone who caused this woman pain, she didn't believe it was the chief of police. Not this time, and she said so. "He's a lot of things, among them jerk, asshole, son of a bitch, arrogant bastard. But he is not duplicitous, Gianna. He is not a backstabber. In fact, one of his best traits is his willingness to look you in the eye and tell you exactly what's on his mind."

"That's what I always thought," Gianna said.

"Keep thinking it, sweetheart. His Excellency did not tell Schmidt to raid your cupboard or give him permission to do so."

Wide-eyed and open-mouthed, Gianna shook her head in disbelief. "I know Schmidt is a self-important blowhard but—"

"He's a fool is what he is, Gianna. A dangerous fool but a fool nonetheless."

"You warned me to watch my back, that he'd have the long knives out, and how right you were. How did you get so wise?"

Mimi rolled her eyes, shook her head, blew through her teeth, and gave the finger to the invisible Deputy Chief Schmidt—and if there were more ways to express disgust, she'd have used them. "No wisdom involved. Don't forget that I've spent a career covering government and politics, which is another way of saying that I covered bureaucrats and politicians, so I know incompetent assholes with long knives when I see 'em. Unfortunately, some do a lot of damage before they're brought low."

Still in disbelief, Gianna wondered how long even a fool expected to get away with such a bold move, wondered how long it would be before the chief discovered it, and, if what Mimi said was true, wondered what she should—or could—do about it. "I can't run tattling to the principal like a schoolgirl."

"He'll make another misstep, probably a bigger one since he got away with this one, and that's when you rat his ass out," Mimi said, and yawned.

"And now you're too tired to tell me about your day," Gianna said through a yawn of her own.

Mimi shook her head. "Not too tired. I'm just not exactly sure

39

what story I may have stumbled upon, but it shows signs that the gentrification skirmishes on the East Side may be about to turn into open warfare."

"You sure you don't miss bureaucrats and politicians?" Gianna asked with a sly grin, and Mimi shot her a dirty look that would have chilled a lesser woman. Her woman laughed and took her to bed with the warning that sleep wasn't in her immediate future.

CHAPTER THREE

Mimi spent the following week learning all she could about the neighborhoods on the east side of town—that is, whenever she wasn't busy being one of the rotating digital content editors, a pursuit she enjoyed more than she was willing to admit to anyone, especially Tyler. However, she was and always would be a reporter, one who was damn glad to be back on the job, and the more she explored and learned about the part of town she'd only previously visited, the more interested she became. Turned out Melinda Franklin was 100 percent correct. It was a mistake to think that what was visible on the surface was the whole story. For starters, she learned that there were four distinct residential communities within the City East designation but that only one of them was a concentrated target of so-called gentrification, and it was the one that would—at least on the surface—be the least expected target. *Gotta get beneath the surface! My new mantra.* She must have spoken the thought because Joe and Carolyn were looking at her strangely. "What?"

"Yeah, what, Patterson?" Joe struggled to conceal a smirk. "Were you away so long you forgot how to work a story?"

Mimi let him have his fun, even if it was at her expense. Both he and Carolyn knew how tough it was to unearth those stories that lurked beneath the surface.

"You've got that look," Carolyn said, giving her a look, "the one that says you're on to something."

"I need to spend a day or two searching property records—"

Joe started twitching. This was one of his favorite things. "Looking for what?"

"Once upon a time in that community there was a grocery store—the elders called it a supermarket—a hardware store, and a café. Not raggedy, cheap places, either, but thriving, well-respected businesses. All the older people I've talked to remember them."

"What happened to 'em?" Joe asked.

Mimi gave a sad shake of her head. "Like a lot of small businesses, the people who owned them didn't also own the physical spaces—"

"Uh oh." Carolyn saw what was coming.

"Yep . . . but here's where it gets strange: The building owners, all of whom now live in the suburbs, had no complaints with their tenants—long-term and well-liked tenants. And the story I hear is that they were pressured to evict those tenants and paid way more money than either the buildings or the businesses were worth." Mimi let that sink in, watching her editor and her friend as they absorbed the information. Before she was an editor Carolyn had been a top reporter. Joe still was, like Mimi herself, and they both smelled the same stench that Mimi did.

"So . . . we've got what?" Carolyn asked. "Three vacant lots?"

Mimi gave her shark grin, shaking her head. Not vacant lots, she explained, but short strips of land on otherwise empty blocks with the same three businesses on each: a liquor store, an off-brand gas station, and a fast food joint . . . not a restaurant . . . a joint. None of the people who operated those businesses owned them, and none of them lived in the area. And almost all of the reported crime in the community occurred in these three areas: drug dealing, prostitution, home and car burglaries, fights, loud music playing at all hours, and the influx of nonresidents into these areas, lured by the crime. And then there were the homeless encampments on each of the three strips.

"What do you think is lurking beneath the surface, Mimi?" Carolyn asked. An editor who'd been a good reporter knew what questions to ask, knew what was involved in crafting a story from hundreds of pieces of buried information . . . making sense of those bits and pieces and forming them into a cogent whole. It was a process, usually a very painstaking one that could not be hurried.

"What are you smiling about?" Carolyn asked.

"I'm so glad you're not the Weasel," Mimi said.

Carolyn's usually calm, peaceful expression morphed into a horror mask. "Oh dear God so am I!" she exclaimed, and Mimi and Joe laughed. Actually laughed out loud, attracting smiles from their near neighbors, especially when Carolyn recovered and joined in the merriment. Such a welcome change from the recent past with their last editor, despite the fact that covering the news these days was a more daunting, not to mention completely and totally unrewarding, experience than ever before.

Confronting today's reporters was a president who lied every time he spoke, who was a racist, misogynist, homophobic buffoon with no knowledge of how the government worked and no desire to learn; a press secretary who lied to reporters about her boss's behavior and mirrored his worst traits; and a public who cheered him on. It was exhausting to watch, much less report on. Sticking close to home for stories was infinitely more satisfying.

"Want some help doing the records search?" Joe asked.

Over the years they'd both spent enough hours poring over and digging through records of various kinds to be adept at it at this point in their careers, so it didn't take long to unearth what they were looking for. Especially since the information wasn't deeply or carefully or even intelligently buried. "Well shit," Mimi muttered in disgust. "I could do without this."

She couldn't count the number of times she'd heard cops on television shows fervently swear a disbelief in coincidences. They didn't happen, pronounced the TV cops. Mimi knew differently. She had empirical proof that coincidences did happen. Which is why, when she studied the info she and Joe unearthed, when she traced the names of the real property owners and not the registered agents back through her memory of social and political and financial relationships, the stink was bad. Really bad. Worse than initially imagined.

"What don't I know?" Joe asked.

"This stuff—the worst of it—leads directly to the mayor, her chief of staff, her husband, and her son-in-law."

Joe looked at her, gape-jawed. "Directly. Which means there's probably more to find when we know where to look."

Mimi nodded and felt miserable. It never ceased to amaze her how really stupid intelligent people could be. And arrogant. They actually thought—believed—that they could get away with it. "This is your story, Joe. Go get it, dude."

"Then what's yours?"

"The people who have been displaced or, worse, evicted, or even worse than that, cheated out of their homes. The people whose neighborhoods have been destroyed. The people who have no place to go."

"But you know the players, their connections to each other and to the city. You know where the bodies are buried and where some are being dug up. You're really the one to write this story—and before you speak the words, I know you swore never to write another graft and corruption story."

And she fully intended to keep that promise. Anyway, she didn't care about such stories any more. Why should a mayor be held to a higher standard than the president? Why should city council people be expected to behave ethically when members of the US Congress and the Cabinet were not and did not? No matter how much the corrupt city officials stole, it wouldn't even be able to pay the tax on what the "First Friends" had been and still were, stealing. Didn't make the city officials' misfeasance and malfeasance acceptable, and they'd pay for it. They should pay for it. Breaking the public trust always hurt the public. But it wouldn't be M. Montgomery Patterson who'd have her finger on the justice scales. Not this time. Somebody else's turn.

✳ ✳ ✳

44

With Eric gone, Gianna had no one she could talk to about her growing unease with Randall Connelly. In the days following the demonstration, he behaved increasingly badly. He was offhand and flippant, feigning disinterest in the fate of the arrested escapees, while constantly asking seemingly innocent questions about their circumstances. In the week since Eric's departure he had become sullen, almost surly, and Tim had told him to straighten up or he'd get benched.

"Benched!" A furious Randall exclaimed. "Whadda you mean, benched? You can't bench me!"

"Wanna bet?" Tim replied.

Since Randall also took advantage of Eric's departure by coming in late to work almost daily, Tim managed to bench him the next day by taking his team on an early morning run in Rock Creek park, followed by a swim at a nearby indoor pool. Nobody knew where Tim and Team T were—or at least nobody admitted to knowing—so Randall had to sit by himself until his team returned. "I'll just hang out with Team B," he announced.

"Not happening," Bobby Gilliam responded almost kindly. "We've got work to do that is team specific."

So Randall Connelly was left sitting alone, watching Kenny Chang and Vik Patel work their computers until he got bored. He whipped out a magazine from his backpack and started to read, which is when Sgt. Alice Long entered the room.

"What are you doing here, Connelly?"

He shrugged but continued reading. "The team left me."

"That means you were late. Third time this week," Alice said. "Your paycheck will reflect—"

That got Connelly's attention. "You better not fuck with my paycheck," he snarled.

"And you better not talk to anyone in this unit in that tone of voice," Gianna said, "especially a senior officer." She had come into the room behind Alice, unnoticed by Randall Connelly. All the color drained from his face though he remained slouched in his chair. "On your feet, Patrol Officer Connelly," Gianna snapped, and he dropped his book and stood up. At that moment

45

Gianna's phone rang. She answered, listened for a brief moment, and all the color drained from her face as she powered off the phone. "With me, Alice," she barked, and made for the door, a concerned Alice Long on her heels.

When they were in the hall, Gianna said to Alice, "Take the back stairs to the basement, Alice, and run. Stay there until I tell you it's safe to return. Deputy Chief Schmidt is on his way here with orders to transfer you to his command, and damned if I'm going to let that happen."

Without a word Alice bolted for the door halfway down the hall, and Gianna knew she wouldn't stop running until she reached the basement. Gianna headed for her cubicle at the rear of the room and beckoned Bobby Gilliam to follow her. "Take your team to the gym," she told him, "and take Connelly with you. Don't come back until you hear from Tommi that it's safe. Go!"

"Right, Captain," he said, and sprinted back across the room. He gathered his team and Randall Connelly, and they exited one side of the double doors that led to their unit as Deputy Chief Gerhard Schmidt and his adjutant entered the other. Gianna kept her eyes on the paperwork on her desk and pretended not to see him until he spoke.

"Captain."

She looked up, surprised, and stood. "Good morning, sir."

He extended a hand that once again was not an offer to shake but contained a sheaf of papers. "These are orders that transfer Sgt. Alice Long to my command, effective immediately," he said.

Gianna took the papers from him and dropped them on her desk. "Alice is away. A family emergency. She'll be back tomorrow or the next day. Sir," she added, making sure it sounded like an afterthought.

Schmidt was flummoxed. Part of his face registered disbelief, the other part dismay. He wouldn't put it past Gianna Maglione to lie to him, but then he knew how serious she was about following the rules. "Please have Sgt. Long report to me as soon as she returns," he said, and turned away. She let him get out of the

46

door before she picked up the phone on her desk, but she got her breathing under control before she punched in Tommi's number.

"Yes, ma'am?" Tommi said.

"I'm going up to the chief's office. Bobby and his team are in the gym, and Alice is in the basement. Once you determine that Schmidt is back in his office you can bring our people home. And Tommi? Do not tell anyone where I am." She picked up the papers Schmidt had brought and walked slowly to the elevator, not because of her leg but to give herself time to get her temper under control. She had never shown the chief of police anger. Frustration on more than one occasion, maybe some pique, but never anger, and she couldn't—wouldn't—do it now.

She was relatively calm when she opened the door to his suite. Capt. Thomas Mintz greeted her warmly if with confusion: She didn't have an appointment with the chief. "Good morning, Captain," she said, shaking his hand. "I apologize for barging in like this, but I need a few moments with the chief. Please."

Mintz gave her an appraising look. He knew Gianna Maglione was a favorite of the police chief, and with good reason. He also knew she wasn't the kind to show up uninvited without a good reason. "Give me a minute, Captain," he said, and he knocked on the chief's door, opened it, and went in. The deep plush of the royal blue carpet silenced all movement. Gianna had never spent much time in the chief's outer office and today was no exception. She barely had time to take in the historical renderings of Washington, DC, before Mintz was back, holding the door open for her.

"Thanks, Captain," she said.

"My pleasure, Captain," he said.

"What's the matter, Maglione?" the chief said when she entered his office.

She inhaled deeply. "If I've done something to upset or anger you, Chief—"

"You haven't," he said, and waited. He was in front of his massive desk, facing her, hands deep in his pockets. His jacket was off and his sleeves were rolled up to his elbows. Piles of papers covered the desk, but in neat stacks, not a disorganized mess.

"I wish you'd tell me why Deputy Chief Schmidt is poaching my senior staff—"

"What the hell are you talking about, Maglione?" Now he was irritated, and he began jiggling the coins in his pockets. He must put coins there every morning when he dressed for that purpose she thought.

"A week ago, he transferred Eric Ashby and Jim Dudley to his command, and this morning he arrived with transfer papers for Alice Long—"

"Stop talking, Maglione!" he thundered. Now he was angry. "Mintz!"

The door opened immediately, and Capt. Mintz entered as if propelled. "Sir."

"Have we received any personnel paperwork from Schmidt in the last week?"

"No, sir," Mintz replied. His eyes never left the chief.

"I would never take any of your people in a stealth move, and it pains me that you think I would."

"That's what Mimi said."

The chief gave her a wide-eyed look of surprise. "Patterson said that about me?"

"Yes, sir. She said one of your best traits is that you looked people in the eye and said or did whatever was on your mind. No secrets and no games."

He nodded. "Mintz, call a Command Staff meeting for 08:30 tomorrow. In my conference room. No refreshments. It'll be a short meeting."

"Yes, sir," Mintz said, gliding silently out.

Gianna exhaled as deeply as she'd inhaled. "I'm sorry, Chief. I guess I couldn't imagine that anyone would take such action without your approval."

"Me either," he said grimly.

"I'm sorry, Chief," she said again.

"You said he came for Alice? But he didn't take her?"

Gianna gave a small, grim smile. "No, sir. I lied and said she was away." She extended Schmidt's papers. "He left the orders with me."

"Good for you, but you must be struggling without Ashby and Dudley."

"Yes, sir, I am. I need a lieutenant and—"

"Mintz!" And when Mintz appeared as if he'd never left, the chief issued another order: "Get me Andy Page." And when Mintz disappeared again the chief looked squarely at Gianna. "You like Andy Page, don't you? Think you could work with him?"

Gianna was struck momentarily speechless, and her boss watched while she found her voice—and her thoughts. "I haven't had a lot of interaction with him, but I like what I've seen. But Chief, I don't want to poach another captain's second-in-command."

He gave her a wry grin. "Nice of you to care, Maglione, but I've already got him, so no poaching involved. Not that I could be guilty of such a thing 'cause I am THE chief and I can deploy resources as I see fit." He paced a few steps, thinking, Gianna knew, how much to tell her about why Andy Page wasn't part of ATTF anymore. It also gave her time to think.

"I like what I know of him, sir."

"He likes you, too. So much that he didn't want to return to ATTF after the assist he gave your unit at the demo, which really pissed off his boss. 'He doesn't want to be here, I don't want him here,' is the message I got, and I've been trying to figure out what to do with him ever since. So, while I'm sorry for what Schmidt did—"

Two quick raps and the door silently opened to admit Lt. Andy Page. He was about to greet the chief when he saw Gianna. His eyes widened in surprise; then a grin split his face, and he rushed forward to greet her, hand extended.

"Captain, good to see you."

"Good to see you as well, Lieutenant. And since I haven't seen you since that scuffle last week, let me thank you again for your help—"

"You two can do your mutual admiration society dance on your own time since you now belong to each other. Page, say hello to your new boss." Page's mouth flew open, but before he could speak the chief told him to wait outside. He saluted and ran to the door as if to make certain there would be no change of mind. "One more change for you to deal with, Maglione, one I don't think you'll mind. I want to give your unit to Eddie Davis. I want to be damn certain that what happened to you will never happen again, and I'm sorry you had to go through it."

"You have nothing to be sorry for."

"You operated so effectively on your own for so long, Maglione, that I guess I thought you always would. But you had no protection—"

"I had you, Chief." And ever since he had removed her Hate Crimes Unit from then Capt. Eddie Davis's oversight, she had answered exclusively to him.

"And that used to be enough," he said grimly. "Time was, nobody would dream of making an end run around me." He sighed. "But times are different." Then he grinned his shark grin. "But not even Schmidt is brave enough to try and end-run Davis." The grin widened, showing teeth. "Though I'd dearly love to see him try."

"Thank you, Chief—for Andy and for Commander Davis. I can work with both of them."

Andy Page was waiting for her, and his face lit up when he saw her. "Captain, I'm really working for you now?" And he grabbed her hand again.

"You really are, Andy." Then she looked at Thomas Mintz, and he gave her a wink and a grin before he silently entered the chief's office again. "And I'm glad you're happy about it. I also hope you can swim because I'm about to toss you into the deep end of the pool."

She took her phone from her pocket, punched Tommi Bell's number, asked her to assemble everyone for a meeting, and then turned to Andy, but he spoke before she could. "You really are about to throw me in the deep end, aren't you?" he asked, but the look on his face was one of pure joy. No hint of fear.

✳ ✳ ✳

"Meet and welcome our new lieutenant, Andy Page, who comes to us from the Anti-Terrorism Task Force—" She was interrupted by a loud, mocking whistle and a bark of laughter.

"What happened, dude; you get demoted?" This from Randall Connelly who was grinning and smirking, looking around the room expecting to meet cosigners to his tomfoolery. He was met with stony-faced disdain.

Andy Page walked to the front of the room. He had everyone's attention except Randall's, and everyone except Randall knew that was a mistake. "You!" Page thundered, and Randall Connelly finally looked at him. To his credit he had the good sense to stand up.

"Sir?"

"Do not ever interrupt your captain again when she's speaking. Got that?"

"Yes, sir, Lieutenant."

Andy turned to face Gianna. "Sorry for the interruption, Captain. You were saying?"

"Doesn't matter. You can handle things." She signaled Alice, Tommi, Tim and Bobby with a glance and they hurried to her side. "These are your sergeants: Thomasina Bell, Administration, and Alice Long, Operations. And these are your team leaders, Detectives Tim McCreedy and Bobby Gilliam." Gianna allowed handshakes all around before she signaled to Alice and Tommi to follow her. "You can have them back shortly, Andy," and she left him to get acquainted with the operational teams.

Tommi and Alice followed her to the back of the room to her cubicle. Since Tommi had already told Alice about Schmidt's visit Gianna didn't feel it necessary to add anything more, so she told them what she knew about Andy Page. Then she told them about their assignment to Commander Eddie Davis.

"You don't look upset, boss," Alice said warily.

"I'm not," Gianna replied. "Hate Crimes reported to him for a while. He's a good boss."

"But what kinda guy is he?" Alice asked.

Gianna gave a sly, wicked grin. "The kind Gerhard Schmidt won't come within one hundred yards of."

"Oh Lord help me!" Tommi exclaimed, looking across the room, and Gianna laughed out loud. She hadn't seen Commander Davis in a long time, and she'd forgotten how good looking he was, and what effect he had on women. He looked like a young Sidney Poitier, a fact that caused straight women like Tommi to all but swoon and which elicited a controlled "wow" from Alice who didn't have a straight bone in her gorgeous body.

Gianna stood up and walked forward to meet her once-again boss, aware that every eye in the room watched them. Grayer at the temples with more crinkles around the eyes, but his pleasure at seeing her was genuine. She extended a hand, but he wrapped her in a quick hug, releasing her just as quickly, and every heart rate in the room slowed. "I am so glad to see you, Commander, and so glad to be working together again."

"You notice that I came as soon as the chief told me," he said.

She led him to her cubicle. "Let me introduce the two people who really run this show: Sergeants Tommi Bell and Alice Long."

"I hear you women run a tight ship," Davis said, shaking their hands, and Tommi stopped breathing for a second while Alice stole a glance at Gianna.

They left, and he waved Gianna into her chair and took the seat across the table opposite her. "We have a lot of catching up to do, but I can see that you have things well in hand here."

"This is as good a group as I've ever had," Gianna said.

He nodded, then got down to business: "Two things right away. First, the chief says we've got to give this unit a name. I'm thinking Special Intelligence Mobile and Tactical Unit."

Gianna processed the information she'd just received. So that's what Eddie Davis did. He ran Intelligence. She nodded. "Works for me," she said.

"Next: You need more people, and the loss of two of your aces made that need acute. You have done remarkable work, Anna, and I don't know how with so few people. I want to add at least eight or ten more. You can decide if you want a third team or if you want to increase the two you have. I'll send some personnel folders over later today. Okay?"

"Fine, Commander," she said, and it was. It was also a relief. She couldn't continue at the same pace and with the same results with so few people, even with those people giving 200 percent all day, every day. It wasn't fair to them. It wasn't fair to her either, for that matter.

"Third thing: I don't like you exposed in this cubicle like you are. I understand why you relinquished your office. Of course the admin sergeant needs a room with a door that locks, but so do you. And Anna—I insist on it. I'll send a crew over right away to look at this space back here—"

"I want and need to be able to see them, Commander, and they want and need to be able to see me," Gianna said. And it wasn't a request.

Davis eyed her steadily and got an equally steady, hazel-eyed gaze back. "We could use lots of bulletproof glass at the top and some kind of reinforced—something at the bottom," he said.

She nodded. He was the only person who called her Anna. When they first started working together, he said he thought Gianna sounded too familiar and Giovanna too formal. He asked if he could call her Anna. She agreed, and he called her Anna as they forged a strong relationship based on mutual trust and respect. The passage of time had not changed that. "I've got a situation that needs your immediate attention," she said to him. She turned her computer around to face him, gave him a headset to put on, and played the demonstration tape showing Randall Connelly's actions. He played it three times, then looked several questions at her. She answered them because she knew what they were. What she hadn't realized was how much she missed him—nor how much like him she had become. She knew that her team thought she was the perfect boss. That was because, she realized, she managed the way he managed: firmly but without getting in the way, and always respecting and trusting the people in her command. He thought in straight lines, but was always prepared for the unexpected. She worked the same way—the way she had learned from him. She told him everything about Randall Connelly and the escape from the police barricade by the demonstrators, about how at least one of

53

them was connected to the group that had bombed Metro GALCO, the Gay and Lesbian Community Organization. She told him about how two of them lived right here in DC on the East Side—and that's when he stopped her.

"At best the little creep is disloyal. At worst, he's a traitor. In any case he puts our people at risk. I want him transferred to my command today."

"Done," Gianna said so quickly that Davis smiled. She couldn't get rid of Connelly fast enough, and she didn't care if her boss knew it. Connelly needed to be where there were enough eyes to keep tabs on him and enough power to bring him down if it came to that. "I'll have Tommi prepare the paperwork."

"I'll send somebody to get it and Connelly within the hour, when I'll also send the personnel files of potential candidates for your review."

"I'll get on that immediately," she said, the relief evident in her voice.

He started to speak, hesitated, then said, "Does Ms. Patterson know how heavily this job has weighed on you?"

She nodded. "At least most of it. Maybe not the heaviest parts."

He stood up. "Well, now that you're not in it alone, maybe you can tell her all of it, especially about the heaviest parts."

"Do you? Share all of it?"

"I do now," he said with a sheepish grin, "after Nell threatened to leave me. And it was not an idle threat." Gianna could see that the thought of his wife leaving him still scared him.

Gianna laughed, kind of, remembering painfully when Mimi did leave her, kind of, and it scared the shit out of her. She stood up, too—a bit too quickly—and grimaced even as she waved away Davis's offered hand. "It's a lot better than it was," she said.

"So I hear," he said, and left.

Gianna summoned her lieutenant and her sergeants and told them everything Commander Davis had told her, beginning with the official name of their unit.

"So the Commander runs Intelligence," Andy said, nodding his head. "Makes sense the chief would put us there."

54

"Just as long as Randall Connelly is somebody else's problem," Tommi said, and slapped her palms against each other. "Good riddance to bad rubbish."

"My grandma used to say that," Alice exclaimed.

"Mine, too," Andy added.

"Where do you think I got it?" Tommi asked, and they all looked at Gianna.

She shrugged. "My grandmao might have said it, too, but it would have been in Italian and lost on me. Though when I think about them, I can imagine it's something they would say." She frowned a thought. "I need to work on my Italian." Then, "Two teams or three?"

"I vote three, Cap," Andy said. "Smaller teams deploy faster, and Commander Davis did call us mobile, right?"

Gianna nodded, then looked at Alice. "You're Ops. Your thoughts?"

"I agree, and I'm wondering if Lynda Lopez can handle being a team leader." Gianna's surprise showed and Alice quickly explained: "She's a damn good cop, she's smart, and she's paid more dues than most. My only reservation is, I wonder whether she's tough enough to be a team leader."

"And that's a big reservation, Alice," Andy said. "Maybe big enough to outweigh all those other good qualities. A team leader needs a kick-ass attitude when that's what's called for, needs to be ready and willing to kick ass if that's what's called for."

Alice shook her head in resignation. "Kicking ass is not part of Lynda's DNA."

"How about Annie Anderson?" Tommi asked, and everybody looked at her, although they were seeing Annie Anderson; and what Gianna and Alice saw was a young woman who could and would kick ass if and when necessary. She had even caught Andy's eye, and he hadn't been there an entire shift yet.

"You might be on to something, Tommi," Gianna said thoughtfully, thinking that Annie was awfully young, but she also was well respected by both teams. "You three do a deep dive into the files the Commander sends over. Get help from the computer heads. I

55

don't want any more surprises." *Like Taylor Johnstone, the junkie, and Randall Connelly,* she thought. "And Andy, you and Alice work up a training schedule. I have a feeling that things have been too calm for too long."

"I'd like to suggest that each team have a member trained in evasive driving and in the use of a long gun." And at the look on Gianna's face Andy hurried to explain his reasoning. "We're a mobile and tactical unit, which means we could be deployed anywhere at any time to do anything, right?"

Of course he was right. His experience working on a tactical team was not only evident but important and useful. He definitely was an asset to whatever it was that the Commander had created. And she'd certainly need an enclosed office with a door that locked if keys to vehicles and long guns needed a place to live. Ditto for the kinds of conversations she'd be having with Page and Alice, who at that moment was giving him the animal, mineral or vegetable look. *What are you, dude?* her look asked.

"I admit that's something I'd never considered, Andy, but I certainly see your point. I'll present it to Commander Davis, but I expect he'll okay it, giving us another reason to get ourselves restructured—and quickly."

"Hate crimes are still important to us, right, Captain?" Alice asked.

"Always," Gianna replied, adding, "especially since hate seems to be bigger and stronger and more widespread than ever." She barely succeeded in keeping the anger from her voice. Tommi gave her Connelly's transfer papers. She read and signed and wondered only briefly what Davis would do with him, but she really didn't care. Good riddance to bad rubbish indeed. She queried Andy Page about his immediate needs, but he said his paperwork was all in order. All he needed was a lanyard and a key.

"We'll all need new lanyards, Tommi, with our new name on them," Gianna said, adding that the old photos of the existing team members would be good enough.

Tommi was nodding and writing. She said, "Special Intelligence Mobile and Tactical Unit, Intelligence Division. Or Intelligence Command?" Gianna shrugged and told her to ask the man himself, and Sgt. Bell almost swooned at the thought.

"Uniforms, Cap?" Andy asked. "At ATTF—"

Gianna shook her head an emphatic *NO*. She'd always thought the ATTF crew looked a little silly in their matching cargo pants and T-shirts. "Maybe jackets that say POLICE, and only if we're going into a potentially dangerous situation and some idiot might confuse us with the bad guys. But no uniforms." She thought Andy looked a little relieved. Then his expression changed as he looked toward the front door. A uniformed patrol officer was wheeling a folder-and-file-filled cart into the room, trailed by a plainclothes sergeant. The three of them quickly stood and hurried to meet their guests. Gianna stood more slowly because her bad leg was always stiff after sitting for a long time, but she walked forward as quickly as possible.

"Captain Maglione, Commander Davis said you'd be expecting these files."

"Yes, thank you."

"If you'd please sign," he asked, and she did, and controlled her smile as her sergeants and lieutenant took control of the cart and all but ran from the room. "And this is the paperwork requesting the transfer of Patrol Officer Randall Connelly to our command, your signature also required." Gianna signed and gave him the corresponding documents transferring Connelly from her command to Davis's. Then she turned to face her team, all of whom were watching her silently and very closely.

"Officer Connelly," she called out, and watched him stand and walk toward her. For the first time he was without his usual smirk or snide grin. "You are officially transferred to Intelligence Command, effective immediately. Please surrender your lanyard and key and accompany these officers."

He was dumbstruck. He tried several times to speak, but no words came out. Someone called his name, and he turned to see his backpack sailing toward him. He caught it just before it hit the ground. He turned back to Gianna to see her extended hand, and he relinquished his ID lanyard and office key.

Davis's two officers saluted Gianna, wished her a good day, and followed Randall Connelly out, one on either side of him in close formation, just as Andy and Alice returned, both wearing wide grins. Gianna went to the front of the room and stood beneath the video screens.

"It's been a very busy day but a very good day, so you all can relax your faces and get your breathing back to normal. We have a lot to talk about, but these are broad strokes: We now belong to Commander Eddie Davis—" and she allowed the loud cheers and whistles that followed, led by Bobby Gilliam, Lynda Lopez, Kenny Chang and Tim McCreedy, all of whom knew him from the old HCU days.

"You're all right with this, right, Cap?" Bobby asked.

"Better than all right, Bobby. Especially since we now have a name," and there was more yelling and cheering when she told them what it was. A stunned and awe-filled silence greeted the news of the new additions to the unit and the formation of a third team. The news that Annie Anderson was to be the new team leader brought them all to their feet and Annie into the air on several shoulders. Gianna knew there'd be no controlling them now. "They're all yours," she said to Andy and Alice, and returned to her cubicle in the back of the room.

CHAPTER FOUR

Rain and winter arrived together on the leading edge of a fast-moving cold front in the middle of the night. Mimi kept hoping that snuggling closer to Gianna would bring warmth, to no avail. The arctic wind slammed the rain against windows that did not rattle in the onslaught because, the real estate agent had stressed, though the building was old it was sound, and had been remodeled expertly and efficiently. Excellent construction notwithstanding, however, winter was here, and heat and blankets were needed. Mimi jumped out of bed and hurried into the bathroom. She grabbed two blankets from the linen cabinet. She wrapped her naked self in one of them and spread the other over Gianna who had curled into a frigid fetal ball. She sighed, unfolded, and Mimi heard her whispered, "thanks, love," as she sprinted down the long hallway to the temperature control panel. The A/C had been off for almost two months, and they'd never used the heat. She pressed the button and hurried back to bed. Two blankets and Gianna's warming body . . . who cared if the heat worked?

Three hours later found her wishing fervently for heat in Florence Gregory's apartment. They sat in the kitchen where the oven door was open for heat, drinking a delicious chai tea and eating scones and muffins she had baked that morning, not because of her guest but to keep the oven going to heat the apartment. And it was a wonderful apartment: spacious and light-filled, beautifully appointed, gleaming hardwood floors that were home to deeply colorful Persian carpets; and Florence Gregory was the ultimate complement to her surroundings. Mimi knew from Melinda Franklin that the woman was in her early seventies but Florence Gregory was living, breathing proof that seventy was the new fifty . . . or that this seventy was not your grandmother's seventy. Only the wariness and weariness in her eyes and the tight lines around her lips suggested that something in the passage of time had taxed her.

"I think perhaps we can sit in the living room now, Miss Patterson. The oven has been on long enough that heat should have migrated that way."

Mimi stood up and helped Florence load a teak tray with their cups and a basket of scones and muffins. Then, carrying the tray, she followed her hostess into the living room, thinking that a city council ordinance that had passed several years ago required landlords to turn on the heat when the temperature demanded it. Surely Florence Gregory would know this. For that matter the building super should have fired up the boiler at first light given how cold it was. These thoughts raced through Mimi's mind in a few seconds and were replaced just as quickly by another: The building had no super. Mimi had walked right into an unlocked lobby that was not as clean as it should have been. In fact, it was flat-out dingy, though, to be honest, it was not really dirty.

Florence was looking at Mimi as if reading her thoughts. "I'm very familiar with your work, Ms. Patterson. I've been reading your stories for years, so when young Melinda asked if I'd speak with you, I readily agreed. If anyone can help our predicament it's you."

Mimi studied the older woman, unable to read anything in the inscrutable mask that was her face. She had scooted back into the corner of the sofa and hugged one of the cushions close to her, like a protective shield. Or for warmth. Additional warmth, for she wore a light blue Spelman College sweatshirt over a turtleneck sweater—the neck and sleeves visible beneath the sweatshirt—and Columbia University sweatpants in a darker blue. She wore thick socks and fleece-lined booties on her feet, and she had a long, multicolored woolen scarf wrapped around her neck. "Why hasn't your landlord turned on the heat, Ms. Gregory? The law says—"

The sound the older woman made in the back of her throat— half growl, half snort, stopped Mimi's words mid-sentence. "There will be no heat turned on here, Ms. Patterson. We had no heat last winter—"

"It was one of the coldest on record!" Mimi exclaimed.

"They want to get rid of us, so we have no services or amenities of any kind in this building—in this complex. The residents here keep the lobbies of the buildings and the grounds clean ourselves, as best we can—"

"That is illegal!" Mimi exclaimed.

"Of course it is," Florence Gregory said calmly and rationally, "and maybe if you can find out who's being paid off in city government and write about it, maybe something will change." She hugged the sofa pillow closer, tighter. A woman under siege.

"How did you survive last winter with no heat? How will you survive this winter?"

She smiled. "Half a dozen space heaters. My nephew bought them for me. They're all on the top shelf in the hall closet, but I suffer from vertigo and I can't get them down. Cameron—that's my nephew—he'll come this evening after work or tomorrow and get them down for me."

Mimi stood up. "Would you like for me to get them down?"

Florence Gregory's eyes widened in surprise, then in gratitude, as she got to her feet. "Would you? That would be wonderful and most appreciated."

Mimi followed her into the hallway where she opened the door at the end and turned on the light. A ladder was already there, probably waiting for Cameron. Mimi unfolded it, set it at the proper angle, and climbed up. She spied the heaters right away, neatly arranged on the topmost shelf. "If I hand them down to you—"

"I'll catch them, no problem. I just can't look up at you or climb that ladder. Serious vertigo."

In just a few moments all six heaters were down and Florence

61

had two plugged in and spewing heat in the living room, where Mimi finally was warm enough to take off her jacket. She was pouring them more tea when Florence returned—minus the scarf that had been wrapped around her neck and carrying an accordion folder of papers, which she gave to Mimi.

"What's all this?"

"It's in chronological order. Begin at the front."

Mimi, holding the folder on her lap, removed the front sheaf of stapled-together papers and frowned as she read. It was a notice from the code enforcement division of the housing department informing Allen Bruce, the registered agent for the River View Development Corporation, that a $5,000 fine had been assessed for failure to provide heat to residents of River View Apartments. Mimi's frown deepened as she realized that the notice was on official Housing Department stationery. How would a resident gain access to this document? Furthermore, despite all the time she and Zemekis had spent combing through property and tax records they had never come across an entity called River View Development Corporation or River View Apartments or the name Allen Bruce. Mimi stopped reading and looked up to find Florence Gregory watching her intently. And expectantly. She was waiting for Mimi's questions.

"Where did you get this document?"

"I did nothing illegal."

"Somebody did, Ms. Gregory, for a resident to be in possession of an official document," Mimi said with a calmness she didn't feel.

"My brother's brother-in-law is a housing inspector. He's been watching River View for a while," Florence said, "and he's shared with me what he could."

"He's breaking the law," Mimi said.

Florence nodded but didn't speak as she continued to watch Mimi, whose next question was really three questions, and they elicited a half smile from the older woman. "Whoever River View is, they bought this complex almost three years ago, and no, I've never met anyone associated with that company. But I've

62

lived in this building since it was built—it'll be twenty years come spring—when it was called 'The Alexis' after the owner's wife. Every building in the complex was named after a woman in his family: his wife, his mother, his three daughters. And the complex was called 'Capitol on the Potomac'." Her smile widened at the memory. "I was one of the first to move in here. It was beautiful. The whole area was beautiful. And the buildings and grounds were well maintained. Almost all the residents were Black and the owners were white and if anybody hated anybody else they kept it to themselves. Not like the ugly stupidity we're seeing today."

Mimi took a breath. And another. "When did the River View people first start trying to force you out?"

"From the beginning. From the moment they took over. It's all there," she said, pointing to the file on Mimi's lap. "Every piece of correspondence from them—"

Mimi shook her head. "I can't take this. I shouldn't. You need these documents for your records—"

Now Florence shook her head. "These papers will be safer with you than if they remain here. Someone has been looking for them—"

"Are you saying you've had a break-in?"

She shrugged. "Technically not a break-in, no. Whoever came in used a key. It has happened twice so far. My things have been gone through. Nothing damaged or broken, but I know when my things have been disturbed, and both times they went through all the papers in my desk and in the file cabinet."

Mimi was looking steadily at her, and Florence finally grinned and told Mimi that these papers were kept under her mattress.

"These papers should be in a safety deposit box at the bank," Mimi said.

"Then you couldn't review them and get at the truth," Florence responded.

Mimi wanted to say something else, but she didn't know what. "Suppose you have no heat all winter? Today was just the first day of cold weather, and it's not even winter yet. What will you do?"

"Same thing I did last year. Besides, this is my home, Ms. Patterson. This is where I live. I won't allow criminals to force me out."

Mimi returned the papers to the file and stood up. "The only thing I can promise you, Ms. Gregory, is that I will read every piece of paper here," she said.

Florence nodded. "That's good enough for me. Thank you, Ms. Patterson."

"You have nothing to thank me for yet."

Now Florence smiled a full, wide, happy smile. Almost a Cheshire grin, really. "But I know that I will."

Mimi cursed under her breath when she exited the building and a gust of icy wind attacked her skin as if she were naked. In the middle of the walkway she turned and faced the building. Above the door, carved into a marble inlay, "THE ALEXIS" was clearly visible. Mimi walked the entire complex—one other high-rise and four four-story structures. She stopped in front of each building, a couple of which were in deplorable condition, while one appeared to be as well-kept as Florence Gregory's building. Each building bore a woman's name carved in a marble inlay above the door: "THE SARAH," "THE AMY," "THE JOYCE," "THE SUSAN," and "THE JEANNE." Nowhere on the property did Mimi see a sign designating it the River View Apartments. She did, however, hear the train screech into its stop, which was even closer than the one she and Zemekis had seen a few blocks away. And though she didn't see the river, she smelled it. She looked up one final time, and in a second-floor window of The Sarah was an old woman wrapped in a heavy blanket, nothing visible but her face. As Mimi watched the blanket slid from the woman's head and one scrawny arm emerged. Mimi walked closer and the woman beckoned to Mimi. She appeared a decade older than Florence Gregory. That or her health care was nonexistent. The old woman beckoned again. Only the arm moved. The dark, deep-set eyes in a face more wrinkled than a prune slow-blinked like a turtle. Mimi tightened

64

her scarf, knowing instinctively that it would be colder in this building, named after someone's Sarah, than in The Alexis.

It was frigid in the dirty, paper-strewn lobby. Not bothering to call an elevator that she doubted worked anyway, Mimi climbed to the second floor, not touching the bannister, even with a gloved hand. When she reached the next landing, the old woman was standing in the hall, the blanket back over her head, and she was very old, much older than Florence. Or maybe just a lot more weary.

"Did Mr. Harris send you?" she asked in an ancient, scratchy voice, the tone almost hopeful.

"No, I'm sorry. I don't know Mr. Harris." The old eyes filled with water, and the old body turned to go back into the icebox she called home, but she stopped when Mimi called her back. "If you tell me your name and how to find him, I'll contact Mr. Harris for you."

She shook her head almost forcefully and the blanket fell away, revealing a full head of wispy snow-white hair. "It don't matter. It's too late. If he hadda done what he said he would, when he said he would . . . but it's too late now! She's dead! The ambulance came and got her last night. And I couldn't even be there to help her." The old woman was weeping now, tears and snot crystalizing on her face.

"Who are you talking about . . . please tell me your name. Who died?"

"My sister. She lived on the top floor of The Jeanne. She didn't have but one leg—lost the other one to diabetes. I told her not to live up on that top floor, but you never could tell her anything. Then when the elevator went out and they wouldn't fix it she couldn't get to the clinic, couldn't get her medicine. And then when it got cold and we didn't have no heat . . . her body was too broke down . . ."

"Who is Mr. Harris and what was he going to do?"

"He works for the aging office in the Housing Department. Ain't none of them people in the government downtown no good to nobody." She went inside and closed the door.

Zemekis was waiting for her in the reading room. So was an order of sautéed broccoli and tofu. He'd already eaten so he read while Mimi ate and filled him in between bites. He mumbled "holy shit" at least half a dozen times, and when Mimi finished eating and told him everything she'd seen and heard, he agreed that they should get Carolyn involved. She joined them, bringing her half-eaten egg salad sandwich, which remained that way as she listened to them. She was silent for a long moment when they finished talking. Then she took two bites of her sandwich. Then she sighed, but not out of frustration. She was deep in thought, and Mimi and Joe watched her think, prepared to sit watching for as long as it took. But because it was Carolyn, they knew it wouldn't take too long.

"First find out who Harris is, then find the paramedics who transported the woman from that location last night, and then lean on the ME until we get a cause of death."

They knew where she was going with this. If the conditions in her building contributed to the woman's death, then the owners and managers could be held accountable. Carolyn proved them right when next she said, "And I think the Allen Bruce in those documents is probably Bruce Allen King—"

"That Ponzi scheme fruitcake who went to federal prison?" Zemekis exclaimed. "Didn't he get a fat sentence?"

Carolyn nodded as she delicately popped the last bit of her sandwich into her mouth. "Twelve to fifteen," she said, chewing.

"Then what's he doing out and how is he involved in any enterprise that involves people and their money?"

"Very good questions indeed," Carolyn said. "I trust you two will find the answers."

That's when Mimi told them about the proximity to the train and the river, and she saw them register the possibilities. Carolyn stood up. "We need big maps showing all these locations—all the neighborhoods, the apartments and houses, the train stops, and where the river runs. I'll take care of getting them made, and then I'll hang them in Tyler's office. You two stay on it. Dig as deep as necessary and let me know if you meet any resistance and

66

I'll get the lawyers involved. Whatever this is, it stinks worse than the Potomac."

"Hey!" Mimi exclaimed. "The Potomac has been cleaned up, I'll have you know. The taxpayers are still paying for it."

Carolyn gave her a wry grin. "Didn't you just tell me you smelled it but didn't see it?" she asked, and she left them.

"What a joy to have a real editor again," Joe said.

"Amen," Mimi said, and it really sounded like praying.

Gianna gave a silent prayer of thanksgiving that Commander Eddie Davis was her boss again. All the time her unit was housed in the chief's office and she answered directly to him she could go days, weeks even, without seeing or speaking to him unless they were in the middle of some crisis or another. Commander Davis called every couple of days, and she saw daily proof of his interest in and concern for her Special Intelligence Mobile and Tactical Unit. Now she was about to seal the deal. "Check out the contents of that cabinet," she said, indicating with a nod a cabinet on the wall near the door and tossing a ring of keys to Andy. He was on his feet in a flash and in front of the cabinet in another as Gianna slid a matching set of keys across the table to Alice. Gianna was ready for Andy's whoop of delight. Alice was not and it startled her, though she caught herself—and her hand, before it reached her weapon.

"Sarge, check this out!"

Alice rushed toward him. "What are you whoopin' and hollerin' about, LT?"

"Look what Cap got us!" he yelled as he tossed a high-powered rifle toward her. She caught it one-handed and with a fluid motion fit the stock into her left shoulder. "Lookin' good, Sarge," Andy said.

Gianna gave her a raised eyebrow. "Are you proficient, Sergeant?"

Alice shook her head. "Not what the Lieutenant would call proficient. Good enough for squirrel hunting with my grandpa

67

in the South Carolina woods when I was a kid, but nowhere near good enough for a Mobile Intelligence operation."

"Cap?" Andy put his weapon back in the rack and was pointing at the key rings hanging there.

"Well, since our unit will be enrolling in tactical and defensive driving courses, the Commander thought we needed our own vehicles," Gianna said, hoping she sounded nonchalant. In truth, Commander Davis had taken her completely by surprise with the three vehicles—one for each Team.

"Wow," the lieutenant and the sergeant said in unison, no fake nonchalance evident.

"I guess the Commander likes you," Andy said.

"I'm guessing the Commander wants us ready to deploy when and as needed, and ready we will be," Gianna said. "Andy, call the Commander's lieutenant and schedule the training—first available. She's expecting your call. Now: What's on for the rest of today?"

"It's a half-and-half day, Cap," Andy said. "Sarge and Bobby are running a strength and endurance training in the gym, and Tommi and I are monitoring a diversity and sensitivity training workshop in Human Resources—"

Gianna cut him off with a rude snort. "You'll do more than monitor if they start that mealy-mouthed, wishy-washy, can't we all get along crap!" She slapped both palms on the desktop and pushed back so hard her chair slammed into the wall behind her, startling herself and her two subordinates. She was not yet used to the fast-moving, high-tech ergonomic chair or the high-gloss wood floor it rolled on. She apologized for the display of temper but made her intentions very clear. "Whoever is running this workshop, make sure they use the terms racist, sexist, homophobic and misogynistic—not feel-good euphemisms—and make sure they define the words and the kind of behaviors and language that correspond to the words. I don't want any of our people to be confused. Understood?"

"Yes, ma'am," they said in unison, and Gianna knew it would be a long time before either of them—before any of them—forgot

Randall Connelly's betrayal. She recalled Connelly's questioning, and its occasional challenging nature: *Weren't people entitled to their own beliefs?* Gianna's answer had not been sufficiently correct. Today her answer would be: *Of course people are entitled to their beliefs. But they're not entitled to work for me if those beliefs jeopardize the people we're sworn to protect.* She sighed inwardly and asked Andy to let her know as soon as the defensive driving and long gun weapons training were scheduled. Asked Alice to make sure their vehicles were in the parking lot, and then asked Tommi to get parking spaces assigned. She stood up to stretch, winced in discomfort that was almost pain, and decided that she'd join the half of her squad being put through their paces in the strength and endurance session Bobby and Alice were running ... though she'd probably regret it.

She resumed her seat and pulled the stack of neglected paperwork toward her. She put on her reading glasses, then looked over the top of them as a knock sounded at the door. The Commander strolled in wearing a big grin.

"Need a little help, do you, seeing the words on the page?"

"Oh, I see 'em just fine. I just don't always know what they say," she said, smiling and walking toward him, hand outstretched.

He took her hand, then looked all around, nodding his approval. "I like this."

"I do, too. You were right. And just a few minutes too late to receive the bows and scrapes of my top guns."

He laughed his good laugh, the one that, along with his good looks, caused grown—and married—women to swoon. "I met them coming in. They do good bowing and scraping, both of 'em. And I thought Sgt. Long was gonna hug me, but it was Lt. Page who grabbed me and cut off my breath."

Still enjoying the moment, they sat across from each other and Gianna waited for him to speak. With a totally humorless smile he said, "We've uncovered connections between Randall Connelly and the group that blew up the Gay and Lesbian Center."

"He was part of our operation that took them down!" Gianna exclaimed.

Davis nodded. "But he was new to them, and they didn't totally trust him so they kept him at arm's length, and he didn't get a chance to warn them that you were on to them and screw up your operation."

Gianna was horrified. How could she have harbored a traitor for so long and been so totally ignorant? And there was Taylor Johnstone, a junkie who almost destroyed their chance to take down an international child sex trafficking ring. Then she had another even more gut-wrenching thought, one that had just occurred—

"Stop it!" Davis snapped.

Shocked. "Sir?"

"You're forgetting how long and how well I know you. You're about to start beating yourself up. Don't. You and your people saved a lot of lives. I still don't know how you managed with so few people—"

"Sir. There were two of them."

"Two of them what?"

"Fuckups. Randall Connelly and Taylor Johnstone. And the chief sent both of them to me."

Davis was stunned into silence as he took in the significance of her words: Someone close to the chief of police was out to sabotage him. Or . . . "Please have Sgt. Tommi send me the complete files on Johnstone and Connelly. In fact, have her walk them over ASAP. I wanna know where those two came from and who sent them. And Anna? I'm thinking you're the likely target of this mischief."

"Me! Why would anyone target me?"

He shrugged. "Why not you? You make a good target."

That stung. "That sucks," she said.

"Not as much as this: We don't have all the answers or all the pieces yet," Davis said, "but we're peeling the onion, and every layer we pull back gives us more info. Coming after you may have been only part of their plan."

"Oh fuck a duck!"

70

"My sentiments exactly," Davis said, opening the door. "I'll keep you posted," he said, and left.

She sat down hard. Too hard, and the pain blinded her momentarily. Then she rolled back down the table to the secure cabinet that held her personal belongings. She changed into her workout clothes and locked the door. She took her time going downstairs to the gym to face whatever Bobby and Alice were doing to the troops. A good workout always helped clear her mind.

Bobby saw her first. "Holy shit!" he muttered.

"Ten hut!" Alice yelled when she looked where Bobby was looking, and everybody stopped what they were doing to salute their captain.

"As you were," Gianna called out with a wave to them, and walked over to Alice and Bobby. "Strength and endurance, right?"

They looked back as if she had a deadly communicable disease. "Are you sure you're ready for this?" Alice asked.

"Maybe not the full monty yet, but I've got to start somewhere, Alice. First, though, let me go speak to my peeps."

Bobby laughed. "Did you say 'peeps'?"

Gianna looked aghast. "Isn't that the correct terminology?"

"For some of us it is," Bobby said, not fully able to control the giggle lurking in his throat.

"For you, too, Cap," Alice said, throwing a hard elbow to Bobby's ribs and walking with her to the crowd of her officers who greeted her effusively, many reaching out to touch her or shake her hand, the veterans as well as the newbies. She chatted with them for a few moments, then signaled Bobby to put them back to work.

Alice put her on an exercise bike and set the resistance at a minimum level for ten minutes. When Gianna insisted that she could go longer and harder, Alice shut her down. "We'll start here, Captain," she said authoritatively, and walked away.

"Is she ready for this kind of workout?" Bobby asked, worry creasing his face.

"I don't know," Alice said. "Let's watch her closely." And they did for the next hour, allowing her a more intensive workout on her upper body and core, and carefully controlling the leg work. Her newest team members were openly impressed by her physical prowess and stopped their own training to observe her until Bobby and Alice ordered them to focus on their own workouts, but they did it gently since, even after several years under her command, they, too, often found themselves in awe of their boss. She didn't push anyone harder than she pushed herself, didn't expect more of anyone than she expected of herself, and routinely gave more of herself than anyone. She was limping slightly when she called it quits.

"Lookin' good, Cap," Bobby said. "Really good."

"I feel good, Bobby. I think."

"Tomorrow is when you'll really feel it," Alice said, "but you know how to move through it."

They watched her leave, both relieved that she really did seem much improved though neither would admit out loud having feared that she'd never again be 100 percent. "I want to be like her when I grow up," Alice said.

"Me, too," Bobby said.

Alice gave him another friendly punch, glad their friendship hadn't suffered when she had passed the sergeant's exam and become his superior, though she shouldn't have been surprised: Bobby Gilliam was one of the least judgmental people she knew and without a doubt the least judgmental man she knew. Then she asked if Bobby would give her a lift home after work, and his answer altered her opinion of him. His response was that she needed a new car, which Alice said she absolutely could not afford, adding that the simple question she'd asked required a simple yes or no answer.

"Relax, Sarge. I'm not bustin' your chops. I'm just saying—"

"I know what you're saying," Alice snapped, "and if I could afford to buy a new car, I would buy a new car. But I'm living check to check," she said, sounding miserable, all the snappishness gone from her voice.

Bobby studied her and quickly withdrew his arm before giving her the hug he knew damn well was out of bounds in the workplace. "You need a tutorial from the Phillips sisters. They've got more money than God, all of 'em. Even the youngsters in that family, the ones still in college, own property."

"I can't intrude on those people like that, Bobby."

He was shaking his head. "They wouldn't consider it an intrusion, Alice. In fact, I think they'd welcome an opportunity to help one of us. They love us. Go see Delores. She's the one they all bow down to."

"She's the one who drives the Bentley, right?" Alice asked.

"The already-paid-for Bentley," Bobby said with a sigh.

An already-paid-for Bentley. Alice was still thinking about that when she knocked on the door to Gianna's newly constructed office and entered. "I'm a little early, Boss," she said when Gianna checked her watch. "I wanted to give you this." Gianna looked at the card Alice gave her. "She's my masseuse, and her hands perform miracles on overworked muscles and joints. And she comes to you."

If anyone knew about overworked muscles and joints it was Alice Long, a regular in iron woman and triathlon competitions. Gianna imagined that she could feel her body relaxing, but she didn't get a chance to say that to Alice because Tommi and Andy arrived and they all took what had become their regular places at the table, facing her. She told them what she'd learned from Commander Davis about Randall Connelly's activities and what appeared to be the good Reverend Jessup's involvement in trafficking underage girls.

"Anything point to Connelly knowing about it?" Alice asked.

Gianna shook her head.

"What is it with grown men and children?" An angry Andy Page spat the words out. "I don't fuckin' get it."

Alice squeezed his shoulder. "I'm glad you don't. I wouldn't want to work with a man who did get it. My gun might have to go off accidentally and mangle his—"

"Enough. Get outta here, both of you. Go do something this weekend that'll make you forget the uglies."

"I'm duty officer this weekend with Team A," Andy said, and both Gianna and Alice smiled. The uglies didn't stand a chance.

* * *

"All that time we spent ruining our eyesight combing through property tax and property ownership records and the name we wanted was in the bottom of the box of papers Florence Gregory gave you." Zemekis rubbed his eyes with his balled-up fists, then resumed his whining and complaining.

"Don't you wonder why?" Mimi rubbed her own eyes and tried not to think that maybe she did need reading glasses as Gianna had suggested.

"Why what?"

"Just a name on a torn-out piece of notebook paper at the bottom of a box of otherwise neat and orderly files. Was she trying to hide it, or did it slip out of one of the files?" Mimi squeezed her eyes shut, remembering that Gianna had also suggested that she keep a little bottle of refresher eye drops in her purse. Her eyeballs were burning. A few drops of cool, soothing saline would be a welcome relief.

"Yeah," Zemekis said. "I did wonder about the name, especially since it wasn't on any of the papers . . . why she had it."

"What I'm wondering," Mimi said, "is what she knows that we don't—"

"You know who he is?"

"I know the name. He builds very high-end, resort-like developments that meld residential with commercial. But he builds them in California and Florida, not, as far as I know, in places where it gets cold and snows." And Mimi shivered. DC was coming off two of the most brutal winters on record. It was already cold, and it technically was still fall. What would Flash Gordon want with a collection of aging apartment buildings in a barely middle-class part of the nation's capital? Unless . . .

"What's that look on your face, Patterson? And who is this guy?"

"Lafayette Gordon, Flash to his friends and admirers—"

"Flash Gordon? Really?" Zemekis mocked.

Mimi explained in detail what she knew about Gordon and

74

his developments, and how she came to know about them. Los Angeles was her hometown, and she and Gianna had good friends who lived in one of Gordon's residential resorts on Florida's west coast—the Gulf of Mexico coast.

"DC doesn't have anything even remotely resembling the Gulf of Mexico or the Pacific Ocean," Zemekis said, "so what could Flash want with us?"

"We have the Potomac River," Mimi said, "which meanders past the US Capital, all the monuments, George Washington's home—"

"The federal government is not about to let Flash Gordon or anybody else, no matter how rich, set a resort development on the banks of the Potomac River."

"The current federal government might," Mimi said quietly.

The look on Joe Zemekis's face mirrored what Mimi Patterson felt in her gut. "Gordon doesn't own any property here," he said.

"We've been looking in the wrong place. We need to check all zoning requests and property easement requests and mixed-use development requests, variances—"

"If Gordon or whoever he's in business with these days gets their hands on those buildings—"

"They'll demolish them faster than you can think that thought," Mimi said, "and everybody who lives in those six buildings will be displaced."

"Evicted, you mean," Joe retorted, anger covering for sadness.

"Could any of them afford to move back in?" Gianna asked.

"Ha!" Mimi scoffed. "Nobody who lives in any of those buildings now could afford to rent a closet in whatever Flash Gordon builds."

"Could we?" Gianna asked.

Mimi yawned. "Maybe. If we didn't want to also eat and pay our utility bills and put gas in the car and clothes on our backs."

They were drinking champagne and luxuriating in the deep, multi-jet Jacuzzi that was part of their master bedroom suite, the

75

feature that had originally sold Mimi on the apartment. It was the working fireplace in the suite that sold Gianna. Now, however, the fact that at the end of their almost always stressful days they came home to each other in the home they shared, should anyone ask, was the reason they had finally sold their original homes and moved in together instead of deciding on a daily basis who would sleep where, and who would be responsible for feeding them. They'd asked each other more than once what took them so long, but they both knew the answer, and neither wanted to spend a lot of time discussing it. "Is knowing about Flash Gordon enough to lure you into writing the 'graft and corruption in high places' story?"

"Nope. My interest is in the fate of those whose lives are upended by the graft and corruption in high places. And thanks to Florence Gregory, a few of them may be on their way to lockup."

"That used to be your job."

"Joe can handle it. Besides, with a lying tax dodger in the White House and a rapist on the Supreme Court and a criminal-loving attorney general, I don't care too much about a few bribe-taking city government officials." Mimi was up to her neck in hot bubbling water. Her eyes were closed, and she'd spoken so calmly Gianna could have mistaken her for someone else had she not been watching her. *Her* Mimi Patterson. The fire-breathing, truth-seeking, hell-raising journalist extraordinaire who'd built a career bringing down corrupt public servants no longer cared what happened to them? She looked so relaxed and peaceful. Sounded so relaxed and peaceful. Who was this snuggled against her in the Jacuzzi after work on a Friday night?

"I'm really glad you're back with Eddie Davis. Seems your jerk of a chief finally did something right," Mimi, eyes still closed, said, and yawned.

Aha—here was her Mimi, not so totally transformed after all. "How long do you think you're going to be angry with him? He is your friend, you know."

"Yeah, I know. But I'm thinking I'll be angry with him as long it feels good to be angry with him. Besides. He deserves it."

76

"He really wants to mend the rift between the two of you."

"He's on the right track. Having Commander Davis watching your back really is a good move—one he should have made a while back. But . . . better late than never. It must be a good feeling."

"You have no idea."

Mimi's eyes popped open and she sat up. "Wanna share?"

So Gianna did. Everything. All of her interactions with Commander Davis, all of the changes he'd implemented, all of her conversations with him and her thoughts about him and his impact on her unit. About his impact on herself. Mimi listened without interruption. Then she was silent and deeply thoughtful for several long moments as a range of feelings swept through her. The first, gratitude that the Gianna she knew so well and loved so much was back—fearless, self-assured, and ready to deal with any ugliness that confronted her. Then she acknowledged her own fear when she saw Gianna's fear in the face of events she could not control. This tough cop was pissed off when she was shot, but she was not fearful. Finally Mimi spoke. A question, not a comment.

"Any more top-level assignments or changes?"

The question surprised Gianna but she gave it a lot of thought, realizing the merit it contained. "Deputy Chief Swanson retired, and Ellen De Longpre is replacing him as acting head of administration; Dick Randolph is going from Internal Affairs to command the East River precinct, and Millie House is moving into the chief's office, to do what only the two of them know."

Mimi was quiet and thoughtful again, though not for long, before she said, "Schmidt's days are numbered. I'm guessing he and De Longpre will be changing places—"

"What makes you think that?" Gianna was startled, but she knew somewhere deep within that there was more truth than speculation in Mimi's words. Mimi knew how political systems worked—almost as well as the chief himself did—and she could see the beauty of this plan: Schmidt wasn't old enough to be forced into retirement, and demoting him would make the chief look bad while firing him would be worse, as if he'd made a mistake promoting the man in the first place. A lateral move, however, would ruffle only the intended feathers: those of Gerhard Schmidt.

"I see you figured it out for yourself, O Captain, my captain. And I make another prediction: that the chief saw the treachery involved in the referral of those shits to your unit and saw that you both were potential targets. Ergo, Commander Davis."

"I definitely feel safer. And comfortable and confident that I can deal with whatever is lurking beneath the surface."

Mimi gave her a speculative look. "What do you think is lurking beneath the surface?"

"People doing bad things to young girls."

"Then they better watch their sorry asses, whoever they are, 'cause the combination of you, Eddie Davis, and Ellen De Longpre spells major trouble for them."

"How do you know Ellen?"

"I know everybody," Mimi said, in perfect imitation of one of the chief's favorite sayings.

"You two think so much alike. Please fix the break between you."

Mimi didn't respond, which Gianna took to be a good sign. Instead she said, "The champagne is gone and I'm hungry. Should we climb out of this wonderful water and find some food?"

Gianna nodded. "I think my muscles have forgiven me, at least for the moment."

"What muscles? Forgiven you for what?"

"I joined Alice and Bobby in the team workout—"

"You let Alice Long and Bobby Gilliam work you out? Are you nuts?"

"They were gentle with me."

"They don't know the meaning of the word. You'll be lucky if you can move in the morning."

With a smug little smile Gianna said, "Won't have to worry about it. We're getting massages in the morning—from Alice's masseuse—who's coming to us."

Mimi's smile was anything but smug. "O Captain, my captain! I think I love you."

"As well you should."

✳ ✳ ✳

Alice Long took her place at the end of the line waiting to get into The Snatch. She was not a fan of bars, but she knew this is where she would find its owner, Delores Phillips. Standing still in one place, unless she was undercover on a stakeout, was not any more of a favorite pastime than bars. She suddenly became aware of the looks she was garnering from the women in the line, but she had long ago come to terms with the burden of her looks. She knew she was gorgeous. She also knew there was much more to her—

"Alice Long! What are you doing back there?" Darlene Phillips, the co-owner of The Snatch, big sister to Delores, and keeper of the door, pulled her into a tight hug.

"Hey, Darlene. How're you doing?"

Darlene leaned in and whispered, "I'm great, *Sarge*. Congratulations!"

Alice didn't ask how Darlene knew about her promotion because Bobby was right about one thing: the mutual admiration between the Hate Crimes Unit and the Phillips sisters ran deep. "Thanks. I didn't think I'd like it, but I really am enjoying myself."

"Cassie would have loved it," Darlene said quietly and sadly. Cassandra Ali, the youngest member of the unit, had been a hate crime murder victim less than a year ago. She and Darlene had been just beginning to get close . . .

"Yes. She would have. After first giving me big-time grief," Alice said with a grin that threatened to break.

"Come on, let me get you outta this cold," Darlene said, taking her arm, "even though I see you're dressed for it." She gave an admiring caress to Alice's jacket. "They got one of those in my size?"

Alice grinned, and this time it held. "They make these for the Hells Angels and those dudes come in sizes ranging from extra-large to hu-normous, so yeah, they've got one in your size, Darlene. Let me know when you want to go and I'll take you shopping," she said, following the big woman to the front of the

79

line to only minor grumbling. Snatch patrons knew better than to challenge Darlene about who she let into her door and when.

"What brings you to see us? I know scantily clad gorgeous women dancing on the bar isn't exactly your thing." The Snatch Dancers were famous far and wide.

"I came to see your sister. Do you think she'd give me a few minutes of her time without an appointment?"

Darlene laughed her deep *heh-heh-heh* laugh, the one she always hauled out at her baby sister's expense. Delores was the serious business-like one who ran a tight ship and brooked no foolishness from anyone. Except perhaps from her big sister, though no one had ever witnessed it. Darlene opened the door. "Go on in. Go past the bar and keep walking to the back. I'll tell her you're coming. She'll be glad to see you."

And Delores did indeed look glad to see her. She met Alice before she'd cleared the bar, hand extended, a smile of welcome on her face. "Sgt. Long! How nice to see you. To what do I owe the honor?" she asked as she led Alice to the back of the cavernous space to a soundproofed large office that was as quiet as the club was noisy. "How's the captain? I spoke with her briefly after her injury. I hope she's healing?"

"She's doing really well, Ms. Phillips. I'll tell her you asked for her."

"Please do. She is one of my favorite people." As was her custom Delores was dressed more like an international banker or the CEO of a major corporation than the owner of half a dozen properties and a lesbian night club and bar—albeit one of the most lucrative and successful such establishments anywhere. The three computer monitors and the charts and graphs on the wall belonged to a woman in charge of a financial operation much larger than a nightclub. She remembered hearing Lynda Lopez say that Delores Phillips wore shoes that cost more than three months of her salary and jewelry worth more than her house. Today was no exception, which left Alice thinking that coming here had been a bad idea.

"I feel like I'm about to waste your time, Ms. Phillips."

"Sergeant, please. If I can do something to help you I will."

"Okay. It's Alice, and Bobby Gilliam told me to talk to you." Delores smiled slightly at the mention of Bobby's name, but otherwise her expression remained polite and interested. "I don't ever have any money and Bobby says there's no reason for it, so he told me to seek your advice because you have more money than God. He said everyone in your family has more money than God. He said even the ones still in college own property."

Delores's smile was wide and full now. "I should pay Det. Gilliam. He has a higher opinion of me than I do, and I think I'm doing all right."

A paid-for Bentley, Alice thought to herself. *A bit better than all right.* "Bobby says since I earn a decent salary and I don't drink to excess, I don't do drugs, I don't gamble, and I don't keep a stable of expensive women ..."

Delores let go one of the most wonderful laughs Alice had ever heard. It began deep in her throat, gurgling upward like an underground stream in a hurry to reach the top. And when it got there it sounded like bells or chimes or someone tapping on an expensive crystal goblet. It was not a mean laugh—Delores was not laughing at her—but a happy, delighted laugh. And, Alice thought, it was a damn sexy laugh. "I didn't know Det. Gilliam was such a funny fellow," Delores said, the laugh tapering off to a suppressed giggle.

"He's a laugh riot," Alice replied with a head shake that said it's a good thing he was her pal.

"And I take it you're here to solicit my advice?"

"If you don't think I'm a hopeless case and a waste of your time, Ms. Phillips."

"It's Delores, and since you don't seem to have the kind of bad habits that usually get people into financial trouble—" and here she had to fight to keep that beautiful, sexy laugh down where it belonged—"I'd be happy to do anything I can ..." Her words trailed off and Alice watched a thought cross her face and take shape. "I've heard a few things about you, too, so perhaps we can help each other, Alice, if you'd be willing: I eat all the wrong things all the time. I don't exercise at all—I tell myself I'm too busy—but I'm in terrible shape and I know it and I don't want to be. I want to be like my eighty-nine-year-old grandma who's still kickin.' Suppose I help you to financial good health and you help me to physical good health?"

Alice was smiling and nodding before Delores finished talking. Physical health and well-being were as important to Alice as being a cop. "You've got a deal, Delores. When do you want to start?"

Delores stood up. "Is tomorrow too soon?"

"It's perfect. I just happen to have tomorrow off." And after agreeing to meet at Alice's at eleven the following morning Delores said she'd walk Alice to the front door. When she opened the office door the blast of sound hit Alice with almost physical force. She stepped backward into Delores.

"Sorry. Should have warned you," Delores said in her ear—the only way to be heard in the now-filled-to-capacity club.

Alice didn't even try to speak. She just followed Delores through a crowd that parted for her. The noise was deafening, and it wasn't just the music, Alice saw, as they approached the bar. For there, in all their splendor and glory, were the Snatch Dancers. The crowd of women was going crazy. Alice watched, mesmerized. They were indeed something to behold. Five of the most beautiful women she'd ever seen, and something for every-one: Black, Asian, Latino and white, each one an exquisite physical specimen. Alice leaned forward and said into Delores's ear, "I couldn't afford the upkeep on one of these women, to say nothing of a stable of them."

Delores laughed her fine laugh, but Alice couldn't hear it. Nor could she see the appreciation in Delores's face for the other woman's understanding of the quality of the performers. Delores was proud of her dancers because they were real dancers, profes-sional dancers whom she paid generously to perform on Friday and Saturday nights, and the women, most of whom were high school or college dance or acting teachers, were happy to earn more in a weekend than they earned in a month on their salaried jobs. There were strict rules. Delores did not permit the dancers to mingle with the customers on the premises, but what they did away from The Snatch on their own time was their own business. When at work for Delores Phillips they retired to a private lounge between sets where there was food and drink, showers, and day beds. At the end of the night there was a private exit at the rear of the club leading into a fenced and locked parking area. An armed guard guaranteed their safe exit from the premises. Unfortunately, not all Snatch customers could be relied on to show the proper respect to the dancers.

Alice hugged Delores at the door, said she'd see her in the morning, and stepped out into the frigid but blessedly quiet night, where she hugged Darlene and gave her a card with her number on it. "We should go get you that jacket," she said. She pulled her watch cap on her head and down over her ears, zipped up her jacket, wrapped the scarf around her neck, put on her gloves, and began the four-block walk to the train station. She felt lighter in spirit than she had on the walk to the club. Delores was going to help her. And equally important, she'd be able to help Delores in a matter as important to her as money management was to the wealthy woman. It was good when there was balance.

CHAPTER FIVE

"You look better than you have in a long while, Mimi," Dr. Beverly Connors said in her calm, measured therapist's voice, though there was the hint of a smile that only Mimi would have detected. The doctor wore an elegant long-sleeved, moss green knit dress with a deep cowl collar, her only jewelry small gold hoop earrings and a circle of entwined platinum and gold on her left ring finger. The only other color in the ensemble was the brightly colored scarf that tied her waist-length dreadlocks back. It was a wardrobe designed to comfort while inspiring confidence. If Mimi weren't already comforted by and confident in the abilities of Dr. Connors, the calm, elegant presence in the armchair facing her would do the job. So would the steady gaze behind the wire-rimmed eyeglasses. Mimi frowned. She saw sadness and sorrow and hurt and pain—nothing calm and steady about Bev's gaze. Patients wouldn't know, but a best friend and ex-lover would. Mimi broke protocol.

"Is it Sylvia?"

The eyes changed immediately, becoming soft and gentle while simultaneously sparkling. The therapist did not break protocol, and Mimi relaxed into the familiarity of their usual doctor-patient routine. "I feel better than I have in a while, thanks to you."

"I'm thinking thanks owed to being back at work might be

more accurate. Have you acknowledged to yourself how much you missed it?"

"I'm not sure how to answer that," Mimi said slowly.

"Why not? You still enjoy your work, don't you?"

"I'm not sure about that, either."

The therapist's brows lifted slightly. "Please explain that, Mimi."

She had known Bev would ask this question, and she tried to put words to her thoughts and feelings. It was still a work in progress. "The newsroom definitely is a much healthier place now that the assholes are gone so I no longer hate going to work." Okay. That was the easy part, and Bev seemed to know that. She waited for more. "But everybody seems to think that I'll pick up where I left off. That I'll keep doing what I always did, the way I always did it. And that's not the case." Mimi had her emotional dukes up, ready to do battle, but the therapist surprised her.

"What's really chewing on you, Mimi? Because I doubt that Tyler really cares whether or not you write another story about corrupt city officials as long as you're back on the job. Are you still blaming yourself for Gianna getting shot?"

And there it was. "It *is* my fault! If she hadn't been protecting me, if she hadn't pushed me out of the way—"

"She was doing her job the way she was trained to do it, Mimi, and you know that. If it had been any other civilian—your across the street neighbor, Mrs. Baker, if she'd been standing next to Gianna—the cop you love would have pushed her to safety and emptied her clip into the little hoodlum. And she'd still have taken the bullet that almost—but didn't—end her life. And now that you've had time to get over the shock, you know that's the truth. Don't you?"

Mimi nodded but didn't speak. Maybe she should find a less proficient shrink. This one, hands folded in her lap, merely watched and waited, which Mimi hated even more than when she pushed and prodded. "Maybe."

"What are you holding back, Mimi? Holding onto?"

"Goddammit, Beverly. Two people tried to kill me in my own front yard! Then there's the bastard who killed himself when I caught him dirty and exposed him, and his wife sued me and the paper."

"The incidents in your front yard, Mimi—both times—you'd be dead now if not for cops: Eric Ashby shot the first one before he could knife you, and you know exactly how Gianna saved your life. And didn't the judge laugh that woman and her frivolous lawsuit out of the courtroom?" Now the therapist broke protocol. "For the record, my dearest friend, I personally am very glad you're not dead."

"So am I," Mimi said, for the first time shifting the focus away from the people whose deaths were the direct result of their own criminality and not because M. Montgomery Patterson was doing her job. "I'm glad I'm alive, too, even if it—"

A piercing scream—a shriek, really—brought Beverly to her feet. She ran to the door. The unmistakable rapid fire of an automatic weapon brought Mimi to hers, and she grabbed Beverly and pulled her backward before she could touch the doorknob. In that instant they played out the scenario they'd just discussed as they heard the sound of the doors locking and metal gates slamming shut. Mimi whipped out her phone and called Gianna. Straight to voice mail. She hesitated less than a second before calling Alice Long who answered on the first ring.

"Mimi? All right?"

"No. I'm in the office of Dr. Beverly Connors in the East Side Families First facility. We just heard screaming and gunfire—"

"Put your phone on speaker and leave the line open, Mimi. I'm getting my lieutenant," and Mimi heard her yelling, heard the sound of lots of feet running, heard her tell someone what Mimi had just told her.

"Ms. Patterson, this is Lt. Andy Page—" he began but several more bursts of automatic gunfire stopped him. Then he yelled, "Team T with a long gun ready to deploy! On your command, Sergeant, when I give the order."

Beverly stood at her office door, ear pressed against it, while

86

Mimi listened to Andy Page interrupt Gianna's meeting with Commander Davis, heard him explain the situation, heard Commander Davis order the deployment, heard Andy call the Commander at the East River Precinct. "Are you still with us, Ms. Patterson?"

"Yes, I am, Lieutenant," she said, going to stand beside Beverly.

"Has there been more gunfire? Can you assess the situation at all?"

"We're locked in Dr. Connors's office—"

"Can you tell if anyone has been shot?" Gianna called out.

Beverly was shaking her head. "I can't tell, Gianna. I can hear crying and some muffled conversation, but I can't see anything."

"Are you two safe and secure in that office?"

"We are. This safety protocol is activated by the front desk receptionist. If anyone has been . . . injured, it would be her—" Beverly's voice broke and Mimi held her tightly.

"Help is on the way," Davis said. "Units from the East River Precinct will be there—I'm told they're there now—"

They must be, Mimi thought, as there was more screaming, yelling, and shooting, which she reported to Gianna and Commander Davis.

"Bev? How many ways are there into that building?" Gianna asked.

"The street on the south side of the building is Addison. There's a gated staff parking lot, topped with barbed wire. There's a door into the building," Bev said, and she gave the code to unlock the gate and the basement door. "They can't see you unless they're in one of the therapists' offices on that side of the building."

"Come on, Bev. Let's go watch the cops arrive."

"No. I need to stay here by the door so I can hear what's happening."

"Wouldn't you rather see what's happening?"

Bev gave her a strange look. "I haven't detected a hint of fear in you since this episode began. Why is that, when what we've essentially been discussing is the fear in you that has kept you paralyzed?"

"There's nothing to be afraid of. We're locked inside a room behind a metal door that Godzilla couldn't break through, and the rescue team is probably outside right now," Mimi replied with the realization that she had not felt a moment of fear. She took Beverly's hand. "Come on, let's go to the window. And I'm thinking you should call Sylvia in case there's been something on the news about this."

Beverly hurried over to her desk and her phone. Mimi went to the window. She guessed that only Gianna's people would use the side entrance while the squad cars from the East River Precinct would converge at the front of the building. She heard Bev end her phone conversation and come to stand beside her.

"Have there been threats against this center? Do you have any idea who these people are or what they want?"

"Yes, and maybe." She hesitated, clearly unsure how much could she safely divulge. True, Mimi wasn't just any reporter and she'd respect a boundary if Bev set it, but still . . . "We've seen several Latinas suffering from physical and emotional abuse at the hands of their male partners for failing to adhere to traditional values. That's not a trope; we've heard it before in several communities. We've had two white women in since Jennifer, and quite a few Black women. But what's different among the Latinas is our sense—"

"Who's 'our'?" Mimi interrupted to ask.

"The other therapists and the social workers."

"Okay."

"Our sense is that 'traditional values' in a couple of cases is a ruse, a front to force the women into prostitution. Or at least into nonconsensual sex."

"Which is rape."

"Yes. It is."

"And 'traditional values'?"

"No birth control, abortion, or work outside the home."

A large black SUV drove up to the gate. An arm reached out of the driver's side window and punched in the code. The gate slid open and the SUV slid in, moving fast. Andy Page and Alice

Long exited the front. Tim McCreedy, carrying a rifle, exited the back, followed by his team of ten. Alice had the door open for them and they filed in.

"We'll be free soon, Bev. Finish what you were saying."

"What most frightened us, Mimi, was the ones who were branded—"

"Branded! What are you talking about?"

"Skin burned with metal. Like the slaves were. Like cattle are. Marked as belonging to a specific man—"

Gunfire and yelling sent them running to the door to listen. Running feet joined the yelling, but it was impossible to tell who was doing what. Then it got quiet. And it remained quiet for several minutes. Then the sound of the door unlocking and the gates lifting signaled the return of normal, though Beverly turned the knob slowly and opened the door gradually. They opened it all the way and saw Alice Long quick-stepping toward them.

"I'm very glad to see you, Sgt. Long," Bev said, shaking the cop's hand.

"And I'm very glad you have the security system that you do, Dr. Connors. It saved lives."

"Ada, the receptionist who activated the system. Is she—"

"One of the intruders cold-cocked her with the butt of a rifle, and she went out like a light and pretended to stay out." Alice gave Bev a pat on the shoulder. "Give her a raise. She earned it. She played possum the whole time, and everybody else swore no knowledge of the security system."

"I'll make sure Ada knows the source of her financial windfall," Bev said.

"Can we continue our conversation—" Mimi began but Bev shut her down.

"We cannot. I need to attend to my colleagues and the patients who were here when all hell broke loose. They must be traumatized."

"I'm a patient."

"And I'll see you next week at your scheduled appointment," she said, pushing past Mimi and Alice and charging down the hall to the front offices.

"Come on, Patterson. Let's get you out of the good doctor's hair. I can't believe I know you well enough to know you're back to normal because you're annoying people."

"Sticks and stones, Sergeant. Sticks and stones. So . . . how many were there and did they say anything? Give any reason for the attack? Are you treating it as an act of domestic terrorism?"

Alice sighed. "You really are a pain in the ass, Patterson, you know that? Talk to my superior officer—"

"She's here?" Mimi asked, surprised, and Alice laughed.

"My lieutenant, Andy Page."

Sheesh. She'd forgotten. "A new day, huh?"

"You better believe it."

"Bev, slow down." Mimi turned away from Alice and ran to catch up with the therapist who was moving like a sprinter. "Who can talk to me about this without violating client confidentiality?"

Bev shook her head. "Nobody I know. Sorry."

Yeah, right. Mimi turned back to find that Alice had caught up to her. "Thanks, Alice. I hope I didn't put you in a bad spot."

"Not to worry. I manage my cop/friend split personality really well. You could take lessons."

"What?"

"You totally fumbled the ball on the friend/patient/reporter thing with Doc Connors."

Did I really? That's what Mimi was wondering when she walked out the front of the building and almost smack into Andy Page. "Oh please excuse me, Lieutenant. I wasn't watching where I was going." She extended her hand. "I'm—"

He took her hand. "I know who you are, Ms. Patterson. Thanks for the assist."

"Glad I could help, Lieuten—" She stopped mid-word as the DCME van drove up and onto the sidewalk. She looked the question at Page.

"Two in custody, one DOA."

"Do you know anything about them? Did they give a reason for an attack on a facility that helps women and children? Are there any people on your radar who target women and children?"

90

"I can't discuss any of that with you, Ms. Patterson."

"Were any staff or patients injured?"

"One minor injury."

"Can you tell me if the intruders were Latino?"

He gave her a scrutinizing look. "You should put any further questions to the Media Relations Office, Ms. Patterson."

"Will they face charges of domestic terrorism?"

"They will face multiple charges but it's too early to be specific."

"Thanks, Lieutenant. I think," she said turning away and walking to her car. She started the engine, turned on the heat, plugged her phone into the charger, and sat trying to decide whether to contact Carolyn or Joe first. She decided Gianna first.

All's well that ends well, my Love. I'm fine thanks to your peeps. A most impressive group, esp. Alice and Andy. And young Tim. Glad you're behaving like a Capt. and orchestrating from afar. I love you. See you later.

Andy Page watched her walk away and when he was sure she was gone, he called his captain. "I just had my first encounter with M. Montgomery Patterson, and if I don't ever have to go through that again it'll be too soon. And after what she just went through! I'd truly hate to be in her crosshairs when she's at full strength."

You have no idea, Gianna thought but didn't say. "Early read on the perps?"

"All Latino males who, according to one of the social workers, don't like their women getting free birth control pills and lessons on how to be their own selves."

"Women controlling their own bodies should be traditional values," Gianna said, and switched gears to her other big concern of the moment: "How's Tim?"

"The adrenaline is wearing off and he's a little shaky. Sarge is sticking close to him, literally. She has a hand on his shoulder and his team is all over him like a comforter. He'll be all right, boss."

She could only hope and pray that was true. "Okay, Andy.

91

Keep me posted." She punched off the phone and stood up to pace a few steps. She was still smarting from Commander Davis's order that she not go to the scene. "You're a captain, and captains don't run around chasing crime. You have a lieutenant, a sergeant, and three deployable teams to do that. And your job is to manage them. Understood?" She was pissed off, but Davis was right: She'd learn more about what was happening in the field moment to moment right here in her office, monitoring all the coms and cameras. She decided it made better sense to focus on the successful operation by one of her teams, the one led by Tim McCreedy, under the direction of Andy Page and Alice Long. A first for all of them: the first field operation of the Special Intelligence Mobile and Tactical Unit. The one Tim would never forget if he lived to be a hundred years old. He had killed a man today.

Gianna strapped on her holster, called Tommi, and asked her to come down and "run the room" because she was going to the scene. She pulled on her coat, put her phone in the pocket and grabbed her keys, all the while trying to decide whether to take Bobby or Annie with her. In the end she decided to go alone. She told the room where she was going, told them Sgt. Tommi was in charge, and left. Annie and Bobby shared a look and a fist bump, and then sage nods with their teams: *We told you she'd go to the scene* was their wordless message. They knew their boss. The newcomers would learn. She stood behind, beside, and with her people. Always.

She received the same response when she pulled up in front of East Side Families First. It was still being treated and processed as a crime scene, and a young cop was trotting her way to give the order to move when she saw who was in the car. She stopped, backed up a step, and smiled when Gianna got out. "'Morning, Captain."

"Good morning, Officer Smith," she said with a glance at the young woman's name tag and followed her to the tape, which another young cop lifted for her to duck under. She signed in and saw that she was being noticed. She saw the commander of the

East River Precinct, Dick Randolph, and went over to pay her respects. They were friends and exchanged a warm hug and a brief whispered conversation, which caused them both to laugh. More than a few people wished they'd heard those whispered words. One of them was Commander Eddie Davis. He was also one of the people who'd known that she would show up here. She'd obeyed his order to command from a distance until Tim McCreedy took down one of the perps. It was a good shoot, the whole thing caught on camera from several angles. But no way would she let a young cop—one of her own—face the enormity of his actions, or the Internal Affairs investigators, alone.

Andy Page and Alice Long walked forward to meet her, Team T members arrayed behind her. "Lieutenant, Sergeant: Excellent job. Congratulations to you and the whole team." Then she faced them, her smile wide. "You guys rock!" And that's when they jumped her.

Commander Davis looked at the chief of police who shook his head in feigned dismay. "I've been trying to teach her proper decorum for almost twenty years. I give up. It's all on you now."

"Thanks, Chief," Davis said in a dry tone rendered ineffective by the twinkle in his eye. Not only did he like and respect Capt. Maglione, but he was glad to have her under his command again. She would always make him look good, as this morning's operation proved. A grunt from the chief made him look up: Internal Affairs was on the scene. He checked to see if Maglione had seen them. She had.

Gianna extricated herself from the Team T group hug, took its leader by the arm, and led him several steps away. Andy and Alice, who also witnessed the IA arrival, corralled Team T so they were bunched together in front of Gianna and Tim, creating a momentary sanctuary.

"I know you didn't wake up this morning thinking this is how your day would go," she said, her hand on his arm.

"No, ma'am." He looked ready to cry.

"Two more things I know, Tim. Are you listening?"

He raised his eyes to meet hers. "Yes, ma'am."

"Everybody has watched every second of this operation and it was a clean and justified shoot, Tim. The second thing is this: There's no way to prepare for it. Even when you know you did right, killing another human being makes you feel sick in the pit of your stomach."

"Is that how you felt when you—in front of Ms. Patterson's house—"

"That's exactly how I felt, Tim. Once I knew I wasn't going to die."

Startled by her words he checked her expression. She was smiling so he made himself crack a weak smile, but he sobered quickly. "I didn't know it would feel this way."

"Nobody ever does. Which is why I strongly advise that you schedule time with the department shrink as soon as we get back home."

"Did you see the shrink?"

"Still seeing him," Gianna said as she heard a spate of dramatic throat clearing. She stepped away from Tim as the IA investigators approached and he went white. He knew they were coming, but that was another experience no cop was ever prepared for, though she knew that Andy and Alice had walked him through it. She nodded at the investigators and received a fish-eyed stare in return. She told Andy and Alice to carry on and went to find her boss, only slightly dismayed to find him chatting with his boss. Probably about her. And it wasn't even noon yet.

"Are you sure you're all right, Mimi?" Carolyn asked.

Maybe the third time was the charm. Tyler had asked if she was sure she was all right. Then Joe had asked, and now Carolyn. The four of them sat at the round table in Tyler's office facing three large maps of the East Side, lots of colored tacks ready to be pinned as soon as Mimi and Joe finished devising a legend that corresponded to the colors.

"Really, you guys, I'm fine. I was never really in danger. Within seconds after the first screams and gunfire the receptionist pushed the button that put the place on lockdown. Dr. Connors and I might have been a danger to each other given how unhappy we both were to be confined like that, but we were in no danger from the perps."

"That's its own story: A therapy center needing a lockdown protocol," Carolyn said. "What a world we live in."

"After the doors were unlocked," Mimi said, "all the clinical staff ran to the front, to the waiting room to check on the clients. Nobody left. The clients were as worried about the therapists and counselors as they were about the clients."

"And I'll bet none of 'em have a complaint about the lockdown protocol," Tyler said. "Run with that story, Carolyn. Now, Patterson. What's your story? I'm assuming that you don't want the details of your therapy on the front page of the paper. Not that there's anything wrong with therapy."

"Nothing at all," Mimi said. "In fact, I highly recommend it. But a much more interesting story is the branding of young girls. What kinda shit is that? Branding young girls like slaves or cattle."

Tyler spit coffee and glared at Mimi as if branding young girls was her fault. He sputtered but formed no words.

"Can you get independent confirmation of that?" Carolyn asked.

"Preferably on the record independent confirmation," Tyler finally managed. Then added, "In fact, I insist on it. If we're gonna write about women—girls—being branded like slaves or animals in this day and time, we're gonna quote somebody high up on the food chain. We're gonna lay this shit at somebody's feet."

Everybody was quiet for a moment, letting that sink in. Mimi had her work cut out for her, though she didn't mind. With a story like this, having somebody high on the food chain corroborating the facts usually led to more experts coming forth with more info.

"What about the traditional values angle?" Joe asked. "I finally got one of Jennifer Gridley's friends to talk to me. She gets counseling at East Side Families First now because Jennifer told her how much she was helped. That'll make for a really rounded-out story: Black women, white women, Latinas—"

"Just don't drop the ball on the East Side gentrification and displacement," Tyler said. "That's an important story." He gestured toward the maps. "We gotta get some pins in some places on these maps."

"Yeah, we know," a grouchy Joe said. "If you can figure out how to add some hours to the day—"

"Which one of you is handling the story on the therapy center attack this morning?" Carolyn asked, fully expecting an answer, but Mimi and Joe quickly distanced themselves from that story.

Already halfway out the door, Mimi said, "I'm not an editor, but if I were, I'd put one of the criminal justice types on it. That was a very smooth operation. All that shooting and only one civilian with a minor injury and only one of the perps down."

"Can you get the Captain to talk to me?" Tyler asked.

Mimi shook her head. "I put several questions to Lt. Page and all I got for my trouble was the suggestion to call the Media Relations Office. If it were my story, I'd start with Commander Davis or the chief. I'm guessing they might divulge a morsel or two given how successful the operation was."

"Successful?" Carolyn's normally calm voice remained that way, but her face screamed disbelief. "A man is dead. How is that successful?"

"None of the hostages is dead, Carolyn. None of the women and children who crowd that place six days a week looking for help, including yours truly, got dead. None of the shrinks and social workers who provide that help got dead. Would it be better if no life was lost this morning? It would. But would it be worse if Dr. Beverly Connors or Marilyn Montgomery Patterson died in the assault? I think so. But then I'm a little biased," Mimi said, smiling as she left the office.

Tyler and Carolyn watched the doorway where she'd stood as if she'd left some part of herself there. Then they looked at each other, two people who'd worked together for more than fifteen years, who had worked with Mimi Patterson for almost that long. People who understood and respected each other. "She's different," Carolyn said even more quietly than usual.

"Yeah. She is. But better different, do you think, or just different?"

"Maybe better," Carolyn said, "because she seems not so angry."

"Yeah," Tyler said again. "That's true. But she's still a royal pain in the ass."

"You can't have everything," Carolyn said, sounding quite reasonable.

"Seems I have less every day, since I'm giving them my intern."

"Think we'll get another intern?" Joe asked while trying to slurp too-hot coffee and burning his mouth. "Ow!"

"What's that saying about doing the same stupid thing over and over and expecting a different outcome?" Mimi asked, her eyes and attention on the sheaf of papers she was paging through. "I'd be happy if we could clone this intern. Look at this report she did for me."

"This is really good work. She's as thorough as we would have been," Joe said. This time he blew on the coffee before taking a cautious sip.

Among other useful pieces of information, the intern (why couldn't she remember the young woman's name?) had delivered Mr. Harris's first name, where he worked, and the name of his immediate supervisor. Turned out Mimi knew this underworked, overpaid civil servant. She picked up the phone and made the call. "Answering your own phone these days, Donald? What happened to the phalanx of gophers who once stood guard over you? Oh, yes. Those pesky budget cuts. Just think: If they'd gotten rid of you instead, at least four of those people could still be employed, given how many of the taxpayers' dollars you collect."

"Whadda ya want, Patterson?" Donald Mathis growled.

"A conversation, Donald."

"Conversations with you usually result in heads rolling. What is it you want to converse about?" Mimi noticed that the man's tone of voice had gone from growling to menacing to almost contrite.

97

"Albert Harris."

No quick repartee, growly, contrite or otherwise. Just long seconds of silence. Mimi was happy to wait. "What about him?"

"Have him in your office, with you, at three thirty when I'll tell you what it's all about," Mimi said, and ended the call.

Hearing all this, Joe asked, "Is this Mathis character likely to know what a lazy, useless son of a bitch Harris is?" Joe finished his coffee in several large and no longer dangerously hot gulps.

"More likely not to care, him being a lazy, useless son of a bitch himself," Mimi said, punching buttons on the phone and leaving a message for someone to meet her for lunch at one thirty at the China Veggie Grill. She extended her arm and wriggled her fingers at Joe, and he returned the sheaf of papers.

"Why didn't she give me a copy of this?"

"She did, Joe. Sasha, that's her name!"

"Whose name?"

"The intern. Her name is Sasha and she certainly gave you a copy of whatever she gave me, but how would you know?" She waved a hand at his desk, as if that could magically transform the jumbled piles of books, papers, and documents that concealed his desktop into the ordered architecture that was her own. He watched as she performed her usual ritual, one he'd watched dozens if not hundreds of times before: She entered the information from Sasha's report into files on her computer. She changed files three times, and when she was finished, she ripped up Sasha's file and tossed it in the trash. Then she opened another file and typed rapidly for several minutes. Joe's computer pinged an incoming, and he opened a file from Mimi with decades of background information on Donald Mathis.

"Thanks, Patterson."

"You're welcome."

"How does it happen you remembered the intern's name? I'm not sure I ever heard it."

"You're hopeless, Zemekis," she said—*but only about the little things*, she thought but didn't say. Joe Zemekis might not

98

remember the name of the young intern he was introduced to a week ago, but he remembered the name of every person he'd written about in the past fifteen years. And while she'd be driven to drink if her desk looked like his, he knew where everything was, and if anyone moved even a single sheet of paper, he knew it—and threw a fit about it.

"My wife says that same thing about me."

"Your wife loves you."

He grinned widely. "Yeah, she does. I'm a very lucky man, if a hopeless one."

"Can you shoot me info on Jennifer Gridley's friends?" she asked, clearing more stuff off her desk, adding more to the files on her computer, and writing in the bound leather notepad she kept in her bag.

"Incoming," Joe muttered, and Mimi looked up to see one of the justice system reporters coming her way, holding a sheaf of papers she was certain was the printout of her account of the morning's event she had sent to Tyler and Carolyn. So, if he had that, what did he need with her? He dragged a chair from a neighboring desk, parked himself beside her, and asked a series of questions already answered in the paper he held. Maybe he hadn't read it. Maybe he wanted to see if she'd tell the same story the same way the second time. When he was finished, he thanked her, stood, and walked away. Mimi called him back and pointed to the chair he left beside her desk. He gave her a strange look and dragged the chair back where it belonged. Mimi picked up the phone to call Carolyn, changed her mind, replaced the handset, and stood up. She took her cell phone off the charger and checked the outside temp. Ten degrees warmer than yesterday—chillier than a normal fall day but not full-bore winter. Yet.

"I'm having lunch with Melinda Franklin. Then I'm going to rat out Albert Harris to his boss. You wanna come with?" Mimi watched Joe's decision-making process dance across his face. He saved the file he was working on, closed his computer, locked his desk, and was ready to go. She knew what decided it for him: the only vegetarian dish he admitted to eating—the grilled broccoli, tofu and rice at the China Veggie Grill—and the chance to meet Donald Mathis in person and watch his reaction to the news that his employee's inaction may have caused the death of an elderly woman.

Albert Harris was about as white bread as a Black guy could be. Nothing about him screamed, *I'm an incompetent, uncaring asshole who left an old woman to die.* Nothing about him indicated that he wondered why he was in his boss's office facing two strangers.

Mimi greeted Donald Mathis with a simple recitation of his name, no banal pleasantries or handshake. "This is my colleague, Joe Zemekis—"

"I'm a busy man, Ms. Patterson—"

"Mr. Harris, do you remember Miss Bernice Days and her sister Mrs. Beatrice Thomas?" Melinda Franklin had readily supplied the sisters' names, adding that Bernice was single, as she told anyone who'd listen, because the thrice-married Beatrice had enough husbands for both of them.

Harris's eyes were guileless behind the rectangular eyeglass frames that everybody seemed to wear. He shook his head. "I don't know anybody by that name."

"They live in the Lady Buildings—"

"I'm familiar with that complex." He looked at his boss. "All the buildings—there are six of them—are named after women—"

"I don't care if they're named after—"

"Miss Bernice said you promised to help get her sister moved out of The Jeanne because of her physical problems—"

"I remember her now. She lost a leg to diabetes. Lived on the top floor of that building and the elevator didn't work." Nobody in this conversation had finished a sentence, but Mimi wasn't about to interrupt Harris now. She waited, knowing that Joe wouldn't break silence. And Donald Mathis seemed to understand that anything he said would only make him look incompetent. So they all waited for Albert Harris. "It was ten stories, I remember that now, and without a working elevator . . . well . . . so I checked for the elevator inspection certificate but there wasn't one. There's supposed to be . . . then I called the building management to find out when the elevators would be working again."

Mimi couldn't help herself. "Who did you talk to?"

"Nobody. I left a message—"

"Did you get a call back?"

Harris shook his head and finally began to look miserable. "To tell you the truth, I guess I let this one slip through the cracks."

Now Donald Mathis spoke up, and not kindly, either. "Get the property manager's number, Harris, and give it to her," he said and pointed to Mimi.

"I don't have it, sir—"

"Look in your file, man! What's wrong with you?"

"I . . . I . . . there is no file . . ."

"What do you mean no file?" Mathis pushed his chair back and pushed himself to his feet. He pointed to the box beside the chair where Harris sat. "What's that?"

"My open case files, sir, but I didn't open a file on her . . . Miss . . . the lady . . . there was no case. I never talked to her so there was no case."

"You talked to her sister," Mimi said, anger and dismay roiling her stomach and ruining a wonderful lunch. "And you had both women's names. You knew what the issues were. Why wasn't that enough to open a case file?"

"That's not how it's done. Only one sister could be the client. I'll get on this right away, Mr. Mathis."

Mimi stood up. "The elevator is still out, Mr. Harris, and I'm guessing you still don't want to climb ten flights of stairs. But two weeks ago, the paramedics climbed those ten flights of stairs with a stretcher and all their gear. But lucky them, I suppose. They didn't have to carry Mrs. Thomas down. That job fell to the techs from the ME's office. Mrs. Thomas died before the paramedics could get to her. The cause of death, in case you're interested, is some diabetes-related thing due to the fact that she hadn't had any insulin, complicated by being damn near frozen to death. No elevator and no heat. Eighty-four years old."

"But . . . but . . . that's not . . . you can't blame me for that!"

Mimi was out the door, but she heard Joe say, "Who do you think should be blamed, Mr. Mathis?"

"So he gets away with it?" Melinda Franklin asked.

They were back together because Mimi wanted to talk to the young woman about something else. A different story, a different conversation, this time, ironically, over salsa and chips at a tiny place Mimi never would have found on her own. Once again Melinda proved how much she knew about her neighborhood. Mimi passed on a glass of wine. She still had work to do and she'd get it done, even if she OD'd on guacamole and salsa and the best homemade chips she'd ever eaten.

After Melinda had conversed in Spanish with the waitress Mimi said, "I don't want to be presumptuous, but can you introduce me to some young Latinas?"

Melinda gave her the kind of look that grown-ups gave to disobedient children, the kind of look that had Mimi explaining in exhaustive detail why she'd asked the question and what she planned to do with the introductions.

"Branded? Like . . . like . . ." She closed her eyes, whispered "Good God," then opened her eyes and stared at Mimi for a long moment. "Are they being trafficked?"

What a remarkable young woman. "Possibly. I have no proof of that but given some of the violence and the control exerted over the women, what you suggest is very possible."

"I can and will introduce you to some young Latinas, but I must be present when you talk to them."

Mimi shook her head. "I can't do that—"

"Do you speak Spanish? No? Then you won't be able to communicate with them or they with you."

"I'll bring an interpreter—"

"From some damn government agency?" Melinda spat the words at her.

"Of course not. From one of the universities."

"Which one?" Melinda demanded. "The one that funnels students into the CIA or the one that funnels them to the State Department?"

Mimi was outclassed, outgunned and outsmarted, a reality she had no choice but to accept. "You and I will need to establish some ground rules."

"Of course."

"And I'd appreciate it if you'd order chips, guac and salsa for me to take home. A double order, I think."

"You let a twenty-five-year-old get the best of you," Tyler said. It was a statement, not a question, made while looking at his computer screen and not at Mimi.

"I got the best of a few people when I was twenty-five," Mimi said. "Besides, we all know which graduate programs used to funnel which students into which government agencies. And, once upon a time, into which newspapers."

"So, you know something your youngster doesn't know," Carolyn said.

"Oh, I know quite a few things she doesn't know," Mimi replied, her grin showing teeth. "Except how to speak fuckin' Spanish." The teeth disappeared. "If girls really are being trafficked—"

"Trafficked again," Carolyn said. "Different girls, same evil."

None of them wanted to think about the international trafficking ring Gianna's team had busted purely by accident just a few months ago: Asian girls, some as young as eleven, smuggled into the country and being raped and brutalized hourly in a warehouse in Midtown. Within eyesight of the Capitol. While the idiots in the White House and the State Department and Congress spent their time spewing hatred and stupidity on social media. So, of course girls might be being trafficked. Latinas this time. Maybe some as young as eleven. And if so, could an anything-but-fake news newspaper reporter and a twenty-five-year-old graduate student do anything about it?

Alice Long stretched slowly and began her early morning run just as slowly. She was nursing an injured calf muscle, and the three-mile trail through Rock Creek Park was a gentle run, as well as a beautiful one, especially at dawn when it was cold as crap. And she was the only runner. Her calf muscle—the sore one—gradually warmed up allowing her to increase her pace, though certainly not to her usual eight-minute mile. She was breathing slowly and gently, too, which allowed her to think about something other than running. Like the time she spent with Delores Phillips. More and more time. More and more enjoyable. True, she was learning a lot about money management, more specifically about budgeting. Delores showed her how she earned more than enough to continue to participate in many of the sports activities she enjoyed, though maybe not those on other continents, as well as buy the new car she so desperately needed. But budgeting was required.

"Do you budget?" Alice had asked Delores.

"I used to," Delores replied. "That's how I got rich."

Alice smiled at the memory that warmed her in the frigid dawn and added another memory. "Don't you miss fried chicken and mashed potatoes and gravy? Or fettuccini alfredo?" Delores had asked.

"Don't have to miss 'em because I eat 'em. Rarely. But I do. I don't deprive myself, and I'm not suggesting that you do." And they'd talked for a long while about food as fuel for the body that, if treated like the intricate machine it was, would deliver like one. And fail if abused. Delores proved that she got it when she brought up cirrhosis of the liver.

"My favorite uncle died from it. He always claimed he was a high-functioning alcoholic, whatever that means, but after so many years his liver no longer functioned."

Alice reached the top of the trail and was turning to make the run back to the lot where her car was parked when movement out of the corner of her eye caused her to stop cold. Reflex response. Even though she hadn't seen the person she knew in her gut that it wasn't another runner or a walker. She eased off the trail into the woods and turned. Two men emerged from the densest part of the wood, which really wasn't very dense now because all the foliage was on the ground. Both had shovels over their shoulders. They crossed the road and took what Alice knew to be a shortcut to one of the parking lots. She walked quickly to where she'd seen the men emerge from the wood, dropped a glove to mark the spot, and then hurried, cell phone in her hand, to where they'd left the trail. She activated the zoom feature of the lens as she spied the two men, taking photos. Their backs were to her. They stopped beside a white SUV, and as they got in she saw their faces. The camera saw their faces. Clearly enough? As they drove away, she clicked on the license plate until they were out of sight. Then she returned to the place where she had dropped her glove, picked it up, put it on, and stepped into the wood. She walked straight ahead. There was no path, but there were footsteps to follow: indentations in and displacement of the frozen leaves led her to . . .

"Oh my dear Lord!" Alice whispered. She was looking at a grave. She was on her knees digging with her hands, piling the dirt all to one side, subconsciously preserving the crime scene because surely a crime had been committed here. A half-assed crime. The covering was mostly leaves and twigs, very little soil, and it was too loosely packed to keep any kind of secret, because it didn't take two grown men with shovels to bury the family cat or dog . . .

"No! Oh Dear Jesus no!" Tears ran down her cheeks, freezing as she seemed to be frozen in place, her eyes on the scene before her: Three young girls were in the half-assed grave, practically naked, and one of them, no more than a child, was on top of the other two. Alice removed a glove and touched the child's face, jumping to her feet and stumbling backward. Still warm. Still alive, maybe? She pressed fingers to both sides of the carotid. Nothing. Still crying, she grabbed her phone in trembling hands and punched a button.

"Whattup, Long?"

"LT . . ." She barely got the choked word out, claiming 100 percent of Page's focus.

"Alice, what is it?"

"Three dead girls in a grave in Rock Creek Park—"

"Talk slow and tell me everything."

She got herself under control and did as he asked. Told him exactly how to get to where she was. Assured him that she was in no danger and then returned to the trail to wait for him. She knew it wouldn't take long, but it took longer than she expected because the captain was with him, both running up the trail toward her. Shit. She shouldn't be running that fast uphill, but Alice wasn't going to tell her that. When they drew abreast of her, Alice led them into the wood, to the grave. Gianna closed her eyes and Andy crossed himself. Then both knelt, as Alice had, but only Gianna reached out a bare hand to touch the face of the young girl on top—the now cold face.

Without having to be asked, Alice gave the already-cued phone to Andy, and he and Gianna watched in silence. Then Gianna pulled her own phone from her pocket and looked a request at Alice.

"Sending photos to you and Andy right now," Alice said. Then Gianna walked closer and hugged her tightly.

"Hell of a thing to have to see first thing in the morning, Allie," she whispered. "But you're on top of your game just like always." Then she walked a little away from them, phone to her ear.

Andy hugged her. "All right, Sarge?"

She hugged him back with gratitude. "I may never be all right again, LT, but I'm glad as hell that it's you and the captain who've got my back."

"Wonder what Commander Davis is gonna say?" Andy said.

"I'll tell you what Cap is gonna say. She's not gonna let him give this away to the feds so they can fuck it up."

106

"We got no choice, Sarge. This is federal parkland—"

"And these days we've got no federal government to speak of," Alice responded. "Even before things got so bad, the Feebies would fuck up a church supper, to say nothing of three young Latinas buried in a shallow grave on federal land."

"So what do you think will happen?"

Alice pondered briefly, then said, "I think Davis will kick this up to the chief, and I think he'll arrange for us to keep it."

And as if to prove the point Gianna hurried over to them. "In the next few minutes all entrances to the park will be closed and our ME will come to collect the bodies. The Commander's Intelligence Unit will be all over the photos." She looked at Alice. "Thanks to your fast thinking, Alice, we're not shooting blanks in the dark."

"So the feds are handing over to us?" Andy asked.

Gianna gave him what Mimi called her "slit-eye" stare. "I don't know what the feds are doing, Andy, but I know what we're doing. We're moving the bodies to our medical examiner's office ASAP. Then some of our best criminalists will search the area to see if 'Dumb and Dumber' left us anything. And we're doing it all really fast so we can reopen the park before some eagle-eyed citizen wonders why DC Police have closed the park at daybreak, instead of the US Park Police who have jurisdiction here."

"Got it," Andy said.

"What's the saying, something before the devil knows you're dead?"

Andy grinned and nodded. "'May you be in heaven a half hour before the devil knows you're dead.' We'll be back at our house drinking coffee before the feds know anything happened in their park."

"There's another saying, about forgiveness and permission," Alice said.

"Let's hope we'll have no need to quote either of them today," Gianna said as she checked her watch. She knew the chief would drive the ME's wagon himself if necessary . . . "Sirens."

They wailed in the distance, grew closer and closer, and then stopped. Silence reigned for a few seconds until the sound of a powerful engine roared toward them from a northerly direction. They looked up toward the end of the trail to see a FDDC paramedic van bounce onto the trail and speed toward them. As it came to an abrupt stop the chief medical examiner jumped out, followed by three of her techs, each carrying a body bag. Commander Davis brought up the rear. Gianna nodded at Alice, and she led the ME and her techs to the pitiful grave site. After a brief consultation, heads close together, Davis and Gianna followed, leaving Andy on the trail alone. He followed with his eyes the backs of his colleagues as they disappeared into the wood. He turned back, prepared to guard the entrance to the body dump, to find the chief watching him. He had never seen the man out of uniform but, Andy thought, he didn't quite look like a regular guy. Something about tailored charcoal slacks with spit-shined Doc Martens, the white silk scarf, the Kangol cap ... He still kinda looked like the chief of police.

"You were right, Page. This is a hell of a lot more fun than counterterrorism."

"Yes, sir, it definitely is. Not to mention that Capt. Maglione is a hell of a lot more fun than my old boss. No disrespect intended," he hastily added.

"A damn sight better looking, too," the chief said, and laughed out loud when Andy blushed a deep crimson. "And way far out of your league, too, son."

"Yes, sir. I know," Andy said. And he did know. He knew that his gorgeous boss and the gorgeous M. Montgomery Patterson, journalist extraordinaire, were a couple and had been for a few years now.

"Keep sharp, Page, while I go see what it is that nobody in my department will know anything about."

Andy watched him as he walked into the wood, moving like a hunter. Turning, he got out his phone to look at the photos Alice had sent. Did these assholes come in the same way they left? And if so, how'd they manage carrying shovels and three dead bodies? But then the bodies weren't those of grown women. They were children; not one of whom weighed more than seventy or seventy-five pounds. Andy recalled the grave. He'd most likely never forget it—the little bodies tossed in like . . .

He studied the photo. It would have been dark when they arrived since it was barely dawn when Alice took the photos. They wouldn't have been seen. Or heard, since the four people exited the wood and were upon him and he had heard nothing. The chief and the commander almost ran to the paramedic van and scrambled in.

"Some looky-loos went around the police line and entered from the forest—"

The ME techs, each carrying a body bag, ran out of the wood and toward the van, which was backing up toward them. The back doors flew open and hands grabbed the body bags. The techs scrambled in and slammed the doors as the ME ran to the open passenger door and jumped in. The van was moving before the door slammed shut.

Alice and Gianna were beside him on the trail, and Andy pretended not to notice that Gianna was limping slightly as she said, "Let's exit the way the bad guys did," and she walked to the edge of the trail and looked down.

"Not a good idea, Cap," Alice said in the tone of voice she used when talking to the team members. She removed her watch cap and gave it to Gianna who hesitated only briefly before pulling it on and down over her ears, then tucking the hair on the back of her head into the collar of her jacket. "You two head down the trail and I'll meet you in the parking lot." A couple returning from a morning walk would be less memorable or noticeable than the three of them together. And she headed down the hill without a backward glance, not wanting to see the looks she was getting from her bosses . . . not wanting them to see the look on her face that said she was regretting her action. Her calf hurt like hell, and she was the one limping when she got to the parking lot. No looky-loos or evidence of police presence remained.

109

"Two hours back at the unit?" Gianna asked.

"Yes, ma'am," Alice and Andy replied in unison.

"And Alice? You'll hear it from the chief and from Commander Davis, but I want to say it again: What you did this morning was exemplary. Thank you."

"Thank you, Captain," Alice said, and hoped they didn't notice her limping when she got into her car.

CHAPTER SIX

Housing Officials' Negligence Is a Cause of Elderly Woman's Death

By Joseph J. Zemekis Jr.
Staff Writer

The head of the City's Housing Assistance Program and a deputy have acknowledged that they "dropped the ball" regarding a request to move 86-year old Beatrice Days Thomas from the top floor of a building without a working elevator or heat. Paramedics, who were summoned by the woman's sister, walked up to the 10th floor where they found the door unlocked and Ms. Thomas on the floor of her bedroom, unconscious. Attempts to revive Ms. Thomas were unsuccessful and paramedics called for the Medical Examiner who pronounced the woman dead.

Richard Harris, a 16-year employee of the Housing Department, responded to a request for emergency assistance from Bernice Days on behalf of her sister. "She said her sister was ill and that she lived alone," Harris said. "She wanted the sister moved from the high-rise building she lived in to the building Ms. Days lived in." Harris told Ms. Days that he would help, but when he walked across the courtyard to the high-rise, he discovered that the elevator was not working. "I called the property management office and left a message. I didn't hear back and, well, I guess I just forgot."

"We dropped the ball on that one," said Donald Mathis, the head of the department and Mr. Harris's supervisor. "Things do fall through the cracks on occasion."

An investigation by this newspaper has uncovered information showing that four different divisions of the Housing Department have failed to correct code violations and collect court-ordered judgements. Documents obtained by this paper also suggest that the registered agents for the property either provided false contact information on their official government filings, or they do not exist. The City Attorney is investigating.

Meanwhile Richard Harris has resigned, and Donald Mathis is on suspension pending results of an investigation launched by the City Council committee that oversees the Housing Department.

The sisters have lived in the same East Side apartment complex since it opened more than 20 years ago.

Did Greed Destroy 80 years of Life and Love?

By M. Montgomery Patterson
Staff Writer

More than sisters, they were best friends. Born and raised in the East River section of DC more than 80 years ago, Beatrice and Bernice Days did everything together. Until it was time to go to college. Beatrice, older by two years, was the adventurous one. "She wanted to go away, to Spelman in Atlanta," while Bernice remained at home to attend Howard.

It takes Bernice a long time to find the words she wants, then to make sentences of them, and it has nothing to do with her 82 years. She is all but paralyzed with grief and loss. And aloneness. Even when they were separated by miles, Bernie and Bea—the nicknames they were always known by—were joined in the knowledge of their mutual existence. Even when Bea was being adventurous.

"She had always wanted to live in New York City. I never understood why, but she did. So she moved up there." Sudden tears fill Bernie's eyes and she weeps silently for several minutes, soaking two crisp, white linen handkerchiefs. Yes, the generation that used hankies still does. She fishes a third from her dressing gown pocket. Just in case. "I used to go up there to visit but I don't like it. Too noisy, too dirty, too many people."

Bea came home often, and on one visit Bernie showed her the new apartments being built in the neighborhood. The sisters liked what they saw, especially the fact that the six buildings were all named after women. Bernie liked that two of those buildings were tall. Not New York City tall, but tall enough that she'd return home to live in one of them. The best friend sisters were together again—in separate buildings—Bernie in The Jeane, Bea in The Sarah, but just across the courtyard from each other. Daily visits commenced.

"We got used to watching them visit each other," said Florence Gregory sadly. An original

113

resident of The Alexis, she and the Days sisters were friends until ill health claimed Bernice and diabetes claimed her left leg last year. "Bea visited daily until they shut off the elevators. She used to try to climb those stairs up to the 10th floor. She was 80 years old! What kind of people shut off the elevators and the heat to make people move out so they can move rich people in?"

The elevator is shut off in Ms. Gregory's building, too, but it's one of the four-story structures so walking is possible. But then Ms. Gregory has both her legs. She does not, however, have heat, the lack of which the Medical Examiner said contributed to the death of Bernice Days Thomas.

"The oven was on in her apartment, but that wasn't sufficient heat for an 84-year-old diabetic who had been without insulin for at least three days," said Dr. Wanda Oland, the City's Chief Medical Examiner. "Cause of death? Complications from diabetes and hypothermia."

According to the ME, the autopsy showed that Bernie had not been taking her full dose of insulin until she had more, and since no pharmacy would deliver up ten flights of stairs and since Bea could no longer walk up ten flights of stairs, there was no insulin.

"I took it to her once," Florence Gregory said. "I'm more than ten years younger and in pretty good shape, but once is all I could manage. Nobody *wants* to walk up ten flights of stairs. I'm sure the paramedics didn't want to. I'm sure the ME didn't want to. They did because they had to."

Florence Gregory is spearheading a group of residents seeking to force the property owners to restore elevator service, heat, and basic maintenance to the property. Their first order of business is to find out who owns the property, since the city doesn't seem to know and since all official correspondence seems to contain fake information, including the legal name of the property. So, everyone calls it by its long-ago given nickname: "The Lady Buildings."

Mimi's desk phone had been ringing off the hook all morning. While she was pleased at the response to her story, she was too busy working on the follow-up to keep talking to people about it. She switched off the ringer and transferred all calls to the newsroom switchboard. She put her work cell phone on vibrate and placed it so that she could see who was calling and answer if necessary. She had afternoon appointments with Florence Gregory and Melinda Franklin. Fortunately, they were in the same part of town. Unfortunately, they were not about the same story, which didn't make Florence happy. She also was not happy that Joe would be at this afternoon's meeting. She wanted Mimi to do all the stories, and she didn't understand why that couldn't happen. Mimi had tried explaining but Florence didn't want to hear it. She didn't want to know how much progress Joe was making peeling back the layers of deceit and subterfuge hiding the true ownership of The Lady Buildings complex. He was almost ready to go to print with a story naming three people in the Housing Department, one each in the City Comptroller's and Tax Administrator's offices, and one in the Office of Management and Budget on the payroll of the owners. Mimi, meanwhile, had the City Attorney almost ready to make Richard Harris and Donald Mathis complicit in the death of Beatrice Thomas since the ME said loudly and clearly that the death was not an accident and could have been prevented.

Thanks to Melinda, however, Mimi also had at least two young women who were willing to talk about men who sold girls for sex and who branded them so they couldn't escape. Was one

115

story more important than the other? That depended on who was asked, but Mimi was more drawn to the story of the exploitation of girls and young women. The continued exploitation of girls and young women around the world—nothing new here, either, any more than there was anything new in graft and corruption in high places. Rich people had been stealing since the beginning of time. About the same length of time politicians had been corrupt. Mimi was just making a choice about the stories that most interested her.

"Check out the digital!" Joe, seated two feet away, shouted.

Mimi parked the file she was working on. The digital edition of the paper, which was always open, boasted two new headlines from the previous hour's edition. She knew without asking which one had Joe all lathered up: *FEDS DENY ROCK CREEK PARK IS BODY DUMP SITE.* "I guess they would," Mimi said.

"Keep reading," Joe said in a tone somewhere between gleeful and ominous. Mimi kept reading, growing more skeptical by the sentence, feeling neither glee nor ominousness: The owner of a camera-equipped drone had it up early one morning about ten days ago. The owner couldn't be specific because the time/date function of the camera was broken. The picture was grainy because it was about six a.m. and because the drone had to stay well above the trees. None of the faces of the several people who were in the woods at the time could be seen clearly, but three of them could be seen carrying black body bags out of the woods and loading them into a DCFD paramedic unit. The owner of the drone tried to share the photos with the Park Service but, to quote the owner, "they weren't the least bit interested." So he sold it to the local TV station that hadn't yet met a dead body it didn't like.

Several people were watching the newsroom TV. Mimi and Joe went to join them in watching the dark, grainy, all but useless video. The only relatively clear image was of the DCFD paramedic van, which was red but looked black. None of the fuzzy people were identifiable. Unless you knew them, which Mimi did. All of them.

"Would you listen to these assholes?" somebody said. "They're actually talking about this shit like they're reporting a real story with real facts. Why wouldn't the Park Police be on the scene? And even if DC was picking up the bodies, if there were dead bodies, it would be the ME, not Fire and Rescue Paramedics."

"You got to consider the source, dude. You know what channel this is, right?"

Somebody turned off the TV and everybody went back to work. Everybody except Mimi. She took her phone to the lunchroom to call Gianna. "Hello, love." She answered on the first ring. "Sorry, can't talk right now."

"Because of what just aired on the lowest of the bottom-feeder stations?"

Dead silence on the other end. Then, "Anybody but you connect the dots?"

"I don't think so."

"Good. We'll talk about it later. I really do have to go." And she went, leaving Mimi to ponder the magnitude of what she'd just learned. For without saying the actual words Gianna had confirmed that a part of Rock Creek Park was indeed a body dump site, that high-ranking members of the DC Police Department had removed the bodies early one morning—and Mimi knew exactly what morning. But all she could do was remember—then keep it to herself. And, of course, wonder how many bodies were buried in the federal parkland that ran the north-south length of DC.

Gianna, meanwhile, was following orders: Say nothing to nobody. Alice and Andy were following the same instructions. If anybody needed to say anything it would be the chief, and so far he hadn't. But truth be told, they didn't have much to say anyway. At least about the bodies and the perps. None of the photos Alice shot had produced any information. The license plates on the white SUV were stolen off a truck in a shopping mall parking lot in Alexandria weeks ago; no matter how hard the techs tried they couldn't produce a clear enough image of the faces of the two men to try for a facial recognition match; and the scene of crime techs got zilch. The presence of the paramedic's van, however, could pose a problem, especially if real reporters like Mimi or Joe Zemekis started asking the real questions. But that was an issue above her pay grade. The chief could handle it if it came to that. Come to think of it, he could handle Mimi, too.

Andy knocked and rushed in, red in the face. "One of the feds is on TV running off at the mouth. Again. Why can't they just shut up if there's nothing to say?"

"You need to calm down, Andy, and stop acting like whatever the feds are saying has anything to do with you."

"I'm sorry, boss. It's just . . . it was a shock seeing it on TV."

"Your mother wouldn't recognize you in that photo, Andy, nor would mine recognize me." *Although my Mimi did.*

"But what about the paramedic van? It's definitely a DC issue, not a US Park Service vehicle."

"The chief will address that if it becomes necessary."

"Yes, boss."

"Where's Alice?"

"At the ME's picking up the report on the girls."

Gianna shook her head. "She shouldn't be doing that, Andy."

"I know. I told her I'd go, but she said she'd finish what she started, that it was her responsibility."

Ah Alice! "Well . . . maybe some good could come of it. Have you ever met Wanda Oland?"

"The ME? No, I haven't." Andy shook his head.

"She's definitely old school—likes dead people better than living ones and treats them with respect. Those little girls died because they were hated, but Wanda will treat them lovingly. She will bathe them and comb their hair and lay them out on a table, not pile them on top of each other in a dirt hole."

Gianna had spoken quietly but Andy heard what she felt. Still, he asked, "What makes you say they were hated?"

"Because you don't rape and torture and murder what you love, Andy. You and Alice come in when she gets back."

"Certain crimes against women are hate crimes," Andy said, then explained himself when Gianna turned to face him head on. "My former boss said you said that if a woman is a victim only because she's a woman, then that's a hate crime."

"What boss was that?"

"Commander Pelligrino. It was a few years ago, when he was a captain, something you said at a crime stats meeting."

Gianna remembered the meeting. A crime stats presentation back when DC had one of the highest crime rates in the nation, including a rash of rapes and murders of prostitutes, though none of them were included in the crime stats. Because they were just a bunch of hookers and who cared anyway? She was the new head of the Hate Crimes Unit then and her angry lash-out at the men at the table—she was the only woman—had put her in Capt. Pelligrino's bad graces for a long time. And even though the chief had added women to the list of Hate Crimes victims, prostitutes remained easy prey. Now, it seemed, so did young girls who were made into prostitutes against their wills.

The young Latinas who faced Mimi and Melinda across the scarred table at the rear of the no-name taco and burrito joint were, to be charitable, sullen and uncommunicative. Even after they'd eaten like it was the first food they'd had in days—and perhaps it was—and gulped enough *horchata* to float a small ship, they still would barely look at Mimi, to say nothing of talk to her. But Mimi looked at them. Studied them, really, and what she was looking at, she realized, despite the heavy makeup, elaborate hair styles, and jewelry, were children. She doubted they had yet celebrated their *quinceañeras*—that's if there was anybody in their lives to throw them the important fifteenth birthday bash. Which might explain the appetites. Growing boys weren't the only ones with bottomless pits for stomachs.

Finally, one of the girls said something in Spanish though she still didn't look at Mimi. Melinda did that. "Her name is Angelica and she said they will get dead if they talk to you, just like the other girls."

"What other girls?" Mimi asked, hairs on the back of her neck at full attention.

"They told somebody about the brand marks and Gustavo didn't like it. They're not supposed to talk about it," Melinda translated, and after a long silence the girls talked some more, and Mimi could see that whatever was said upset Melinda.

"Gustavo doesn't like it when the girls go outside their own kind. That's what the other girls did, and that's what these girls are doing by being here with us. We're not their kind."

Mimi knew that there was a new kind of animosity between Blacks and Latinos and that it was due in large part to the bad feelings between West Coast Blacks and Latinos, but that didn't lessen the impact of hearing that some Latinas could be dead because they had Black friends. "Melinda, ask them how they know the other girls are dead. Maybe they just ran away."

Melinda asked, and the terror was so immediate that Mimi knew the answer: These girls had witnessed the murder of the others. That would be how Gustavo kept them in line. She raised her palms to calm them and spoke one of the few Spanish phrases she knew: *"Lo siento! Lo siento!"* She asked Melinda to make a better apology for her and changed topics: Did the girls all live together? How many and where? And what was Gustavo's last name? How old was he?

Melinda spoke, then listened for a long while as the two girls took turns talking, now and then sneaking glances at Mimi. And the more she learned, the more concerned she became. These two were the only ones left since Gustavo killed the other three. They all lived in a house with two adult women whom they referred to as *Abuelita* and *Tia*, Grandmother and Aunt. So adult women were helping Gustavo enslave girls and sell them to be raped, not hesitating to kill them if necessary. They didn't know the address of the house, just that they had to ride the *tren* over the river to get here to this meeting. They didn't know Gustavo's other name or age—just that he was old. And mean.

"How are they able to be here?" Mimi asked.

"The grandmother and auntie told them to go earn money."

Mimi got the message and fished the agreed-upon sum out of her pocket, covered the bills with her hand, and slid them across

120

the table. The older of the two girls scooped the money up and counted it without separating the bills. She'd had lots of practice getting paid. The two girls got up, ready to go. Mimi didn't want them to leave, didn't want them to return to their lives. "Ask them if they're branded," Mimi said quickly, and Melinda asked just as quickly. After a brief hesitation and a longer consultation, they answered, then all but ran the few steps to the door and out into the cold.

Mimi waited for Melinda to be ready to answer the final question: "A dollar sign and the letter *G* on their buttocks. Right cheek. He makes them with paper clips that he twists into a *G*; then he heats them with a blowtorch."

Mimi was glad she hadn't eaten because she felt sick to her stomach. If there had been food in there, she'd be in the bathroom right now. "Thank you," she said to Melinda.

"Can you do anything to help them?"

"I have to try," Mimi said.

"Count me in," Melinda said.

"This Gustavo asshole kills people!"

"So do some of my homies," Melinda said darkly.

Unable to come up with a suitable retort, Mimi changed the subject. "I take it Florence Gregory is annoyed with me."

"Pissed-off big time is more like it! She loved your story on the Days sisters and she thought you'd be back over there today. Instead she got Mr. Zemekis—"

"Who is a great reporter and a very nice man." Mimi was trying not to let her annoyance with Florence Gregory show, but that was an uphill slog. "After his story, the city attorney's office is looking for somebody to prosecute and the housing agency is looking for someone else to fire. What more does she want? My editors cooking and cleaning for her?"

Melinda's phone beeped an incoming text message, so while she checked, Mimi checked her own phone, which had been vibrating in her pocket for the last half hour. Zemekis three times, Tyler twice. She read Tyler's messages, then pulled up the digital edition as he'd asked, and she saw why: *POLICE CHIEF*

BELITTLES FEDS. AGAIN, the headline screamed. She didn't need to read the story. Instinct told her it was about what did or didn't happen in Rock Creek Park, and since the headline didn't implicate the chief and two of his top officials, namely Gianna and her boss, she could read it later.

Zemekis had his hands full with Florence. She was following him and the two interns everywhere they went, asking questions and, worse, demanding answers. Mimi sighed inwardly and tamped down her irritation with the older woman. How must it feel to be considered unworthy of heat, elevators, maintenance, and other basic services? To be treated as nothing more than pawns in somebody's real-life Monopoly game? The phone rang in her hand and she almost dropped it. Zemekis. A call and not a text? Oh Lord. He really did strangle Florence.

"What's up, Joe?"

His excitement caused him to talk so fast Mimi could hardly understand him, and when she finally did, she stood up in a hurry, glad she was on this side of town. Melinda got up, too, looking as excited as Mimi felt. She'd received the same news: City officials, at least a half dozen of them, had shown up at The Lady Buildings complex with a phalanx of maintenance workers, along with employees of the electric and gas companies. Their mission: to restore all legally mandated services to the six buildings in the complex as well as perform the basic maintenance that had been ignored and neglected for months. And for a change the city attorney's paperwork had teeth, in the form of liens against the properties. Seemed the city was charging the owners for all the work done and leaving them no choice but to pay or forfeit the right and ability to sell the property.

When Tommi asked Andy and Alice to meet with her in the captain's conference room they did so without question. They couldn't imagine what she wanted but if Tommi requested their presence, she got it.

122

"My daughter—you know I have a daughter, right? She's thirteen, and she thinks she might know one of the girls you dug up in Rock Creek."

Whatever they had tried to imagine Tommi wanted, it wasn't this. "Can you walk us through this, Tommi?" Andy asked, gently and carefully. "How does she know . . . ?"

"Oh God I'm sorry. Let me tell it like I'm a cop and not a mom. She overheard Mike and me talking last night. We thought she was asleep in her room, but she had her pillow and bedcovers on the floor outside our bedroom door. She's been sleeping there since her friends went missing and we didn't even know it."

"Take a breath, Tommi," Alice said taking her hand. "You're a cop and a mom and the best of both. You've talked about her—Sandy's her name, right? You've talked about her a lot, Tommi, and she sounds like a really smart girl with her head screwed on tight and straight."

"That's exactly who she is, and that's why we got so worried when she ran into our room asking questions about those dead girls, whether we knew who they were. If only we'd closed the door."

"Why does she think she might know who one of them is?" Andy asked.

Tommi explained that Sandy's BFF, a girl her own age named Evangelina, had disappeared suddenly without a word. "They tell each other when they're going to pee, so for Lina to just disappear, well, it worried me, too." The major source of her worry, Tommi said, was an uncle who had recently moved in with Lina's family and didn't like her spending so much time with Sandy. "He told Lina to stay with her own kind, so they would see each other at school and text and tweet. But when Lina's big sister, Carmen, dropped out of high school is when I really got worried. Carmen was a good student and she loved school. She planned to go to UDC, she talked about it all the time. Then Lina stopped going to school."

"Tommi. You know you're talking about these girls in the past tense."

Tommi inhaled. "I've got a real bad feeling about this, Allie."

Andy tried not to show surprise at Tommi's nickname for Alice. He spent a lot of time with both women and he'd never heard it. But then they spent time with each other away from him and the captain, and they were more like each other than they were like anyone else. "Do you know this uncle's name, Tommi, or where he came from?"

"I don't, LT, but Sandy probably does."

"Then we'd really appreciate being able to talk to her, Tommi. When can you bring her in?"

"She's upstairs in my office. I'll go get her. But first, you guys, a couple of ground rules: Andy, I want her to talk to Alice, please, no disrespect. And I don't want her looking at pictures of dead bodies."

Alice and Andy readily agreed, then asked if the conversation could be recorded and Tommi agreed just as quickly. When she left to go get her daughter, Alice and Andy exchanged a long, worried look. Questioning a child was tough, even a smart one with her head screwed on tight and straight. But the child of a coworker? And if her best friend had been raped, mutilated, murdered, and buried in a park in the middle of the city . . .

"You'll just have to play it by ear, Alice."

"Suppose it is her friend, Andy? Do we tell her the truth?"

"I think she already knows the truth. I'm pretty sure Tommi does." He tried not to think too hard about what an ugly mess adults had made of the world that children had to live in. "I better call the captain and let her know what's up in case she comes back and wonders why people are in her office."

"Good idea," Alice said, taking deep breaths to calm her nerves. She'd rather take on a perp with a gun or a knife than talk to this little girl, this daughter of her friend, about some of the ugliest shit on the planet, the kind of shit children don't ever recover from. Grown-ups, either, for that matter.

Sandy Bell didn't look frightened, but she did look sad. Her red-rimmed eyes and runny nose told the story. She hugged her mom and Tommi left them. She shook Alice's hand when it was offered and she sat down beside her, which Alice took to be a good sign. She looked all around the room, then at Alice. She was ready.

"I'm so sorry that the first time we're meeting, Sandy, I have to talk to you about things I know are painful."

"It's all right, Sgt. Long. My mom told me all about you. She said you're a kick-ass cop and if anybody can find out the truth about what happened to Lina, it's you." Tears formed in her eyes but she wiped them away. Alice went over to Gianna's desk and got the box of tissues from the shelf behind it and put it in front of Sandy.

"I'm glad your mom thinks so well of me, Sandy, 'cause I feel the same way about her. And we're thinking you might be able to help us find some answers to a big problem that's been bugging us for a little while."

Sandy took her phone from her pocket, punched it on, opened the photo gallery, and pushed it over to Alice, who had to work hard to contain her emotions. If she lived to be a hundred, she'd never forget her first glimpse of the still-warm dead girl's face. What she was looking at now was that same girl's bright, smiling—alive—face. Evangelina. Sandy Bell's BFF. And Carmen, Lina's big sister. No photos of the third girl, and they couldn't show Sandy her dead face. They'd promised Tommi no photos of dead girls. Alice scrolled through the photos.

"Who's this guy?"

"Uncle Gus. They hate him, Lina and Carmen do. He makes them do things they don't want to do." She was crying again, and Alice let her. Did she know what things Uncle Gus made the girls do? She couldn't bring herself to ask that question, and she was glad she didn't need to. She'd read the autopsy reports.

"Who are these women? Lina and Carmen's mother?"

Sandy was weeping again and shaking her head. "Señora Maria Reina went away, too. Gus said she didn't want to live with Lina and Carmen anymore, but they didn't believe him." She was

125

crying harder now and Alice held her tightly. Oh how she wanted to get her hands on this Gus asshole and wrap them around his neck. She looked up and saw Gianna and Andy watching them.

"Would it be all right, Sandy, if Capt. Maglione and Lt. Page came in?"

Sandy stopped crying and sat up straight. She wiped her face and blew her nose. "Ready?" Alice asked, and beckoned to Gianna and Andy.

Sandy gazed at Gianna in wide-eyed wonder, a clear case of heroine worship. "Captain, my mom told my dad you walk on water."

Gianna threw her head back and let go a gut-busting chortle. "You know your mom rides those waves with me, Sandy, and I couldn't get anything done without her. She's my rock."

Sandy's smile almost cut through her pain. Gianna sat across the table from them, Andy beside her. Alice asked Sandy for permission to share the photos from her camera.

"Is it Lina and Carmen? The bodies Sgt. Long dug up? Is it them?"

"I'm so very sorry, Sandy, but yes, I think so."

She collapsed into Alice's arms. Andy got up to go call Tommi while Gianna and Alice tried to calm the child. They didn't want Alice to find her daughter any more traumatized than she already was.

"It's them, Mommy," Sandy said as soon as Tommi entered, "but the Captain is gonna get who did it. Right?"

"I will do everything I can, Sandy, I promise you that. And what would help is if we could have copies of those photos, please?" Gianna wrote down her number and Sandy sent the photos. Then Tommi thanked them, took Sandy's hand, and left the three operational cops to do what they did. The first thing Gianna wanted to do was listen to the recording. "I've got a really bad feeling about this," she said. It only got worse after what she heard from Sandy. She picked up the phone and punched in Commander Davis's number. Andy and Alice stood up to leave. She shook her head. They sat back down.

Gianna started talking when Davis answered, and without giving him a chance to speak she said, "Suppose there are more of them. More dead women. Suppose Rock Creek Park really is a burial ground."

Alice and Andy sat still and quiet and watched their boss sit still and quiet as she listened to her boss, not knowing that Commander Davis had not spoken. He knew her well enough to know if she asked such a question, she believed she knew the answer. "I'm sending you some photos." She nodded at Alice who opened her own phone and sent all of Sandy's photos to Commander Davis. "Two of the dead girls when they were very much alive. The man who runs them. And the two women who help him—"

Now the Commander did speak: "Goddammit! Here's me wondering what could be worse than raping and murdering little girls and the answer is, grown women helping. We'll meet later today," and he hung up.

"How close do these people live to Tommi?" Gianna asked, and the looks she got meant they didn't know. "Ask Tommi to come back, preferably without Sandy if that's possible."

Andy stepped out to call Tommi. Alice sat watching Gianna, waiting for her to speak. Wondering if she would. But Andy returned almost immediately with Tommi. "I was already on my way to thank you. To thank all of you—"

"We owe you the thanks, Tommi, for trusting us with your little girl," Gianna said. "That couldn't have been easy for you."

"No, it wasn't. But if she knew who the dead girls were, all of us—me, Mike, and Sandy—wanted to help."

"How close do you live to Lina and Carmen?" Gianna used the girls' names. She couldn't bring herself to call them "dead girls" to a woman who'd known them.

"Next door . . . kinda," Tommi said, and explained that there was a vacant lot between the two houses, and she felt the energy shift when she said that, so hurriedly added the pertinent details: A fire "of suspicious origin," according to the fire marshal, had leveled the house. After several months of constant harassment, the city finally cleared and leveled the lot. "Lupe wanted to plant a garden.

She said like one her Mama had back home, but Gus wouldn't let her, the bastard. Then one night I saw him digging over there—"

"Digging where, exactly?" Andy asked.

"At the rear of the lot, near the fence by the alley."

"Please tell us everything you know about that family, Tommi, beginning with their last names and where they're from. And are Gus and Lupe really related?" Alice and Andy were ready to take notes. Gianna kept her eyes on Tommi as she began to talk, and as soon as she revealed the surnames of Guadalupe and Gustavo, both of whom were from a Guatemalan village on the Mexican border, Andy was up and out of the room.

"Were they legal, Tommi? Do you know?" Alice asked, and Tommi gave her a wild-eyed look of disbelief.

"I don't know, and I don't care, Alice. Those little girls were born here, that much I do know!" Anger replaced Tommi's grief, misplaced as it was.

"Whoa, Tommi," Alice said, palms raised in surrender. "I'm not doing the ICE search-and-destroy thing here. Just trying to find info that will let us background Gus, find out if he has a criminal record, known associates, and to determine whether Lupe really went home." *And left her little girls with a bastard like Gus,* she thought but didn't say.

Tommi's anger dissipated as quickly as it flared, leaving only the grief. "I'm sorry, you guys. I know better. I know how this works. And you don't think Lupe went back home any more than I do. She wouldn't leave those girls of her own free will any more than I'd leave mine." The tears flowed then, but she pulled out a packet of tissues and wiped them away, becoming Sgt. Tommi once again. "He killed her like he killed her girls and—wait a minute—you think he buried her in the vacant lot next door?"

Gianna reached across the table and took Tommi's hand, meeting the woman's dark, sorrowful gaze with her own hazel one. "The only thing we think, Tommi, is that we have to consider all the possibilities. That's all we're doing right now: looking at all the possibilities from every possible angle. You know the drill." And maybe the park wasn't the burial ground; maybe the backyard was.

Andy returned then and gave Tommi an *atta girl* pat on the back. "Good job knowing how the last names work. That'll help a lot."

"I asked Lupe about it—why she and the girls had the same last name, but none of them had her husband's last name—"

"What husband?" Gianna and Alice pounced on this piece of information like starving lions on raw meat.

"Guillermo. He went Out West to the fields, traveling all over picking everything from berries to lettuce to corn to apples—to whatever grows, I guess. And for a while he sent money back to Lupe, but then he stopped. Seems he met a woman ..."

So Guillermo might be a bastard, but he wasn't a likely lead. Andy asked Tommi if she knew his two last names. She did. He wrote them down, and left, walking fast. Every bit of information was helpful, even if all it did was confirm a negative, helpful because that meant time and resources wouldn't be wasted running down a dead end.

"Thank you again, Tommi, for your patience," Gianna said. "I know how hard it is to remain focused on the job when it crosses the line into your home life." And she did know. They sometimes forgot because she handled it so well. Killers had come after Mimi Patterson twice, and Gianna had almost lost her own life protecting her. Alice wondered how well she really handled it, or did she just do a good job of masking her pain? *No way I can ask her*, Alice thought, but she knew she needed to tell someone how the images of the girls in the Rock Creek Park graves constantly danced behind her eyes, keeping her awake most of the night.

"Really, Captain, you don't need to thank me."

"I do have one more question, Tommi: Does Gustavo know what you all do, you and Mike?" Tommi's husband, Mike Bell, was a postal inspector. A cop, too.

Tommi laughed a real laugh. "Yeah, he does, and he hates it. That's another reason he told Lina and Carmen to keep away from us. He was trying to teach them to hate cops, but they liked us too much, and they grew even closer after Lupe left."

129

Andy burst through the door, excitement radiating off him like heat waves. "A lead, folks. We got ourselves an actual lead. Check this out: Gustavo really is Lina's and Carmen's uncle, but he's not Lupe's brother. He's Guillermo's brother."

Dead silence in the room as the information was processed and then as possible scenarios took shape in their cop minds. All were dismissed except one: Guillermo sent Gustavo into his home when he knew he wasn't coming back. Maybe he knew what would happen to his wife and daughters, and maybe he didn't, but all were willing to bet that Guillermo knew what kind of man his brother was. And no decent man would send the most indecent of men into his home, filled with women. Gianna spoke first. "Tommi, you and your family need to get out of there. Now."

"But . . . but . . ." Tommi sputtered.

"No buts, Sarge," Andy said.

Tommi collected herself and told them that she and Mike planned to move in the next couple of months. They were looking for a place on the East Side near a private girls' school that Sandy already was accepted for the winter semester beginning in January. "We just haven't found a place to live yet. One that we can afford. I didn't realize how expensive it was over there—"

"Hotel for the next several nights until we figure out the details—"

"We can't afford that."

Gianna waved her arm around the room. "Commander Davis seems to have an unlimited budget. I'm sure he'll figure it out. Do you think the school will admit Sandy a couple of months early? If the request comes from the department?"

It was a lot to wrap her mind around. Almost too much. She could organize and run the unit almost without thinking about it. Throw in a hitch, glitch or challenge and she was at her best. But this? "I'll ask the school. And I need to discuss all of this with Mike. And Sandy. Are we really in danger, do you think?" But she knew the answer.

Gianna stood up and went to the door. "You three work out

130

the details. Do whatever you think is necessary." She opened the door. "Alice, a moment please?"

They stepped outside the office and closed the door. Alice was relieved to see the room empty. The three teams were in class or in training, which was a good thing, Alice thought, because the shit was about to hit the fan, and they needed all the learning and training they could get. That feeling churned her gut, and that's what she was thinking about when Gianna blindsided her.

"I feel your hurt, Alice, and your struggle with how to handle it. And I strongly recommend that you talk to someone about it. This is not an order or a departmental mandate as if you'd been involved in a shooting." She stopped talking and watched Alice for a bit, not so much waiting for a response as seeing if the words sank in.

"I thought I'd get past it, Cap, but I haven't, and I don't know why."

"I know why, Alice. Because you're a good and decent human being. And because you're a woman who witnessed the aftermath of the brutalization of three little girls. I had to discuss it with my therapist, and she was so concerned she put it at the top of the list of things we discuss—ahead of my being shot and almost dying." *Crimes committed against women because they're women are hate crimes.* The words and their truth reverberated in her brain.

Alice wanted to cry. Gianna knew it. But neither of them wanted that to happen in the squad room, so Gianna touched her shoulder and walked away, telling Alice that she'd be in Davis's office, learning if the shit had already hit the fan.

The air was almost festive in the courtyard of The Riverview Apartments, now known almost universally as The Lady Buildings—if frigid air could be considered festive. Maybe at an ice hockey rink . . .? Practically all of the remaining residents of the buildings were outside watching city officials perform their due diligence—their long *over*due diligence. The courtyard was being cleaned, as were the building lobbies, and a worker on a ladder was cleaning the grime from the marble inlay into which the "Lady" names were chiseled. Engineers from the building department carted toolboxes and ladders into the buildings, the gas company technicians with their gear were up and down from the basements, and Mimi and Joe were shocked into near speechlessness. They alternated between conducting interviews for their respective stories about the events unfolding before them, and expressing their amazement that what they were witnessing actually was happening. Mimi's favorite scene was playing out between a wealthy-looking man wearing bespoke everything (why people couldn't say *hand-tailored* Mimi didn't know) and the city attorney who was there in person. He was a dour man who, though of average height, always managed to appear to be looking down his nose at whomever he was speaking to. Now, as he peered at the bespoke fellow, a ghost of a smile lifted his lips. Should she be counting miracles? First, Ryerson was on the scene, then he smiled . . . kinda?

"Joe, will you look at that? Ryerson actually smiled."

"Yeah. Like a shark smiles."

"Who is that?" Mimi asked. Joe would know since the sharks were his story.

"That's the attorney for the property owners demanding that the liens be lifted. Ryerson already told him that's not happening until he meets the owners in person."

"Playing hardball, our Ryerson, and that's a game he likes. Especially when he's written the rules of the game."

"And if that chump was from around here, he'd know that."

"Where's he from, in his bespoke wardrobe?"

"What a stupid word. *Bespoke.*" Joe said the stupid word like it emitted a foul odor in his mouth.

"You wouldn't think so if your friends and family saw you wearing a bespoke suit and overcoat."

"Anybody who knows me would ask what they said when they spoke."

Both reporters got a good chuckle out of that. Melinda Franklin appeared and wanted to know what was so funny, so Joe told her. She thought it was funny, too, and added that she had to look up the definition the first time she encountered the word. "Would it kill them to say *hand-tailored* or *handcrafted?*" she asked, sounding as if she really wanted an answer. Then she shifted gears. "It seems Florence was right. The free press can still work miracles," she said.

Mimi looked all around the courtyard, then she shifted her gaze to The Jeanne, and up to the top floor. "Would any of us be here right now if an eighty-four-year-old woman hadn't died up there because greed shut off the elevators? Let's be honest: That's why we're all here, the city attorney included." And since there was no adequate response to that, no one said anything. Until the energy shift that had elements of the crowd reacting in totally different ways.

A group of seven—women, men and children—entered the courtyard, and a cheer went up as a dozen people rushed toward them, outstretched arms in both groups. "They used to live here," said Melinda. "They were some of the first to leave when things started to get really bad, especially the ones who lived on the high floors and had children."

"Back up, motherfucker!" came the loud command from another quarter, and the focus shifted to two of the grounds crew who were trying to separate the two lawyers, but the angry corporate lawyer wasn't having it, and he was much stronger than he looked. Or maybe he was just more pissed off than City Attorney Ryerson, because the two grounds crew guys were having a tough time separating them. Finally, two more workers joined the fracas, and the four of them—two on each lawyer—moved the suits away from each other.

Joe rushed toward the lawyers, and Mimi rushed toward the two groups of Lady Buildings residents, former and current. Time to go to work. But before she could introduce herself there was Florence Gregory, making the introductions and crediting Mimi with the day's activities. Mimi stopped her with a raised hand. "Two stories in a newspaper don't lead to all of this, but a couple hundred letters and calls to the editor and City Hall do.

And so does citizen participation in the process—people like you, Ms. Gregory, and Melinda Franklin. People who don't rest or keep quiet until people like the city attorney show up to listen and to see."

"Your modesty is impressive, Ms. Patterson," Florence said, her tone dry as the Kalahari, "but I know why Mr. Ryerson is here even if you don't."

Okay. She wasn't going to win a war of words with Florence Gregory. No point in trying. So she addressed the crowd: "You think what's happening here today represents permanent change? Or enough change that you want to return?"

They all tried to talk at once. Finally, a big guy with a big voice who was waving a piece of paper won. "This is my original lease," he boomed. "And this is the returned certified and registered letter I sent telling them that I intended to break my lease. I broke my lease, informed management, and nobody responded— the letter came back to me unopened—so my lease isn't broken. I can move back in today, and I plan to do just that."

"Me, too," several voices called out.

Mimi raised her hands for quiet. "Are you saying that there is no landlord of record here? That there's no legal landlord?"

"Yes! That's what we're saying!"

Mimi conducted half a dozen interviews. She visited each of the six buildings to see if the elevators were operational and if the heat was on. She and Joe both took photos of the workers and the city attorney. She had enough information for a story, but she couldn't write one without a conversation with the newspaper's lawyer: If the residents had leases and the buildings had no registered owner, were they legal tenants, or squatters? It was a fascinating question and there was no easy or clear answer. Joe already had Ryerson on record as saying he could find no recorded transfer of the deed to the property. She shivered. The wind was picking up and she was hungry. She looked around for Melinda. She wouldn't mind a return visit to the Mexican place. This time she'd eat. Then she checked the time. Shit. She called Carolyn, told her about the story, asked to have one of the

134

lawyers available when she returned, and looked around for Joe. She saw Florence Gregory rapidly closing the space between them. *She's seventy-how many?* Mimi wondered, and added a visit to the gym to her end of the day schedule.

"What's next, Ms. Patterson?" Florence asked.

"I return to the paper to write my story, Ms. Gregory."

"And what story will you write?"

All right, enough! "Ms. Gregory—"

"Patterson!" Her name, loudly yelled. She looked around to find the source. Joe was standing with City Attorney Ryerson, waving his arm at her, Ryerson looking down his nose at Joe who was at least a couple of inches taller. Bespoke attorney nowhere to be seen. This was going to be very good or very bad. Florence had followed her gaze and frowned her continued annoyance at Joe, but Mimi didn't much care. She excused herself and walked away from Florence Gregory, angering the woman, but her vocal objection was literally lost on the wind.

As Mimi got closer, she could see Joe writing rapidly in his notebook, holding his phone in the same hand to record Ryerson's exact words as he talked. Mimi took out her own phone and activated the voice recorder in case whatever Ryerson was saying could affect her story, too, and she guessed it would since Joe had summoned her.

"So, I think they most certainly have the *de facto* right to return to their homes if not the *de jure* right," Ryerson said before he nodded at Mimi and strolled away.

"He's talking about the people who left and came back today?" Joe nodded. "You got interviews, right?"

"A bunch of 'em," Mimi said. "We're more than covered on that front. I even shot photos of the original leases with the names of the original landlords."

"Good," Joe said, nodding as the crease in his forehead deepened.

"What's up with you? Where's Sir Bespoke?"

"That's what's up with me. He is royally pissed off about Ryerson's legal take on permitting the return of those who left, and

135

he's gone to have somebody send private security guards here to prevent that from happening."

"Oh fuck a duck!" Mimi exclaimed, poaching one of Gianna's favorite curses.

"Any chance you can call the captain, get some of her people over here? The way they handled the takedown at Women and Children First was masterful."

"I'll let her know what's happening here and maybe her people get sent, maybe not." She texted 911 to Gianna and prepared to wait.

Gianna, still meeting with Commander Davis, looked down at the phone when it vibrated, then back at Davis. "May I, sir?"

"Of course."

Gianna's quick callback surprised both Mimi and Joe. She answered and began talking immediately.

"Slow down and start from the beginning. I'm with Commander Davis and I'm putting you on speaker," Gianna said.

Mimi and Joe took turns explaining the events of the day, occasionally taking a breath in case there was a question. There wasn't—not from cops as experienced as these two. There was no response until the end. "That asshole really said he's sending a private security force into that complex to prevent people from moving back in?" Mimi didn't know Davis well and Joe didn't know him at all, but both winced at the tone of his voice.

"That's what he told City Attorney Ryerson and that's what Ryerson told me," Joe said.

"Thank you both for the call and the information," Davis said, and the call was disconnected.

"Does that mean they're sending somebody?" Joe asked.

"I'm thinking yes," Mimi said, "and I think we should alert Carolyn and Tyler in case this thing goes sideways. I'm also thinking this, Z: Why the all-of-a-sudden interest, concern, and action from Ryerson? This situation isn't new. What's your gut saying, Joe?"

"That Ryerson is taking aim at some higher-ups."

"Like the mayor," Mimi said, and it wasn't a question.

"Who do you want to send over there?" Davis asked Gianna.
"Alice and Team A."

Davis nodded. They'd already decided to send Andy and Team B to monitor Mike and Tommi Bell's move. Davis had approved a month in a corporate apartment, giving them time to find a permanent place to live, to their relief. With Mike on the speaker, they'd agreed to immediately move all the clothes, toiletries, important papers and photographs, and anything they couldn't live without. The Bells had an attached, closed garage and they could load their cars without being seen. Andy and Team B would observe from a block away in case Gus or one of the women got curious and approached the Bell residence. The formal move would take place once there was a home to move everything to, which made Tommi happy because she'd been bemoaning the fact that nothing would be wrapped and packed and organized, organization being her strong suit. For his part, Mike was so glad to be getting out that he was prepared to call one of the social service groups and have them take everything and start new in their new home.

Even if the Bell family didn't make use of a rental truck that cold, windy night, three other families did. The Smiths, the Richardsons, and the Allens had almost completed their families' move back into their former homes in The Lady Buildings with help from friends and neighbors. More than one of the returnees remarked, either in sadness or in anger, how different the return was with the help of working elevators from the escape carrying their belongings—and their children—down the stairs. A ripple of unease moved through the crowd when Team A from the Special Mobile and Tactical Unit arrived, but the calm authority of Sgt. Alice Long calmed their fears when she assured them the police were there for their protection.

"Protection from who?" several people asked.

The answer was the arrival of armed security guards from a private company, who blanched and backed up at the presence of the real cops. So did Sir Bespoke when he arrived. He sputtered and whined and complained and postured. Nobody paid even minor attention to him. He tried to order his hired guards to stop people from moving their belongings into the buildings, but Alice locked eyes with their commander and put her hand on her Glock as Team A lined up behind her in military "at rest" posture. The security guards didn't want any part of this, and they backed up and away, ignoring Sir Bespoke's call for their return.

"Feel free to call City Attorney Ryerson if you like," Alice said politely.

"Who the hell are you?" Bespoke demanded. Nastily.

"Sgt. Alice Long, Special Mobile and Tactical Unit of the Intelligence Division of the Metropolitan Police Department," Alice replied, no trace of polite remaining.

Bespoke was about to say more when he saw Mimi and Joe, notepads and phones at the ready. He turned and left without another word. Mimi and Joe took lots of pictures. Alice watched as Annie deployed her team at strategic locations after she made certain that the security guards were gone. She sent two of them to follow Bespoke who had disappeared into one of the buildings.

"That young woman is all right," she heard behind her. Mimi had watched Annie as closely as Alice had.

"A whole lot better than just all right. She's a star, Patterson. Your captain had better watch her back because that kid is gonna be chief someday."

"From your lips to God's ears," Mimi said with feeling. The last thing she wanted was for Gianna to become the chief of police, and Gianna didn't want the job. She hoped and prayed.

"You don't want her to be chief?"

"I want her to do whatever makes her happy."

Alice gave her a raised eyebrow look. "And what about what makes you happy, Ms. Patterson?"

"She makes me happy, Sergeant."

Now Alice gave her a look that Mimi couldn't decipher. Her face had gone from playful to serious with a hint of sad. She looked around, then stepped closer to Mimi. "Can you put me in touch with Dr. Connors?" Without a word Mimi pulled up Bev's number in her phone and passed it to Alice. "Can I tell her you referred me?"

"You can, but you won't need to," Mimi said. "She knows who you are and that you saved our asses that day at the therapy center."

Alice started to say something, but Annie calling her name loudly and urgently grabbed all of her attention. She returned Mimi's phone and followed the sound. Annie was standing in the doorway of The Alexis. She whispered something to Alice who nodded and started to follow her inside. Loud shouts from the building lobby galvanized the cops, and they broke into a run. Mimi followed on their heels.

The hostile energy in the lobby was an electrical charge. A mad-as-hell Bespoke was going toe to toe with a group of about a dozen also mad-as-hell residents. He yelled at them and they yelled back. Mimi activated the video recorder on her phone, not at all certain there was any point to it: She couldn't understand what anyone was saying. Then the big man with the big voice, the one who had prevailed outside earlier, did so again.

"We don't want you or your office in our building!" he shouted

Bespoke flushed scarlet and yelled back—screamed, really: "This is my building, do you understand? My building! And I can do what I want, and what I want is to put my office in here."

The last words were heard clearly because his opponents had gone quiet at the words, "my building."

"Did you just say that you own this building, sir?" Mimi called out.

Bespoke sought the questioner, and he blanched when he saw who it was, but he did not speak.

"If you claim to own this building, does that mean you claim ownership of the other five in the complex?" Mimi queried, but

Bespoke's lips were firmly zipped shut. She pushed forward to get closer to him, still recording. He saw her coming and began to backpedal. Then he turned and ran toward the rear exit of the building. The residents' derisive catcalls followed him, but Mimi didn't. She shut off the video and called Joe as she headed back outside where it now was fully dark. She briefed him and told him she'd be back in the office soon—with food and coffee.

CHAPTER SEVEN

Gianna's glum face matched that of her lieutenant. Despite a 24-7 surveillance over the last week of the house where Gustavo and the two women lived, they had developed no new information—and they'd been so certain that they would. After all, Gustavo and his crew were in the business of selling girls for sex, and he'd murdered three of them. Two girls remained, but they stayed in the house all day with the *abuela* and the *tia*, while Gustavo spent his days and nights in a raggedy-ass bar on a raggedy-ass part of the waterfront so dangerous that cops avoided it unless there were dead bodies in the street. And there often were.

Andy's phone signaled an incoming text message. He read it and passed the phone to Gianna. She read it, and worry replaced her frustration at a stalled case. She reread Alice's text, then grabbed up her own phone, scrolled a list, and punched a button. "I need you to get dirty, Bobby, and go meet Alice who's undercover somewhere with Watkins. Andy will send you the address."

"What's got you spooked, boss?" Andy asked as he sent a text to Bobby Gilliam.

"I'm spooked because Tony Watkins is spooked. He's the best undercover cop I've ever seen, and if he's worried enough about something to send for Alice, who's the second best—"

Now Andy was spooked. "He wouldn't put her in harm's way, would he?"

"Not intentionally, but if he's not trusting his own people, I want somebody to have Alice's back. Tony's too, if necessary."

"Suppose Bobby needs somebody at his back?"

"He'll ask if he does. And if he does, Andy—"

"You don't even have to say it."

Gianna didn't say it, and they returned to a discussion of what Gustavo was up to, in addition to getting drunk every night as they watched the surveillance video of him and his house. The previous day's video was the most interesting. A woman showed up at the house at three thirty a.m. and she attacked the woman who opened the door—they couldn't tell whether it was the *abuelita* or the *tia*—with what looked like a two-by-four, and the woman went down. Then she attacked Gus with the same quasi-lethal piece of wood when he appeared, and he went down. The woman was waving the two-by-four around and screaming—no audio on the videotape—until a girl appeared, fully made up and scantily dressed. The woman slapped her twice, then hugged her and dragged her from the house, after first bashing Gustavo with the two-by-four again. Which left one girl in the house. And no more girls had appeared. Could it be that the man was shuttering his operation? They didn't think so. Predators didn't turn over new leaves. Especially predators with no other source of income who liked drinking the night away . . . every night.

"He's gotta be bringing new girls in from somewhere," Andy said, and Gianna agreed, but they had no way to find out how or from where, nor could they hope to find the woman who'd avenged her daughter with a two-by-four. She'd dragged the girl up the block to where a beat-up old hatchback was parked. Another woman helped the mother push and pull the girl into the car and it took off, moving faster than it looked like it could. But it was dark, there were no streetlights, and the car didn't have lights—or the driver didn't put them on—so the image the drone captured was useless; with the possible exception of the license plate, which was from Mexico, but they couldn't tell from what state. So, in truth, they had nothing.

"Not totally nothing, boss." She gave Andy a look that two months ago would have frosted his liver. He hurried to explain: Given the hits Gustavo and the woman had taken from the angry mom swinging the two-by-four, medical attention would be required. Ice packs and Band-Aids wouldn't do. So follow them to the doctor, and whoever that was would be another link in the chain, and maybe even someone who didn't want to lose a medical license. Or be charged with practicing medicine without a license.

"You're all right, Andy Page. I think I'll keep you." Gianna clapped him on the shoulder. Andy grinned and his liver relaxed.

The drunk was singing "roll me over in the clover" loudly and off-key. Sgt. Alice Long and Det. Tony Watkins stopped their whispering and looked wide-eyed at each other though they couldn't see each other. Couldn't see anything in the predawn blackness behind the grocery store where they huddled together. Especially how much they resembled bundles of rags nestled beside the line of disused shopping carts. Tony had said this spot was safe, that it wasn't frequented by the homeless, which is why it was a good meeting place for undercover cops.

"Roll me over in the clover, roll me over and do it again," the drunk warbled.

"You can't carry a tune for shit, Bobby Gilliam," Tony whispered.

"What are you doing here, Bobby?" Alice hissed.

"Boss sent me," Det. Bobby Gilliam replied *sotto voce*, kneeling in front of them. "Good to see you, Tony. What's up?"

The story Tony Watkins told was almost unbelievable, and had the story come from any other cop Alice and Bobby might have been skeptical. But they knew this man, trusted him. They also believed him, especially when, after relaying the info he had for them, he said: "Get me outta that unit! Please. I can't work for that guy any longer. Can you get me a face-to-face with Eric Ashby?"

"We're gonna get you a face-to-face with Capt. Maglione, like in the next hour, my friend," Alice said, getting to her feet. "Do you have to go back to your squad to get clean?" she asked Tony.

He shook his head. "Clothes are in my car, but I need to go home to shower."

"You can shower at our house," Alice said. "Let's move."

"You do sergeant real good, Legs," Tony said.

"You oughta see her in action," Bobby said.

"Yeah, yeah, yeah. Beer's on me tonight." Alice let them hear the smile in her voice, but she kept to herself the pride she felt that these tough as nails cops, two of the best cops she knew, had reverence and respect for her.

An hour later Tony Watkins told his story to Capt. Maglione and Lt. Page. They listened without interruption, and if asked Tony would have said they seemed more angry than shocked or surprised. Then they took him through it again, this time asking questions and seeking his opinion.

"I have no proof of anything, Captain—"

"I know, Tony, but you're a good cop with good instincts and I want to know what you think," Gianna said. Then she added, "But the fact that you're here tells me what you think. Doesn't it?"

"Yes, ma'am. I guess it does," Tony replied.

"Tell me about the fake cops, every detail," Andy said.

"Their uniforms were real, but those guys were bogus as fuck." Tony got pissed off just remembering it. "Middle of the morning, middle of a public area, they charge me, weapons drawn. I open my jacket to show my badge and gun and call out that I'm on the job. 'Not in this sector, Bub,' the fat one said. I said I was after info on the missing girls, and the one with all the hair said that was none of my business and anyway the girls were okay because their preacher knew where they were—"

"Exact words, Tony, please. About the preacher."

Tony closed his eyes. "'Nothing to worry about, Bub. Their preacher knows where the girls are, and he told their parents. So there's nothing to investigate.' One of 'em got more hair than a mop; the other one's fifty pounds overweight—no way they're

144

cops. And we don't call our divisions sectors." He opened his eyes and looked from Alice to Bobby to Gianna, to find that they all were looking at him. Then Alice and Bobby shifted their gaze to their captain, and Tony followed suit.

They watched her, looking for some clue, but aside from a slight narrowing of her eyes as she thought, there was nothing. Then, finally a question, but definitely not what they were expecting: "What's the song you were singing, Bobby? Let's have a few bars."

Bobby stood, cleared his throat in dramatic fashion, belted out two verses, and took a bow. Gianna laughed until tears came to her eyes. She got herself under control and asked how he came to know the song.

"It's a World War II ditty. I heard my dad sing it, and he heard his dad sing it, and he learned it from the British soldiers. It's about—"

"I think I know what it's about, but thanks for being so willing to provide the intel." Then, as if the levity was what she needed to organize her thoughts, she shifted gears. Two hours later she and Tony Watkins faced Commander Davis across his desk, and if it wouldn't have ruined his reputation with Capt. Maglione, Tony would have run screaming as if being chased by zombies. While women saw a sexy movie icon when looking at Davis, Tony saw a man who could wrestle alligators and win without breaking a sweat.

"If you don't mind, Det. Watkins, I just have a couple of questions."

"Yes, sir," Tony said, as the urge to flee lessened.

"You said mothers of missing girls told you they didn't think we—the police—were taking them seriously? Were they Black mothers or white mothers?"

"Both, sir," Tony said. "Seems like we're mistrusted and hated across the board."

"We obviously need to do something to fix that," Davis said, "and we begin right now. Second thing: What made you bring your concerns to Captain Maglione?"

"She's the only high-ranking officer I trust. Sir."

"Good instincts, son. That's why I want you working for me. I'm transferring you to my command effective immediately."

Tony closed his eyes, muttered "not a zombie" under his breath, then thanked both Gianna and Davis. "You all just saved my marriage."

Davis stood up, and Gianna and Tony followed suit, but he waved Gianna back down. He shook Tony's hand and thanked him for his good work. "There are many ways I can and will help you, Watkins, but in the marriage-saving department you're on your own. Now if you'll wait in the hall for a moment, I need a word with the captain before I take you to meet Lt. Ashby."

"Yes, sir. Thank you, sir." Watkins saluted and left.

Davis locked eyes with Gianna, and she heard every word he didn't say. What he did say was, "Those fake cops—I want 'em arrested and charged now. Right now, captain!" Gianna saluted and left. In the hall she shook Tony's hand and thanked him, but before she could say more, Davis grabbed him and off they went.

She didn't waste any time dispatching Andy and Tim to take down the fake cops, and she hesitated only briefly before deciding to join them. Davis would be pissed but she didn't care. Too many missing girls, and if cops had anything to do with it, fake or otherwise—

"Ah . . . sorry, but not a good idea, Cap," Tim said.

Gianna looked at him. "What's not?"

"You going on the fake cop takedown—" Tim raised his hands, palms out, to halt whatever Gianna was about to say, and he starting talking fast, over-talking and outtalking her. "You're way too angry, Cap, and if those creeps say anything stupid or sexist you'll take their heads off."

Gianna inhaled deeply, and on the exhale the fire and anger left her eyes and she managed a small but genuine smile for Tim. "You're right, Tim. Thanks for having my back." She waved a hand of dismissal at them. "Go get 'em. And Andy? If a smack upside the head is necessary, well . . . just don't leave a mark."

Even with their hands cuffed behind their backs, the fake cops had trouble believing that the real ones were arresting them and that no violation of their rights was involved because they had no right to impersonate police officers. They still didn't understand why not, even as they were stripped of the police uniforms and dressed in the DOC coveralls provided by the Central Jail. "Ask your lawyer to explain it to you," Tim snapped, kinda regretting that he'd talked the captain into standing down.

Mimi Patterson and Sarajean Conover eyed each other across the barely furnished living room in the apartment Sarajean called home. The furniture was plastic patio or yard furniture: two Adirondack replica chairs and a bench of the same design. Sitting on them was tough but it couldn't be helped, Sarajean explained, because the cushions were the beds for the children. Colorful sheets hung at the windows, but they didn't need to keep the cold out. Heat flowed from the simple and functional wall grates steadily, as if mocking the just-restored radiator heat in the elegant Lady Buildings.

"How old are your children, Ms. Conover?" Mimi asked.

"Two, three, and four," Sarajean replied. Mimi studied the girl—and she was a girl if a weary and worn-down one—she hadn't yet seen her 20th birthday.

"They must keep you busy."

Sarajean nodded. "They're a handful all right. Especially the boys. Jerry trains them so they don't listen to me. He says boys give orders to girls; they don't take orders from girls. I told him I'm their mother, but he said that don't matter: They don't have to do what I tell 'em to do 'cause that'll just make 'em weak. I tried to tell him that I'm not just some girl, that they have to obey me 'cause I'm their mother. But he said that would just make them pussies and not real men."

Mimi controlled her anger. Barely. "Is Jerry at work now? Are the children at nursery school?" She fervently hoped not to make Jerry Conover's acquaintance this day.

"Nuh uh. He don't work no more. He does jobs for Rev. Jessup. All the men do. And the children is over at Miz Williams'. She takes care of a lot of the children and I help her 'cause I ain't got no money to pay for day care. Ima go over there when I get through talkin' to you and help out with the children."

"You don't work, either?"

Sarajean looked appalled. "Me? Work? Oh no! That's what's wrong with this country today: women workin' outside the home 'stead of takin' care of it. That's the man's job, to take care of home and family." She made the pronouncement proudly, with a happy smile.

"But Jerry doesn't work. He's not taking care of his family. Who's paying the bills? Who's buying the food?"

Though she appeared a little confused, Sarajean opened her mouth to respond as a knock sounded at the door. Mimi wanted to tell her to ignore it, to answer the questions because she wanted to hear the answers, but Sarajean was headed to the door. "That'll be Becca and Brandi," she said, and Mimi was for the moment mollified. Sarajean had made good on her promise to invite friends to talk with Mimi. Perhaps with three of them weighing in . . .

The new arrivals were obviously related. Sarajean told Mimi they were cousins, but they looked like sisters. Twins, almost. Both were dark-haired and dark-eyed, quite tall, and if Becca hadn't been pregnant enough for both of them, they'd have both been thin to the point of skinny. Like Sarajean, Becca and Brandi didn't get enough to eat. These might be married women with children, but they were little more than children themselves, still growing into bodies that needed feeding on a regular basis.

"I appreciate being able to meet you and talk to you—"

"You're going to pay us, right?" Becca interrupted Mimi to ask, making it sound like a demand.

"Wrong," Mimi snapped back. Becca shrank back, looking confused. "Reporters don't pay for information."

"My husband said you did," Brandi weighed in.

"Just one more thing your husband is wrong about," Mimi said, standing and gathering her belongings.

"Wait. Where you going?" Sarajean asked.

"You all expect to be paid. I don't pay for interviews. So staying here is a waste of my time and yours," Mimi said.

The three young women looked at her as if she'd addressed them in Urdu or some other equally foreign tongue. "Well, we don't have nothing else to do," Becca said.

"But I do," Mimi replied. "You young ladies have a good afternoon."

"What is it you want to know from us?" Sarajean asked.

"How and why all of you ended up here, literally in the middle of Washington, DC, the only white people in a Black and Latino neighborhood."

And what she heard left her speechless, which was a good thing because the three young women talked for a long while about what they believed and why and how those beliefs had brought them to Washington: Rev. Jessup led the MAGA Church and he taught that white people now had a chance to take back what belonged to them from the people who had been getting a free ride for hundreds of years. They now had a voice in a place that mattered: in Washington, DC. Where they could live rent-free just like Colored people had been doing forever 'cause they're lazy. Where they could get free food just like Colored people had been doing forever 'cause they don't work. They could stay home all day and get free money just like Colored people had been doing forever. It was their turn now—white people— and Rev. Jessup would show them how because the time was right. Because now they had a voice in the highest place of all.

"God?" Mimi asked. "In heaven?"

Better! Not up in heaven but right here on Earth. In Washington, DC. In the White House. The White People's House.

"Do you like living in the same apartment complex with people you hate?"

Horrified expressions from the three girls. They didn't hate anybody, the girls exclaimed.

"These are people you just called lazy freeloaders—"

"But not the ones where we live," Sarajean exclaimed.

"They're real nice to us," Becca said.

"And they all go to work every day," Brandi added.

"So you all are the only ones who don't work," Mimi said.

"We think the ones who live here must be different from all the other ones," Sarajean said.

Of course they are, Mimi thought. "Is your rent free? Is your food free?" she asked, knowing the answer.

Becca and Brianna offered puzzled frowns and head shakes. "The lady in the office said everybody got to pay some rent. But we do get food stamps."

But if the men don't work, where does the rent money come from? Mimi wondered. Receiving only blank stares, she changed the subject: "Are you all from the same hometown?"

The three of them exchanged a glance, deciding who was to be the spokeswoman. Brandi. "Little places called townships. They're not really towns or cities, and that's why they share a school and we all went to the same one. That's how we know each other."

"Did Jennifer attend the same school?"

Violent shakes of three heads—two dark, one blond. "We ain't allowed to talk about her. She got us in so much trouble!"

"Got you in trouble how?" Mimi asked. "She's dead."

Heads still shaking. "She broke all the rules."

"She did everything we're not supposed to do."

"And nobody knows where she got that gun."

"Or who taught her to shoot it."

"But we all got beat because of her."

"What do you mean, you got beat?" Mimi was loath to interrupt the damning and damaging flow of words but she needed clarification on the matter of the beatings.

"Rev. Jessup ordered the beatings, and he told our husbands they better make sure it hurt. He said he wanted to see black and blue marks on Sunday."

What the hell kind of alternate universe was this? Mimi didn't care. Alternate or parallel universe was a make-believe construct. These women were living real lives in a place where a preacher could order their husbands to beat them black-and-blue and the

150

husbands complied. A world where someone named Rev. Jessup could order people to move away from their homes, to take up residence in a strange city in a community of Black and brown people the good reverend described as lazy, useless, and anti-American. A place where a man called reverend discouraged men from working at real jobs for real salaries and instead paid them for performing unspecified tasks at unspecified times. The more these young women revealed of their lives, the more concerned Mimi became.

Did any of them have cell phones? No.

Did the husbands have cell phones? Yes.

Did they television at home? No.

Did they have landline phones? No.

Did they communicate with their families back in Pennsylvania? No.

Didn't they miss their families and their homes? Yes, but communication was not allowed because they were on a new path to righteousness, one where Rev. Jessup paved the road, and people at home might not understand.

What was Rev. Jessup's first name? Unconcerned shrugs all around. They didn't know, had never heard it spoken.

Does Rev. Jessup live here with you?

No, he lives in Virginia.

Where in Virginia?

Falling Waters . . . No, Church something.

Falls Church? Mimi asked.

Yes. That's it. Three heads nodded up and down.

Is that where the church is?

Oh, no. The church is right here.

Right here where?

The apartment complex has a community meeting room. Church is held there.

Every Sunday?

Unless Rev. Jessup is called away.

Is he often called away?

Not a lot, they said. Just when those little girls went missing, and Rev. Jessup spent a lot of time with their mamas and the police helping to look for them.

Mimi thanked the women for their time and offered her card, but there were no takers. They knew that was how Jennifer came to her bad end. No reporter's card would get one of them in the kind of trouble Jennifer found for herself.

She stood outside, grateful for the damp chill after the stifling heat of Sarajean Conover's all but empty apartment. She wondered if Becca and Brandi had furniture. As her body began to find a comfortable body temperature, she realized that her butt, which had become numb, was beginning to hurt. She looked at her watch: More than two hours on the hard plastic seat. Why hadn't she thought to fold her coat and use it as a cushion? Afterthoughts were like hindsight: Perfection always came too late to do any good.

Mimi studied her external surroundings, which she hadn't done on her way in. This was city-owned property, built some ten years ago to provide decent, low-cost housing for large families. The units were all two, three and four bedrooms, and there was a waiting list to get in. How, she wondered, had Sarajean, Becca, Briana and Jennifer all gotten in at apparently the same time; how had they all jumped ahead on the waiting list? How was it possible to hold a church service in a city-owned building, a service that almost certainly did not welcome the majority of the residents of the community? And who was Rev. Jessup? Maybe some kind of alternate reality was happening here after all.

Mimi took one last look around. The buildings and grounds appeared to be clean and well maintained. Not elegant or spotless but well within acceptable bounds. All the utilities, including the elevators, seemed to function. And as she watched, two teams of Housing Department police officers began to make their rounds, keeping a close watch on the younger children playing in the courtyard and on the older ones doing not much more than just hanging out, like kids of a certain age did everywhere in the world. The lights came on. Grown-ups came home from work, to be greeted by their children, who followed them inside. Time for them to do homework while the adults prepared dinner. Mimi walked to a spot in the courtyard where she could see all the front doors and called Carolyn.

"I want to hear the recording when you get back, Mimi."

"Think I'm making it up?"

"Nobody could make this shit up. Not even Margaret Atwood."

"Can you put the interns on Jessup? Not much to go on, I know."

"Not to worry," Carolyn said calmly. Carolyn always said everything calmly. "Where are you off to?"

"Gonna meet Zemekis at The Bluffs."

"Joint byline?"

Mimi laughed and disconnected the call. Joe's story, his byline. She shivered. She was cold now. She was hoping to catch sight of at least one of the white men coming home but apparently, they weren't in a rush to get home as were the lazy, good-for-nothing people who'd worked all day.

Mimi surveyed her surroundings, more than a little dismayed by what she saw. The Bluffs Apartments were three blocks and a world away from the complex everyone now called The Lady Buildings, which had been built to last, had been built to be homes for people. For families. The Bluffs, on the other hand, were barely shelter and had never been much more than a roof. These buildings were uglier and less structurally sound than the city housing she'd left barely an hour ago. Mimi knew nothing about construction, but even she knew that these buildings were poorly constructed from materials barely meeting the minimum codes and standards. And now the complex had been sold to a group of out-of-state developers and was slated to be demolished. Mimi tore her eyes from the ugliness of the buildings and looked at the vista that gave The Bluffs its name. If the view from the Lady Buildings was impressive, the one from here was breathtaking. With the foliage stripped from the trees near and far, the Capitol Dome and the monuments were visible in the distance. New, modern, well-built units here would command high rents. Only one problem: The people who lived here weren't going down without a fight.

The residents' meeting was at seven p.m. because practically everyone who lived here also worked. Those who didn't have outside jobs were, Mimi learned, retirees who provided free or very low-cost child care. The complex didn't have a community room so the meeting took place in the lobby of the front building because it had a kind of terrace at the rear. Opening the door meant the crowd could spill out there. It also meant that fresh air could circulate. Fresh but bitterly cold air.

Mimi and Joe worked the crowd, introducing themselves and identifying those who seemed to be the organizers, though several people made it clear that no one person was in charge, that they all were in this fight together. The meeting was called to order at precisely seven, and after a brief prayer the city council member from the area was introduced—to loud boos, hisses, and catcalls. Mimi and Joe weren't surprised. The man was useless and all but invisible in the community except at election time. Mimi was willing to bet he'd won his last election, since he supported the sale of The Bluffs to the out-of-state developers.

The next person who tried to speak was from the development group and he wanted to discuss relocation assistance, but he was less welcome than the councilman.

"You tell more lies than that dumbass president!" somebody yelled, and when the crowd surged toward him the man scooted away like a desert jackrabbit.

Then, as if borne in on the night air, City Attorney Ryerson appeared, and he got a cheer. "Well, well, well," muttered a surprised Joe Zemekis.

"You didn't know he was going to be here?" Mimi asked.

Joe shook his head, whipped out his phone, and called Carolyn.

Mimi saw the crowd watch Ryerson. Clearly, they expected something from him, perhaps some announcement or action that would save their homes as he'd done at The Lady Buildings. Her phone vibrated in her pocket. A text from Gianna, wanting to know when she'd be home.

154

On my way she replied and returned the phone to her pocket. She was loving how much they both enjoyed coming home at a reasonable time. No more working around the clock, getting home barely able to remain awake long enough to greet each other, to say nothing of sharing dinner and conversation. This was Joe's story and she was happy to leave it to him. She'd already talked with Carolyn, and the editor knew that Mimi had more interviews tomorrow with other imperiled young women. Not that she enjoyed listening to young women so devoid of joy and hope that accepting brutality at the hands of men who professed to love them seemed the only acceptable option. But she'd still rather write about them than another crooked politician or government official. And she was so sure that Ryerson was up to no good. But . . . not her story. Joe may not have known the city attorney for very long, but he knew the type very well.

Florence Gregory all but tackled her before she managed to clear the front door, but Mimi didn't stop walking. If Florence wanted to talk, she'd have to do it while in motion, which Mimi knew would annoy, irritate, and generally piss off the older woman, who continued to cling with both hands to the belief that Mimi Patterson's job was to report what Florence Gregory thought she should report.

"Why are you leaving, Ms. Patterson? This meeting has barely begun."

"Because covering this meeting isn't my assignment; it's Joe's," she said, as she continued to walk. And as Florence continued to keep up.

"He's not as good a reporter as you are. You should be covering this story."

Mimi stopped walking and faced Florence Gregory, taking an extra few seconds to get her anger under control. "In the first place that is absolutely not true, and you have absolutely no basis for making such a statement. And I take assignment orders from my editor. Now, if you'll excuse me—"

"Then perhaps I should speak to your editor."

"Carolyn Warshawski," Mimi said, spelling Carolyn's last

name and providing her phone number. "I'm going home. You have a good evening, Ms. Gregory."

The closer Mimi got to where her car was parked the further Florence receded from her consciousness. Her only thought was that she was going home to Gianna. And Gianna's only thought as she unpacked their dinner from the Greek market was that Mimi would be home soon. She loved Greek food. Gianna smiled at the thought. Mimi loved good food, no matter its ethnic origin. And fortunately they lived in a city where every ethnic group was represented—as was their food. Greece was close enough to the Middle East that hummus and pita bread happily and comfortably joined spanakopita and Greek salad, with baklava to sweeten and round out the meal. And they happily discovered that champagne went well with everything.

Finally, after years of worrying about the inherent professional conflicts their jobs brought, they now comfortably shared the details of their workday. They trusted each other, and anything said in the privacy of their home remained private. They'd had so many discussions about how women were treated that they didn't need to have another one. Mimi did, however, need to release some steam about the preacher named Jessup who resided in suburban Falls Church, Virginia, while his congregants lived in a city housing project. Gianna sat up straight, hazel eyes boring into Mimi.

"Falls Church?"

Uh oh. Mimi sat up straighter, too. "That's what Sarajean, Becca, and Brianna said. I haven't had time to verify. Does that mean something to you?"

"It just might," Gianna mused, and told her about Randall Connelly's connection to people who lived in Falls Church, and their connection to the bombing at the gay and lesbian center that had leveled the building. And about the two recently arrested fake cops who, so far, had refused to say who they worked for or where they obtained authentic police uniforms and equipment, though Gianna was betting Randall had a hand in that, too. He would know where cops bought their uniforms and equipment.

156

"Would he know how to help them investigate two missing girls?" Mimi asked, and gasped as Gianna threw her champagne glass into the sink, shattering it and sending glass shards flying. Mimi hurried to stand behind her. She wrapped her arms around a Gianna who was as stiff and immobile as a concrete pylon, and just held her until she relaxed. Then she returned to her seat in the cozy eating nook and waited for Gianna to explain.

"I'm sorry. That was—"

"One weight too heavy?" Mimi asked with a smile.

Gianna nodded her head up and down, then shook it from side to side, then got a fresh glass and brought the bottle of champagne to the table. "These two girls bring to ten the number who've recently gone missing. We found three murdered but haven't yet been able to arrest the man we believe responsible. We have nothing to tie all the girls together except their youth. And the worst thing . . . cops may somehow be involved."

Mimi was speechless. No wonder Gianna had hurled the glass. More girls endangered so close on her takedown of the traffickers who brought in underage Chinese girls and kept them in a warehouse, available to men all day and all night. Was there a new ring operating? And if cops indeed were complicit—yes, it was too much weight. At least Commander Davis would shoulder some of it. But it still was too much.

"Do you need to break something else? I'd be happy to help."

Gianna gave her a warm smile and leaned across the table to kiss her. "I feel better just thinking about you breaking something."

Yep. She was all right. "So . . . back to Connelly. Randall is a prize asshole, no doubt, but do you think it's a stretch even for him to move from stupid right-wing violence to harming young girls? Would he even be able to manage it?"

"Davis has him on such a short leash it's a wonder he can manage to swallow. But is he capable?" Gianna shrugged. Given what she'd recently learned, she wouldn't put it past him. "Davis is looking for charges to file, though the little shit may not have done anything actionable. But only because he didn't have time."

157

Gianna was pissed about that. The little shit put her life in danger, and those of her team and the public.

"Does he have actionable information on the people in Falls Church?" Mimi asked, but instead of answering that question, Gianna wondered whether Mimi planned to attend the good Reverend Jessup's service on Sunday.

"Wouldn't miss it," Mimi said, and she knew from the look on Gianna's face that several members of the Special Intelligence Mobile Unit wouldn't be missing it, either.

"But you didn't hear that from me," Gianna said, adding another piece of baklava to their plates.

"I only hear words of love from you, O Captain, my Captain."

"You're so full of it, Patterson."

"Whatever do you mean, ma'am?" Mimi said, going for innocent.

"I'll race you to the bedroom," the Captain said, no innocence present.

"Oh dear Lord! Please tell me you haven't been working out with Alice and Bobby again."

"Only every day," the captain muttered as she sprinted toward the bedroom, balancing baklava in one hand and a flute of champagne in the other. The reporter strolled behind, not worried about missing out.

"I want to share something with you," Alice Long said to Delores Phillips. "If that's all right." The lights were low in Delores's elegant apartment. The fireplace burned warmly and brightly.

"Of course it's all right. Anything." Delores's voice didn't register the unease that was threatening to cramp her stomach. Alice looked and sounded so sad. Delores had never seen her like this. She didn't let herself hope that whatever Alice wanted to share, it wouldn't mean the end of their association. They were together several evenings a week and all the weekend days that Alice didn't work, and they'd long since evolved from discussing only nutrition and finances.

"Dr. Connors said it would be helpful if I had someone I could talk with—"

"Who is Dr. Connors?"

"My . . . the therapist that I see . . . I've been learning to talk openly with her, but she said I need other people in my life that I can share with. And, well . . . you're the person in my life I feel I can share with."

Delores was overcome with emotion. This stronger-than-iron woman had just willingly exposed her vulnerability. She moved closer to Alice on the sofa and waited for her to talk. She could see how difficult this was, so she took her hands. "No rush, Allie."

Alice looked at Delores. Allie. She'd never called her that before. Did that sound like love in her voice . . . or was that wishful thinking . . . ? She inhaled and started talking. She told Delores everything about finding the three little girls buried in the shallow grave in Rock Creek Park. She told her how she'd touched the child's still warm face. She told her how she'd interviewed the girl's best friend who happened to be the daughter of a friend and colleague (the only other person who called her Allie). She told her how she couldn't get the image of the grave out of her mind and how it kept her awake and how it began to intrude on her awake mind. Which is when the captain had told her to talk to someone. Which is when she got Dr. Connors's number from Mimi Patterson. "Both of those women talk to therapists. Women I respect and admire. So, if they can, I can, and that's where I was at seven o'clock this morning."

"I respect and admire you, Alice Long," Delores said, squeezing her hands in her own. "And it honors me that you trust me enough to share this with me. And I'm so sorry that you had to witness something so ugly, but I'm so glad you're the one who helped Sandy. That little girl is alive and loved and she knows it. That has meaning." Then she took Alice Long in her arms and held her while she wept.

They sat for a long while on the sofa after Delores had dried Alice's tears and made them both large mugs of chai tea and put more logs on the fire. They watched it burn, watched the flames dance and gyrate. They sat close and took comfort in each other. Alice recalled in great detail that it was Delores who blew the whistle on the international sex trafficking ring operating in sight of Capitol Hill, in a warehouse that just happened to be adjacent to a warehouse that she used for storage. Delores had witnessed young Asian girls being taken inside and men coming and going twenty-four hours a day. She gave the keys of her building to the chief of police and told him to do whatever it took to rescue the girls and prosecute the men who ran the operation. Her family's restaurant fed the cops who worked around the clock to make that happen; and she had refused to accept payment. But from that day to this, when it seemed the same thing was happening again, what Delores did not understand was men profiting from the abuse of children.

"Entitlement is one of those concepts that's been taken way too far."

Delores was aghast. "They think they're entitled to rape and kill in order to make a few bucks?"

"To kill, to hate, to judge, to steal people's babies at the border." Alice was disgusted. "Entitled to do whatever they want. And it's hundreds of millions of dollars."

"How do you do it every day? How can you stand to do it every day?"

Alice shrugged and managed a small smile. "Somebody has to. And I'm in good company: From Dr. Connors to the captain. They see and hear worse than I do."

"Makes for some rough days, Sgt. Long," Delores said.

"I can handle it if I have you at the end of those days."

Delores squeezed the hand she still held. "I'll be right here."

"Okay: One more thing and I swear that's all. I love you, Delores. I didn't plan on it, but I do, and I hope that's all right."

Delores Phillips laughed her beautiful laugh and then she showed Alice Long how much love it contained.

✳ ✳ ✳

160

Andy was in a lousy mood Sunday morning when he took a seat toward the middle of the rows of folding chairs for the Rev. Jessup's service. The fake cops had made bail and disappeared. The addresses they gave were as fake as their claim to be cops, which wasn't crime enough to hold them without bail. Andy didn't want to contemplate the time and resources they'd expend tracking them down. Best to focus on the right now.

He saw that Mimi Patterson was in the front row and that she was, as far as he could tell, the only Black person there. Three of his people were present and taking photos and videos of everyone, especially of Jessup, who'd been clocked from the moment he arrived. At the moment, he was staring daggers at Mimi Patterson as if his evil-eyed glare would make her jump up and run for the nearest exit. She sat as still as a bronze statue, arms and legs crossed, gazing back at him as if waiting for him to begin the service. She was one cool woman.

"You can't be here," Jessup thundered, pointing at her.

"Of course I can," she replied calmly. "This is the property of the District of Columbia and it is open to the public."

"This is a private church service," Jessup pronounced, "and only members of the church are allowed."

"Do you pay to rent this space?" Mimi asked.

"I don't have to rent it. I live here!"

"No, you don't," Mimi replied, holding Jessup's furious stare, letting him know that she knew what she was talking about.

"Get out!" Jessup thundered.

"I don't think so," Mimi responded calmly.

As Jessup jumped down off the platform that held him above his flock and started toward Mimi, two Special Intelligence cops took seats in the front row flanking Mimi, while two others made it clear that they were photographing Jessup's every move. He stopped threateningly close to Mimi, who hadn't moved an inch and who continued to lock her calm but cold stare with the preacher's hot, angry one. Then a man rushed toward Jessup and whispered in his ear and pointed.

"Ah shit," Andy Page muttered. "I'm made," he whispered as Fat Fake Cop, named Elvis Lane, pointed his way and ID'd him to Jessup as a cop. No wonder they couldn't find him. The preacher glared at Mimi, glared at Andy, and then strode back to his platform, crossed it, and all but ran to the back door where he was photographed every step of the way to his Lincoln SUV. He climbed into the back, Shaggy Haired Fake Cop flung himself into the driver's seat, and the big vehicle burned rubber getting out of the parking lot. The cameras rolled until there was nothing to see. But if Shaggy thought he was getting away he was mistaken. Half a mile away the big Lincoln slowed down, its occupants feeling safely away from the morning's unpleasant threat. They were suddenly swarmed by half a dozen cop cars and a dozen vest-wearing, automatic weapon-bearing, order-shouting cops.

"Turn off the vehicle and hands where we can see 'em. Now!"

And within seconds both men were on the cold ground, handcuffed, and relieved of all personal possessions, including two cell phones each.

Back inside the church service, Mimi finally stirred. She turned to look for the intern she was told would be assigned when she heard a loud argument.

"That's that damn reporter. You brought her here!"

"I didn't. I swear I didn't," Sarajean Conover screeched, the fear palpable in her quivering voice.

"You lyin' bitch!" And the sound of flesh hitting flesh. Hard.

"I'm not. I swear I didn't know she was coming!"

Sarajean's husband hit her again, knocked her to the floor and kicked her, and in an instant he was on the floor himself, surrounded by cops. He was handcuffed and started screaming about his rights and about police brutality and how white people couldn't get justice and how he had a right and a duty to punish his wife.

Andy Page pulled him to his feet while the team patted him down and relieved him of his watch, keys, phone, wallet, cigarettes, lighter—and a second phone, which brought a big change in Andy's mood. "Shut up," he said to Jason Conover, who was still screaming about his rights as a white man in America.

162

"Read him the rights he does have," Andy told one of his cops.

"You have the right to remain silent," the cop said to Jason. He said it until Jason stopped screaming about his rights as a white man in America.

Mimi nodded to Sasha, the intern who'd been dispatched to keep an eye on things this Sunday morning, and left her to talk with anyone who'd talk. She knew that Gianna would have a full report within minutes, if she didn't already, so no need to call. She walked out into the cold and suddenly blustery Sunday morning. She buttoned her coat, put on her hat and gloves, and headed to her car, looking up at the dark clouds racing across the sky as if trying to catch something. A snow sky. Snow was on the way.

CHAPTER EIGHT

Every brain in the room was firing all synapses, including those who had worked all night. Including Gianna, Andy and Alice. Including Team Leaders Bobby, Annie and Tim. But all eyes were on their captain as she walked the front of the room, eyes that moved between her and the images on the screens behind her, images that shifted and changed as she talked to them about what was happening. And a lot was happening.

Thanks to the arrests of Clemson Jessup (who, to nobody's surprise, was no more a minister than he was an open heart surgeon), Elvis Lane, and Shaggy a.k.a. Wilmer Flint—and their six cell phones—a definite link was established between the group who bombed the gay and lesbian community center (almost killing Gianna), those who almost escaped from the enclosure of the White Is Right demonstration, and those who moved to DC from rural Pennsylvania to collect free benefits. And Randall Connelly definitely was behind the fake cop uniforms and equipment. They could not, however, find out anything about the missing girls. Yet. Jessup hadn't said a single word since requesting a lawyer, and the two fake cops really were as stupid as they looked. But the burning question was whether Connelly had any knowledge of the missing girls, and he wasn't talking either. He and Jessup shared a lawyer.

"If he has, I'll bury him so deep he'll be an old man before he sees the light of day," an angry Commander Davis had said earlier that morning during Gianna's regular briefing.

164

"And I want to know how he and that other one you busted down, Maglione—what was his name?—I want to know how they got their jobs in this department." This from Deputy Chief Ellen De Longpre who, as Mimi accurately predicted, replaced Schmidt as head of Intelligence. Today was her first day in the new job.

"Taylor Johnstone," Gianna replied, only slightly unnerved by the new Deputy Chief's unexpected presence at her early morning meeting with Davis.

There was movement, too, on the murders of the three young girls who were buried in Rock Creek Park. It seemed that the 24-7 surveillance had finally paid off. Two nights ago, a panel van pulled into the vacant lot behind Gustavo's house and backed all the way up to the back door. Close. Almost touching. So close that the technicians were still trying to figure out who got out and entered the house, but they were certain that people did. Several people, small people, people who could be young girls. The dark-colored van had no tags, but one of the drones tracked it to a fenced lot in one of the Maryland suburbs where it remained, and where the drone kept watch on it and on everything and everyone moving into and out of that gated compound. However, as welcome as this new information was, it raised more questions that needed answers, and they didn't have them. "Three steps forward, two steps backward. That's how it feels sometimes," Gianna said to her squad. "We've gotta walk those backward steps forward and we don't have a lot of time. There are maybe a dozen young girls out there counting on us."

"What if we can't—"

Gianna raised her hand, cutting off the question before it got asked. "We don't have that luxury. Does everyone understand that? We don't have the luxury to entertain that thought."

She felt the energy shift in the room before she saw the why: Deputy Chief Ellen De Longpre stood in the doorway. How long had she been there? Gianna hid her surprise and went to greet her new boss, whose long stride quickly narrowed the distance between them, and who still looked better in a uniform

165

than anyone she knew. Except perhaps herself, to hear Mimi Patterson tell it.

"Deputy Chief. I didn't know you were coming." Gianna's smile was owing to thoughts of Mimi and she saw that De Longpre misinterpreted, but that was all right.

"We didn't really get a chance to talk at this morning's meeting, Gianna, and it's been such a long time since we did talk. I hope it's all right that I've come unannounced."

"Of course it is. Come, let me introduce you." De Longpre followed her to the front of the room where they had every-one's total attention. "Everybody, please welcome Deputy Chief Ellen De Longpre who, as of this morning, is the new head of Intelligence."

"'Afternoon, Chief," they said in unison.

"I've known and admired your Captain for a long time. She's one of the very best in this department, and you're very lucky to be able to call her boss."

Hearty clapping and foot stomping greeted this statement, but only Alice saw—and interpreted—the look the deputy chief gave the captain. *Oh, shit,* she thought to herself as she watched the two women walk toward the office. But she was sure that the look was one-sided, that whatever long-time-ago feelings the chief may have had, the boss didn't share them in this day and time. She'd seen how her boss looked at Mimi Patterson. And she just saw how she looked at Ellen De Longpre: the same way she looked at Commander Davis. With respect. And that was all. She hoped.

"It's good to see you, Gianna," Ellen said when they were seated in the office. "And I'm so very proud of you."

"And I of you, Chief. You earned it. You've paid a lot of dues."

"I've mostly been in the right place at the right time."

"I admire the modesty," Gianna said with a smile, "but I've heard nothing but good things about you, Chief. You earned this."

Ellen laughed and withdrew one of her many fountain pens from a pocket, beginning to roll it between her palms. It was an old habit. "Don't you think you can finally call me Ellen? After all, you're a captain now."

"And you still outrank me," Gianna said with more edge to her voice than she really intended. There had never been anything more than conversation between them, and Ellen had shut that down because as a sergeant she couldn't risk a relationship with a lowly patrol officer. Or, at that time, with any woman.

"I owe you an apology, Gianna—"

"No, you don't. I mean that, Chief. It was more than fifteen years ago, and we both were pretty far in the closet with the doors locked and bolted."

"A place you no longer live," Ellen said quietly.

"Thank the dear Lord."

"And Ms. Patterson is—?"

"A miracle of creation," Gianna said with a hearty laugh.

"You're very fortunate," Ellen said with quiet wistfulness.

"That's what she tells me on a regular basis."

Ellen stood up to leave. "Is it possible . . . do you think we can be friends?"

Gianna saw, heard, and felt the sadness. "Are you all right?"

Suddenly the deputy chief looked the ten years older than Gianna that she was. "My . . . partner . . . died four months ago. Cancer."

"Oh Ellen, I am so very sorry. I didn't know."

"No one knew." The bitter words flew from an angry mouth. "We still lived in that dark closet so no one that we could have cared about knew we were suffering. She was an executive at an insurance company, and they were kind, but they believed that their colleague was a single woman with no family. They didn't know that she was someone's lover. And my work colleagues didn't know that I'd lost the most important part of myself."

"The chief would have understood," Gianna said.

Ellen nodded sadly and agreed that he would have. "It's such a different department today than when we were young and starting out. Not nirvana but a damn sight better than it was."

"I'll say. I've got you and Eddie Davis for my bosses."

Ellen stood up, gave Gianna a pat on the back, and headed for the door. Gianna stood and followed. She was still thinking about Ellen grieving alone, trying to imagine the unimaginable pain.

"What's on your mind, Gianna?"

"Let's get dinner some night soon, Ellen."

The deputy chief's eyes filled with tears that she refused to let fall. "Thank you. I'd like that and I'll look forward to it."

When Mimi knocked on the door of the apartment where three teenaged girls were waiting to meet with her, it opened immediately. However, the woman who let her in was a woman—not a teenager. She introduced herself as Clara Carruthers, the mother of one of the girls and the guardian of the other two. "That's a snow sky," she said, looking past Mimi at the sky. "Been threatening for two days."

Mimi agreed and introduced herself, but before she could state her business Clara spoke again. "I know who you are and what you want and the only reason you got in here is because Dr. Connors said I could trust you."

Mimi hid her surprise but was silently thankful for the confirmation that Bev was closely tuned into the plague of abuse that was killing the spirits and claiming the lives of young girls in the nation's capital. Mimi had received information that Clara's daughters—all of them—had been victims of sexual battery. Apparently, it was true. "I appreciate the vote of confidence. I've known Dr. Connors for a long time."

"That's what she said. So here are the rules: You can ask the girls anything you want—I already know everything they'll tell you—but when you write your story, you can't use their names, say where they live, or mention me, 'cause that'll give them away. If you agree to that I'm going to bed. I just got home from working two shifts and I'm dog tired." She looked it, but no amount of weary could detract from the gravity or force of her words: She meant what she said.

"I agree to your terms, Ms. Carruthers. I don't want to do anything to put your girls at risk."

"Good. Y'all can come on out now," she said in the same conversational tone she'd used standing six or seven feet from Mimi, but the girls entered the furniture-stuffed living room from a closed door. Three of them. Clean and well dressed but all with the same sunken, haunted eyes. All much too thin to be thirteen and fourteen years old. Too thin to be considered healthy—like Sarajean Conover and her friends.

Mimi walked forward to meet the girls, hand extended. They looked at it as if it held danger.

"Shake the lady's hand, y'all," Clara said quietly. "That's what you do when you meet people: You shake their hands."

One by one the girls took Mimi's hand as Clara identified them: Carla, Darla, and Denise. Limp hands until Mimi applied a little pressure, and two of them got the message and tightened their grip. The third did not.

"I'm glad to meet all of you, and I really appreciate your talking to me," Mimi said. "But I need to ask while you're still here, Ms. Carruthers, why the girls aren't in school today, because if you kept them home to talk to me—"

Clara Carruthers' shoulders sagged, and the rest of her body followed. "The school won't let 'em in 'cause they don't have no records—"

"Just me and Darla don't have records 'cause we didn't never go to school, but Carla, she can go," Denise said.

"That ain't why," Darla chimed in loudly, the one who hadn't increased the pressure in her handshake. Nothing limp about her voice as she spoke up. "Tell her, Ma Clara! Tell her why we ain't got no school records."

All three girls turned eyes on their mother. Mimi followed suit, and it was Mimi the woman spoke to though she wrapped her girls in a tight hug, Carla and Darla in one arm, Denise in the other. "Their mama—Darla and Denise's mama—she named them after her favorite drinks. She named these girls Whiskey Sour and Tequila Sunrise."

169

Mimi was speechless. *What the hell did you say to that?*

"That look on your face? That's how I felt when I first heard it. The school at first didn't believe it. Then everybody, the principal, the teacher, the students, they all made fun of the girls, so they stopped going to school. Then their mama—"

"She started selling us—"

"What do you mean, selling you?" Mimi asked, voice barely recovered and working to keep it steady.

"What do you think I mean?" Denise snarled.

Hearing the words, seeing the girls, knowing just a small part of what they had endured—it was too much. Mimi didn't know if she wanted a story this badly.

"I'm hungry, Mama. Do we have any food?" Carla asked.

Clara winced and shook her head. How much did it hurt to tell your children there was no food? "I'm gonna try to borrow some money from Teresa when she gets home. She knows I get paid on Friday and how many double shifts I been working. I think she'll front me a few dollars."

Mimi saw a chance to escape. Briefly. "Let me go get some food, Ms. Carruthers. I don't mind and I'll be right back." She was still putting on her coat when she got outside, hat, scarf and gloves still stuffed in the pockets. She inhaled deep gulps of the cold air, glad that it hurt her lungs. She had never before run away from a story. Maybe she'd been at it for too long. Maybe she should be one of Tyler's digital editors, sitting inside at a desk all day, watching a screen, only imagining the horrors that lurked beneath the surface of the stories, never having to hear the details or see the faces and bodies that remained after the horrors.

She hadn't planned to go to the grocery store, but once inside it felt like the right thing to do, to buy enough food, real food, to last the family for a while. She filled the cart with large bags of rice and dried beans, boxes of cereal, gallons of milk, sacks of potatoes, onions, flour and corn meal and grits, cooking oil, salt and pepper, a four-dozen carton of eggs. Loaves of bread and tubs of butter. She pushed the cart up and down the aisles, seizing items she thought would be useful and needed: toilet paper,

paper towels, napkins, tampons, sanitary pads, dish soap and body soap and laundry detergent. And a huge bottle of multivitamins. It turned out she needed three carts, and when they were filled, she needed help rolling them out to the parking lot and lifting them into the trunk of the car. Back in the parking lot at Clara's building she called and asked if the girls could help her unload the car.

"You're back here? I thought you'd left," Clara said, accusatory bitterness heavy in her voice. "You were gone too long to pick up some chicken or burgers and fries. Can the girls help you with what?" But before Mimi could punch off her phone the girls came barreling out the front door and to her car.

"Are you all strong enough to lift these out?" she asked, opening the trunk. Mimi had backed up to the sidewalk, so the carts were a relatively easy roll to the front door once they were out of the trunk.

Denise understood first. She looked from the food to Mimi and back again. Then she lifted one of the carts out. "Can y'all roll this inside without spilling out everything?" she asked the younger girls, sounding both protective and demanding. Sounding like a mother.

They nodded a wide-eyed assent and two pairs of hands grabbed the handle and pushed the cart forward. Denise and Mimi got out the other two. Mimi shut the trunk and moved the car to a parking space. By the time she got to the front door, the girls and groceries were inside. Clara's expression was astonished disbelief.

"I never had this much food in one time in my whole life. I wish I knew some better words than thank you, Ms. Patterson, but they all I got. Thank you so very much."

"You're very welcome, Ms. Carruthers. I know you want to feed your children, so why don't I come back later—"

"Can I go outside and talk to Ms. Patterson?" Denise asked.

Clara gave her a long, questioning, searching look. Dr. Connors had said she was dealing better than the other two girls with the trauma of their lives. *She doesn't understand why such ugly*

171

things happened to her, and she'll probably never forgive her birth mother, but she truly wants to move forward, which is why she's so ready to put the past behind her. Clara would never forget the therapist's words, and she'd never stop wondering when the full force of what happened to her would hit the girl. She nodded and Denise headed for the front door. Mimi followed.

"Do you want to sit in the car where it's warm?"

"I like the cold. If I'm cold I know I'm not dead."

"Is that the only way you know you're not dead?"

"Not the only way," Denise said, "but the best way. That place where we had to be with the men was always too hot. Even in the summer it felt like the heat was on. And I used to pretend to be dead so I wouldn't have to think about what the men were doing to me, so I didn't feel it. 'Cause if you're dead you can't feel, right?"

Mimi nodded. "I think that's probably right."

"I hate summertime. When I'm grown, I'm moving to a place where it's always cold. Where is a place like that, Ms. Patterson, where I could live and be safe, where wouldn't nobody bother me?"

Mimi considered. No point in telling the girl the polar ice cap was melting, or that perhaps no place was really safe for women. "Maybe some places in Alaska and Canada. And Russia. Maybe in Iceland."

Denise gave a slight smile, liking the thought of never being hot. "I guess I better really study geography when I get back to school."

"Do you want to go back to school?" Mimi asked.

"Oh hell yeah. We're gonna have a normal life with Mama Clara. We already got normal names." She frowned. "Mama Clara said we got to make 'em legal, get a lawyer and go to court and get rid of the stupid ones." Her young face contorted in deep thought. "Maybe that's when we can go to school and learn stuff. Like geography."

"What's your birth mother's name, Denise?"

The girl shrugged. Because she didn't know, or because she

172

didn't want to know? "I don't remember. She was always chang-ing it. But her favorite one was Shalimar, after a perfume. How stupid is that? Calling yourself after a perfume."

Stupid, maybe, Mimi thought, but a damn sight better than Whiskey Sour and Tequila Sunrise. "Do you know where she lives?"

"The cemetery. Deep in the ground where worms and bugs eat her."

"How do you know she's dead?"

"'Cause Mama Clara killed her. And before you ask how I know, I know 'cause I saw it happen. She beat the shit out of her with a baseball bat. Best day of my life."

All of a sudden, the sky was spitting ice pellets. Denise looked up and smiled. Mimi looked up and frowned. "Let's get you inside so you can eat, and I need to say good-bye to your mom so I can go to work."

Clara, a sweater pulled closely around her, was on her way to get them when they appeared at the door. An excited Denise called out that it was snowing, and the younger girls abandoned their food and ran out the door with their big sister. Clara gazed after them proudly. "They're good girls," she said softly.

"Yes, they are—thanks to you. You can be proud of them."

"I am proud of them. And I hope they can . . . heal. Get better. Get happy again. Children should be happy. Even poor Black children."

No woman should sound so sad talking about her children's happiness. "You're making that happen for them, Ms. Carruthers, when you show them they're loved."

"What if love isn't enough?"

"It's been enough for millions of children, everywhere in the world, for hundreds of years."

Clara gave her a steady gaze. "Especially if there is someone to help feed them. Love needs food, too." She opened the door and called the girls in to eat—scrambled eggs and grits and biscuits—and for the first time Mimi saw them as the children they were, chattering excitedly about making snow women and building snow castles. They ran to the table and pounced on the food, not caring that it had chilled. They were hungry and they ate like it. Mimi watched them, and she watched Clara watch them.

"I'm not going to write about you or your children, Ms. Carruthers. I'm going to write about the men. Denise mentioned a place. Where does it happen? And do you know the names of the men involved?"

Turned out Clara Carruthers knew everything, and she told it all to Mimi, and Mimi told it all to Carolyn and Tyler. The only thing she left out was that Clara Carruthers had beaten Shalimar Grigsby to death with a baseball bat behind the Playpen, the former Midtown Inn, a no-tell motel well known to the sex, vice and drugs cops, but which apparently now operated under the radar. "One thing Denise told me that got my attention. She said the man who owns it, or runs it, is a fake, a phony."

"How so?" Tyler asked.

"His name is Patrick O'Shaunnessy, or something like that. And he talks with some kind of accent when people can hear him. But when he thinks nobody is listening, or if it's just the people who work for him, there's no accent." Mimi took a breath. "Denise said he stopped his playacting in front of the girls after a while, like they didn't matter. Which is why I want to write about the men and not the little girls they brutalize and traumatize for life," Mimi said to her editors.

"I agree," Carolyn said, and Tyler nodded his assent. Then he asked her to lay out all the details, everything she knew. She did, and then came his questions:

"So, only Blacks and Latinas, no Asians or Caucasians?"

"As far as I know, but I'll put that question to Clara."

"Did the police investigate Shalimar Grigsby's murder?"

"Don't know. Clara said she'd been dead several days before she was found."

"I want to know everything about this location. And when we get that nailed down, I want to know how the men know the girls are there."

"As I understand it, the girls are always there."

"The Black girls and the Latinas?" Carolyn asked.

"This is an interesting aspect," Mimi said. "I'm chasing down a lead that three of the Latinas just disappeared, and the source heard the man who ran them had them killed because they had Black friends and talked to the cops. By the way, he was the one who branded his girls—"

"He *what*?!" Carolyn exclaimed.

"With hot metal. Like slaves and animals. With his initial: *G*."

Carolyn made a sound in her throat, got up, and strode from Tyler's office.

"Another thought," Tyler said. "If the girls are all Black and brown, are the men? Or are they all white?" At that, Mimi wanted to follow Carolyn out of the room, but it was more than a legitimate question; it was a pertinent and necessary one. Even if his accent was fake, was Patrick a fake white man?

Tyler and Mimi looked at each other for a long moment. "Are you going to tell Gianna?"

"She already knows most of it. I'm thinking to write the story and let the chips fall where they fall, and that'll be on the heads of the sex crimes and vice cops. And on a very unhappy chief of police."

"You're gonna throw him under the bus like that?"

"No," Mimi said with a head shake. "I'll warn him first."

"And I'm sure he'll really appreciate that," Tyler said. "But I want a police response included in the story. From vice or sex crimes, even if it's a 'no comment.' If the cops don't know that place exists, I want that in the story. If they do know it exists and haven't shut it down, I want that in the story, too."

Tyler's expression changed then, from that of her editor to that of her good friend. And he called her Mimi instead of Patterson. "How's everything, Mimi?"

"Really good, Tyler, thanks. Gianna is stronger every day, and so am I. I've just about stopped blaming myself for almost getting her killed."

"I'd say that's a big step," Tyler said, hoping he didn't sound as relieved as he felt. "Home stretch from here, huh?"

175

"Yeah, but walking, Tyler, not running. Just so Gianna can keep up."

He mocked her and didn't try to hide it. "She'd outrun you with that cast still on her leg."

They enjoyed the moment but knew it couldn't last. Work and duty called. Mimi stood up, but grabbed a last moment of closeness with her friend. "When do I get to meet the new man in your life?"

"I was thinking we should go to dinner, the four of us. Soon."

"Say when and where and we'll be there," Mimi said, her hand on the doorknob.

"Patterson? A story like this leaves skid marks, you know?"

"Yeah, I know," she said, exiting the office and heading to her desk. She was already feeling sideswiped. She knew the direct hits were just around the corner. She wouldn't be cancelling her standing appointment with Bev any time soon.

It was a busy night and the sun had barely set. Maybe the bad guys wanted to get home and warm before the predicted snowfall got started. Whatever the reason, all of Gianna's team members were deployed and all were busy. She checked her watch and texted Mimi, letting her know she wouldn't be home any time soon. *No worries. See you when I see you and love you always.*

"Snow is starting, Captain, and it's coming down in a hurry. At least for now." This from Kenny Chang who monitored the weather feeds when weather was an issue.

"Thanks, Kenny. Let me know if it starts to accumulate."

"Yes, ma'am . . . what the—"

Then Gianna heard what Kenny heard: Some kind of ruckus at the downtown synagogue. Three of her people were undercover there due to a dramatic uptick in hate mail and phone threats because two blocks in all directions were newly designated "Quiet Zones," eliminating skateboarding and illegal go-kart bikes.

176

"Gotcha, you little bastard!" someone exclaimed.

"Who's that, Kenny?" Gianna asked, hurrying over to stand beside him and watch his live feed.

"Lev Asher. He was inside the synagogue when two fools came in the front door with spray paint cans."

She watched as Lev wrestled a paint can away from a person whose face she couldn't see, after which he dragged him to the front door and handcuffed him to it. Then he was down the steps and running. "I'm going after the second one. Enough snow on the ground I can follow his footprints."

"I'm on my way to you, Asher!" Andy barked. "Just a couple minutes out. Your location and direction?"

Andy and Alice were roving and tasked with providing mobile backup, and both were now in play. Bobby and Tim were at the downtown mosque, also recently designated as a Quiet Zone, to the dismay of some local residents, who wanted the Muslim call to prayer that was subject to the new restriction. Wasn't gonna happen, which didn't sit well with a few vocal area residents who had decided to show their dissatisfaction. Alice was en route to provide backup for them.

"Boss? Something else happening in the synagogue," Kenny said.

Gianna went to look. The woman rabbi ran into the sanctuary. Fast. She was being chased. And somebody—one of her people— was chasing whoever was chasing the rabbi, but the perp had a head start, and he had something long and heavy-looking in his hand. He swung it at the rabbi and she went down. Tameka Thompson, weapon out, was giving chase, but she stopped short. She looked after the perp, then down at the rabbi, and made her choice. She knelt beside the rabbi. "Need paramedics here! Head injury. No, ma'am, I'm not leaving you. Quiet, now, help is coming. Right, y'all?"

"Right, Thompson. Less than a minute out."

"And the rabbi says there might be another one somewhere in the building. And LT? Hurry up because if there's another one and he comes for us, the rabbi says I for sure cannot fire my weapon in this sanctuary."

No, Gianna thought, you for sure cannot. Even in states where any damn fool could legally carry a gun any-and-everywhere, ministers of all denominations had spoken out against bringing them into their sanctuaries. And religious men and women of all denominations, no matter what the threat, would not allow a weapon to be fired in that place of reverence.

"Cap? Lev and me, we got three of 'em, and I'm on my way in to find Thompson, and the ambo is here. And if there's one still inside, we'll find him. And Cap? They're kids. The three Lev and me got are thirteen, and the fourth one is fifteen. And they're standing out there in the snow giving the Nazi salute and shouting 'Heil Hitler' and generally looking and acting stupid. Can I smack them upside the head, please?"

"No head smacking. Let's have them unbruised when we take their booking photos, please, Lieutenant." *Because we will be booking and charging the little bastards,* Gianna thought. *Especially the one who cracked the rabbi's skull.*

"Yes, ma'am," Andy said.

Gianna walked to the front of the room and looked up at the screens. All dark and quiet and she'd heard nothing from Bobby and Tim. No news, good news. She hoped.

Mimi was packing up to leave when her desk phone rang. She answered, hoping that it would be Melinda Franklin returning her call and not Florence Gregory, who continued to stalk her. It was Melinda. She sat back down and told her about Clara Carruthers and her girls. Told her everything except the truth about the demise of Shalimar Grigsby. Then she asked for a favor. "I need two kinds of help from you, Melinda, if you can: A pro bono lawyer to get the girls' names changed legally and then to help Clara navigate the foster care and adoption system. She took the girls in because they had no place to go, but there was nothing legal about it."

"Shouldn't be a problem. What else?"

"Some tutoring. Even if they get into school they'll be so far behind—"

"Got it. This is a good thing you're doing, Ms. Patterson."

"Not looking for a pat on the back, Melinda. Just trying to help someone whose help maybe saved two girls from too much of life's ugly too early in their own lives."

"So what's your next move?" Melinda asked.

"Who says I've got a next move?" Mimi retorted.

"You've always got a next move, Ms. Patterson."

Mimi couldn't disagree. "I've got to get the Housing Department to give Clara one of those units for large families. They're in a one-bedroom."

"Good luck with that one," Melinda said in the jaded tone of one who knew how the system worked and didn't work, and she disconnected.

Mimi looked across the desk at Joe, who was also packing up to leave. "Is Don Mathis still feeding at the public trough?" she asked.

"He is, and he figures he has you to thank for that."

"How? If I had my way, he'd be collecting unemployment and food stamps."

"And he knows that," Joe said, "which is why he thanks you that he still has his job. You could have dropped the hammer on him, but you didn't and he's grateful."

"He didn't feel the hammer only because I didn't feel like making the effort."

"He doesn't know that part," Joe said, getting to his feet. "Tomorrow is a new day with new challenges. You coming?"

Mimi groaned. "No philosophizing, please, trying to make it sound noble."

"It is noble, the work we do on behalf of an ungrateful public." He struck a pose as if he held sword and shield.

"I'm going to see if Mathis is still in his office."

"He is," Joe smirked. "He still has his job and he's still the boss, but only if he acts like a boss, and bosses work late hours. What do you want with him?"

"I want him to put Clara Carruthers and her girls in one of the big units for families. I'm guessing there may be a vacancy or two over there."

179

"Yeah there are!" An evil grin spread across his face. "Seems the Housing Department brass didn't know church services were being held on the property, didn't like it, and especially didn't like that certain kinds and colors of people were prevented from entering the residents' community room on Sunday mornings."

"Imagine that!" Mimi exclaimed.

"And when one of the men beat and kicked his wife with cops and reporters looking on—well, that family was evicted immediately."

"What I'd like to know is how all those people got their apartments at the same time, and whether they jumped the line ahead of people who'd been waiting awhile."

No response from Joe, who was checking the weather on his phone. He pulled on his cap and overcoat. "Unless you need to see Mathis in person you should head home and call him. Snow's really coming down."

"Oh shit, I forgot about the snow!" Mimi exclaimed, grabbing her phone to make her own weather check. She pulled on her coat and hat, picked up the phone, and called Donald Mathis, told him she'd be calling him when she got home, hung up the phone, turned off the lamp and the computer, and followed Joe out of the fast emptying newsroom: Everyone who was off the clock was heading out of the building, especially those who lived in the suburbs and who foolishly drove to work instead of taking the train. Mimi and Gianna lived in the heart of the city. Gianna drove a department-issued sedan and Mimi usually took a Lyft or a taxi, but she had driven today because of the meeting with Clara and her daughters. And good thing she had, because of the grocery store run, though that trip was unplanned. No rush to get home, though, since Gianna wouldn't be there. And she couldn't rush even if she wanted to. *Let it snow, let it snow, let it snow,* she hummed to herself. Then reminded herself that while she loved the holiday season and its music, she intensely disliked snow.

✳ ✳ ✳

180

"We need backup. Now!" The urgency in Bobby's voice sent chills up Gianna's spine, and she wasn't alone.

"Where are you?" Andy hissed.

"At a bus stop—" Gunfire interrupted Bobby momentarily; then he yelled, "Go get that son of a bitch, McCreedy! Don't let him get gone."

Gianna didn't hear Tim's response, but she didn't need to. She hurried to stand beside Kenny, and she didn't need to tell him what she wanted. He manipulated the mouse and changed the screen shot. Gianna was looking at a raggedy, run-down, ill-lit mini-mart on a raggedy, run-down street, streetlights mostly absent. No people were visible, and the building looked dark. "Everybody left when the snow got heavy," Kenny said.

"Where's the bus stop?"

Kenny manipulated the mouse and zoomed in on a leaning structure that would have provided absolutely no protection from the elements even if somebody waited there to catch a bus. Gianna looked more closely and realized that there was no bus stop route sign. This no longer was an operable bus stop, which no doubt was why the shelter was all but on the ground. No people here, then.

"Which way did Tim run?" she asked Kenny, and he showed her. Enough snow had accumulated that even in the darkness she could see his footprints. She needed to hear from Bobby—

"We got one of them, boss," Bobby said, breathing heavily.

"How many were there?"

"Two," Tim said.

"Four," Bobby said.

They'd spoken simultaneously. "Guys?" Gianna said.

"Sorry," they said together.

"One at a time, please. Take your time, catch your breath. Andy and Alice will be with you in a moment."

"Two perps and two vics, Cap," Bobby said.

"Captain?" she heard in her comm.

She exhaled gratefully. "Alice?"

"We got bodies. Two of 'em."

181

Short-lived gratitude. And the way Alice sounded—

"One perp down," Andy said in her ear, sounding as tight and tense as Alice had. "And one young girl, approximate age twelve."

"Goddammit!" Gianna threw a chair across the room, then calmed herself with the thought that there would be no arms wrapped tightly around her because she wasn't at home. "Send the address to my phone, please, Kenny," and she left the squad room to go to the scene.

Andy, Alice, and Bobby stood looking down at the two bodies that the gently falling snow was making look almost pretty. But they were not pretty. "This is some fucked-up shit," Andy said in disgust.

"I'm sorry, LT. It just happened so fast—" Bobby began.

Andy punched him on the shoulder. "You damn well better not apologize, Bobby Gilliam. If I could raise this bastard from the dead I would, and then I'd shoot him myself. Whatever he had planned for this little girl, she might be better off dead. And I'm going to help Tim look for the other one before she gets dead, too. You guys stay here and wait for the captain."

And not one of them questioned whether their captain would come. She always went to her people when they needed her, and they needed her this night.

"Fuck a duck!"

Uh oh. "Boss? You all right?" Alice asked with her eyes shut and her fingers crossed.

"I am now, Alice. Thanks. I see the lights strobing. I'll be with you in a minute."

And she was, out of her car and moving toward them as if the ground weren't icy and slippery. "Tell me," she said when she reached them.

"At first we couldn't believe what we were seeing," Bobby said: Two grown men, each with a young girl by the arm, dragging them toward a dark-colored cargo van. The girls were crying and screaming. The men slapped them into silence. "We came on 'em

182

by accident! If we hadn't gone to investigate a drunk and disorderly ..." Bobby ran out of words as the potential fate of the girls took over his thoughts.

"How'd we get two dead bodies?" Gianna asked, and despite her calm tone Bobby knew to start talking faster.

"We pulled over, jumped out of the car, yelled that we were the police and ordered them to release the girls. And that's when they started running, dragging the girls, but one of them fell and the dude dragging her left her and took off. Tim went after him. The other one slipped and fell and lost his grip on the girl and she broke loose and ran. The fucker shot her. And I shot him. And Tim caught the other one, but the little girl got away."

"Where is Tim now? And the other little girl?"

Bobby pointed into the darkness. "The lieutenant went after him when he got here, to help him."

This was a story he'd tell many times before this night was over, but she had enough info to call Davis. She took Bobby's weapon and body camera and stepped away. She looked for Andy and Tim but saw only darkness. And before she could say anything else, Alice was beside her. "Andy went to look for the girl who got away, and he left Tim guarding the other perp." Good info to have, she thought, as Eddie Davis answered his phone.

She started talking immediately, and he listened until she stopped talking, and then she listened to silence for several seconds until he said, "I'll be there in a few. Send the location address to my phone," and he disconnected.

She walked over to stand beside Bobby who was still staring down at the two bodies. Davis was calling out the ME and the crime scene techs. A biting wind was preventing the snow from covering them and completely destroying the crime scene. File in the category of being thankful for small favors. "Bobby."

He lifted his eyes from the corpses to look into hers. "It was so fast. Too fast. I didn't know he was going to kill her, Captain, and I just couldn't react fast enough to stop him—"

"Don't do that, Bobby. Don't blame yourself for not thinking

183

like a murdering, baby-raping piece of shit." Though her tone was harsh, her voice was not loud, yet Alice seemed to hear and she moved several steps closer to them. "Alice, go help Andy. If that other child is dressed like this one, she might already have frozen to death. And make sure Tim has the other perp secured. I want to hear from you every five minutes. I mean that. And that means you, too, Andy Page."

"Yes, ma'am!" she heard in her comm.

She walked a tight circle around the bodies, then pointed to the cargo van. "Anybody been near that?"

Bobby shook his head. "We've kept eyes on it to make sure nobody else did, either."

"Good," she said, walking toward the van and hoping that it was empty, that there wasn't another child inside. She didn't get there because Davis's SUV skidded into view. "Go get in my car and get warm, Bobby. Not a request," she added, walking toward Commander Davis and taking him over to the crime scene.

"How did I know you'd be here," he said. It wasn't a question so she didn't have to answer. She filled him in on all of the night's events, ending with the fact that two of her people were still waiting for a city attorney at Central Booking. He whipped out his phone, pulled up his contact list, punched a number, and waited. Briefly. "Ryerson. Eddie Davis here."

Gianna watched, listened, and learned as her boss calmly explained the situation and just happened to mention how nice it would be if the concussed rabbi could know that the people who had invaded her sanctuary and attacked her had been charged and arrested. After warm words of gratitude Davis punched off his phone and grinned at Gianna. "The great man himself is on his way to Central Booking. And I'd like to meet Thompson and Asher. Is Gilliam all right?" he asked as Gianna gave him Bobby's weapon and body camera.

"He's pretty broken up about the little girl."

"Yeah," Davis said, staring down at the little body. And that's when Gianna remembered that he had a daughter. She let him have his moment. "And McCreedy has the second perp in custody?"

"Yes, sir."

"Is he bruised and bleeding?"

"I sincerely hope not," Gianna said.

"Anything else?" he asked, and Gianna pointed to the dark blue cargo van. He nodded understanding and looked relieved as the ME and crime scene investigation trucks arrived. Then the comms went live.

"We got blood," Andy said.

"Not a body, just blood," Alice quickly clarified.

Gianna ran for her car. "I'm coming to you, but you'll have to lead me in." Then Bobby was running toward her and Davis was ordering him to stop. "He'll be all right, Commander. I promise."

"He better be," Davis said, without rancor. He completely trusted Capt. Maglione, and she completely trusted her people and that was good enough for him. He went to speak to Dr. Oland, and sicced the CSIs on the cargo van.

Gianna cursed the darkness while Bobby took directions and navigated. "There they are." He put the spotlights on and they got out, Maglites and weapons in hand, and slow-walked to their colleagues, hypervigilant. "Somebody is losing a lot of blood," Gianna said, following the trail with her flashlight. And it was a trail, not just a few droplets.

"I hope it's his ass," Bobby growled, pointing to the cuffed perp on the ground. Gianna looked down at the perp, did a head-to-foot scan. No blood, which meant the little girl was bleeding. Badly.

"Has he said anything?" Gianna asked.

"Aside from calling me and Tim cracker motherfuckers and pasty white cracker motherfuckers, not a word," Andy said.

"Let me have a word with him, see what he calls me," Bobby said, standing over the perp, who lay unmoving on frigid ground, his eyes closed as if he were napping.

"Get him on his feet. And if you don't mind, Bobby, I'll have the word," Gianna said. "Then if he calls me a pasty white cracker motherfucker, you can have your chat."

185

"He's got a Maryland driver's license says his name is Ronald George, but it's as phony as a seven-dollar bill," Andy said.

Gianna stood facing the man. "I don't care what your name is or where you live. I want to know where that little girl is and why she's bleeding, and you're going to tell me. Or you can tell the fellas you'll be sharing a cell with at Central Lockup downtown, which is where you're headed."

"I don't know where she is," Ronald-or-not said quickly. "She got away when that cop was chasing me and screaming that he was the police and telling me to stop running or he'd shoot me, the motherfucker."

Gianna's steady, flinty gaze didn't waver, but Ronald's did. He looked wildly around and seemed suddenly to realize that he was surrounded by cops, that he was ass-deep in a bucket of watery shit, and there was only one way out. He started talking and they were listening, but they weren't interested. He had enough face time with cops to recognize the flat face of disinterest. But he couldn't tell them what they wanted to know—not and live. The Cartoon would kill him.

"Can I have that word now, boss?" Bobby asked. Gianna nodded and Ronald smirked. They thought he'd talk to the Black cop, who walked over and stood before him. Ronald had to look up. The cop was a big dude, which is why he didn't notice the slight movement in the cop's right arm. Then his left hand was in a vice and the pressure was forcing the bones to rub together and he couldn't breathe, to say nothing of being able to speak. The grip loosened slightly, and Ronald told them almost everything. The vise tightened and he told them the rest. Bobby walked away and Ronald dropped to his knees and Tim took off running.

"The bastard tossed a phone and I missed it. I'll find it."

"Get him up," Gianna said to Andy. Then to Ronald, "Show me on your leg where you cut the girl and tell me why." When he showed her, Gianna wanted to slap him. Maybe more than wanted to because sudden pressure on her right arm forced her

186

gaze away from the perp to rest on Bobby. "What are you doing?" she snapped at him.

"Keeping you from doing something you don't want to do, Cap."

She glared at him, but they'd worked together so long her glare no longer had any effect. She walked a few steps away. "I really do want to hit him, Bobby."

"I know you do, but you can't."

"But you could break all the bones in his hand?"

"I wanted to break his balls. Besides, his hand is fine. And another besides: I'm just a lowly detective, not a captain in charge of an elite unit of the DC Police Department. You know I'm right—right?"

Gianna nodded, touched his arm, and said, "Get him in the car."

"I'm not going to Central Lockup, right?" Ronald whined.

"Damn right you are, you piece of shit," Bobby snarled at him. "Because of you that child is probably dead."

Gianna followed the blood trail back to where Tim was searching for the phone, and then forward. "She got in a car. That's why the trail ended so suddenly. But where exactly are we? Is this some kind of weird back of beyond?"

"I think I know, Cap," Bobby said slowly, "and you're not too wrong. You know too, Legs," he said to Alice. "The area Tony told us girls were going missing from—"

"You're right!" Alice exclaimed. "This would be an easy way to get in and out of that area without being seen, and nobody who wasn't completely familiar with the area would know to look back here."

"But where is 'back here' exactly? And why wouldn't the cops investigating the girls' disappearance just keep driving until they got 'back here'?" Gianna asked.

"Because they couldn't," Bobby said, and explained that about ten years ago there had been a plan to revitalize this neighborhood that included construction of a transportation hub that would

187

run only express busses to and from different parts of the metro area and multiple units of affordable housing. So existing housing was demolished, streets were closed, and—nothing. The project was dropped or cancelled or, most likely, the developers just walked away.

Tim hurried to them and held up the snow-covered phone. "At least we can find out who he called and that might help us figure out if anything he told us is true. But I did not see a car. I would have noticed if one passed me, and I'd have noticed headlights coming toward me."

So who had grabbed the girl and where did he come from?

Gianna was back at the original crime scene with Bobby, the second perp, and the snow-covered cell phone Tim found.

"I trust you'll find the answer to that question," Commander Davis said, "which leads me to ask: Why are you so certain the girl is dead?"

"Because the idiot cut her femoral artery trying to carve an arrow, and if the bleeding isn't stopped quickly you die," Gianna said, and Davis knew she spoke from experience. The limp was almost history. The memory never would be.

"And he was marking this girl as someone's property?"

Gianna nodded, and added: "He wanted the arrow to point to her—"

"Don't say it! I might kill this son of bitch myself." He stalked over to the squad where Ronald George huddled in the back seat and snatched open the door. "Get out." Ronald stumbled getting out and stayed down. This cop frightened him more than all the others combined. The snow fell hard and fast. "Who told you to cut that child?"

"The Cartoon," Ronald answered without looking up.

Davis looked the question at Gianna and she shrugged. "We haven't come across that name—"

"But you will, Captain, and you'll do it soon."

"Yes, sir."

"Anything else?"

"We gotta take good care of Ronald George or whoever he is in lockup tonight, Commander, because he might be our best or only way into whatever is going on over here," she said.

"And what do you think that is?"

What exactly did she think? She told him: that a low-life POS was paying other low-life POS's to steal girls from their homes to be sold into sexual slavery, and some police officers knew about it. He didn't flinch when she spoke. And when she said, "I think we need a Sky Eye—" he cut her off with, "Already ordered."

"Thank you, sir."

"Thank you, Captain, for your good work. Now go home and get some rest, and send your people home because I want all boots on the ground bright and early."

She went to find Bobby, to make certain the Internal Affairs jerks weren't giving him too hard a time. To find Tim to make certain that he wasn't giving himself too hard a time. To find Andy and Alice to make certain they were taking care of themselves.

"You all right, boss?" they inquired of her before she could ask about them.

"Where's Tim?"

"Giving the IA guys the evil eye. You know how he feels about Bobby," Alice said.

Gianna did know. Bobby thought of Tim as a little brother, and Tim idolized the older detective. "You two should go home. The Commander has this scene secured."

"We'll go when you go, Cap," Andy said.

And Gianna would go when Bobby was free to go—which was now as the two big detectives approached them, both wearing big smiles. Genuine smiles. Gianna knew them both well enough to know that. "I'm going home now, and I want all of you to do the same. Have a good meal and a good sleep. We've got a lot of work to do, and it starts first thing in the morning." And the Mobile Intelligence Unit went home. Just as the snow turned blizzard-like.

"Goddammit. Fuckin' snow!" were the last words they heard as they gratefully left the scene of the double homicide in the capable hands of Commander Eddie Davis and Dr. Wanda Oland, the ME. Gianna wondered if Mimi was still awake . . . she wouldn't mind being awakened even if she was. The thought warmed and sustained her on the drive home.

CHAPTER NINE

Nobody was sorry that the snow had stopped—nobody but the kids who were looking forward to making snowpeople and sledding down hills. Most other humans, especially those who had to make their way to work come hell, high water, or snow, would rather have clear roads. Of course, if the temperature dropped before the slush ran down the drains, then everybody would wish to have the snow back because ice was the worst. Gianna, the Philadelphia native, unbothered by snow, slush or ice, drove to work. Mimi, the Los Angeles native who was bothered by all of it even after many years in DC, took a taxi, and was pleased to see that, true to his word, the housing department's Mathis had a fax waiting for her, and the information it contained was better than she'd allowed herself to hope.

Gianna was met by a bland-faced Commander Davis and a grim-faced Deputy Chief Ellen De Longpre when she arrived for her early morning meeting with them. They both were standing so Gianna remained standing.

"'Morning Deputy Chief, Commander," she said, copying Davis's bland mien.

"Captain, I'd first like to congratulate you and your people on outstanding work last night," De Longpre said.

Gianna sighed, closed her eyes, and said, "I'm ready. Drop the other shoe."

Because her eyes were closed she missed De Longpre's barely stifled grin, but she opened them in time to see the nod to Davis who said, "You were right to be concerned about Ronald George, whose real name is George Ronald Price. He was killed in prison last night—"

"How?" Gianna snapped, as if speaking to a subordinate. "He was supposed to be in isolation, under guard." She got a grip and began the apology that was owed her superior.

"He was," Davis said, waving off her apology. "He was in the hospital ward under guard. A 'doctor' with the proper ID came to check his vitals at five thirty. At shift change. When he was left alone for exactly ten minutes."

Nobody said it. Nobody needed to say it: There no longer was any doubt that somebody was paying off cops. Somebody involved in the trafficking of little girls for sex. They stood together in miserable, helpless silence for a moment. Then Davis spoke.

"You were also right about putting a drone up. We may have lost Ronald but we got this one," Davis said, as he pulled up video of a car with two passengers dumping the body of a little girl less than a mile from where her now-frozen blood stained the sidewalk.

Gianna scrutinized the time stamp. A little more than four hours ago. "We're drafting warrants for both of them now," De Longpre said, as if reading her mind. "And if they do anything except go to the toilet before the warrants are signed, we'll arrest them. We know where they are and who they're with. What else do you need?"

Gianna inhaled deeply, exhaled slowly, and gathered her thoughts. Then she told them what else she needed.

Mimi took one of the newsroom cars to Clara Carruthers's place after first stopping at the grocery store to buy chickens. Gianna pointed out that not everyone was a vegetarian, a fact Mimi

192

should keep in mind. Mimi agreed. It hadn't even crossed her mind during her first shopping trip for Clara and her family. She never visited the meat aisle when she was shopping, and even though Gianna ate chicken occasionally, and fish more often, she bought them fresh from a market in Chinatown. Today Mimi bought lots of chicken because, well, four people had to eat and three of them were teenagers.

Clara opened the door to her knock, surprised to see her. She was surprised that Clara was awake but glad that she was. "I have something for you," Mimi said. "Two things, actually."

Clara accepted the sheaf of papers Mimi gave her and read the top page. She kept reading it, over and over. Then she forced her eyes from the paper to meet Mimi's. "Is this for real?"

"It definitely is," Mimi replied.

"I have a three-bedroom apartment in one of the multi-family buildings? They told me there was a four- or five-year waiting list to get in there."

"There was, but space opened up just the other day—"

"Those people who got evicted for fighting in the church, or whatever it was!"

Mimi nodded. "Are you interested?"

"You know I am, but why are you helping me like this, Ms. Patterson? I don't understand it."

"Do you understand why you're taking care of two children who aren't yours?"

"'Cause it's the right thing to do," Clara said defiantly. "'Cause I killed their mama," she whispered, her voice pained and shamed.

"Yes, you did. Probably before somebody killed those little girls because they were living on the street. Or in the Playpen," Mimi said in her own whisper.

"Thank you. Thank you so very much," Clara said. "I know I can't ever repay you, but I hope you know how grateful I am."

"You raise those girls to be the kind of woman you are and that will be thanks enough for me," Mimi said.

Then she heard cheering and noticed for the first time that

193

someone else was in the apartment: Melinda Franklin as well as another young woman, and they were seated with the three girls at the dining table, books and papers spread out before them. "They're having a spelling lesson," Clara said, proudly and happily, and Mimi watched the fear and worry and misery drain from her face. She realized that Clara Carruthers was a young woman, perhaps not yet thirty. She gave Clara the bags of chickens and walked away, as much because she didn't want to hear any more "thank-yous" as she wanted to speak to Melinda and the girls.

"We're having a spelling bee, Ms. Patterson," Carla exclaimed, the most animated Mimi had seen her.

"Ooooh, can I play?" Mimi asked, and was rewarded by a loud and universal chorus of noes, so she leaned toward Melinda with a whispered "thank-you" of her own. When Melinda introduced her friend as an attorney with a newly established legal cooperative, she knew how Clara felt. She thanked both women as Clara walked over to the table holding aloft the lease that would allow her and her girls to move within the next few days, and that was it for spelling. The girls wanted to pack immediately.

Mimi asked Clara if they could talk and followed her into the bedroom where she closed the door. "I know you'd rather be asleep after having worked all night," Mimi said and apologized before Clara could speak. "I'm sorry to bring up hurtful things, but I'd like to know everything you know about the Playpen and the people who run it."

Clara was already shaking her head back and forth. "I don't know anything about that place, Ms. Patterson. I only know what the girls told me, and I only been there one time: When I went to get my baby outta there."

"Was Patrick there? Did you see him?"

"He wasn't there, just some Mexican man—"

Holy shit! The branded girls from the restaurant? "What Mexican man, Clara?"

"I don't know who he was. He had a little girl by the arm. I thought she was, you know . . ." She started to shake. Mimi took her by the arm and led her to the bed.

"Sit down, Clara, and catch your breath. If you really can't talk about this, I'll understand, and I won't ask you again."

"It's all right, Ms. Patterson. I got to tell somebody all of it, and that somebody might as well be you. I haven't even told Dr. Connors all of it." She closed her eyes, inhaled deeply, and began talking.

"I got pregnant when I was sixteen, had Carla at seventeen, and got disowned by my parents. It's just been me and her ever since, on our own. I found out my Carla was in trouble when I was sorting her clothes to wash and there was blood in her panties. I thought her period had started, which surprised me 'cause I think of her as my baby, but when I asked her, she just started screaming. It took a while before I got the story, that Denise and Darla's mama—I can't call them by those other names—she took my Carla with them to that place. Carla didn't know where they were going, but she was tired of being home by herself all the time while I worked. And I couldn't blame her."

"You can't blame yourself, either, Clara."

"That's what Dr. Connors said, but I'm the one who was supposed to protect her, to keep her safe. Anyway, the next night I left work early to surprise Carla. I brought her the fried shrimp and fries she likes but she wasn't here." Clara got lost in her memory of that night, a night she'd likely never forget.

Up and down the hallways, pounding on doors, screaming for Carla. "Carla! Where are you baby? Come to Mama, Carla! CARLA!" Out to the street, screaming for Carla. At the bus stop, Mrs. Burns from on the first floor. "I just saw your Carla with that ho going up Eighth Avenue. She was dragging her by the arm and Carla was crying. Here, take this." The baseball bat Mrs. Burns took with her everywhere. For safety. Running, running. Carla told me where Shalimar Grigsby took her: A place called the Playpen. On Eighth Avenue. By the liquor store. Running. Running and swinging the bat, and screaming for Carla. Pulling open the door and running into the Playpen screaming, "CARLA! CARLA! WHERE ARE YOU, BABY? CARLA?" Denise and Darla running to her, grabbing her,

195

wearing tacky, whorish fake robes and tacky, whorish makeup and carrying their regular clothes. "WHERE IS CARLA?" Denise pointing to the hallway. "In the first room on the right." Making them take off the tacky, whorish shit where they stood. "Drop it on the floor and put on your clothes and go outside and wait." Then the Mexican man dragging the little girl by the arm came from hallway. "What the fuck are you doing, bitch?" "You kiss my ass, motherfucker. CARLA! CARLA!" First room on the right. Door not locked. Fat white man's fat white ass in the air, pumping.

"CARLA! GET OFF MY BABY YOU FAT UGLY BASTARD!" Swinging the bat. Hitting his ass, his back, his head. Hitting and hitting until he's off Carla and on the floor, looking up at her, mad and scared, but mostly mad. Carla looking blind. Scared. Worse than scared. Not seeing her mother. Covering her nakedness with my coat, carrying her from the room, heading for the front door, Mexican man in the way. "Where you goin' bitch?" Swinging the bat, hitting and hitting. Outside with Carla. Shalimar running and running, shouting and cursing me, grabbing her girls. The bat, part of my arm, hitting and hitting, chasing and hitting, following Shalimar around to the back of the Playpen, the bat chasing and hitting and hitting and hitting. No words. The only sound the bat hitting and hitting. Then, "Mama Clara? Can we go home with you?"

"Denise called me Mama Clara and that was that, though I think it was the next day before I called them Denise and Darla. I don't know if Denise told Darla what I did to their . . . to Shalimar. I don't think she had to."

"Where exactly is this place, this Playpen?"

"On Eighth Avenue at Field Street, by a liquor store. You'll know it when you see it. Nothin' but drunks and junkies hanging around."

"Thank you, Clara. I can't imagine how difficult that was. But it looks like you and your family will be starting new lives in a new place."

"A new life in a new place. I like how that sounds."

"One thing, Clara: Keep seeing Dr. Connors. You and the girls. A new start helps but it's not a cure."

"How long before they get cured, Ms. Patterson?"

Oh God. What would Bev say? "I don't know, Clara. Healing is a slow process and it's different for everybody. It takes as long as it takes. There's no clock or calendar."

"I won't ever forget you, Ms. Patterson."

"I won't ever forget you and your girls, either," Mimi said, and she thought about them while driving to Eighth Avenue and Field Street to see with her own eyes the house of horrors, the hellhole, a place called the "Playpen." Like the brutality was a game. Like the little girls in there were playing his game. And was that a detective squad car parked in front?

Alice and Andy were quiet after Gianna briefed them on her meeting with Davis and De Longpre, and she gave them time and space to order their thoughts—as her bosses had done for her.

"It could be days, weeks, even, before we know who those little girls were, or anything about the perps," Andy said.

"And those girls who went missing before—whose mothers were ignored by the cops—they're not going to welcome us with open arms now," Alice said. "And I don't blame them."

"Not to mention that missing girls or their moms aren't IA's top priority," Andy added sourly. "They're looking for bent cops."

"So let's focus on what we can do something about," Gianna said, redirecting their anger and frustration. "Thanks to our eyes in the sky, we may have movement on Gustavo. Kenny and Vik have been watching the drone feeds and nothing until last night. They started watching early this morning, three days' worth, and it seems that the two women leave every evening for a night on the town, returning shortly after midnight—before Gus returns."

Andy and Alice watched her. There was something she wasn't saying . . . until she said it. The women came and went via the front door, and the house was empty when they left. So tonight could be a good time to lay hands on that ground-penetrating radar machine.

197

"What are you thinking?" Andy asked.

"That it's time we found out if Lina's mother is buried in the backyard."

Andy was gone in a flash, across the room to his cubicle, leaving Gianna and Alice to continue to watch the drone feeds.

Andy came their way at a trot, grinning widely and rubbing his hands together in glee. "We'll have the machine as soon as the sun goes down. When those women go out the front door, we can get to work in the backyard."

"Good work, Kenny and Vik. Keep eyes on it and call me if you need to," Gianna said, and led Andy and Alice back to her office where they planned and strategized for the next hour. They had to agree that even if the ground-penetrating radar machine saw evidence of bodies in the backyard, they'd do nothing until they had Gus and the women under arrest. And they discussed several different scenarios if they had proof that Gus had brought more girls into the house, but they agreed on one major point: They would do all in their power to prevent those girls from being raped and brutalized. "Keep one team with you tonight and send everybody else home to bed. Let the crime scene techs operate the equipment. They'll start as soon as the women are clear of the neighborhood."

"And if the techs get a positive result?" Andy asked.

"Mark the location and get them and their machine out of there, fast."

Andy nodded, saluted, and left. Alice was standing but she didn't leave. "A word, Captain?" and when Gianna nodded, she closed the door.

"Is something wrong, Alice?"

"No, ma'am. At least I don't think so . . ."

Now Gianna was concerned. She stood up and closed the distance between them. "Talk to me, Alice."

She took a breath, but then a hint of a smile eased some of Gianna's worry. "I don't think this is a conflict of interest, but Delores Phillips and I—we're seeing each other and—"

Gianna had her in a tight embrace before she could complete the sentence. "Oh Alice, that is just wonderful. Congratulations to you both. I am so happy for you." She released her and backed up a few steps. "When did this happen? How did it happen? Is it all right if I ask?"

"Oh, yes, I want to tell you. I am so happy and so . . . overwhelmed . . . and I have Bobby Gilliam to thank." At Gianna's expression Alice wished she could duplicate Delores's laugh. Then she recounted how it happened that she and Delores became a couple. "Mimi told me some time ago that when I stopped thinking and worrying about not having anybody, that's when it would happen, and it did. The only thing I was thinking about was how to stop spending every dime I earned, and Delores made it so easy. Not only do I have a new car, but I actually have money in my savings account."

"Is your new car a Bentley?" Gianna asked, and Alice left her standing there with a big grin on her face. Alice and Delores Phillips, totally unexpected but totally wonderful. Two of the best women she knew were together. She grabbed her phone to call Mimi and share the news but decided to wait until she got home. But an incoming text from Mimi suggested that likely wouldn't be for a while: She, Joe, their interns, several other reporters, and a couple of photographers had just been dispatched to a disturbance at The Bluffs Apartments. Gianna hurried over to Kenny and Vik and asked them to pull up anything at The Bluffs Apartments on the East Side. She knew that the unrest over the gentrification issue could boil over at any time. Was this that time? Disturbance could mean any number of things, none of them good, and could have any number of possible outcomes. Gianna shut off her brain. If Mimi sent a distress signal, that's when she'd worry about a disturbance at The Bluffs. Until then she had enough of her own stuff to worry about.

CHAPTER TEN

The Bluffs disturbance that evening was the kind that quickly degenerated from name calling, to pushing and shoving, to rock and bottle throwing, which is when Mimi and Joe ordered the interns out of harm's way and into the lobby of one of the apartment buildings. It was also when the police joined the party. Fortunately for all concerned, all they had to do was show up and the activity quickly dialed back to name calling, and there it remained for the rest of the evening because the police stayed put.

Mimi talked to a dozen residents but could not get a handle on the exact cause of the unrest. Joe tried in vain to locate a representative of the apartment complex—the property manager, the leasing agent, even the maintenance man—somebody who could speak for the property owners or at least say that he or she couldn't speak for the owners without permission. He also couldn't find anybody from city government—from the mayor's office, the city council, or the housing department. Maybe that's what the residents were pissed off about? Their evictions were looming, and they didn't have anybody to talk to about it. A few dozen families were about to be on the street with no hope of finding another place to live in the nation's capital and they wanted somebody to care. Perhaps in this day and time that was asking too much . . .

Mimi's phone vibrated in her pocket. So, apparently, did Joe's, for both reporters grabbed their phones, checked the screens, and turned to look toward the building where their interns were beckoning.

"If we're not careful, those kids are gonna have our jobs," Joe muttered.

"I just hope they have a story for us," Mimi said. "In which case young Sasha is more than welcome to mine because she'd deserve it."

"You seem not to mind relinquishing this job," Joe grumbled, sounding every bit as accusatory as he felt as they made their way through a still restless and hostile crowd to their interns. "You recognize any of these cops?"

Mimi shook her head; she'd been checking them out, too. "Must be from the East River Precinct, which makes sense: This is their home turf."

"But Maglione sent her crew—"

"Different scenario," Mimi said. "A top city official was there that time, and the owners had called in armed security guards. That could've gotten real ugly, real fast."

Joe acknowledged that there was a difference in the two situations as they reached the interns, who had official-looking papers and were flanked by angry-looking residents. Mimi and Joe introduced themselves and received a polite, almost warm greeting. Sasha introduced the residents, then told Mimi and Joe to read the documents.

"Holy shit!" Joe exclaimed. He whipped out his phone, and while Mimi held the papers he took photos of them. Then he excused himself and Mimi knew that he was calling Carolyn and that his second call would be to City Attorney Ryerson.

Mimi reread the documents, which were letters addressed to individual residents, on the letterhead of something called the "City East Development Partnership." "Had any of you received a communication from this organization before these letters?" she asked, and all the residents responded in the negative. The first letter, dated ten days earlier and signed by Jonathan Sturgess, Vice President, was an offer: If the recipient agreed to vacate his/her unit by the end of the month, City East Development Partnership would pay $2,500.

"That's my letter," said a very tall, very thin man pointing to the letter Mimi held. "I called the next day and asked for that Jonathan Sturgess, and the lady who answered the phone said he didn't work there. I told her I was holding a letter from him that he wrote two days before and she hung up on me."

Mimi reread the second letter, dated the following day and signed by Gwendolyn Carter, Human Resources Manager, rescinding the terms of the previous letter, citing "an organizational error" and apologizing for any misunderstanding.

"I tried to call her, too, the next day but nobody answered the phone. I kept trying all day from work, every half hour: voice mail."

So many red flags waved at Mimi that she expected to see the bull come stampeding through the crowd at any moment. No doubt something hinky was afoot, but what? Maybe Joe had an answer because he was striding their way with a sense of purpose. "Tyler and Carolyn want us back at the paper sooner rather than later."

"May we have your contact information—" Mimi began, but she should have known better, should have known that Sasha would already have the contact info for everyone she spoke with, and she smiled at the young woman and touched her shoulder. "So just this one last thing," she said to the gathered residents, "and it's only a suggestion. Don't accept any offers from management, and don't agree to do or not do anything. Please let Joe Zemekis know if you receive any more mail from any person or company claiming to own or represent this property. We will find out all we can about these two letters and who sent them, and we'll let you know what we learn. It could take a few days so please be patient. We're on this."

She and Joe spent another half hour talking with the residents before taking their leave. They thanked the interns for their assistance and sent them home, then went in search of a taxi. "What did Ryerson say, Joe?"

"He said, and I quote: 'Greedy bastards. They just hung them-selves.' He wouldn't tell me exactly how, but he said the people who live here most likely can continue to live here. At least until the lawsuit he intends to file moves through the system."

Alice Long was on her way to meet Michelle Rivera and she was seriously considering activating lights and siren. The woman's voice was quivering when she called—Alice put it on speaker—and Gianna told her to go, right now, when she told them who Michelle was and that she had something "very, very important" to share. Alice just drove, didn't try to imagine what was so important that Michelle had asked her to come right away.

She remembered Michelle primarily because she was different from the other transgender women who'd crossed her path. She was quiet, withdrawn, and so fearful that she had decided that she wanted to go home, to her parents' home, rather than risk a beating, a rape, or worse at the hands of people who hated her, and she had asked Alice if she would drive her to her parents' in a Virginia suburb. Alice told her that she couldn't leave her assignment but that on her next day off—

"Never mind," the terrified woman had said. "I'll just stay here. I could get beat to death at home, too."

"You're a double target, Michelle, that's just a fact. Prostitutes are targets and always have been, and transgender women are targets—big targets these days—"

Angry now. "So it's my fault some sick fucker wants to kill me?"

Alice shook her head. "Nobody's fault but the sick fuckers who do the violence. But we don't have enough cops to stop all of them and protect all of you."

Now this woman was waiting for her in a diner to share some-thing "very, very important." Alice parked in front of the diner—one of the perks of driving a copmobile—and went inside. It was warm, almost too warm, and the sound and smell of food sizzling on the grill was making her slightly nauseated.

She looked around for Michelle and spied her in the last booth, scrunched into the corner, holding a cup between both hands, looking tiny and frightened and more than a little worried. She was trusting a cop.

"Hey, Michelle," Alice said, sliding into the booth opposite the frightened woman, giving her a warm, and she hoped, relaxing smile. It didn't work.

"Thank you for coming, Sergeant," Michelle said in a near whisper, voice still quivering.

"Something has frightened you very badly, Michelle. What is it and how can I help?" Alice extended her hands across the table, palms open. Michelle didn't take them but she did start talking.

"There's a man, a very bad man, named Patrick O'Shaunnessey, and he's starting to do business with an even worse man named Gustavo Ordonez-Gutierrez."

Alice's world tilted on its axis. *Gus!* Was Michelle really about to hand them Gus? She didn't say anything. She leaned farther across the table, closer to Michelle, and nodded to her, a signal that she should continue talking, which she did: Patrick called her yesterday. He used to be a client, but she cut him off because he was rough, violent. He thought it was all right to hurt her and he refused to stop, so she refused to see him "even though the money was always good. He thought paying a lot meant he could do what he wanted. I hadn't seen him in six or seven months—until yesterday." She took a sip of whatever was in her cup, frowned in distaste, and pushed it away.

"What is that, Michelle? Coffee? Would you like another cup? Or something to eat?"

"It's tea and yes, another cup, please. With honey. And some buttered toast." When the order was placed Michelle continued: Patrick needed her to serve as a translator for him. He was going into business with a man he did not trust, a man from Mexico, who pretended he couldn't speak English very well though Patrick knew that to be a lie. He would pay her five hundred dollars. "That's a fortune for me, Sergeant, so I said yes, as long as there was no sex, and he laughed. He said that I was too old

204

for his friend, that he only liked real girls and he liked them very young."

"Where was this meeting, Michelle?"

"At this place Patrick owns. It used to be a ... a ... motel? Not a hotel that is built tall but a place where the rooms are all on the same floor. Motel, yes?"

"Yes, that's right." *Fuck a duck! A motel.* Now Alice looked hard and close at Michelle. She'd heard a slight accent, but now she knew that Michelle was not a native-born American. Nor was she merely a small woman, she was a very young one. Beneath all the makeup and copious hair, she was, at most, seventeen years old. Not American-born and anyway too young to know when motels were king, but on the stroll long enough to be familiar with the no-tell motel. "Where is it located, Michelle? This motel."

Michelle took out her phone and looked up the address, which she read off to Alice. "It's not a nice neighborhood. Junkies and hookers, dealers and pimps."

Alice wasn't expecting Embassy Row. "How does their business work? What did you translate for Patrick?"

"Gustavo wants his girls to live at the motel with all the other girls, and he wants his own room there so he can watch them, but they did not agree on how much he will pay to Patrick. Gustavo says Patrick wants too much."

Alice's brain was in overdrive. *All the other girls. What other girls? How many? How many girls does Patrick have?* "So, they have to meet again?" And when Michelle nodded *yes*, Alice crawled all the way out on the limb. "I don't want you to be alone with them again, Michelle. It's too dangerous." How much to tell her? "We knew about Gus, but he disappeared before we could get to him—"

"He was in Mexico. He just got back with the girls."

"How many girls, Michelle? Do you know? And where are they?"

"Five or six, and they are at his house until he moves them to the motel."

205

"Do not talk to Patrick if he calls, Michelle, and do not go back to that motel. Promise me you won't. Please."

Michelle looked at her long and hard. She drank the rest of her tea and ate the rest of her toast, all the while watching Alice. She wiped her mouth, then asked: "What do you know, Sergeant?"

"Gus has killed three girls that we know about, and at least one woman—we think the mother of one of the girls. We were watching him, gathering evidence, when he disappeared."

"You have to get him before he puts those girls to work. They are little girls, Sergeant, children. Do you understand?"

Alice nodded even as her stomach clenched and bile rose into her throat. "I do understand, Michelle, and as soon as we see those girls moved into that motel, we move in. Believe me, we don't want them . . . whatever happens to them."

"I can tell you. I know because it happened to me, starting when I was nine. My father and his friends. Because I told my mother that I was really a girl, he said he would treat me like a girl . . ."

Alice closed her eyes, but she saw Lina and Carmen and the other girl in the grave. She opened them and saw the sad, broken, but still strong Michelle. "Where do you live, Michelle?" And when she shrugged Alice had the answer: She was homeless.

Alice made a split-second decision, pulled up the contacts in her phone, and punched a number. "Jose, my love. How are you?" She listened for a few seconds to his surprise and delight at hearing from her. Then, "I need a favor, Jose. Right now, tonight." And she told him in broad strokes about Michelle needing a safe place to be, just for a little while, and when he readily agreed, she thanked him profusely, adding, "We'll be there shortly."

"Be where?" Michelle asked warily.

"Do you know where the new City Alphabet Soup Center is in midtown?"

Michelle nodded and almost smiled. "That's a good name for it. I thought it was finished when they added the *T* for us, but then they added some more letters." Alice stifled her own smile. "Alphabet Soup" was what Delores's mother called *LGBTQIA* once when her two lesbian daughters and Alice were at her home for dinner. "What do those new letters mean?" she had asked, then roared with laughter when the three of them couldn't agree without going to the internet. "How am I supposed to keep up if you three can't?"

"Jose Cruz runs the help line. He's a good man and a good friend, and you'll be safe with him and Emelia, his sister."

Michelle considered. "What if I hate it there?"

"Then call me and I'll come get you. Otherwise, I'll see you as soon as we have Gus and Patrick locked up and all the girls freed."

"Okay, I will go to Jose and his sister, and I will stay there." She slid out of the booth and stood up facing Alice, barely reaching her shoulder. "And I hope that the men in prison do to Patrick and Gustavo what they do to little girls. And boys."

"One more thing, Michelle, please. What's the motel called?"

Gianna and Andy listened without interrupting until Alice finished talking. Then they sat speechless for several very long seconds processing it all, fitting all the pieces together, doing all the things Alice had done in her head even while Michelle was talking her through it. They had him. Gus. They had everything they needed to take him down, bringing the Patrick asshole to the ground with him.

"Drones with audio all over that Playpen. Deep and complete background on that Patrick freak and on the property. And what else does he own? I want to take everything he's got. And now that we know for certain girls are in Gus's house, I want to be damn certain we see when they leave. Andy? Damn certain."

"Yes, boss."

"And boss?"

"Alice?"

"According to Michelle, Gus likes young girls. He might already be raping them in that house—"

"I know, Alice, but we can't see inside the house, and we lose too much if we take the house now, even if we could get warrants. I'm sorry. We need all the pieces."

"Yes, ma'am."

"Surveillance outside the Playpen?" Andy asked.

"Definitely. Around the clock. And we're around the clock, too, until we wrap this up." Then she laid out exactly what she wanted and how:

Closeup photos of the men entering and leaving the Playpen.
Same thing for anyone else entering and leaving.
Photos of their vehicles and the license plates.
A schematic of the Playpen from the city engineering department.
Surveillance of all the ways into and out of the place.
Neighborhood surveillance—a four-block radius.
Tails on Patrick and Gus whenever they leave the Playpen.
Twelve-hour shifts for everybody—unless something pops.
One of us always on overnight; we'll rotate.
And keep a very close eye on the weather; be prepared for the worst.

"Did I leave anything out? Andy, Alice, anything to add?"

"You left Tommi out of the loop, boss," Alice said.

"She and Mike are packing—"

"She's gonna be really pissed off. She's gonna feel left out."

They were right. Gianna knew it. "Twelves for Tommi, too, but no overnights. Call her, Andy, before she hears about it."

"Have we IDe'd the women helping Gus?" Alice asked.

"Nothing solid," Gianna said, "but we're still on it. We've got good photos so if they're in anybody's database we'll know it ... what are you thinking, Alice? You want to show the photos to Michelle, see if she recognizes them?"

Alice nodded. "She's from down there, I don't know exactly where, and she didn't exactly want to tell me."

"If she's illegal, keep her well away from any operation. She's not mentioned in your report from the other night, is she? Good. Let's keep it that way."

208

"Suppose she calls and says she doesn't want to stay with Jose ..."

"She'll have to. At least for the short term." Gianna's tone made it clear that discussion of the matter wasn't an option.

"I'll get the photos printed," Andy said to Alice.

"I'm thinking—hoping—that we have another intel source. Michelle said there are already girls in that place, and Gus is bringing more. They live there, and so does Patrick. Somebody has to cook and clean ..."

Andy was up and pacing and thinking out loud. "Which means there almost has to be a back entrance or a side entrance ..."

"Maybe even a basement," Alice added, sensing the possibilities. "And any workers most likely would be women—"

"Who'd be scared shitless at the thought of life in prison—" Andy.

"Which they'd definitely be facing given the charges we'd lay—" Alice.

"So, do we wait until Gus's girls—"

"No!" Gianna and Alice said together.

"As soon as we get confirmation that people work there, as soon as we get photos, as soon as we follow a few of them home and see where and how they live, we make the attempt to turn one of them."

"And if there are no takers?" Andy asked.

Gianna shrugged. "Can't make them talk. But they sure as hell better not alert Patrick. Whoever talks to them, make sure they understand that." She stood up and stretched. "Good work tonight, Alice. Thank you for giving us Gus on a platter."

Andy gave her a one-armed hug, echoed the captain's congrats, and then said, "I wish the Seals had the equivalent of oorah—"

Alice pulled out of his embrace. "Andrew Page! You were a Seal and I didn't know?"

"No big deal, Sarge. And nobody calls me Andrew but my mother."

"Yes hell it is, LT!" and she gave him the Nancy Pelosi seal clap.

Gianna shooed them out with the directive that they get busy on the schedule while she prepared the report she'd give Davis and De Longpre first thing in the morning.

The two top cops read Gianna's report thoroughly, and she watched their faces go from grim to relieved to something resembling satisfied, though she knew that given the kind of cops they were, they'd never be satisfied knowing that this level of brutality was occurring in their city. Davis spoke first.

"Do we know for certain that he's bringing girls here from Mexico?"

"From Mexico or perhaps Guatemala or both, but yes, he is bringing minors across the border—our border—for purposes of prostitution. Sex trafficking."

"Your deployment of resources is, of course, excellent, Captain, but are you sure you have sufficient personnel?" De Longpre asked.

"Enough people, yes, but we could use more drones. We've got a couple of crucial locations uncovered," Gianna said.

"All you need," Davis replied. "I'll shift some from traffic immediately. Have Page call Ashby to make the arrangements. We'll take an inventory and let you know when we can free up others. Will that be all right?"

"More than all right, thanks. Andy and Alice are still fine-tuning the schedule so unless Gus moves the girls tonight, we have a little time to put things in place. I'll get it to you the moment it's finalized."

Gianna headed for the door. "By the way," she said, turning back. "If I may ask, where are the vice and sex crimes people? Shouldn't they be all over the Playpen? Shouldn't that place have been shut down long ago?"

The deputy chief's mood changed, her lips tightened and thinned. "You're not the only one asking those questions, Captain," she said, "and believe me the person who should have the answers will have them."

210

"Oh I believe you," Gianna said, rubbing her neck in the way that said she was glad it wasn't her head on the chopping block. She thanked them both for their support, and they both thanked her for a job well done. De Longpre added: "As much as I appreciate the work you're doing on this case, I'm very sorry that it has to come so close on the heels of the Asian sex trafficking ring you busted just a few months ago. That one was children; this one is children. I'm sorry it has to be you again. I can't imagine."

Gianna let the pain and the sadness and the fury take their turns moving through her before she made eye contact with Ellen De Longpre and said, "You'd think that we women had actually done something to deserve the hatred visited upon us."

Ellen held the eye contact and answered, "Perhaps we have. We have persisted, haven't we?" And when Gianna was gone, she said to Eddie Davis, "I don't know her as well as you do, but she seems different somehow. Am I reading her wrong?"

"You're right. She is different. More . . . relaxed . . . easier."

"Yet she still gets more accomplished than most. How?"

Davis looked up at the ceiling as if he could see straight through it to the sky. "I think those two back-to-back life-threatening events changed her, though I couldn't tell you how exactly." And they left it at that.

Gianna knew exactly how the two near-death experiences had made her stronger. And better. And the two people she answered to, because of the kind of people they were, would make it possible for her to keep the promise made to herself, and to Mimi, to steer clear of life-threatening situations. When she could. There could well be some lives threatened in the next forty-eight hours but hers wouldn't be one of them.

Gianna walked to the front of the room and they got quiet, knowing it was about to get serious. She told them in broad strokes what was about to happen, told them their lieutenant and sergeant would supply the details. "What I want to tell you is this: We're going straight at these people with everything we've got." Then she left it to Andy and Alice to provide the details of

211

the mission, along with the schedule that would tax all of them to the limits. She walked slowly to her office with the prayer that Gustavo would move the girls sooner rather than later, because the sooner this mission was over, the better for everyone. Except for Gustavo, Patrick, the people who helped them, and the men who gained pleasure from raping little girls.

Mimi's phone, set to vibrate, did a slow dance across her desk. She was totally oblivious, so intent was she on the story she was writing. Or trying to write. She'd already tossed two drafts, and given the difficulty she was having with this, the third, it was doomed to a similar fate. There was no easy way to write about the trafficking of young girls for the sexual gratification of grown men. The words didn't flow with ease or grace or brilliance. The task was complicated by the fact that DC owned the dubious distinction of having the highest rate of human trafficking in the US, which specifically meant bringing children of both sexes and adult women across the border for purposes of forced prostitution. Atlanta was such a close second that it sometimes got ranked first. Neither city was anxious to claim first place and neither seemed to be doing anything to rid itself of such a hor-rific distinction.

Mimi had two big problems. If women and children were being forced into prostitution, she didn't care where they came from; and everybody—cops, city officials, and most community activists—seemed to be ignoring the large numbers of young Black girls going missing right here in DC. The mothers of these girls believed, in fact they insisted, that their daughters were being kidnapped and sold into sexual slavery, but they had no proof, so police insisted the girls were runaways. And until she met Clara Carruthers she'd had no reason to believe that girls were being snatched off the street and sold.

"Answer your damn phone, Patterson!" Zemekis hissed at her across the desk.

She didn't recognize the number, but she answered anyway.

She didn't recognize the voice or the name the woman gave. She mentioned Jennifer and Becca and Brianna. But Mimi was certain she'd never met this "Gwen," who confirmed it when Mimi asked, "Do I know you?"

"The girls all had your card. Jennifer and Becca and Brianna, and I overheard all the husbands talking about you, cursing you, saying you had to be dealt with. Then they all got arrested. The reverend, too, and I knew it would be safe to talk to you. That none of them could hurt me anymore. So, do you want to hear what I have to say, Ms. Patterson?"

Well shit. She couldn't say no. She didn't say no. She arranged a time and place to meet; then she went to explain to Carolyn why her story wouldn't be finished when promised.

"Really, Mimi? Again?" Carolyn was not pleased.

"I know, and I'm sorry. Truth is, Carolyn, the story is kicking my ass and I need this distraction. And who knows? If she's the last of that group still around and if she wants to talk, there may be a story."

Carolyn gave her a look.

Gwen was a distraction all right. For starters she looked nothing like the other women Mimi had met, and the fact that her meeting place of choice was a coffee bar in a bookstore was another major departure. Gwen sported an Emma Gonzalez-like buzz cut and was dressed in all black—leggings, sweatshirt, hoodie and Doc Martens. She had a cappuccino in a cup the size of a soup bowl and the largest éclair Mimi had ever seen. She didn't have the way too skinny, almost emaciated look of the other girls, but it would take a lot more cappuccino and pastry before this young woman rid herself of the vestiges of starvation, for despite her current appearance, she'd have looked just like the others a month ago; of that Mimi was certain.

"Your call definitely surprised me, Gwen," Mimi said, sitting down. She removed her hat and gloves, unzipped her jacket, and sat back, waiting for Gwen to speak. After a moment she did.

"I know you told the other girls you don't pay for information, but you will when you hear what I have to say." Mimi sighed, zipped her jacket, put her hat and gloves back on, and stood up. "Wait, don't you want to hear what I have to say?"

"Your MAGA man is the one who is friends with people who own papers that pay for information. You should call one of them."

"I don't want anything to do with people like that anymore. I hate them!"

Mimi sat back down. "Why do you hate them, Gwen? You're here in DC because of them, aren't you?"

"They're liars, all of them. And worse." Those two words were almost whispered, and the girl shivered when she said them.

"Worse how?" Mimi unzipped her jacket and removed her hat and gloves. She wanted Gwen relaxed, comfortable.

Gwen told the whole story, in detail. Mimi put her recorder on the table between them, asked if she could record, and switched it on when Gwen nodded. Mimi took notes as she listened, but she stopped writing and listened in disbelief when Gwen described Clemson Jessup's relationship with the wives of the men who ostensibly worked for him. In truth, the men were paid to give Jessup access to their wives.

"He called us his concubines and his harem, and he made us be skinny." She took a big bite of the big éclair and licked the cream from her fingers. "We could never eat or drink anything like this when he was in charge of us."

"Why, Gwen? Why be skinny?" And when she heard the answer Mimi wished she hadn't asked, but it was too late. Gwen told her.

"He wanted us to look like little girls so he could pretend to be ... you know ... with little girls. But he said he needed to do it with us older girls because the kids, they were too small down there and he was so big, too big, to do it with them." She made the kind of totally disgusted face that Mimi wished she could make. "He always bragged about it, how he was hung like a horse." Her expression changed from disgust to sad in an instant.

214

"I tell myself to find the good in what happened and not to think on the bad."

"What was good about any of that, Gwen?"

"For one thing, we found out that our piece of shit husbands didn't care anything about us. They only cared about being in Jessup's army and getting all the money he paid them. But only me and Jessica got mad about it." Then the tears began. "Poor Jessica. She thought the only way out was to kill herself. She didn't even manage to kill her bastard husband. She killed her own self."

"And what about your husband, Gwen? What happened to him?"

"They killed him," she said, wiping her eyes.

"Who killed him? When?"

"That time after you came to the church. You remember that time?" Mimi said she did. "When Jessup got caught Bob said he was leaving, going back home. He wasn't gonna wait around to get arrested. So Jessup told the other men to kill him so he wouldn't talk, but I didn't know he was dead until one of Jessup's men came to give me money—"

"I'm sorry to interrupt you, Gwen, but what man? Came from where?"

"Where Jessup lives in Virginia. One of the men who lives there. And he brought me a lot of money because he thought I knew Bob was dead, but I didn't. I just thought he went back home like he said he would and didn't take me."

"Do you know the man's name?"

He told her his name, she said, but she didn't remember it. She just remembered that he was younger than Jessup. And, she said, she was a little afraid of him. "He told me I better not leave town, that I better wait for Jessup because I was his unfinished business."

"Do you know what he meant, Gwen?"

She nodded. "That's why I wanted money from you, so I can leave before he gets out." Now she looked frightened and frantic. "He'll make me get pregnant—"

"Say what? Explain that, Gwen, please," Mimi said, hoping she sounded calmer than she felt.

"We couldn't be with our husbands, only with Jessup, and all the babies were his. That's the organization he was making. His church. And I'm the only one who didn't have a baby. I'm his unfinished business. And now he's getting out of jail—Connelly. *That's* his name. He came over this morning and gave me some more money and told me to get ready to receive my master. It was an hour before I stopped shaking. And after what he did to his own little girls, I knew what he'd do to me."

"What do you mean, after what he did to his own little girls?"

"He sold 'em to this rich guy he's friends with."

Mimi was speechless. This was not just a story. This was . . . she didn't know what the hell this was.

"I'm not lying. You think I'm lying but I'm not—"

Mimi tried to calm Gwen. "I don't think you're lying, Gwen. I honestly don't. I'm just having a hard time wrapping my mind around what you're telling me. That's all. It's a lot to take in."

"That's why Pastor Jessup told us not to talk to anybody outside the church. He said nobody would understand."

"He's right about that," Mimi said, but before she could question Gwen further the girl began to come undone.

"I got to get away before the reverend gets out!"

"Are you sure he's getting out?"

"That's what Connelly said."

Connelly. Randall fucking Connelly. And Jessup was getting out of jail. Did Gianna know? "Gwen, do you want me to see if I can stop Jessup from being released?"

The girl reached across the table to grab Mimi's hands so fast that she knocked over her empty cappuccino cup. "Can you do that? Can you really?"

Mimi nodded. "But I need to send a text right now. All right?"

Gianna was with Alice and Andy when the message came and she stopped talking midsentence. She read and reread the message; then she passed the phone across the table so they could read it, too: *DO NOT LET CLEMSON JESSUP LEAVE JAIL! I'LL EXPLAIN SHORTLY. RCONNELLY ALREADY OUT?*

216

Gianna was on the landline to Davis. Andy and Alice didn't know what to do, wouldn't know until Cap had some word from Davis. It was a short conversation, and a mostly one-way one. "He'll call me back. But if Connelly got released then Davis didn't know it, nor is he aware of Clemson Jessup's pending release."

"Where can you go that's safe, Gwen? Not back to where you live."

"I was going to the mall to see a movie."

"Good. Do that and stay there until I call you. Please."

"You really think you can find out if Jessup's gonna be free?"

"I'm pretty sure I can. And if he's getting out, Gwen, I'll arrange for you to get enough money to get safely away from here."

"Do you promise me?"

Mimi nodded and shook the girl's hand. "I promise, Gwen. Now go."

Mimi took a taxi back to the paper. She called Carolyn en route, asked her to grab Joe and meet her in Tyler's office. She played Gwen's interview for them and they were as speechless as she'd been.

"What's Gianna have to say?"

"Haven't heard back yet—" she was saying when her phone rang. Gianna. She listened for several long moments, then disconnected. "Jessup's very carefully crafted plan to be released is stopped in its tracks for the time being. If Gwen's account can be verified, he'll be looking at additional charges that will make bail impossible. As for Randall Connelly—he's still in lockup, unable to make bail. Gianna's people are looking to see if there's another Connelly connected to Jessup and his church."

Tyler sat back in his chair, eyes closed, thinking deep thoughts. "Start piecing this thing together. Joint byline, you two, and I don't want to hear anything but okay from you, Patterson. We'll play this one close and careful. Meanwhile ..."

"Is the mayor still refusing to talk?" Carolyn asked, knowing Tyler wanted to get back on track with the story about the landlords and city officials, which they could write and publish immediately, while they waited for more facts about Jessup and the horrible abuse Gwen accused him of.

"The mayor's press secretary is still refusing to talk," Joe responded sourly. "But to tell you the truth, I don't think she's even talked to the mayor. I don't think anybody has. I don't think anybody knows where the mayor is."

"She's elevated hiding to an art form," Mimi said. "She's always done that. When she was on the city council and found herself on the wrong side of a vote, she'd hide out, disappear for several days."

"How'd she get elected mayor anyway?" Joe asked. He had been in South America covering a different brand of election corruption when the current DC mayor was elected. "She doesn't even seem to like the job, to say nothing of barely putting forth any effort to do it," he said, looking directly at Mimi. She appeared to be about to answer, but then jumped up and ran to the bank of old metal file cabinets at the back of the newsroom. Joe ran to his desk. He grabbed armloads of files and hurried back to Carolyn's cubicle. "If she has what I think she does, we need the tables in Tyler's office."

"Looks like she does," Carolyn said, getting to her feet and heading to Tyler's office while Mimi came their way with her own armloads of files.

"Hot damn!" Joe exclaimed, and the evil grin on Mimi's face telegraphed that she was thinking the same thing that he was thinking: The mayor was well and truly fucked.

"I didn't give her much chance to win," Mimi said when they were gathered in Tyler's office, the files open, the papers spread across two tables, "even though she was outspending everybody. Even though she'd had a term on the council. Even though she was a DC native with deep roots in the city. She didn't attend one of the universities here. Her husband was from out of town. Her children went to private schools out of state. Her parents

218

retired and moved to some island in the Caribbean. She might as well have been from the moon. That was my thinking."

"I remember you wrote a story about how all her big money donors were from out of state," Carolyn said.

Mimi shrugged. "Didn't seem to bother anybody. The voters, that is. Her opponents jumped all over it, but she never addressed the issue, never responded to questions about all of the out-of-state money. She just kept producing these slick—and expensive—TV ads showing her doing and being ... well ... slick."

"Well, we've certainly never seen any of that slick from her," Carolyn said.

"Maybe we have," Mimi said. "Suppose she's the mastermind behind this whole stupid scheme?"

"And is it ever stupid, to say nothing of arrogant." Carolyn was getting madder by the minute. "What made them think they could get away with it?"

"They almost did get away with it, Carolyn," Mimi said. "What firebombed the mayor was the housing crisis she created. The residents of the targeted apartments refused to go because there was no place for them to go to. But if they'd managed to empty all those buildings and start demolition—"

"No stopping them then," Carolyn agreed. "Bastards."

Joe paged through the campaign contribution reports all candidates are legally required to file and was comparing the names to those of the now-proven-fictitious property owners, and his grin grew wider and wider. All of them. Right here. The new owners of the properties and the campaign donors—same people!

Mimi was paging through her files, including the stories she wrote during that mayoral campaign. "You knew her husband was her campaign manager, right? Well, now that I'm going through this stuff, I'm seeing where I screwed up royally: he worked in the housing department before he quit to run her campaign."

"Ryerson knows all this stuff, right?" Carolyn asked, and when both her reporters nodded yes, she asked, "So why indict everybody except Her Honor? She's a walking example of malfeasance, misfeasance, and nonfeasance if ever there was one. Surely she's not getting a free pass?"

Mimi shook her head. "Ryerson is isolating her. He left her out on the limb all alone because there's something he doesn't have yet that he wants—"

"The money," Joe and Carolyn said in unison.

Mimi nodded but not in satisfaction. "This is Ryerson patting himself on the back. He probably figures isolating the mayor, making her the fall guy, takes the heat off him and makes him the knight in shining armor, fighting for the good of the people. But if you check those documents Florence Gregory gave us—"

"Those illegally obtained documents," Carolyn said darkly.

"We didn't obtain them illegally," Mimi said, "which means we can use them, and if Ryerson howls, let him. He could and should have done something about all this two years ago, and these documents prove that. Does he really think that because he finally stepped up and did his job the people will reward him with the keys to the city? Yes, it's good that he saved people from losing their homes, but it should never have come to that and Ryerson knows it. And anyway, we're protecting our source."

The three of them sat silently for several long moments, the editor and one reporter contemplating the possible downfall of the mayor and the city attorney, the other reporter realizing with surprise that she felt more sadness than anger. Should she share this with her colleagues who also were her friends? She stood up.

"I have two thoughts to leave with you, my friends. The first is do you ever wonder why people continue to equate stupidity with poverty? The stupid people in this scenario are not the poor people being pushed out of their homes. The other is please don't ever forget that we're in the middle of this story because greed and stupidity left an eighty-four-year-old woman to die a horrible death." She was at the door, halfway out of it, before she turned back. "Here's a story for you, Carolyn—"

"You mean another one?"

"Yeah, okay. Another one: Any idea why the Vice and Sex Squad cops expend so much time and resources entrapping and arresting prostitutes while men buy and sell little girls—and little boys—hourly and with impunity?" And she was out the door ... but she wasn't gone a second before she turned back. "And remember this conversation when our city attorney announces his run for mayor." Then she was gone.

NEW CHARGES FILED
IN MAGA CHURCH CASE:
RYERSON CALLS IT A CULT

By M. Montgomery Patterson and
Joseph J. Zemekis Jr.
Staff Writers

Clemson Jessup, 40, the self-proclaimed pastor of the now defunct MAGA Church and currently in jail on fraud charges, faces a host of new charges, the most serious of which are a murder that is a result of his operation of a criminal organization, and rape and sexual abuse. City Attorney Max Ryerson said all the charges—the new ones and the old ones—are directly tied to his association with a right-wing hate group based in Idaho and which operates locally out of a house in Falls Church, VA. Until his arrest, Jessup lived in that house with at least half a dozen other men, all of whom are currently under arrest and who also face additional charges.

"We believe Jessup headed up operations of this group here in the DC area. At least a dozen young men took orders from him and performed a variety of criminal acts at his behest."

Ryerson said the worst of these acts involves Jessup's routine rape of the wives of the men he controlled. "He owned our husbands, and he said our husbands owned us and they could do whatever they wanted with us. And they wanted to give us to Rev. Jessup," one of the women told investigators.

The woman, whose name is withheld because this newspaper does not print the names of rape victims, also said that the husbands were not allowed to have sexual relations with their wives and that all of the children born to them were fathered by Clemson Jessup. "We are, of course, investigating that claim," Ryerson said. And if it is proven to be true? Ryerson shook his head. "I don't know, to tell you the truth. This is uncharted territory."

The woman also said that Jessup ordered the murder of her husband because he wanted to leave the organization and return home. "He just wanted to have a normal life," she said.

Every inch of space on the long table in Gianna's office was covered. They had learned a lot in just a few days, the most important thing being that Patrick's real legal name was O'Brien, which made it possible to learn that in addition to the Playpen, he also owned a multimillion-dollar townhouse in Georgetown, two mini-mart-type stores on the East Side, and a boat docked at the marina, all of which let them guess at how lucrative a business the rape of young girls was. She pulled the *Warrants* pads closer. On the *Warrants–Persons* pad she wrote Patrick O'Brien a.k.a. Patrick O'Shaunnessey, just beneath the name *Gustavo Ordonez-Gutierrez*. On the *Warrants–Property* pad she listed all of Patrick O'Brien's property, including his bank accounts—the ones they knew about. Alice and Andy would add everything else, but she wanted to be the one to add these names.

Thanks to the original paperwork filed by the original owner of the Playpen when it opened, they knew there were five ways, in addition to the front door, to enter and exit if they remained functional; and Gianna bet that only Patrick knew about them.

Although it was their intention to take Patrick and Gus by surprise, giving them no opportunity to run, all those exits would be covered. Simultaneous raids on their homes would result in the arrests of everyone there, even if they later were released. She reread last night's reports and rewatched last night's video feeds. Then she went out into the squad room to watch the live feeds. She could watch them in her office, but she liked watching with her peeps, and they liked having her do anything with them.

"I was just about to call you, Cap," Vik Patel said, not looking away from his screen, and his intense focus on whatever he was watching galvanized Gianna. She stood beside him but didn't speak. He knew she was there, and he'd speak when he had something to say. She recognized the image as the block the Playpen was on, and Vik was playing with camera angles on the liquor store up the block. No, she realized, he was manipulating the camera angles in the drone. The liquor store was on the corner, and then Vik and the drone turned the corner. Halfway down they turned into an alley that looked barely wide enough to accommodate a vehicle but which opened onto a wide driveway with a loading dock. Two panel vans were parked there. Both looked familiar and Gianna's gut roiled.

"Oh, no," she whispered.

"He's not in there, boss," Vik whispered back.

"Are you sure, Vik?"

"Yes, boss. Those vans just arrived, and one guy got out of each of them and went in, no other people inside. But this is what you need to see," and he switched to another screen showing the front of the liquor store. A car pulled up and parked in the loading zone. A man and a woman got out and went into the store. Gus was the man, and the woman was the *tia* from their house, the one next door to Sgt. Tommi. Gus looked different, but she knew it was him. The *tia* looked same.

"When was this, Vik?"

"About an hour ago."

The car was still parked in the loading zone, but Gianna asked anyway: "They haven't come out?"

223

Vik shook his head and began manipulating camera angles. Gianna walked away a few steps and took out her phone. She punched a button. "Andy, I need you to come back right away. There's something you need to see that I think will mean reworking our plan. Soon."

The call disconnected. Andy hadn't spoken, but he didn't need to. She knew he'd come barreling into the squad room in—she went into her office to check the schedule, to see where he was, to see where Alice was, because he wouldn't leave without telling her. She guessed he'd arrive in fifteen to twenty minutes. She went back to stand near Vik. One of the big front screens showed the loading dock in real time, the two vans still parked there. The other showed the front of the liquor store in real time, the sedan still in the loading zone. Too wired to stand looking at stationary images, she returned to her office to make some notes: *Who were Abuelita and Tia? Get IDs on them NOW. Get arrest warrants.*

Get the warrant to dig up that backyard NOW.

Did anyone live with Patrick O'Brien? FIND OUT.

DMV! Registration of all vehicles—in whose names?

She reread all of the daily and nightly reports to make certain that she'd missed nothing, not even the smallest thing. Andy Page barreled in. She started talking before he could. Then she led him into the squad room and over to Vik, who had images cued up, ready. Andy watched three times, his lips a thin white line in his colorless face.

"We're sure he's not in there?"

Gianna nodded. "Pretty sure. We know he didn't take any girls into the Playpen or the liquor store, and this is the first time we've seen the vans at that loading dock. What we don't know is whether there's a way into the Playpen from an adjacent building." She inhaled deeply before adding, "I think we'd know if new girls were in there because we'd have seen an uptick in ... visitors ... and we haven't. Unless they've got a secret entrance, too, that we don't know about."

Andy was on his phone, speaking in a low, urgent tone. To Alice, Gianna guessed correctly, when he punched off the phone and said that every office and agency of city government that might have diagrams or schematics of the liquor store and loading dock would feel the presence of a Special Intelligence Unit officer in the next few minutes. He touched Vik on the shoulder. "Great work, Vik. You might just have saved this operation for us. I owe you a meal and a beer."

"Thanks, LT. I appreciate it, but what would really be special is if you could get me out of exercise class. The sarge and Det. Gilliam are punishing me. The cruel and unusual kind."

Gianna and Andy walked away laughing, glad for Vik's timely release of the tension that had them wound way too tight. "Funny guy, Vik Patel," Andy said when they were seated in Gianna's office.

"I didn't know how funny," Gianna said, still smiling.

Smile gone. "Everybody on the street in the two-block radius around the Playpen, around the clock, and eyes on every entrance and exit that we know about, around the clock, until we get some intel on the liquor store and the loading dock."

"Starting when?"

"As soon as it gets dark," Gianna said. "And Andy, that car Gus and the *tia* parked in the Loading Zone in front of the liquor store. Had you ever seen it?"

Andy shook his head. "Not even in the parking lot of that place in Maryland where the vans are stored. You don't think he drove those girls up here in that sedan?"

"I don't know what to think, to tell you the truth, Andy. I just know that I'm really sick and tired of Gustavo and the sooner we can put him away, the better."

Andy's phone rang. He did more listening than talking before punching off. "That was Alice. Michelle did not recognize the photos of the *abuelita* and the *tia*, but she did think that Patrick has new girls coming in this week—"

"Why are we just hearing about this?"

"Patrick's been calling . . . and calling. She finally answered, she said, to tell him to stop calling. He said he really needed her, that he'd pay her more money, but he needed to negotiate with Gus what he called the 'fine points' regarding how much the girls would charge. Gus thinks his girls are worth more than Patrick's girls, but Patrick thinks only the age of the girl should determine price. The younger the girl—"

"Goddammit, I've a good mind to shutter that hellhole tonight!"

Andy knew better than to speak, so he waited in silence, watching her think and feel and reach some decisions about their course of action. She walked around to the other side of the desk where she'd been working, grabbed the two *Warrants* pads, and gave them to Andy. "Everything you can think of, Andy, and right now, so I can get them to Commander Davis. Then look at these notes and tell me what I've forgotten or left out or just didn't know about."

He was reading and nodding his head. "The Warrants ones I can do right now. That other list—when we get intel on that liquor store—"

"Sorry I'm taking out my frustration on you, Lieutenant."

"No apology necessary, Captain." He'd never had a superior officer apologize to him, whether he deserved it or not, and he most definitely did not deserve an apology from her right now. This was why he considered her one of the great ones.

"I'm going to make contact with the emergency services people to tell them what we might be looking at—kinda like what we had to deal with at that warehouse with the takedown of the other sex trafficking ring—just without the language barrier. So they'll be ready," Gianna said.

He'd never have thought of that and said as much. "That would be a lot to spring on somebody with no notice."

"I just hope it won't be as bad as the other raid. I hope we get these girls out before too much brutality is done to them." *As if there's an acceptable amount of brutality*, she thought but didn't say.

"They've already suffered too much," Andy said, as if she'd voiced her thought, and took his leave to call Alice to tell her of the new info and the changes.

"Not a problem, Loo," Alice said. "I'll be a presence on those two blocks around the Playpen starting at sundown, and I'll keep you posted."

"Boss, we've got a problem," Alice whispered.

"What kind of problem?" Gianna didn't whisper but because she was out in the squad room, she kept her voice low.

"The Mimi Patterson kind."

"Can you be more specific?"

"She just parked across the street from my location and immediately began taking photos of license plates, including all of ours. And to put your mind at ease, she's driving one of the newspaper vehicles, not your pearl Audi convertible."

Alice thought she heard the captain stifle a laugh, but she couldn't swear to it. "We gotta get her gone," Gianna said. "Go make her a deal, Alice: If she leaves now, she'll get access to everything we get. But she's gotta go. Right now."

"Copy that, boss," Alice said, out of her vehicle in a flash. She crossed the street in front of Mimi's car so she would see her and approached on the passenger side. Mimi unlocked the door. "Good evening, Ms. Patterson," she said, settling herself into the passenger seat.

"Sgt. Long. Fancy meeting you here."

"I think you've got me beat on that one."

"Yeah. Well. What can I say? The job is what it is, as you well know. By the way, you look fabulous. Not that you don't always, but there's . . . something . . ."

"Your Dr. Connors has a lot to do with that. She's amazing."

"She's the best there is. What's the rest of it?"

"Well . . ."

"Oho and aha! By Jove, I think I've got it. Unless my eyesight is failing, that's the look of love."

"Your eyesight is fine."

"That's wonderful, Alice. Congratulations! Anyone I know?"

"Well . . . as a matter of fact . . . yes. Delores Phillips."

Mimi reached over, grabbed Alice, and hugged her tight and as close as one could on the seat of a midsize auto. "How very wonderful, Alice. Congratulations to you both. I'm so happy. Does Gianna know?"

Alice was as stunned by Mimi's reaction as she'd been by Gianna's. They both were truly pleased and happy for her and for Delores. Alice hugged Mimi while looking for words to respond. "Thank you," was all she could manage.

"I want to hear all the details—"

"And you will, but not tonight. You gotta get outta here right now. I'm authorized to offer you total access to whatever we come up with here, but you gotta leave right now."

"This comes from your lieutenant?"

"From my captain."

"In that case, an offer I can't refuse," Mimi drawled, starting the car.

Alice opened the door, then closed it and looked at Mimi. "It means a lot to me that you two can be so happy for us."

"It means a lot to both of us—and I know I can speak for Gianna on this—that two of the people we like most have found each other."

Alice opened the car door, quickly exited, closed the door firmly but quietly, and all but disappeared into the night. Mimi started the car, put it in gear, and moved slowly forward, not turning on her lights until she was a block away. Alice nodded approval and called Gianna, telling her that all was well.

Alice alternated between walking the four blocks and driving them, parking her car at a different location each time, farther and farther away from the Playpen. Her backup was half of Team B and half of Team T, some of them on foot and some in vehicles, and all of them with eyes on her even if she didn't always see all of them. She was relieved at midnight when Bobby Gillian and the second half of his team, along with the second

228

half of Team T, signed on. They would remain until eight o'clock the next morning.

Gianna felt guilty about going to bed, but she had total trust in her team, especially Alice, Bobby, and Tim. She also needed the sleep. She hadn't had much of it lately and she'd hate to have to bench herself. She didn't want to fall asleep before Mimi got home—what the hell was she doing at the Playpen?—but that was a discussion they'd have in the morning, she thought, as she felt herself drift off to sleep.

She was jolted awake at 1:30 by the ringing of Mimi's phone. Though it was on the bedside table practically next to Mimi's ear, she didn't hear it. Waking up in the middle of the night was not a thing Ace Reporter Patterson did well, when she did it at all.

"Mimi, wake up! Your phone is ringing."

"Make it stop," she mumbled. "Turn it off."

It was her work phone so Gianna knew she couldn't do that. She looked at the readout. "Mimi, it's Clara Carruthers—"

That got her attention. She sat up, groggily, and Gianna put the phone next to her ear. "Hello?"

Gianna could hear a woman's voice, obviously upset. Mimi appeared to be listening but since her eyes were closed Gianna wasn't sure. "Mimi? Do you hear her?"

"Clara? Clara, please calm down and say it all again slowly." She put the phone on speaker so Gianna could hear.

Clara took a deep breath. "Okay. It was on the news. You know how they play the eleven o'clock news late at night? Well, there he was talking about he arrested some drug dealer for attacking him but that's a lie, Ms. Patterson! I'm the one who beat him. I told you about that, how I had to beat him off my Carla in in that nasty motel!"

"I remember, Clara, but why was he on the news talking about it—"

"That's what I'm trying to tell you, Ms. Patterson. He's a cop. The one who was raping my baby—he's a cop!" Now Mimi was awake. Gianna had turned on the TV and was scrolling through the channels looking for a news program.

"What's his name, Clara?"

"Boite. Lucas Boite. And I'm sorry for calling so late and disturbing you."

"Not a problem, Clara," Mimi said. "And if I can't find that story tonight I'll see it tomorrow and I'll call you. Will that be all right?"

"That'll be just fine, Ms. Patterson. Thank you."

"How are you and the girls doing, Clara?"

"Oh Ms. Patterson, it's like we're different people."

After the phone call ended Gianna looked closely at the love of her life. "You know I gotta ask how you know about the Playpen."

Mimi told her the story. Almost all of it. She left out Clara's murder of Shalimar Grigsby, but she told her everything else, including the Latino man holding the young girl by the arm. Listening, Gianna was transported back to the beginning of their relationship when it seemed that Mimi was reporting on everything Gianna was investigating. Back then the cop did not trust the reporter, even as she was beginning to love her. How could she trust her? But she had learned that Mimi Patterson's word could be trusted.

"Did you see this Boite?" Gianna asked.

Mimi shook her head. "I wasn't there."

"But you believe her?"

"Absolutely," Mimi replied, adding that she'd met all three girls.

"Three girls. All of them Black, Mimi?" And when Mimi nodded in the affirmative Gianna thought she knew what brand of ugliness was being peddled in the Playpen: Black and brown girls. And she was willing to bet that all the customers would be white men. "I need to meet with Clara, Mimi. She's been inside that place and she can tell us things we can only speculate about. And she may know about . . . other girls."

"I'll ask her, Gianna. In fact," she added, accurately interpreting the look in the hazel eyes, "I'll strongly recommend that she meet with you. Where?"

"Place of her choice, but soon, Mimi."

Mimi sent Clara a text message first thing the next morning asking Clara to call when she could. Her phone rang within the hour, and Mimi wasted no time explaining the reason for the call. Clara wasted no time responding in the negative, adding that she didn't trust one cop to investigate another one.

I wouldn't ask you to talk to Capt. Maglione, Clara, if I didn't trust her.

You really trust her, Ms. Patterson?

With my life.

What do you want me to tell her?

Everything you told me except the part about killing Shalimar Grigsby.

Why shouldn't I tell her that part?

Because she'd have to arrest you for murder.

But she won't arrest me for almost killing a cop?

You were protecting your child from a rapist.

They ended their conversation with Clara surprising Mimi by saying she wanted to meet with Gianna at her office because she wanted to see what it was like. Mimi said she'd pick her up. Clara said thanks, but she'd take a taxi. Mimi, liking the newly assertive Clara, called Gianna and told her when to expect Clara Carruthers. Gianna promised to show her gratitude, and Mimi assured her that she'd be expecting an appropriate show of gratitude.

Gianna was still imagining appropriate displays of gratitude when Andy and Alice knocked and entered, and she filled them in on Clara Carruthers and the story she had to tell them.

"That's major," Andy said. "We could know exactly what we'll be looking at when we breach the front door, instead of guessing."

"I just hope she can deliver that kind of detail. After all, the woman was on a mission to stop her little girl from being raped."

"By a cop," Alice snarled.

"By the time Clara gets here we'll know all there is to know about Mr. Boite." And they knew she'd filled in Commander Davis. Of course she would; an informant had accused a cop of rape. That was a shitload of trouble and you put it on someone

231

else's plate as soon as possible, which is what Davis would do if the allegation against Boite proved to be true: It would become Deputy Chief De Longpre's problem, and given what they'd so far learned of her, she'd be pressing the chief of police to fire his ass, take his pension, and let the city attorney's office throw the book at him. Serve him right.

Gianna asked Andy to make certain all the warrants were in place or in process, and she asked Alice to be present for the Carruthers interview. She believed that this entire investigation would take a major turn before the end of the day, and that Clara held the key. Andy, too, thought they were close, but he also thought there was something they were missing . . . something they'd overlooked . . . something that would rise up and bite them in the ass if they weren't careful. He scrutinized the warrants so carefully that his eyes burned, and he asked Alice to backstop him. If there was something to miss, then they'd both missed it. And if Clara disappointed . . .

But she didn't. Clara Carruthers was everything every cop hoped for in a witness. For starters, she didn't allow her inherent distrust of cops to deter her from sharing with them every detail that she could recall from her visit to the Playpen. Either they'd believe her and help, or they wouldn't, but she'd say her piece. They listened, the captain and the sergeant, until she'd stopped talking, without interrupting even once. Then, the first question came from the sergeant:

"How'd you happen to have a baseball bat, Ms. Carruthers?" she asked.

Clara smiled and explained that Mrs. Burns, her neighbor, took the bat with her everywhere she went. "Part of our neighborhood is kinda okay, but part of it is just terrible, and Mrs. Burns always said if she had to go down, she'd go down swinging."

Alice smiled, too. "A woman after my own heart," she said, adding, "but how did she know you'd need the bat?"

"Because she knew where I was going, and she knew why. Don't forget, she saw that Grigsby woman dragging my little girl by the arm, and she knew where she was taking her. People knew that woman sold her own girls for drug money, so if she'd sell her own . . . anyway, that corner is dangerous, and it's worse since the gambling started."

"Gambling?" asked the captain. "What gambling? Where?"

For the first time Clara was uncertain in her recitation. "Somewhere in that liquor store. This is what I've heard. I don't know for certain 'cause they only let white men in there   "

"How do you know this?" Gianna asked.

"Because some of the Black men who're always around that store for whiskey or drugs, they heard about the gambling and wanted to play but the white man who owns the store told them only white men allowed."

The captain was quiet. Clara could see her thinking. "Do you think Lucas Boite was one of those men?"

Now Clara was shocked. "You know his name. You found out about him. That means you believed me about what he did to my little girl!"

"Of course we believed you, Ms. Carruthers."

Clara's tears started. Her chest heaved and she wept silently for several seconds. Gianna gave her a box of tissues, and she wiped her eyes and blew her nose. "We didn't think you cops believed us. We been telling you for—oh, for a long time now—how our girls been going missing, but nothing happens. The cops tell us the girls are running away but we know better. Somebody is taking our girls. If I hadn't gone to get my Carla, the cops would've told me she had run away from home." Her tears started again, and she missed the look Gianna and Alice exchanged. They both were aware of the missing vs. runaway conflict. What they'd missed was the level and degree of distrust the official reading of the situation created within the communities of those girls.

"We can't speak for all cops, Ms. Carruthers, but we can tell you that we do believe you and that in a matter of a few days, you will see proof of that," Gianna said.

"Can you and the sergeant go check out those places on the East Side, too?"

233

"What places?"

"There are some places girls go missing from. Some stores . . . not big places, just little raggedy places, where they buy cigarettes and beer and condoms and marijuana rolling papers. The girls hang out there because the boys and their drugs hang out there, and then the girls just disappear."

"Where does this happen, Ms. Carruthers?" Gianna asked.

"Over by River Valley Road somewhere—"

She stopped talking at the sound Alice made. She still had the warrant papers Andy had given her to check out and she passed them to Gianna, pointing to properties owned by Patrick O'Brien. On River Valley Road. She was already on her feet, headed for the door and Andy when Gianna stood up.

Clara looked alarmed. "Did I say something wrong?"

"No, Ms. Carruthers, you said something so right, and we feel so stupid for not seeing it until you said it." Gianna took the woman's hand and ushered her out the door when Tommi came in. She introduced the two women and asked Tommi to escort Ms. Carruthers to the elevators and get her a ride home if she wished it. "I can't thank you enough, Ms. Carruthers," Gianna said, and rushed to the two big screens at the front of the room where Alice and Andy watched Kenny and Vik manipulate drone cameras.

"Did we fuck this up, Sarge?" a miserable looking and sounding Andy asked.

"If we did, LT, I'll kick my own ass," Alice said, matching him for misery.

Clara Carruthers stopped walking and stood watching the screens. Then she looked at Tommi. "She's really going to do something about all this, isn't she?"

"Yes, ma'am. You better believe it."

At that moment Vik Patel stood and pumped his fists. Then he hurriedly sat back down, typed on his keyboard, and said to the screen before him, "We've had eyes on all of Patrick O'Brien's properties, including these on River Valley, since we got the list. The video starts here and continues up to the present moment."

"We know where this is. Brace yourself, Patel, because I'm gonna kiss you," Andy said with a whoop, some fist-pumping of his own, and some odd-looking hops.

"Oh God, Loo, no. Please don't." They all needed the laughter to release the tension—and the fear—that had invaded them, fear that O'Brien had transported girls to the Playpen and they'd missed it.

They watched three nights of relative non-activity outside both mini-marts, barely a mile from where a dark-colored cargo van had dumped the body of an eleven-year-old girl less than two weeks ago. The fact that it was freezing did nothing to deter the hanging out and loitering. Then on the fourth night—last night—one of the girls they'd seen before arrived, on foot as usual, holding the hands of two much younger girls. The three of them went inside the store and emerged a short time later, each of the younger girls eating from a bag of chips. The older girl stood a little apart from them looking toward the road as if waiting for someone. And she was. A black panel van pulled into the parking lot, stopping away from the store and the people, and the girl walked toward it. She talked to the driver for a moment, and then, with a cup in each hand, she walked back to the younger girls and gave each of them one of the cups.

"No!" Alice said. "Goddammit no. Boss, we gotta take him now!"

Gianna grabbed Alice's arm and pulled her in close, kept her close, as they watched the two little girls go limp while the man driving the van picked them both up, one in each arm, and put them in the back. He gave the older girl a wad of bills, which she carefully counted. Then she walked around to the passenger side and got in. The man got back into the van and drove away. But he didn't go far. Just to the parking lot of the next mini-mart, the other one owned by O'Brien, where they watched the exact same scenario play out. Gianna kept holding Alice, who was shaking, either from rage or because she was weeping. Gianna didn't know and she didn't look to see.

235

Both Vik and Kenny tightened their angles on the van. As soon as the license plate was visible Andy wrote it down and ran for his desk. The face shots of the men were iffy, at best. The faces of the older girls, the ones who were paid for delivering the younger girls, weren't much better. All were dark and grainy because there were no streetlights or any other light to help. Gianna knew that her techs wouldn't let that van out of their sight, but it was out of theirs in a few seconds. Even the taillights disappeared into the frigid darkness. Alice sighed deeply and slumped, and Gianna released her, but she didn't move away.

Andy returned and stood with them. They'd know all there was to know about the black van and its owner very soon. One thing they did know, though. Whoever he was he had four drugged little girls in the back of that van and two older, apparently willing and complicit girls, and if they didn't rescue them very soon, no matter how long they continued to draw breath, their spirits would be dead.

CHAPTER ELEVEN

The drones followed the black panel van to the loading dock behind the liquor store where the driver got out, and where they were able to get a decent photograph of him. While they waited for a result, they put the final touches on their takedown plan. Gianna, Andy, and Alice agreed that if Patrick's girls were about to be in play, Gustavo wouldn't be far behind. If he wasn't already in town, he soon would be. Their biggest decision: when to raid the Playpen and make arrests.

"When we see men—customers, clients, whatever they call themselves—going in," Andy said.

"How many do we need to see?" Alice asked.

"I'd like to arrest more than one or two of them," Gianna said.

"Which means allowing several—or all—of the girls to get raped," Alice responded.

Heavy silence before Gianna replied, "Yes, maybe." She let the silence hang before she continued. "I keep thinking about why that van parked at that loading dock, and I keep thinking there's a good reason for that . . ."

"You think the girls go in there, and then through the liquor store somehow," Andy said, "and then into the Playpen."

"But we never got any plans or schematics from the city on that liquor store or the loading dock," Alice said.

"Then I expect Gus to show up at the loading dock any time now with a van-load of girls. And if all those girls go in through there, then we'll own that dock just like we'll own the front door of the Playpen," Gianna said.

"Visible presence, boss?" Andy asked.

Gianna shook her head. "Not until we're ready to make arrests. It's possible that some of the . . . men . . . use that back entrance, too. And by the way: Why haven't we heard anything about Lucas Boite? If he's one of the men who frequent that place, I want to know about it, and whether other cops are involved, too."

"Yeah," Alice said, "it would take more than one cop looking the other way for that place to stay in business as long as it has. And when you consider the other crime in the area—that liquor store is a crime magnet."

"Andy?" Gianna said.

"I put in the request for info on Boite—"

"Do I need to call the commander?"

Andy shook his head back and forth. "No, ma'am. I'll call him again. Right now." He had his phone in his hand. "The guy has always given us everything we've asked for, and done it quickly. I don't want to send Davis crawling up his ass if it isn't necessary."

Gianna nodded. She understood protecting a source, and she respected Andy for wanting to protect his. However . . . "I also want last quarter's crime stats for the area."

"You got it," he said, hustling away.

Gianna let it all out. "I want to get them all, Alice, the men and the women, because I want those two women who help Gus, and I want those two girls who helped drug those little ones. I want their parents, goddammit! I want the owner of that liquor store, of that loading dock, the drivers of the vans who deliver the girls. I want all of them, Alice, facing so many charges it'll take their lawyers a week to read 'em all."

"I know, boss."

Andy was galloping back to them. "Boite is dirty, boss. That's what was taking so long. My guy had to do a tiptoe through the tulips to get the info without tipping off Internal Affairs. But I don't think they know about his, ah, proclivities. Is that the right word? They know he's been fudging his monthly crime reports. Seems he didn't report a homicide, and they already know he's lying about how he got beat up. They know a drug dealer didn't do it. And head knockers and rollers are really pissed off about that little media thing he did, the one Ms. Carruthers saw on TV."

"Well, good thing he's a fool, too; otherwise we wouldn't know anything about him. The crime stats?"

"Should be in your email, boss."

"Thanks, Andy . . . what homicide didn't he report?"

Andy shrugged. "I don't know all the details, but a woman was beat to death over there somewhere—a junkie hooker—and Boite didn't want it to go against him." The woman Clara Carruthers beat with a baseball bat. All the pieces, one by one, clicked into place.

Gianna left them watching the screens, watching and waiting for Gus and his girls. Watching the loading dock, watching his house. Watching the sun come up. "Do you think he's close?" Andy asked.

Alice nodded. "I agree with the captain. If Patrick has girls ready to go to work, Gus doesn't want to miss out. Or lose out. This is all about money, don't forget."

"Then what's taking him so long? What's he doing?"

"Branding them would be my guess," Alice said.

"Oh fuck me and damn him straight to hell," Andy said, hands balling into fists.

"You guys!" Kenny called out, and they hurried to stand beside him. Like Vik, he didn't look at them. He kept his eyes on his keyboard. Andy and Alice glued their eyes to the screens. Two sedans entered the loading dock parking lot. Patrick got out of one of them, and Gus got out of the other, the same one he'd parked in the loading zone in front of the liquor store. This time, however, he was alone. Patrick went to speak to the driver of the van that had his girls. Gus looked at his watch. Waiting for his van?

"Guys?" This time Vik summoned them, and he was so fidgety they knew what he had was good. "Look!" And he put the image from the drone up on one of the big screens. The *abuelita* and the *tia* with two Black women were heading for the back door of the Playpen. Andy called Gianna, loudly, because neither he nor Alice wanted to leave the screen. She came at a run.

"Tell me we're in play." They told her everything, and Vik replayed the image of the four women entering the building from the rear. "Where did they come from?"

Vik reversed the feed on his screen and backtracked the four women to their arrival six minutes earlier. One of the Black women drove one of the small SUVs, and she'd parked directly beneath one of the few operable streetlights on the block. Vik aimed the camera at the license plate, then at each woman's face. Andy was ready and writing, and this time he made the call where he stood. "I need a plate, please, and if it comes back to a Black woman, I need her DL info and photo. And I'll wait, if you don't mind."

"How much is this costing you, LT?" Alice asked.

Andy groaned. "You don't want to know."

"But I do," Gianna said, "so I can get you reimbursed." She well knew that it could take days, if not weeks, to obtain this kind of information. Andy had been getting crucial info almost immediately, which meant that his source was hopscotching over other cops who were waiting for much needed info to help Andy, at great personal risk to him or herself. Definitely an expensive proposition, and Gianna would get him repaid.

His phone beeped, and Andy gave a satisfied grin as he forwarded the info to Gianna and Alice. "Somebody give me a pad and pen, please."

Hands produced the requested items and she began writing, talking as she did, as much to herself as to Alice and Andy:

"Six women to be arrested—four adults and two teens

"Four men—Patrick, Gus, liquor store owner, loading dock personnel.

"All the johns in the Playpen.

240

"Other men—van drivers if they're still on the premises (if not, the next day).

"Anyone inside the Playpen (except the victims) at the time of the raid.

"Is that everybody?" she asked.

"What about the two who buried Lina, Carmen, and the other girl?" Alice asked.

"You think they're the van drivers?" Andy asked.

Gianna was writing furiously. "We have decent photos of the van drivers, yes?" And when Andy nodded, "Decent enough to compare to the gravediggers?" Andy didn't know but said he'd find out. "Good save, Alice—thanks for plugging what could have been a huge hole in our case."

They moved to her office to discuss the next matter: "Okay, deployment of personnel and munitions." It was a lengthy discussion and she'd need the approval from Commander Davis for some of what she wanted to do, but she fully expected that he'd back her, so they planned as if they already had his okay. They'd use their own people for the major arrests, and personnel from the transport trucks for anything else. Four major areas: front door, back door, the liquor store front door, and the loading dock.

"Force as necessary?" Alice asked, and Gianna nodded, then added, "But we protect those little girls. Let's make sure nobody tries to use one of them as a shield, which means we take down the major players hard and fast. Also, let's separate them: Keep Gus and Patrick separated; the *tia* and the *abuelita*; the two Black women; the two big girls. And don't let any of these people talk to each other. We'll have our own in each of the transport vehicles and make sure they don't." They went over it again and again, punching holes in the plan, patching the holes, then punching more, until they were too tired to keep it up.

"Captain!"

They were on their feet, out the door, and across the room in an instant, and they didn't need a briefing. They could see what was happening: A van pulled into the loading dock, and the *tia* and the *abuelita* came out to meet it. Gus's girls, and they all had

241

to be carried into the building. The two male van drivers carried two girls each, one under each arm, as if they were bags of rice or cornmeal, and the women carried one girl each. Six of them, appearing to be between ten and fourteen. Andy exhaled heavily, and Alice stopped breathing. Gianna kept her eyes on the loading dock door. After several minutes—perhaps long enough to take the girls through the liquor store into the Playpen—the two men exited, climbed into the van, backed up and headed out into the alleyway.

Gianna had already activated her comm. "Take 'em down, separate 'em, take their phones, wallets, and keys, and have the van hauled to the impound lot."

"Yes, ma'am," she heard. "And you want the men to Central Lockup?"

"Yes, but keep them separated. And that's an order, not a request."

"Yes, ma'am."

Then the two Black women, the van driver, and the two older girls took the four younger girls inside. They were gone longer than Gus's drivers—at least half an hour—which was good because that allowed time for the takedown in the alleyway and the removal of the van.

"How much time do you think we have?" Andy asked.

"I think until sometime tomorrow," Gianna replied. "They've got to get the girls settled, acclimated to the environment, maybe fed—I hope fed—and maybe rested."

"They don't give a damn about those girls," Alice snarled. "Fed and rested? I doubt it. Maybe drugged again so they don't resist what's about to happen to them."

Gianna and Andy stayed silent. Then Gianna said, "We'll be ready when we need to be. Deploy personnel, Andy; then you and Alice take your positions. And take the long guns."

They took them but they didn't need them. The blinking and flashing neon lights of the Playpen went on at seven the following morning. Men entered the front door almost immediately, as if they'd been waiting, and through the front door of the liquor store and through the loading dock door. Gianna gave the takedown order, and nothing happened for several long seconds. Commander Davis watched with her, and neither of them spoke. Then men began scurrying like roaches when the light is turned on— out of the front door of the Playpen, out of the liquor store and the loading dock, half of them naked or nearly so. And cops were waiting for them as the transport trucks rolled up. The naked ones had no phones, keys or wallets to confiscate, so they were hand-cuffed and helped, not gently, into the transports, but they were almost docile in their compliance. No one fought or attempted to escape.

"You sons of bitches!" Davis exclaimed, striding closer to the big screens for a better look at the naked men. "Those two are cops—you sons of bitches."

"Would one of them be named Boite?" Gianna asked innocently.

"It would. You know him?"

She shook her head. "Just heard some things but no solid evidence. Until now."

The four women were met at the back door but unlike the men, they did not go gently. They screamed and cursed and kicked but calmed down when Annie Anderson coldcocked one of them, then left her on the ground moaning and bleeding while she handcuffed the other woman. Gus's women became quietly defiant, as if they expected to be rescued soon—no worries.

Gus came barreling out the front door of the liquor store and skidded to a halt when he saw the transport trucks. He turned and raced back inside, but a bunch of cops were waiting for him at the door of the loading dock. He released a stream of Spanish, which everyone assumed was profanity and which everyone ignored as they took his wallet, two phones, keys, and a huge wad of cash. Then he made the mistake of spitting on Bobby Gilliam, and it took three people to help him to his feet. When he was upright Bobby leaned in and spoke to him, punched him in the nuts, then backed away and yelled, "Feo piece of caca!"

"What did he say?" Commander Davis asked Gianna.

Gianna controlled the grin that wanted to break free. "He called him an ugly piece of shit."

"I want to know what he said before that," Davis said. "Somebody?"

Silence on the comms, a long one. Then Tim McCreedy answered. "He said 'that was for Alice.'"

The liquor store owner and another man who refused to identify himself were in cuffs and the store was padlocked. Everybody was accounted for—except Patrick O'Brien. Alice led the team inside. Every inch of the Playpen was searched and cleared but there was no sign of him. Social Services and paramedics were sent in to tend to the girls, but Alice's hackles were up. She was certain that they hadn't overlooked O'Brien inside the building, and she had a tight feeling in her gut about him. She focused her attention on the girls. As much as she didn't want to look at them, see them, she had to know if they were all right.

"Drugged," a paramedic told her. "And raped, of course, but they're all alive. At least they were when they left here."

"Maybe if they're lucky they won't survive."

The paramedic gave her a hard look. "Really, officer?"

"It's sergeant and yes, really. What these girls—these children—endure day and night has got to be worse than being dead. At least you can't die but once—" Alice stopped midsentence when she spied one of the girls who'd sold the two younger ones to Patrick's lackeys. She was sitting on a bed waiting to be examined by a paramedic. "You! On your feet, hands behind your back." She walked over to stand in front of the girl. She was heavily made up and wore a skimpy negligee, but Alice recognized her. "I said, *get up.*"

The terrified girl rose on shaky legs. "What did I do? Under arrest for what?"

"Sex trafficking, endangering a minor, prostitution, pimping—"

"No, I didn't do none of that! Who told you those lies?"

"We've got video of you selling two little girls in the minimart parking lot on River Valley Road—"

"I didn't sell them!"

"You brought them to that parking lot and you took money. We saw you."

The girl was shaking so hard she could barely speak. "I was doing what somebody told me to do. She told me to bring the girls and to get the money and that's what I did. That's all I did, and I gave her that money. I didn't keep not one dollar!"

The girl was telling the truth; Alice was certain of that. "What's your name and how old are you?" Alice let the girl sit down so she'd stop shaking. She asked the medic if the girl could have something to drink, and after polishing off a bottle of orange juice in what seemed like a single gulp, the girl was able to speak coherently: Her name was Patty Thomas—Patricia—and she was fourteen. "Where did you get that money, Patty, and who did you give it to?"

"I got it from a man who calls hisself 'Transformer'—people call him Cartoon behind his back—and I give it to Roberta. I don't know her last name. She works for Mr. Patrick. He's the one bought them little girls, and I give her the money soon as she got here."

"Don't we know those names, boss?" Alice asked.

"Indeed we do," Gianna said quietly, as another piece clicked into place: Cartoon, named by Ronald George as the man who told him to carve an arrow into the leg of a twelve-year-old girl. Transformer. *Gotcha, you piece of shit.*

Alice kept talking to Patty, hoping to make it sound and feel like conversation and not like the interrogation it was. "Do you know how long Roberta has worked for Patrick?"

"Longer'n me," she said. "Can I have some more juice?" Alice nodded at the paramedic who was standing close and the juice was produced. Patty drank it slower this time, but she drank all of it again. That was hunger. This girl was hungry.

"So you've worked in this place for a long time?" Alice asked.

Patty shook her head. "No, ma'am. This my first time here in this place. I was working for him at that house in Georgetown, me and some other girls."

"When was this, Patty?"

"I started when I was eleven and stopped this year when he said I was too old. He got some more younger girls for 'cross town, and he said us older girls have to come here."

"But those little girls we saw you with—"

"He have some of us over there 'cross town for his special friends, and he have some of us over here for whoever want to come."

Alice stood and walked a little away from Patty and the paramedic. "Are you hearing this, boss?"

"We are, Alice. I'm here with Commander Davis. Is she saying, Alice, that we've got our very own Jeffrey Epstein?"

"That's what it sounds like to me. What should I do with her?"

"Give me a few minutes, Alice, but I think you can uncuff her."

"Yes, boss." And she apologized as she uncuffed Patty. "I thought you were one of them, Patty. I'm sorry I frightened you so much. Are you all right now?"

"Yes, ma'am," Patty said, then asked, "You sure you a cop?"

"Positive," Alice said laughing. "Are you hungry?"

"Yes, ma'am." She looked at the paramedic for the okay to give the girl some food, and the paramedic shrugged an okay.

"All right. I'm going outside to see what my people have to eat."

Patty grabbed her hand and pulled her down to whisper in her ear. "He on the roof," she whispered.

"I'm sorry? What?"

"Mr. Patrick. He on the roof. That's why y'all cain't find him. He up on the roof."

Alice straightened so quickly she knocked the girl over. She pulled her up and asked how he could get to the roof. Patty explained that a closet in one of the hallways had pulldown steps to the attic and the roof. Cursing under her breath and phone in hand she ran out the front door of the Playpen, phone in hand. "Captain."

"I heard. Do you know where this closet is?"

"Patty told me. Boss . . . do we have access to a dog?"

"A dog! What are you—"

"I'm thinking if Patrick hears some snapping and snarling and growling, he'll come down sooner rather than later. I, for one, am in no mood to make nice with him."

"Nobody is, Alice, and yes, there's a dog but we haven't needed it. Yet. I'll take care of it. But Alice, I need you calm."

She took a deep breath. "Yes, Captain. I'm in control, I swear." No response to that so she asked, "Do we have any food I can take to Patty?"

"I'll have someone take her something. You stay put. I think you should be the one to see Mr. O'Brien's descent into reality," and she cut the call.

Alice shut off her phone and looked up to find Andy looking at her. "All right, Sarge?"

"Fuck no, Andy. That bastard started raping that child when she was eleven—"

"I know, Allie, I heard," he said gently, and she knew he was remembering how she was, the morning she discovered three little girls buried in a half-assed grave in Rock Creek Park. "So, let's make sure we get him safely off that roof and safely into custody and safely into prison where the inmates will enjoy and appreciate his presence. And we'll do a much better job of watching his ass than they did up in New York with that Epstein freak. There will be no quick and easy out for Mr. O'Brien in this jurisdiction."

Just then a K-9 officer and the largest German shepherd Alice had ever seen came their way. "Do you know where we're going and what we're doing?" the officer asked.

Alice nodded. "Does your partner bark and growl and snap and snarl on command?" She got a walleyed look as an answer, so she explained that the perp was on a ladder to the roof and they wanted him to keep climbing, to have a good reason to keep climbing, and then to descend to the ground.

"Oh," the K-9 cop said, "Bella and I can do that, no problem."

"She definitely is a beauty," Alice said, and she and Andy watched man and dog enter the Playpen. Then they backed up to the sidewalk, so they'd have a clear view of the roof when

247

Patrick O'Brien made his appearance. And it didn't take long. He had a backpack slung over each shoulder, and even at a distance they could see the wild look in his eyes. He planted himself in the middle of the roof looking at all the cops waiting to end his life as he knew it. Then he looked behind him. Alice was pretty sure that Bella wasn't on the roof, but she also was pretty sure that Patrick had no plans to backtrack to see if she was still behind him.

"Come down from there, O'Brien!" Andy called out.

"How'm I supposed to get down?" he whined.

"Jump," several people called out.

Alice walked over close to the building. The front was covered by thin ivy and some other dense foliage, most of it weeds. She pulled at it and enough of it parted that she could see lattice work. She told him about it and suggested he use it to climb down.

"As old as that wood is? It'll disintegrate before I'm halfway down!"

"I'll bet Bella will help you decide. She's 150 pounds of 100 percent pure German shepherd waiting for you on the ladder."

O'Brien crept to the edge of the roof holding a backpack in each hand. What to do with them? He clearly wasn't an athletic guy so wearing them while he climbed down wasn't a real consideration. "Leave them up there while you climb down, O'Brien, or throw them down. Either way they're ours," Andy called out.

"Make a decision and do it quick, asshole," Alice snarled. "It's too cold to stand here playing with you."

As if reality finally gave him a head butt, he threw the backpacks down and looked ready to cry when the cops pounced on them. Then he turned and extended a foot over the edge, seeking the lattice. He found purchase and, grasping the edge of the roof, he lowered the other leg. Then he was on the quasi-ladder and began his slow, cautious descent. He made it halfway before the wood splintered and he crashed the rest of the way down. But he landed in bushes and overgrowth, so he wasn't injured. Maybe he was thinking that it was a good thing he didn't bother to take better care of his property, because he just lay there looking up at the dozen cops who were looking down at him. Then hands reached for him, hauled him up, pulled his hands behind his back, and cuffed him. He was read his rights but did not respond when asked whether he understood them.

"I asked you a question," Tim McCreedy said almost politely.

"Yes," O'Brien whispered.

"Yes what?"

"Yes, I understand my rights."

"Good. Now understand this: We have warrants to search this property, your house in Georgetown, your boat, both the stores on River Valley Road, all your vehicles. We have warrants to access your bank accounts—"

O'Brien started screaming and cursing, then howling and then crying. He kept trying to free his hands wanting, no doubt, to hit someone, but that wasn't happening, so he did what seemed the next best thing: He kicked Tim. Big mistake, almost as big as the one his partner made spitting on Bobby. O'Brien was aiming a second kick when Tim grabbed the leg and pulled up. O'Brien went down. Hard. And showed no willingness to get up. The cops had to help him. Had to all but carry him to the transport vehicle after they relieved him of his wallet, watch, three phones, keys, and two USB flash drives. "Can't wait to see what's on these," Andy said as they were dropped into a plastic bag. "And yes, we have warrants for computers and computer equipment. And recording equipment." O'Brien didn't bother to respond. He just went limp.

Alice's phone rang. "Captain?"

"Do you have the strength to hang in there a little while longer until the crime techs arrive and the girls are transported?"

"Of course."

"Thanks, Alice. For everything. Again." Gianna rang off and Alice told Andy what was happening. Then she went to check on Patty and found the girl curled up in a ball, fast asleep.

"She ate the food you sent in. Then her eyes closed, and she went out like a light," the paramedic said.

Alice looked down at her with a mixture of sadness and relief. Maybe her nightmare was over, but the road to wellness would be long and treacherous. "And the others? How are they?"

"Three transported to the hospital in guarded condition, and the others, once they come out of the drugs, may be able to be moved."

"To where?"

The paramedic looked around, then pointed. "She can tell you. She's the Social Services rep in charge. Name's Catherine something."

Catherine heard her name and walked toward them. She looked at Alice and gave a tired smile. "You must be Patty's police officer."

Alice nodded through her own tired smile and introduced herself. "Do you have a placement for her and for the others?"

Catherine nodded. "Thankfully, yes."

"Can you tell me where Patty's going and tell her I'll see her in a few days—"

Catherine frowned and shook her head. "You need to tell her yourself. If she wakes and you're gone, she'll think you've abandoned her. Please don't do that. She trusts you, and that's major for a child who's been through what she has." Alice nodded her understanding and reached down to touch Patty awake. Catherine grabbed her arm. "And don't touch her, Sergeant. When these girls are grabbed or shaken awake—"

Oh dear God. And this girl had lived like this since she was eleven. Once again Alice indicated she understood, and she leaned down. "Patty. Patty," she said in a calm tone. "It's me, Patty, Sgt. Long."

The girl's fear-filled eyes shot open and she jerked up to a sitting position. Then she immediately calmed. No need for fear. "You came back. Did you get him?"

"Yes I did, and yes we did, Patty, thanks to you."

"Is he going to jail?"

"For the rest of his ugly life. And you're going to a place where you'll be safe."

Patty looked deep and hard into her eyes. Then she looked at Catherine. "Can I have my own bed, by myself, nobody in it with me?"

"That's a promise, Patty."

"And I'll come to visit you tomorrow and you can show me your bed."

"How'll you know where to find me, Sergeant Alice?"

"Because Catherine is going to tell me," and she took her notebook and pen from a pocket. She turned to face Catherine who recited an address which Alice wrote down. Then she gave both Patty and Catherine cards, and she looked at Patty. "That's my phone number. You call me if anything is wrong, Patty, okay?"

Patty whispered, "okay" back and Alice took her leave.

DC Police Shut Down Sex Hotel
Sex Traffickers Arrested as Dozen
Young Sex Slaves Freed

By Joseph J. Zemekis Jr.
Staff Writer

Officers of the Special Intelligence Mobile and Tactical Unit of the Metropolitan Police Department staged an early morning raid at the Playpen, a former motel on Eighth Avenue, and arrested nine men, including two police officers, and charged them with a wide array of sex crimes. The Playpen is known to be a place where men can freely buy sex with underage girls, almost always against their will. Two of those arrested, Patrick O'Brien and Gustavo Ordonez-Gutierrez, managed the operation. O'Brien owns the Playpen and Ordinez-Gutierrez, a Guatemalan national, also was charged with transporting minors across the border for purposes of prostitution. Commander Eddie Davis, head of the Intelligence Unit, said

Ordonez-Gutierrez will face federal sex trafficking charges in addition to the half dozen charges DC will file against him. "But our charges will take precedence," he said. City Attorney Neil Ryerson confirmed that. "These crimes occurred in our jurisdiction and we will prosecute them to the full extent of the law." When asked if Ordonez-Gutierrez's crime didn't begin the moment he crossed the border into the United States transporting five underage girls, Ryerson replied, "Perhaps if federal officials were more focused on the huge problem of sex trafficking instead of stealing children from their parents at the border, they'd have arrested Ordonez-Gutierrez before we did."

Also arrested at the Playpen were Lidia Ramirez, Maria Guerrerro, Roberta Robinson, and Tyra Smith who monitored and managed the girls, "preparing them for their sessions with the customers," one of the women told police. They will face the same charges as the men, and two of them, both Guatemalan nationals, will also face trafficking charges.

No one could say exactly how long the Playpen had been operating. Best guesses ranged from three to five years. When asked how such an operation, especially one victimizing young girls, some little more than children, could go undetected by police for so long when police were customers, Davis replied, "That may be your answer." He added that a full investigation into the matter already was underway under the direction of the Chief of Police.

We have also learned that Patrick O'Brien ran a separate operation from his Georgetown townhouse involving girls as young as eleven and available to "special" friends. While all the girls at the Playpen were African-American or Latina, all the girls at the Georgetown location were white or Asian,

252

usually Thai, according to a woman there who identified herself as O'Brien's housekeeper. According to police, she has agreed to cooperate in exchange for a reduction in the number of charges she faces. However City Attorney Ryerson said he has "made no such commitment to this woman."

All of the young girls were removed from both locations. Several remain hospitalized in "guarded" condition while the majority are in the custody of the Department of Social Services and housed in group homes. Authorities acknowledge that identifying all the girls will prove difficult, especially those brought into the US by Ordonez-Gutierrez. "We don't know where or how he gained access to those children," Intelligence Commander Davis said, "and he's not telling us. None of them speak English so we have interpreters standing by to question them when the doctors give us permission." As for the African-American girls? "We're assuming they're all English speakers," Davis said, "but we don't know for certain how or where O'Brien got them as he's not talking, either."

All of those arrested are being held without bond until a status hearing is set.

Fate of Young Sexual Assault Victims: Uncertain to Dire, Say Professionals Who Treat Them

By M. Montgomery Patterson
Staff Writer

"Some of them may never recover—mentally or physically."

That's the assessment from a therapist who treats the young victims of sexual abuse. "When

253

that kind of trauma—and I use the word torture, because that's what it is—begins as early as age 10 or 11, truthfully I have no tools with which to help them."

The three therapists interviewed for this article agreed to talk on the condition that they not be identified, not because they fear for themselves, but because it may be possible to identify the victims through them, and they are committed to safeguarding their identities because many change their names once they've escaped sexual slavery. I have met and talked with five such young women.

Girls, really. The oldest is 15. All were victims of the two men just arrested and charged with running the sexual slavery operation at the Playpen on Eighth Avenue.

The first three I'll call X, Y, and Z.

X and Y were sold to Patrick O'Brien when they were 11, sold by their mother who was a drug addict and prostitute who used the money to feed her habit. The girls are now 12 and 15 and have been adopted by a woman whose own daughter was kidnapped and sold to O'Brien. This woman, called Mama by all three girls, found out where her daughter was and broke into the Playpen wielding a baseball bat and rescued her daughter, Z, who also was 11 at the time and good friends with Y. Both younger girls remain severely traumatized. They're just beginning to talk again, but neither girl sleeps through the night without being jerked awake by nightmares.

Mrs. M keeps close watch on her three girls. She's really worried that the two younger ones are largely nonverbal, and that the older girl wants so much to put the ugly past behind her that she sometimes denies that it ever happened. She'll talk about it to her therapist if prodded, and she talked to this reporter about her ordeal. But only once.

Since that one time, she has refused to discuss the matter, preferring instead to talk about finishing high school and going to college and moving away from DC. She's adamant on that point: One day, she will get far away from her hometown. She's blocked the memory of Patrick O'Brien. But what Mrs. M is always alert for is any sign that one of her girls may be suicidal. "I'm so afraid that I'll miss something, that I'll fail one of them. But not even the doctors can tell me exactly what to look for because they don't really know." The three therapists interviewed for this story confirmed that. "This is uncharted territory," said one.

"Yes, we're seeing more and more children—girls and boys—who have endured this kind of trauma, but there really are no studies of the long-term effects," said another. "We're relying on information about children of war zones. That's the closest experience to sexual trauma."

The "two Marias," as they refer to themselves, share a similar experience with X, Y, and Z—up to a point. They were sold to Gustavo Ordonez-Gutierrez when they were 10 or 11—they're not sure which—and they lived in Guatemala and Mexico, in tiny, dusty border towns where people moved easily and freely between the two countries. Ordonez-Gutierrez brought them to the US in the back of a panel van, beneath the floorboards, to his house in DC. Along with three other girls, they worked out of this house until several weeks ago when the three girls disappeared.

"We thought Gus killed them 'cause he always

255

said he'd kill us if we crossed him," said Maria No. 1, "and they always crossed him 'cause they hated him."

"And they told him how they crossed him," said Maria No. 2, "which really made him mad. They were born here in the US and they had parents until Gus came to their house; then the parents disappeared, too."

Questions about the disappearance of the parents of three girls who also disappeared brought shrugs, downcast eyes, annoyance, and finally hostility, silence, and a threat to end the interview even though they hadn't finished their meal at what they said was their favorite restaurant.

The girls insisted on being called Maria No. 1 and Maria No. 2 because "All gringos think we're all named Maria and Jose, so call us Maria." This was the second conversation with them. The first occurred several weeks ago, when Gus was in Guatemala or Mexico finding new girls to bring to DC to replace the ones who went missing. They were left in the care of women Gus called *abuelita* and *tia*—grandmother and aunt—even though the Marias insisted he was not related to them. They told the girls to "go earn money." They soon realized the older women had no understanding of American money, so the Marias converted their earnings to one-dollar bills and turned over less than half, and before Gus returned they took the money and ran. This is what separates the Marias from X, Y and Z: They escaped.

They laughed hysterically at the news that Gus and the two women were arrested and wished them lifelong incarceration. Then they wept. "We're really free now," Maria No. 1 said. "We can stop living in squats and get a real apartment."

"None of your business," snapped Maria No. 2 when asked about the dangerous living conditions in a squat.

"Gus and all those men were dangerous. The squat is home and the people who live there— they're our family."

"We don't want to talk to you no more," Maria No. 1 said, and they held each other and wept again.

The Marias have never received counseling and said they'd refuse it if it were offered. They said they didn't need or want to talk about their experience—another thing they shared with X, Y and Z. But unlike them, the Marias had no desire to go home. There was no one in "that other place down there" who wanted them, no one to call Mama. "They're the ones sold us to Gus."

"They seem to be coping so far," one of the therapists said, "but there's no way to predict how they'll do long term. The only thing I can tell you for certain is that they are every bit as damaged as the other girls."

"We don't need no head doctor," Maria No. 2 said, "but we need another kind. Can you get us one who can get that mark off?"

Gus branded his girls with a *G* and a $ on their buttocks.

The Deputy Chief and the Commander were reading Mimi's story when Gianna entered the office. They looked up at her briefly before returning to the story. Gianna sat down and waited for them to finish. She fully understood. She'd had the same reaction to the story when she read it for the first time seated across the breakfast table with the reporter. She had read the story a second time, then took the reporter back to bed and kept her there so long they both were slightly late for work. The bosses finished their reading, but before either could speak, Commander Davis's adjutant knocked softly, opened the door, and told him the city attorney was there. Davis nodded and Max Ryerson stepped in.

"I'll start at the top," he said sounding officious. "You are to be commended, Deputy Chief, for a job very well done."

"I did absolutely nothing, Mr. Ryerson, except stay out of the way of the people who did the heavy lifting," Ellen De Longpre said, pointing at Davis and Gianna and heading for the door. "I wish the department had a hundred more of them." And with that she left.

Ryerson continued as if he hadn't been interrupted. "Commander, Captain, you have my gratitude for making my job easier than it has been in a very long time. All I had to do to indict was follow your warrants. A superior performance."

"Thanks, Ryerson. Glad to be of service," Davis said.

"I'll share one bit of information with you, if I may, something no one else will know for at least a couple of weeks. I'll be tying Mr. O'Brien to the housing fraud scheme. He and an investment partner bought those River Valley Road properties for the mayor's son-in-law and would have profited handsomely had housing been built there. That investment partner: one Richard Connelly. Uncle of your Randall." Another question answered, another loose end tied up.

Gianna cleared her throat and they all looked at her. "We recovered recording equipment and devices at the Playpen, the Georgetown residence, and the boat. We'll be cataloging it soon."

Ryerson smiled broadly. "So, I expect you'll let me know if I'll be filing additional charges against . . . anyone. And perhaps this knowledge will induce the mayor to be . . . more cooperative," he said, and left after shaking everyone's hand again.

Gianna prepared to leave, too. "I get final clearance from my doctor today," she said, one hand on the doorknob. But her boss wasn't ready to let her go yet.

"Are you all right, Anna? This was a horrifying case, and coming so soon after that other operation you took down . . . I can see that the leg is back to 100 percent. But how about your—"

"Thanks for your concern, and yes, the shrink has cleared me, too."

He had more than her health on his mind. "Do you understand, Anna . . . can you understand . . . how do people do this kind of thing to their own children? That Roberta woman, she was selling children that could have been her own daughters or granddaughters. And Ordonez-Gutierrez . . . how do they do it? How do they justify it?"

She'd had this conversation with Mimi and with Beverly more than once as the case progressed, as the facts emerged. How does a grown man have sex with a child? How do people victimize their own? She was hoping for answers that would make it easier to do her job. She didn't get them. "I've had the same questions, Commander, and I didn't like the answers and I don't think you will either: It's not a new phenomenon, either thing, and it's not likely to stop any time soon. And if you're looking for logic . . ." She shrugged.

"Well, that doesn't make me want to rush to work in the morning."

"Me either."

He sighed. "I suppose I'll take the good news where I can find it, and I'm very glad for your health and healing. On both counts. I don't mind telling you I was more than a little nervous," he said.

"Well, I do mind having to tell you that I was, too," she said, saluting him and taking her leave. While it was true that she was going to the doctor, her most important stop was at the home of Margie and Richard Baker, Mimi's former neighbors who'd saved her life that day she was shot and lay bleeding to death in the middle of the street. Retirees both—a nurse and a Marine master sergeant—they wrapped a belt around her leg and packed the wound, preventing the femoral artery from pumping all of her blood into the street and ending her life in the process.

She was barely out of the car when Richard sounded the alarm. "Margie, Margie! Come see who's here. Hurry up, woman!"

Margie ran out the front door dragging a string of Christmas lights, and her face lit up when she saw Gianna. "Lieutenant," she exclaimed, and ran toward Gianna, her arms extended.

"She's a captain now," Richard bellowed, and saluted before he wrapped Gianna in a bear hug. "You are a sight for sore eyes, I'll tell you that."

"Still putting the bad guys away," Margie said, "and this last bunch were just about as bad they get."

"That they were," Gianna said.

"And Mimi's story in the paper. It brought tears to my eyes," Richard said. "Those poor little girls. Will they ever be whole again?" She knew his tears were genuine, for the Bakers had three daughters and four granddaughters, and little girls were precious to him, to both of them.

Gianna didn't have an answer for that, and they didn't expect one. Richard abandoned the hedges he was stringing lights on, took the bags Gianna was carrying, and the Bakers invited her in for hot cider and homemade fruitcake. She happily joined them knowing it wasn't necessary to thank them for saving her life. Mimi had already been here several times with that message, as well as telling them how much she missed them. They were good neighbors and good people, and they'd be regularly invited to the new home Mimi and Gianna shared.

The Bakers weren't the only ones stringing Christmas lights. Andy and Alice were overseeing the transformation of the Special Mobile and Tactical Unit squad room into a place of joy and festivity. The huge wall screens showed Christmas scenes from all over the world, and carols played on a loop. Gianna had bought many gallons of cider and eggnog and ordered turkey and dressing and all the fixings from the Phillips Family Restaurant, and half a dozen cakes and pies. The chief, the deputy chief, and the commander all were invited, and they all joined in the

260

festivities. Davis brought Eric Ashby, Jim Dudley and Tony Watkins along, and they helped celebrate.

Gianna managed to separate herself from the crowd and stand a little away, watching. Her people had done one hell of a good job shutting down the sex rings and they knew it. But many of them were feeling a little PTSD. They'd never been so close to the victims of sexual predators, had never seen child victims. They needed this party, needed something that felt normal. They needed the closeness of their lieutenant and their sergeants and their team leaders, people who would take them to see the department shrink if necessary. They needed to feel the respect of the chief ofpolice and the deputy chief and the commander and their captain. And they needed to know that the job they did was the job they did.

Gianna had Tommi, Alice, and Andy work up a schedule that gave everybody at least three days off during the holidays. Gianna and Andy were on call all the time while Alice and Tommi alternated, as did Kenny, Vik, and the other techs.

"You throw a good party, Maglione," the chief said. "Thanks for inviting me."

"Thanks for coming, Chief. And I saved you a whole pecan pie."

A light snow fell as Mimi and Joe arrived at the Lady Buildings for the lighting of the tree in the courtyard. Florence Gregory had invited them, and they were too curious to do anything but accept. It was dusk when they arrived and there was a crowd. There also was a huge Frasier fir tree at the back edge of the courtyard facing the buildings. The tree was planted in the ground there. And it was decorated.

"How'd they get all those ornaments and lights on that tree?" Joe exclaimed. "It must be fifteen feet tall."

"It's beautiful," Mimi said, looking all around. Things certainly had changed at the Lady Buildings. The grounds were pristine. There was a decorated wreath above each door, and twinkling lights were visible in all the lobbies. But the Frasier fir that apparently was a permanent fixture—

"Thank you both for coming," Florence Gregory said behind them, interrupting Mimi's admiration of the tree.

"Thank you for inviting us," Mimi said.

"This is really beautiful," Joe said.

"An infusion of new blood," Florence said, "that we didn't know we needed." She surveyed the gathering with the same curiosity as Mimi. "We have eight new households, all in the last month."

"Is the city still your landlord?" Joe asked.

Florence still didn't like him, for reasons unknown, but she answered him with a nod, then added, "And it's working better than we dared hope."

"You mean better than *you* dared hope, Ms. Gregory?" Mimi smiled as she challenged the older woman. Florence dug deep and rose to the challenge, but someone calling Mimi's name interrupted.

"Ms. Patterson!"

"Sgt. Tommi! What are you doing here?" A surprised Mimi hugged Gianna's sergeant. "Not that I'm not happy to see you."

"We moved in last week—"

"One of the eight I mentioned," Florence interrupted. "How do you two know each other?"

"Looks like the tree lighting is about to commence," Joe announced as three people approached the tree, one of them holding an electrical box. Joe, Mimi, and Tommi stepped closer to the tree. So did the crowd, leaving Florence surrounded by her neighbors. Three people stepped forward to sing "O Christmas Tree," and amid loud cheers and applause somebody pressed the button and the huge tree glowed.

"Do you see who that is!" Joe exclaimed.

Mimi did, and she almost didn't recognize Beatrice Days. The old woman was transformed. She was held—supported—by a young woman on either side, and Mimi recognized both of them. "Be right back," she told Joe and threaded her way through the crowd. She and Melinda hugged, and Mimi recognized the other young woman as the lawyer who had helped Clara's girls. She also recognized the young lawyer as Melinda's lover.

"We live here now," Melinda said, "and serve as property managers while the city finalizes a property management contract. We also watch over Ms. Days."

"I'm glad to see you again, Ms. Days," Mimi said, but the old woman's eyes said she didn't know who Mimi was. Mimi hugged her anyway. "Lunch or dinner soon? Both of you?" Mimi asked. Both young women nodded, then told Beatrice Days it was time to get her inside. And it was time for Mimi to head home. She looked for Joe and found Tommi.

"My husband, Mike, and my daughter, Sandy."

"Daddy and me made Christmas cookies with lots of sprinkles, and my mom says you can take them to Captain Gigi." The little girl held out a bag, and Mimi could smell the cookies. They'd be lucky to make it home.

"There you are." Joe stood behind her. He and Melinda exchanged a warm greeting and agreed to meet the next day so he could get a tour of the new and improved Lady Buildings complex . . . and learn how it got so improved so quickly. As they made their way to the exit, they took a last look. The place and its residents were ready for Christmas. All except Florence Gregory, who stood alone in a crowd of happy, festive people.

"I wonder why that woman is so unhappy," Mimi said.

"I wonder where you got baked goodies," Joe exclaimed.

"Sandy and her dad baked Christmas cookies."

"Gimme," Joe said, reaching for the bag.

Mimi backed away. "Can't. They're for Captain Gigi."

"Captain Gigi! I love that."

"She will, too."

CHAPTER TWELVE

"I don't know whose idea this party was but it's brilliant," Cedric enthused, wrapping Mimi in a bear hug. "Everything is beautiful and perfect, especially that tree! Just waiting for us to decorate her."

Mimi returned the hug with love, for Cedric and Freddie were two of her most favorite people. Then she looked up at Freddie who, uncharacteristically, hadn't yet spoken, and who was looking down at her wearing an odd expression. "What's wrong with you? Why are you looking at me like that?"

"I'm not sure. You're different somehow," Freddie said, as he grabbed her into a rib-crushing hug. "You both are."

Mimi pushed him away and looked at Cedric. "Your husband is a pain in my ass," she said. Then to Freddie, "If you can explain and define 'different' I might listen. Otherwise—"

Freddie grabbed her again. "In all the years I've known you, you've never taken the time to plan a party, not even in college."

"I didn't plan anything in college, as you well know, because neither did you. It was always a by-the-seat-of-our-pants performance." Especially the double dates with her girlfriend of the moment and his boyfriend of the moment.

Freddie stifled a very unmanly giggle as he no doubt was remembering the same thing she was and continued with his observation of the present day. "And you and Gianna always worked such long hours that when you weren't working, you were sleeping. Now you've both stopped those crazy fourteen-hour days and we can tell, your friends can, and we like it, Mimi."

"You're right, Freddie. Of course you are, and I'm sorry I snapped at you."

"Not to mention that frequent and adequate sleep has really improved your disposition."

She ignored that comment and searched inside the bags of ornaments Freddie held, ready now for the tree decorating to begin. "We always wanted a big tree but because we lived in two places, we had two small trees—the tabletop kind—one at her place and one at mine." She gazed across the expanse of the living room at the eight-foot tall Douglas fir, imagined it decorated and lit, and felt an enormous sense of peace. She and Gianna had done a bit of decorating in preparation for the party. There were candles of all shapes and sizes in holders of all shapes and sizes everywhere, and they had hung aromatic fir boughs woven through with tiny white lights around all the doorways and arches, and of course on the fireplace mantel. Huge logs burned and blazed, and the wide hearth was adorned with baskets of pine cones and pots of poinsettias. But the real decorating would be of the tree. And the dining table when the food was served.

"A tree trimming, housewarming, holiday party. Like I said— brilliant," Cedric enthused with another hug, and his holiday bow tie blinked a kiss at her.

"It's gonna be a tree-decorating, eggnog-drinking, fruitcake- eating, carol-singing good time," Freddie exclaimed, and Mimi gave him "the look."

"Nobody said anything about singing."

"There has to be singing," Freddie insisted. "Why don't I make a list of my favorite carols—"

"I told you, didn't I, that the Creole Cajun Kitchen is catering, and all your favorite foods will be on the table?"

Freddie's eyes widened and he began to salivate. He turned quickly away from them and headed for the kitchen, and Mimi thought, she would have to remember to apologize to the catering staff. She knew how he felt about the food of his home state of

Louisiana and she shouldn't have told him, should have just surprised him when dinner was served, but she had to get his mind off singing carols. A sing-along definitely was not on the menu.

"The man hasn't lived in Louisiana since he left high school to attend college in Los Angeles, but you'd think he left there just yesterday," Cedric mused.

The doorbell chimed, and Gianna opened the door to admit Beverly and Sylvia, and Ellen De Longpre. Mimi went to help Gianna play hostess but not before begging Cedric to haul Freddie out of the kitchen—by force if necessary—and they both laughed at the image that produced. Freddie had played ten years in the NFL as a defensive tackle and had maintained his fitness. Cedric, himself physically fit after years as a marathoner, was a poet and college professor by profession and wouldn't dream of forcefully hauling anybody from anywhere, even if he could have hauled his husband. Which he definitely couldn't have.

Both Mimi and Gianna were pleased that every guest so far had embraced the request to wear holiday festive attire—whatever that meant to them. Freddie and Cedric both wore tuxedo pants, Cedric with a white silk, long-sleeve T-shirt, sparkling silver suspenders, the red and green blinking bow tie, and silver elf boots with toes that curled. Freddie's footwear of choice—Doc Martens, as usual—paired with a formal tuxedo shirt minus the sleeves, putting his formidable muscles on display, and a long red and green blinking tie with Santa Claus faces.

Shades of red—from cranberry to crimson to claret—and green and gold were the colors of choice for most of the women, Mimi and Gianna included, and the attire definitely added to the festive occasion. Ellen vacillated between wishing she'd stayed at home and being glad she hadn't. She expected that she'd be the only single here, and riding the elevator up with Beverly and Sylvia confirmed her suspicion. But they were so friendly and warm that Ellen was glad she wasn't spending yet another night at home alone. She needed to be among warm, friendly women.

"I'm guessing that we're going to the same place," Beverly Connors said as she introduced herself and her wife, Sylvia

266

Rogers, and when Ellen introduced herself she thought she saw a tiny flicker of recognition in Beverly's eyes, but she was certain that neither of these women was a cop. And what difference did it make anyway? It was a cop's party and everybody present would be queer. *Time to get out of the damn closet, Ellen,* she chided herself. Gianna's warm welcome, and the introduction to Mimi Patterson and her warm welcome, put Ellen at ease.

A young woman employed by the catering company collected the coats and hats, and Mimi and Gianna collected the ornaments everyone had brought to decorate the tree. Everyone seemed to know each other, and that, momentarily, had Ellen again wishing she hadn't come, but a drink and a tour of the truly wonderful apartment shifted her thinking again, and meeting Gianna and Mimi's houseguests from Florida, Sue and Kate, ultimately relaxed her. They were from Dunedin, a place Ellen and Iris had often visited, so she had something to talk to somebody about.

"Who are we waiting for?" Beverly asked. "I want to start decorating that tree."

"Tyler and Scott and Alice and Delores," Mimi answered, "and I'm sure they'll be here soon."

"If Tyler doesn't get himself stuck at work," Kate said darkly. "You know how he is about work." Tyler had known Sue and Kate for many years, and he had introduced them to Mimi and Gianna, and the women became friends.

Mimi did know; she once was the same way. "If he gets himself stuck at work," she said even more darkly, "he'd better stay there."

But Tyler was not stuck at work. At that moment a taxi bringing him and Scott entered the curved driveway of Mimi and Gianna's building and the doorman opened the door for them. At almost the same moment the doorman, who saw everything thanks to ten years on the job, saw the black Bentley he'd been told had the garage gate code and an assigned parking space drive in. The police captain had asked that he call up when the Bentley arrived so that someone could come down to the garage and make certain the car was in the correct space, and he made the call. He

267

hadn't known what to expect from these two women, the police captain and the newspaper reporter, but they treated him with more courtesy and respect than many of the people for whom he'd opened doors and accepted packages these last ten years.

Delores followed Gianna's directions once inside the garage to the parking space that was reserved for her, and when she got there a young woman was waiting. "Good evening Ms. Phillips, Sgt. Long. Captain said to tell you that both spaces are reserved for you," and the young woman gave Delores a card to put on the dashboard identifying the vehicle as a legitimate guest of the building. They thanked her and opened the trunk to take out armloads of flowers and bags containing several vases.

"Would you like for me to take those up for you? I can get a cart—"

"No, we'll take the flowers," Alice said, "but if you have a cart, there's a box that needs to go up. If you can take that on the cart, we'd appreciate it."

"I'll be right back," the young woman said, sprinting toward a storage room. She vanished inside and was out in seconds pushing a cart to the rear of the Bentley. She put the box—a case of Veuve Clicquot—on the cart. Very carefully. "I have to use the freight elevator to bring this up and enter through the kitchen door. I'll meet you up there," and she pointed them toward the passenger elevator. She didn't look at the bill Delores Phillips slipped into her hand until she was in the elevator headed up. *Holy shit, a hundred dollar bill!*

Tyler and Scott had barely cleared the foyer when the doorbell chimed. "Alice and Delores," Mimi and Gianna sang out in unison, and their genuine excitement and pleasure at seeing the two women helped cover their astonishment at the transformation in Delores. How many times has someone said of another person, "She looks like a new woman"? Delores Phillips really did. She was transformed, and yes, love definitely contributed, but so had adopting the "Alice Long Physical and Nutritional Plan." Delores had helped Alice attain financial good health and she, in turn, had helped Delores attain the physical equivalent.

"We're so glad you came," Gianna said. "And these flowers!"

"We hope you like flowers," Alice said, "because Delores loves them and can't go into the florist shop without buying every available bloom. Then we have to go buy vases—" and she held up bags of vases.

"We love flowers," Mimi said, "but it's a good thing you got vases because we've never loved this many flowers at one time."

As Gianna took their coats Delores said, "I must ask one question: How did the young woman in the garage know our names?"

Mimi shook her head in mock dismay. "Seems that my lovely one is known far and wide by an ever wider assortment of the citizenry."

Gianna was amused. "Young April is an academy recruit and she works here part-time. She recognized me, and to help with her rather dire finances I send work her way."

"We couldn't have had a better meet-and-greet committee," Delores said.

"And speaking of which, we brought up the flowers, but young April brought a box up on the freight elevator. She should be in the kitchen with it now," Alice added.

Mimi took the coats from Gianna and headed for the coat closet and then the kitchen while Gianna took them into the living room. Introductions were made where necessary, and hugs and kisses were exchanged where they weren't. More logs were added to the already roaring fire, everyone had a drink and a plate of hors d'oeuvres, which were some kind of shrimp and crab delights, and the business of decorating the massive tree began. Of course everyone had an opinion about how to proceed, and silliness ensued, which required more drinks. The one point of agreement: Lights had to go on first, and such a large tree required a lot of lights. As they were the tallest, Freddie and Cedric, using step stools instead of the ladder because they didn't need it, started at the top and inside the boughs, closest to the trunk, and worked outward. Sylvia, Alice, and Delores began midway and followed the same procedure, Kate; Beverly and Sue handled the lower boughs, and in short order the tree was lit.

That important accomplishment called for another drink, which led Freddie to call for the singing of carols, and he started singing along to an instrumental version of "Good King Wenceslas" emanating from some invisible speaker. Loudly, and in a surprisingly decent baritone. Delores added a lovely contralto and Tyler, of all people, supplied a tenor. Ellen, who hadn't enjoyed herself in so long that she didn't remember the last time, added a soprano and received some assistance from Kate and Sue. Mimi pulled up the lyrics on her tablet, and the singers did resemble a choir as they moved close to each other and held the tablet in front of themselves. The non-singers began adding ornaments to the tree. Then the song was over and everybody started adding ornaments. There were a lot of them, and every one of them found a branch to hang from.

Mimi turned off all of the lights in the living room, dining room, hallway and foyer so they could fully appreciate the beauty of the tree, and it was something to behold. A few whispered "wows" and at least one "holy shit" summed up the response to the beauty of the tree. "You guys rock," Mimi exclaimed.

"Thank you all so much," Gianna said.

"We're going to start this tradition when we get back home," Kate said.

"And in case you two don't know it, this is our new tradition: tree trimming at Mimi and Gianna's," Delores said, and a rousing cheer went up.

"Tree trimming and carol singing at Mimi and Gianna's every year from now on," Freddie said, and everybody clapped and cheered, and it went on for a while. Ellen joined in despite a huge wave of sadness that swept through her, and it wasn't just because she missed Iris but because of all they'd missed out on by living behind their closet doors. *Fear is a bitch,* no doubt about it. They could have had friends like these, had parties like this, but fear had forced them to keep their secret. Yet here was Alice Long who worked for Gianna, and Tyler Carson who was Mimi's boss. Hell, she was Gianna's boss and here she was at Gianna's home. She studied these people, friends who obviously loved each other and enjoyed each other. But more importantly, lovers who liked and enjoyed and respected each other. She watched as Gianna leaned into Mimi, as Mimi's arms went around her, as Mimi leaned in and whispered something that made Gianna snuggle closer. Alice held on to Delores and the woman clearly loved it, wouldn't have stepped away from Alice's side if a bomb had fallen on the building. Beverly and Sylvia regularly shared looks of love and gentle caresses. Even the men were unafraid to display their love and affection for each other. Was it too late for her to have this? Ellen wondered. Had the opportunity passed her by?

"I have an announcement to make and then we can eat," Mimi said, getting everyone's attention. "There will be a tree un-trimming party on January first—" The laughter propelled them into the dining room and to a feast that kept them quiet and eating until not another person could manage another bite. Then they returned to the living room and the roaring fire and the magnificent tree, with cups of mulled cider or eggnog, and got comfortable. And sang carols until it was time for dessert.

Acknowledgments

Everyone who lived through 2020 has their own words to describe the journey and therefore doesn't need mine. But we got through it in our own, individual ways, probably with a little help from our friends. And the women of Bywater Books always were there: for me, with me, beside me, behind me, and in front of me—leading the way. Thank you to Marianne K. Martin, Salem West, Kelly Smith, Fay Jacobs, Ann McMan, Elizabeth Andersen, and Nancy Squires.

Let me go further and tell you that Fay Jacobs is more than just an editor. Yes, she does everything a great editor should do—which is to help a writer find her way to a better novel. But more than that, "FayJ" is the *Penny Whisperer*. She put up a literary signpost, and I saw and heard every single plot point, scene shift, and character action needed to complete this journey for Mimi and Gianna. Fay was pure magic amid the 2020 madness.

Then there are those other Bywater Women—the ones who write the books. And oh! What books they write! I have been sustained and nourished by them.

I had no idea it was possible that I'd never miss libraries and bookstores—or even my favorite Greek market.

The publication *You Can't Die But Once* in December 2020 is absolutely the best present I have *ever* received. Yes, 2020 changed our lives, and our celebrations, but it didn't take this bit of joy away from me!

About the Author

Penny Mickelbury is the author of three successful mystery series and an award-winning playwright. She is a two-time Lambda Literary Award and Golden Crown Literary Society Award finalist, was a writer in residence at Hedgebrook Women Writers Retreat and is a recipient of the Audre Lorde Estate Grant. Her novel *Two Wings to Fly Away* was awarded an Independent Publishers Bronze Medal in the Historical Fiction category, and she is a recipient of the Alice B. Medal for her outstanding body of work in the field of lesbian literature. Prior to focusing on literary pursuits, Penny was a pioneering newspaper, radio, and television reporter. In 2019, she and other members of *The Washington Post's* Metro Seven were inducted into the National Association of Black Journalists' Hall of Fame.

At Bywater Books we love good books about lesbians just like you do, and we're committed to bringing the best of contemporary lesbian writing to our avid readers. Our editorial team is dedicated to finding and developing outstanding writers who create books you won't want to put down.

For more information about Bywater Books, please visit our website.

www.bywaterbooks.com

CPSIA information can be obtained
at www.ICGtesting.com
Printed in the USA
JSHW040934071120
9398JS00003B/12